For Megan & A.

Blood & Sand

The First Book of Rue

Aisling Wilder

Wilderwood Press

Galway, Ireland

x Aisling Wilder 10/20

Published by Wilderwood Press
11 Henry St, Galway, H91 X49N
wilderwoodpress.com

Blood & Sand/ Aisling Wilder -- 1st ed
978-1-8381152-1-0

I would like to thank all the people who helped in the creation of this book. Thanks to the old IC gang, for watering the seeds, thanks to everyone at Writers Beat, and to my beta-readers Ionia, Sorcha, Deirdre, Darragh, and all of you who helped, encouraged and rooted for me along the way.

A special thanks to the Sublime Seven (you know who you are!) and my critique partners and fellow authors Sara Burr, A. S. Howell, Christine Matthews and my lovely editor Madelaine Miles. Your feedback, critiques, empathy and patience (even when I'd disappear for weeks at a time only to pop back into existence with more questions!) is something I will always appreciate more than words can express.

Finally, thanks so very much to Monika Ozdarska, for your help, your patience and your wondrous and magical cover design!

This book is dedicated to Órla.
My angel, my muse, my compass and my comfort.
I love you.

*'The mind is its own place, and in itself
Can make a Heav'n of Hell, a Hell of Heav'n.
What matter where, if I be still the same?'.*

—JOHN MILTON

BLOOD & SAND

Prologue

Asharru

My name is Asharru, and today I must be perfect. For today I will be chosen. The sun has yet to rise, but I have been awake for hours while priestesses bathed and anointed me with scented oils, plated my hair tightly to my scalp, then dressed me in new white linens.

My heart beats hard in my chest as I am led in silence to the steps of the temple, to stand with the other girls who have come of age.

The eastern sky grows pale as we wait, the Great Ziggurat looming above us, huge and dark against the growing dawn. It is more than a little frightening, knowing that soon I will ascend its steps, even though I know them better than most. Although I have never before climbed them—only those in the priesthood are allowed to—I have often run my hands along the lower edges, tracing my fingers across every dip and crack in the painted mud-brick and wondering what it would be like, when this day came.

As I have always known it would.

I was born here, in the temple complex in the city of Ur, the capital city of the Sumerian empire. My city is the greatest city in all the world. Our god-king makes his home here, and our temples are the highest in the land. As a girl-child born to the temple, this moment was arranged soon after my birth. I was born to this calling.

Born to the gods.

A crowd gathers behind us, their murmurs growing as more girls join our ranks, and I cannot keep myself from staring at the newcomers. Until now I have never met a child from outside. The temple born are not allowed to play with other children, or even to leave the complex. But sometimes we climb up the walls and watch them, or more often, tease them; throwing rocks and stones at them, and threatening them with the anger of the gods if they dare fight back.

I peer around, craning my neck to see if any of those I teased are here now—but just then, one of the priestesses catches me looking, and glares at me, so I stop, staring straight ahead again and trying very hard to hold still.

I am not used to this. Being still. Waiting. Until now I have been allowed to do as I wished, and have spent the sun-drenched days of the last six years running and playing games with the other temple-born in the narrow streets amidst the tangle of tiled buildings. I wish I could go and play now, but then I remember what is about to happen, and catch myself, concentrating on holding still again.

I am frightened by what is to come, but I am also proud.

After today, I will no longer be a child. After today I will begin my education. I will learn my letters and numbers, and how to read and write them. I will learn the history of my people and my city. I will learn to read the paths of the stars and planets, and to see how they move the world of men, and most importantly, I will learn the secrets of the Anunnaki; our divine teachers.

It is a lot, and fear rises again, my heart thundering even harder—then harder still as from above, there sounds a long, low blast of a trumpet horn, then the drums begin to pound, and the priestesses in charge of us guide us up the steps of the Ziggurat.

The sun stretches his first golden arms into the pale blue sky as we climb the steps, the mud-brick cool and smooth beneath my feet. I bite my lip as I climb, concentrating on each step, making certain I do not trip on the hem of my new linens, or bump into another of the girls.

As we near the top, I see my mother, the High Priestess, standing tall and beautiful. She is surrounded by the other priestesses, every one of them staring down at us as we are led up to face them.

The priestesses into whose charge we have been given move among us then, pushing and pulling us into a semi-circle, then pressing on our shoulders with stern whispers and gestures, making us kneel on the painted dais.

I am trembling now, and I continue to worry my lips between my teeth, stealing glances at the girls to either side and wondering if they are as frightened as I am.

There is another long, low blast of the horn, and the drums stop, leaving a ringing silence to settle around us. My mother steps forward then, and into that silence begins to recite the words that will dedicate us into the service of Inanna, Goddess of love and war; daughter of Nanna, God of the moon.

I gaze out over the city, as the other priestesses join in, chanting prayers and invocations. I try to listen, but their voices blend together, until I cannot tell one from another. The sound makes me sleepy, and so I let my gaze stray from the altar before me to the view beyond.

I have never in my life been up so high. From here, at the house of the god, I feel that I can see the whole of the world. Far to the south, a line of hazy blue mist cloaks the delta where it meets the sea. Closer in, past the walls and stretching to the river, are acre upon acre of fields, orchards and gardens; the irrigation ditches that feed them shimmering silver in the sunlight. Nearer still, the city gates, the canals, and the city itself: a tangled maze of gardens and houses, markets and people.

Most of the citizens of Ur are gathered at the foot of the temple to witness the ritual. Many of their daughters have been chosen. It is not only the temple-born who may go into the priesthood, any child may be chosen. Many parents give generously to the temple so that the gods might name their children. They are good people, the people of Ur.

My people.

I test the words, whispering them to myself in the same way my mother says them, with a certain seriousness. It is the place of the priesthood to give to the people the word of the gods. The people must carry out those commands, but the priests and priestesses are tasked with making every instruction clear. If they do not—if we do not—then the gods will be angered, and the empire will fall.

The heat of the new summer morning beats down upon my shoulders as I squint against the waking sun to look up again at my mother. The ceremony seems to go on forever and I wonder how she has memorised all those words, knowing that soon I will be expected to do the same. At last, after what feels to me like an eternity, she stops, and we are made to stand, one by one, and step forward to receive her blessing.

I am third in line, and my mother offers me a proud smile as she lays her hand on my hair and speaks the blessing, aiming her voice so the crowds gathered below can hear every word.

I cannot hear her, however, for, at that instant a sound fills my head, building like music until the very stones seem to ring. At the same moment, the light of the rising sun falls into place in the stone archway above us, its warm rays hitting me full in the face, bringing tears to my eyes. There is a gasp from the masses gathered below, and I am filled with pure joy.

The gods have accepted me. They have blessed me in front of thousands.

I cannot stop smiling as my mother speaks the final words of dedication, and I am guided to stand beside another girl in the long row of neophytes. The ceremony moves on, but I keep crying and smiling. The other girls gape at me. Not all of them have been affected the way that I am. But I do not care. With absolute faith, I believe. My heart grows warm inside my chest, and I feel like dancing, I'm so happy. I am chosen. Cherished. A true daughter of Inanna.

Forever.

Chapter 1

Smoke and Screams

S moke and screams fill the air. I can't breathe, can't see, as I fall, and fall. I flail in the dark, reaching for any help, any hold to stop my descent—and hit the ground. Hard.

Gasping for breath, I scramble to my feet and try to run, but the earth beneath me slips away, and I can't find enough friction to move. Panic thunders through me, as I stumble and fall. Then, a sickly orange light shivers and stabs the darkness.

I know this place. I've been here before.

Wake up.

Black sand surrounds me, stretching out in every direction. A warm wind whips up, and a sound follows; a deep, hollow roar that fills me with dread. I look up to a sky on fire; the arms of a hundred rising suns raging toward each horizon. Cold terror fills my throat, and I struggle to my feet, trying to run again as monstrous, shadowy shapes explode from the sand to surround me; their leering, familiar faces bathed in ash and blood.

Wake up.

Razor-clawed hands snatch me up, rip and slash me, flesh and bone until I am torn and dangling like a rag doll between them. I beg for release, but they only grin and close fists of iron, crushing me until my bones crack and splinter.

Limp and hanging helpless in their grasp, I manage one ragged, rasping breath—and the sand rises up, surging into me like a living thing; filling my mouth, my throat, my lungs with a billion shards of black glass, each one slicing through me until I am fragmented; a thousand parts pain.

Wake up!

A hot wind, black with blood, lifts me, spinning me to the edge of the earth and dropping me into the centre of a roaring sun. I am blind, helpless, hopeless; my disembodied screams silenced by molten fire. And all the while someone, somewhere, is laughing; a high-pitched, maniacal howl that grows to a lunatic scream—and I gasp upright, tearing in panic at tangled sheets.

Safe. Whole. Not burning.

The scream is a siren splitting the night as a police car speeds past on the street below my window. I release a shuddering sigh as the dream slips away, leaving only fading fragments, like reflections in broken glass, as I remember where I am.

Home. In bed. Hungry.

Extracting myself from the sheets, I get up, making my way across the dark flat to the fridge. My pale arm reflects the dim blue light that flickers on as I tug the door open and stare disbelieving at a pile of wrung out IV bags.

"Shit."

I forgot. Fresh out.

Wait, this doesn't make any sense. Jude was just here, wasn't he? Bleary-eyed, I lean in and rummage through, squeezing out a few of the bags in denial, hoping a drop might be left. But no.

I stand up, leaving the fridge door open as the room comes into focus. Rubbing a cool hand over my face, I turn to the sink and drop the bag in my hand. Piled next to the basin are more bags. Empty. The counter and sink are stained crimson.

"Shit!"

This is wrong. Very wrong. Wide awake now, I check the doors, front and back, then the security shutters on every window. Locked tight. I check the alarm. Still armed. No one could have got in. Not without waking me.

I move back to the sink, grip the edge with both hands and stare at the dark stain around the drain. The sharp tugging in my gut tells me that I did this, no one else.

I dumped it all out.

And judging by the way I feel now, it must've been a while ago. I try to remember, try to see myself doing this. But I come up empty.

My stomach groans at the thin, metallic scent, and makes me painfully aware of the burning ache inside. I wipe at the sink and counter with my hands, licking my fingers in vain hope, but there's not much there, and what's left has gone off.

Way off.

Fighting panic, I dart to the fridge and rip open all the empty bags, one by one, licking the plastic clean. Not enough. Fuck. Okay. Have to calm down. I stand there for a moment, taking a few deep breaths. But instead of calm, the terror from the nightmare rises again.

Swearing under my breath, I hurry back across the flat and grab my mobile from the bedside. I left it charging, thank the gods, but it's set to silent. Another thing I don't remember doing. I hit last call and wait.

"Where the hell have you been?"

Okay, he's upset. I must've slept longer than I thought.

"Listen, Jude, I need some more."

"You've been out of touch for three weeks, Rue! Would it kill you to pick up the phone?"

"Probably not." I sigh. Better make nice, he's in a bad mood, and I should've called. "I just tend to sleep a lot when it's like this. Summer. You know."

"No, I don't know. You've never done this before! You know, friends are supposed to tell each other about things like this so friends won't be sick with worry when friends don't ring them back!"

"Yeah." I close my eyes, rubbing at a needling headache. "I'm sorry. It hasn't been this bright for this long for a few years, and—anyway, look. This isn't something I want to talk about right now."

"Right. You and the phone thing. No one's listening, you know. These days, nobody cares."

He thinks I'm paranoid. Maybe I am. But I'm still alive. I wince as the headache moves to the back of my skull, like it's got a mind of its own. Fucking hell. I start to massage it away again, then what he said sinks in.

"Three weeks?"

"And a bit."

"Shit."

"What's going on with you? Are you okay?"

I shake my head and run a hand through my sleep-tangled hair. "I'm fine. Only I really need some more. Tonight."

Jude sighs on the other end. "Okay. I'll leave now. But it'll be a while."

Shit.

I'm already shaking, and my skin is coarse and dry. I can feel it, drawing in around my bones. Nearly a month with nothing. This isn't good. Sleeping so long, blacking out, wasting it all like that—

"Rue?"

"Yeah?"

"Will you last?"

"Yeah, don't worry."

I end the call, throw the phone on the bed, clean up the mess, make certain everything's back in its proper place, and head downstairs to my library. Have to stay in control.

Twisting my hair up, I push a couple of chairs out of the way and lay out a small round Persian rug. I do a short meditation, then move into Asanas. The practice is one of the few things that have kept me sane over the years, but tonight I struggle to stay focused. Every time I close my eyes, images from the dream rise, taunting me. Trying to shake it off, I slip into what is usually an easy rhythm of ancient forms I'm sure modern practitioners would love to get their hands on; moving smoothly with each breath. In. Out. Again.

Not working.

Frustrated, I try another short meditation, then move into my usual martial arts practice. Tonight, every stance is off, however, and it's difficult to stick with it. I'm impatient. Restless. Hungry. After an hour or so I give up, and head for the shower. I can feel my blood stir, weak and weedy through my veins; and my heart jumps and flutters in my chest, arrhythmic. Starved. Not good. I turn the tap to cold and get in. The water brings relief, for the moment anyway, and I stand under the spray for a while, trying to calm down.

That damn dream. Every time I sleep, it's always the same, and I can't shake the feelings that come with it. Panic. Terror. Helplessness.

That's the worst of it. Being out of control. The images flash through my mind again, the lingering emotion mingling with my hunger, making me anxious. Edgy.

Fuck it. I need to get out. I'll take a walk, clear my head and kill some time before Jude gets here.

I turn the tap to hot and finish washing, then get out, dry off, and dress quickly, sunblock first—better safe than sorry—then jeans, T-shirt, harness boots, a couple of light scarves, hoodie, gloves, and my favourite leather jacket. Layers are important, and I like mine in varying shades of black. I grab my phone and a pair of sunglasses as I head out.

I live in a restored Georgian house. It's one of many such buildings on the quays, and one of a handful of properties I own around Dublin. I use the top two floors to live in, the next for storage, the ground floor I lease to an antique bookseller, and the cellar I've converted to a garage. On the whole, it's convenient, private and safe. Plus, the shop gives me extra security during the day. The owner and his employees don't know much about me, only that I've a keen interest in old and rare books, and so charge an exceedingly reasonable rent. Such things make for loyal, unquestioning tenants.

Which is very good for someone like me.

Taking the back stairs all the way down, I cut through the hall behind the bookshop to the lane outside, re-setting the alarm before leaving.

I stand for a moment on the cobblestones, taking in the evening. It's late summer, and although it's after ten, the sun has only just set behind the buildings. Its dying light is reflected in the Liffey, giving the city a scarlet glow as night creeps up the eastern sky.

Out of habit, I carefully scan the street and surrounding buildings, doorways and rooftops. Tonight no one's there, but you never know.

Letting out a long breath, I put on the sunglasses and walk to the quay at an easy stroll. The night is warm, the air heavy with the iron scent of summer; a mingled miasma of buses, cars, trains and a hundred thousand swarming people.

I slip through Saturday night crowds smoking outside pub doors, making myself unnoticeable—although I notice them; the life and heat radiating from their bodies in tempting waves, the rivers of red that run beneath their skin. Again, the thing in my gut twists and stabs, sharp enough to make me gasp, so I move faster, farther away. Past the Custom House, past new bridges and century-old warehouses, until I'm meandering deep into the old and empty industrial streets that border the river as it widens toward Dublin Bay.

Giant cranes loom over soon-to-be shiny new glass and steel towers, being built to replace crumbling old warehouses of brick and stone. Their half-finished skeletons rest like bones in some colossal elephant graveyard, shadows crisscrossing one another, creating patterns of light and dark that would usually entrance me.

But tonight, I'm too restless, worried and hungry to be entranced by anything. I still can't believe I dumped everything out. It isn't like me to waste anything; every drop is precious. And to pour it down the sink? I wouldn't ever do that. But I did. Okay. So why? Frustration claws at me, threatening any calm and birthing a growing anxiety; like I've forgotten something important, and when I remember, it'll be too late.

At the next street, I turn and head for the docks. I need space. The night grows darker as I walk, bringing some relief from the shaking in my veins. I pick up the pace, and soon enough reach the North Wall, winding my way out through the Docklands. It's quiet enough here, and I calm down a bit, letting the night enfold me like a mother's embrace. It's then, as I've nearly relaxed, that I hear the gritty scuff of a misstep on gravel behind me. As I round the next corner, I glance over my shoulder—and a shadow darts back into a lane.

I'm being followed.

Chapter 2

Dawn

The day dawns bright and hot, the rooftops beyond my window shimmering in the heat of the morning sun. I have been awake for hours now, long before the sun, having spent the night praying and meditating as I prepare for the next stage of my service to the gods. I am tired, but also elated. And impatient.

I stand by the window, breathing deeply of the morning air as I wait for what is to come. After all this time, I still am not good at waiting. I turn from the window, pacing the small room I have shared with two other priestesses for the past twenty-one years.

No longer.

This night all will change. For this night, I will undergo the rites that will make me High Priestess. Then I will have my own chambers, and priestesses to attend me, and my word will be the word of the gods. For I have been chosen. I will be my mother's successor. She has named me so.

There are some who whisper behind my back because of this. They say it always would be thus; that the priesthood is corrupt and in the hands of familial dynasties. I hear what they say. And I ignore it. It is nothing more than envious mutterings borne of small minds. The gods themselves have chosen me. In my heart, there is no doubt. I am ready.

I do not know why it must take so long.

As the sun journeys swiftly across the winter sky, I try once more to meditate, to calm my mind. Yet it will not be still. My thoughts wander, as

I wonder what it will be like, to finally be High Priestess, to clearly hear the words of the gods, and to give them to my people.

My people.

I smile as I whisper the words to myself, my heart blooming with pride and love. I love my people. And so, like the gods, I will care for them, and they will love me, even as they love the gods, and the city will flourish, for the gods will be pleased at my good guidance.

A soft knock at the door rouses my from my musings, and three younger priestesses enter my chamber, to bathe and dress me in the finest new linens, to oil and braid my waist-length hair and coil it around my head, and to place about my person the beaded jewellery of bronze, gold, and precious stones that the people have tithed to the temple.

After the women wash and anoint me with scented oils, they lead me from my chambers, and deep into the temple complex until we reach a small windowless inner chamber, before which stands my mother, the High Priestess, and all the other priestesses of the temple gathered to witness the ritual.

I kneel, bending my head low, my heart thundering as it did twenty-one years past, when I was but a child.

Then, as the sun tracks low across the winter sky, my mother steps forward, laying her hand upon my head, her voice soft, yet clear.

"Daughter of Inanna, Priestess of Ur—my daughter—you have learned your lessons well."

She smiles own at me, leaving her hand to linger a moment more upon my head before stepping back, her tone growing sombre as she speaks in ritualistic timbre.

"Know you how to read the paths of the sun, the moon and stars, and foretell the future from the past?"

I nod my head, responding as I have been taught. "I know."

She carries on. "Do you comprehend the mood and mind of nature? Do you discern the energies that move around all living things?"

Again, I nod. "I do."

She pauses then, and steps closer to me once more.

'Will you commune with the gods and their children? Will you dress, bless and feed them day and night, giving to them the sacrifice, and receiving from them instruction, so that you may apprise the people of their will?

I bow my head. "I will."

I hear the smile in my mother's voice as she steps forward again, holding forth a graven ivory cup, filled with a vile smelling liquid.

"Then drink, Daughter of Inanna, so that you may be imbued with the wisdom of the gods."

She presses the cup to my lips, and I tilt my head back, swallowing down the thick brown liquid made from sacred roots and herbs gathered by the light of the last full moon.

The taste is as foul as the smell—more foul even—and I gag as I drink, but do not allow myself to be ill. I will not fail in my quest. I will meet the gods.

Once I have finished the drink, my mother steps away and nods to the other priestesses, who lead me deeper into darkness, guiding me to kneel on the cool tiles in the centre of the empty chamber. They say not a word to me as the draw heavy curtains across the windows, only bow as they withdraw and shut the chamber door, leaving me alone.

I am to stay here, in silent meditation, communing with the gods until evening, after which I will be anointed High Priestess, in front of all the people of Ur.

My people. I smile, then laugh aloud, and put my hands to my mouth in surprise. My lips feel numb, my tongue thick behind my teeth, and my flesh feels soft and giving as river mud. I run my hands over my face, then my arms, squeezing and pulling at my skin, and then gasp in shock as the two serpents inked into my forearms twist and writhe, then slither away from my person altogether, curling around each other, changing colour as they coil and turn, undulating faster and faster, until I am dizzy and must close my eyes.

As I do, the walls and ceiling of the chamber melt away, unveiling the sky above and the dark expanse of night beyond the blue; endless and swirling with light. I watch as galaxies spin in great spirals, stars turning in each curving arm; watch as worlds dance around stars and moons around worlds. All in perfect synchronisation.

It is beyond beautiful.

I see the world whence our gods came, and the one beyond that, the home of their gods, and all at once, I understand; that the gods have gods as do those gods in turn. One day I see that I too, and all my people, will be as gods to another people in a future world far beyond my comprehension.

This knowledge fills me with wonder, and I begin again to laugh, and then to weep. As I do, the visions take a darker turn, and I watch world after world burn and fall from the sky. Thunder and fire crash together and this world, my world, also burns. I cry out as I hear the cries of the people in the city below. They are burning. Dying. I reach for them, trying to help—and fall face down on the floor, awake, sick, and horribly aware that outside the walls there are screams.

And they are real.

Struggling to my feet, I stumble out into the courtyard. Black smoke billows from the buildings below, blotting out the sun, and an orange glow fills the darkening sky. My city is on fire. With a cry, I run out into the temple grounds. As I round a corner, the screams grow louder, and I hear the clash of weapons, the cries of women and men, the bellowing of horns, and know what is happening.

Raiders have come. An army of them. We are overrun.

Even as I think it, dark shapes run out of the smoke toward the Temple complex.

I turn and run the other direction, trying to make it indoors before I am seen. Running around the side of my dwelling, the one I share with my mother and sisters, I stumble and fall over a pile of smouldering rags, hitting the ground hard.

Stunned, I lie there struggling for air as I register what I see. What I thought to be a heap of cloth I now recognise as the charred and blood-drenched remains of my mother.

Her eyes are open and staring, her skin blackened and torn; her rich jewellery ripped from her, and what is left of her clothing burnt and shredded. The dark shaft of an arrow juts from her chest, the tarred fletching still smoking. My mother. The High Priestess. Dead. Murdered.

I scream, and keep on screaming, scrambling back away from the sight—and then the men are upon me. One lunges for me, grasping my legs, while another grabs my arms, yanking them painfully behind me.

No.

Tearing myself from their grasp, I kick the one at my feet in the face and then lunge backwards, bloodying the nose of the one holding my arms. The men let go, then shout at each other and at me in their coarse foreign tongue as I struggle to my feet and run once more, back to the courtyard, no thought in my mind but to flee.

I do not get far. There is a whistling sound, like wind through long river grass, and I feel a sharp blow from behind. Startled, I look down at the glistening black point of an arrow protruding from my abdomen.

The pain hits then; cold fire blooming from the wound. My blood pours hot against my skin, my breath fails me, and I stumble, falling to my knees at the edge of the courtyard. The men surround me, their rough hands pulling at me, their harsh voices ringing in my ears.

Someone turns me over and holds me down, tugging at my bracelets and rings, my clothes—and I cry out as the arrow pushes deeper in. My vision blurs as the men take what they want, leaving me bloodied and bare. They must know I am dying, but it matters not to them as they rob me, stripping me of my jewels and linens, and then moving away.

All but one.

I choke, drowning in my own blood, as he leers over me, pressing his stinking weight down against my naked flesh. He would take more than the rest. I meet his eyes, dark to my blue and full of greed and a vile lust. He sneers and tugs free his tunic, ripping aside my undergarment and thrusting himself inside me. I scream at this new pain, fighting for breath, my mind reeling as I push at him, striving desperately for escape.

He stabs himself into me, over and over, grunting like an animal, and as he does so, I feel the hilt of his dagger dig hard into my thigh.

A weapon.

Straining in agony, I reach, stretching as far as I can, and my fingers close around the hilt. Yanking the dagger free of its scabbard before he can react, I drive the curving blade into his throat. A wound for a wound.

His grunts turn to a gurgling gasp as his eyes open wide in shock. Using all my strength, I shove him off me as he dies, crying out as the arrow in my gut breaks off in the process. Rolling away, I get to my knees, blinking against the cold sweat that washes over me. Dumbly, I look down at the arrow still protruding from my skin, and clenching my jaw hard against the pain, yank it from my gut. Blood gushes from the wound and down my thighs to pool around my knees where I kneel. I drop the arrow to the sand as my body grows hot, then desperately cold. My mouth feels dry as the desert, a wave of vertigo washes over me, and my entire body begins to shudder. But I cannot stop now. Gazing down the smoke-filled street, I see more darting shadows, hear more shouting voices. They cannot find me here. I must flee. Clenching the dagger tightly in one trembling hand, I crawl, then stumble to my feet.

Desperation drives me on, as I half-run, half fall down the narrow passage that leads to the Great Temple. The smoke of the burning city stings my eyes and fills my lungs as I weave toward the safety of the Ziggurat. The enemy will not destroy the Temple of The Great God. Surely, they are afraid to. There I will be safe.

Reaching the shelter of the last building before the open courtyard of the larger temple, I stop, disbelieving. The temple square is filled with the smoke of a hundred burning buildings, the ground strewn with the bodies of my dead brothers and sisters. Priests and priestesses, acolytes and children, lying where they fell. The temple. Desecrated.

Unthinkable.

These men have no fear of the gods. There is no sanctuary.

I hear shouts and the sound of running feet behind me. I will have to risk discovery to make the temple itself. But if I must die, let me die at a place of my own choosing.

Pushing myself forward, and pressing my hand tight against the wound in my gut, I stumble across the courtyard toward the steps. In the smoke, no one sees me. Yet. I reach the bottom step and climb; forcing myself upwards by will alone.

I am a third of the way up when I hear a cry from below and know I am seen. Sobbing with effort, I will my feet to move faster, as I hear more shouts and running feet behind. Faster still, I struggle up the steps, through the lower arch and up, leaving a trail of blood and using my hands as much as my feet; the rough mud-brick scraping the flesh from my fingers as I claw my way toward the shrine at the top. The House of the Great God Nanna.

The men below are gaining on me. To them, this is a game. I hear their taunts as they hound me, herding me to the top, where they will seek to take me again. I know it. That knowledge more than anything else drives me on. I crawl up the last remaining steps and fall through the final archway into the shrine. At last.

Wielding the dagger before me, I glare at the men as they approach. No. They are not men. They are animals that would desecrate this Holy Place, cowards that would ravage a Daughter of Inanna. They are no better than the beasts of the hills they hail from. I spit at the first one that enters the shrine and slash wide with the dagger.

The others soon catch up and surround me, shouting and laughing at me and at one another in their own tongue, assuming I will not understand. But I do. They call me black-headed whore and worse. One lunges at me, and I slash his arm, cursing him in his own tongue, which causes the other men to jeer louder, laughing at him as he stumbles away.

I press back against the doorway built into the inner shrine wall; the silver inlaid tile cold against my fevered skin. The door leads nowhere. As a priestess, I know this. It is for ritual only; to represent the way the Great God of Night may walk into this world. It will offer no escape.

19

Another of the men circles in, and I lash out again, nearly collapsing in the process. My blood spills into an ever-widening pool beneath me, and I know as well as my attackers that I have little time left. And still, they will not leave me to die in peace.

But they will not have me.

I will give myself up to the care of the gods, I will go into the underworld and walk there as one of the Winged Dead forever. A few moments more, and all will be over. The knowledge gives me a moment of beautiful clarity.

From the top of the temple, the whole city is laid before me, the dwellings ruined and smoking, the people dead, or dying. Then my vision wavers, and for a single moment I behold the city as it was, whole and beautiful; white-washed buildings shining in the sun, coloured banners fluttering in the breeze from the silver river. My vision wavers once more, and I watch as a great wind rises to stir the sands until they cover the top of the Great Temple where I stand. Until nothing is left but sand and silence.

The vision passes then, and I look to the West as the great golden sun slips beneath the horizon, lighting up the sky in glorious shades of blue and orange, red, violet, and blinding, blazing gold.

It is time.

Glaring at the men that torment me, I slash wide with the dagger one last time to keep them away as I cry to the gods with all the breath I have left.

"Nanna! Great Lord of Night! Father of Inanna who is Mother of us all! I am here at your door! Your Daughter's Daughter calls you! Save me from the unbelievers! Take me now into your darkest arms!"

And, closing my eyes, I drive the dagger deep into my breast, falling into death's waiting embrace.

But I am not yet dead.

From behind me, I hear a deep rumble, then a terrible crashing, as brick and mortar shatter to dust. I feel a breath of cool air as a shadowed form moves over me, and then terrified screams and the sound of armour shattering, of flesh torn and bone broken. To my dying mind, it is as if the temple itself has come to life, the very stone rising to my defence. But this cannot be so.

Lightning rips the heavens asunder and rain begins to pour. I gasp for air, but can no longer breathe. And as I slip slowly into the world of the dead, I feel I am lifted in strong yet gentle hands, and carried down into merciful darkness; darkness that surrounds, comforts and covers me completely, until I know no more.

Chapter 3

Brave or Stupid

Changing direction abruptly, I turn the next corner and head for the tallest of the buildings under construction. At the same time the wind picks up, and I catch the faintest hint of a sweetly familiar scent on the air. So familiar it nearly turns me around.

I frown, shaking myself out of it, and pick up the pace. If it's hunters behind, I'll be damned if I'm giving them any advantage. I've met hunters before. Our exchanges have never been pleasant.

I reach the skeletal frame of the building and climb up, hand over hand. It'll take them a good bit to catch up with me, and in the meantime, I can suss how many they are and how strong.

A final tug lands me on the half-finished roof. It's quiet up here. The view downriver and out over the Irish Sea is exquisite, but I barely take it in as I move around the edge, searching the streets below for my pursuers.

For a few minutes, I see nothing. No one. Then, a woman steps sideways out of a lane across the street. She looks very young. And very scared. She's carrying a small crossbow with an even smaller torch taped to it and is holding the weapon out in front of her awkwardly, aiming at every dark corner.

Great. A newbie. I really don't need this right now. I scan the streets and buildings all around for her friends, but I don't see anyone else. Which is odd. Either she's alone—which I doubt, hunters always travel in packs—or her friends are exceptionally good at hiding.

Troubled, I go back to watching the girl. I doubt she can see me up here, but even so, I step back as she stops and peers up at the building, a flash of reflected streetlight glinting off her glasses. She hesitates a moment, then crosses the street into the building site. Brave girl.

Brave or stupid.

The wind picks up her scent again, and something inside me shivers at the familiarity of it. I wrack my brain trying to think where I could have met her before, but come up empty. Frowning, I move back across the roof as she steps into the maze of construction below. She's managing to be pretty quiet; I'll give her that. And I still don't see any others. Maybe she's alone. Or maybe she's bait. Either way, I'll wait.

It doesn't take her long to find the half-constructed stairs. I follow her progress through the building, moving to keep her in sight, and staying alert for her friends, wherever they might be.

She stops on a landing a long moment like she's heard me, although that's unlikely. I can hear her breathing, in short, shaking gasps, as she stares wide-eyed around her. She's in complete darkness except for her torchlight, the beam flickering left and right as she ascends, but I can see her clearly, night vision being a nice side benefit of my condition. She's plainly petrified, but after a minute she swallows hard, takes a deep breath, then continues up.

Hunger pulls again in my gut, sharp, biting; a hollow, impatient need. It would be so easy now, the thing inside me whispers. Take her, and damn the consequences. But no. I'm not so far gone. I wait as she moves up the last few stairs, slipping back into the shadows as she steps out from the stairwell opening, and onto the roof.

I study her as she moves out into the night, searching, that crossbow held in front of her like a shield. She's a little older than I thought. Mid 20's, maybe. Fair-skinned, wearing wire-rimmed glasses, with a spattering of freckles across her nose and honey-coloured hair that curls and frizzes around her face, glowing against the streetlight like a halo. A pretty girl. Again, I feel I've met her before, but I still can't place it.

It doesn't matter anyway. She's followed me, and she's got a crossbow with a wooden bolt knocked in place. Which means she probably knows what I am and may know where I live, which makes things complicated. I have to try and talk to her, find out how much she knows and where she got her information. Which won't be easy, as I'm sure she assumes I will try to kill her.

I hate assumptions. Especially when they're about me.

I wait until she's a few feet away, then step out into the open, all casual and easy. "Nice night for it."

She gives a little shriek, and the crossbow bolt comes speeding towards my torso. She's fast. But I'm faster.

Snatching the bolt out of the air, I hold it up to the light, inspecting it as I take a few steps toward her. "This is well made. Where'd you get it?"

She doesn't answer, as she's too busy fumbling to reach into her somewhat complicated combat-trousers pocket. I pause, waiting for what I know is to come, as she drops the crossbow to better get at her pocket. Sure enough, after a few frustrated seconds, she gives a little cry of victory and jerks out a canister of pepper spray. Aiming wildly, she lets loose in my direction, covering me in a misty cloud.

Only it's not pepper spray.

I smirk. "Let me guess...holy water? Sorry, but that doesn't really work on me."

She's trying not to cry now, and underneath her fear, I sense an aching grief. Feeling sorry for her, I stop, watching again as she fumbles with a chain at her throat, which she then breaks off, holding the attached cross charm up at me.

"Stay back!" She glares, meaning to be frightening, I know, but she succeeds only in looking more terrified.

I give her a smile, trying to put her at ease. "Nice necklace. Is it silver?"

She winces, and I take a slow step forward, my hands up in front of me in the universal gesture of 'hey, I'm not gonna hurt you'.

"Look, I don't know who you got your information from, but they left out a few things."

She's trembling, but doesn't lower her hand. "I know enough! I know what you are. I know what you did!"

I reach up, ever so slowly, and take off my sunglasses, putting them in my pocket as I take another step toward her. If I can meet her gaze, I may be able to calm her down. I have some skill there, although I'm far from being able to read minds, or control them. It happens naturally when I drink from someone—this empathic energy exchange—but over the years I've perfected the skill beyond feeding.

I smile at her, and tune in.

"Take it easy. Let's talk about this, okay? First, about what you think I am, and second, about what you think I've done."

Her eyes widen as she sees my own, and I realise belatedly that mine've got to be incandescent with hunger by now.

Shite.

Terrified, she scrambles for the crossbow, grabbing it up and holding it in front of her again, even though it's no longer loaded.

"Stay back! Or I'll..."

She trails off, and again I feel sorry for her, as I watch her realise she's completely out of options. She swallows hard, and her lower lip trembles slightly, as she looks up to meet my eyes, pleading, like so many others before.

"Please..."

The torch attached to the crossbow shivers in my direction as she trembles, glinting off my eyes, which makes nothing better. I blink in the light, and she takes another step backwards, bumping into a half-constructed wall. I close the distance between us with a few more steps, then stop again. I honestly don't know what to do. I don't want to kill her. But I can't let her go. I stand there a moment, staring at her.

She's shuddering, pressing flat against the wall, as if she would pass right through it if she could. Her heart is thundering in her chest, but she holds my gaze, even in her fear. This close, she's beautiful. So beautiful my heart catches in my throat.

I feel the heat from her body, smell the sun on her skin, the scent of her hair. That's where it's coming from. Those honey curls smell faintly of vanilla. Tuning in again, I sense her emotions, so strong they make me tremble. Fear is there, of course, but there's more. Grief, panic, desperation—and under that, so deep I can hardly feel it, is something absolute and abiding. Something quite simply good.

Something else inside me gives a little twinge, like a memory of a memory. I'm just thinking of what to say to try and calm her down, just reaching further for her mind with my own, wondering why she makes me feel I know her, wanting to get to know that goodness—when her eyes widen again, her pupils dilating further as she sees something over my left shoulder.

Shit. Company.

I don't even have time to turn around before the shotgun blast rips through me from behind, and everything goes black.

Chapter 4

Dusk

Cold. Pain. Darkness.

Where am I? I cannot see. My eyes are open, yet a veil of night lies across my vision. I cannot comprehend what has happened. My last memory is of the knife, blooming cold fire in my breast; of falling, dying.

Am I dead?

The thought darts across my mind, and I begin to shake uncontrollably. No. I feel. I cannot be dead.

Can I?

I panic, choking and struggling to breathe. Then someone speaks, close by, and a cool hand brushes my cheek.

"You are dying, Daughter."

The sound of a voice so close fills me with disquietude, and I crane to see through the darkness, to find the source even as it speaks again; in tones resonant and even.

"It is your strength and will that have brought me to you. You called, and I have come. And now I offer you a gift if you would live. Or is it truly your wish to walk forever with the Winged Dead?"

Death—no. To be dead is to hunger and thirst forever, wandering the endless night of the Underworld. No, I do not wish to die. A shudder tremors through me, followed by an icy chill, and I struggle again to see the speaker, shaking my head, seeking all around me as I try to answer. I have no breath left in my lungs. Yet I am compelled to speak. Once more, I focus all my will, forcing my lungs to draw air and give utterance.

"No."

The voice sounds pleased as it whispers, now very near my ear. Cool breath moves against my skin.

"I thought not. Then take my gift, and live again."

I hear a rustle of fabric, feel cool lips—a kiss—at the curve of my throat, and then a sudden stabbing pain which turns into a coiling pleasure such as I have never known. It washes over me in waves, one tumbling against the next, and I cry out, reaching, grasping for a hold, as I am carried far out on its tide, drowning in ecstasy.

Then the bliss fades, and I too fade, until everything—pleasure, pain, the struggle for life—dissolves to a pinpoint of light, and simply ends.

I am nothing. I feel nothing. I want nothing. There is no 'I', only a great and peaceful everything. It is beyond sublime, and I want to stay. I belong here, at the end and beginning of all things.

But then a great weight pulls at me, tearing me away, ripping me out of harmony and oneness into chaos. Molten liquid spills onto my lips, into my mouth, down my throat, and from there, into every part of me, until I am filled with fire. I scream and claw at my skin, trying to tear the pain away, but strong hands hold me down, and bind me with heavy ropes as I rage for release.

The voice returns, speaking louder now, but I cannot hear the words. Gradually, the pain lessens, only to begin anew, as once more comes a sharp stabbing, this time at the crook of my arm. Pleasure builds within me once more and is lost in further agony as more liquid fire pours down my throat and into my very core. I scream again, and again, begging, pleading for release, to no avail. All the while, the voice keeps speaking, murmuring words I do not understand. But now at least, as through a lens of blood, I can see someone shining in the shadows. A face with eyes of silver, and skin as luminescent as the moon.

"Nanna?"

I think I know the moon-god in my last moment of sanity, and then I am lost to the torment within, and nothing is known anymore.

The suffering seems to last forever. I lose any thought, any true consciousness; only jolt awake in flashes of the room, the ropes, the pain, and always the ever-patient presence of the speaker. One last time I feel a sharp stabbing, this time at my wrist, and once more there is such sweet pleasure, and torturous fire. Only now I need the liquid that burns me. I must have it. Only this one thing can quench the ravenous ache within, and as I struggle against the bonds that hold me, I am certain I am dead and in the Underworld, and this torment my eternity.

Then the pain passes, and I wake to a terrible thirst, as if I am the desert, and could drink the sea. The speaker is still there, and this time there are more shapes surrounding me, in a wash of colour and light. And then, close, so close, I smell and feel a warmth; a moving tempting object, radiating life and heat. I do not know what it is, but I know I need it more than I have ever needed anything.

It is there. Just out of reach.

Someone is screaming, begging, in a voice filled with terror. I strain against the ropes that hold me, and they snap like dead reeds. There is a sudden sharp twinge in my jaw that is just as swiftly gone, and then I am on top of a warm and soft and living thing that cries out once and is silent. I bite down, hard, as instinctively as a babe suckling to its mother's breast. A thin and fragile material gives way under my teeth, and then I am drinking sweet, blessed, thirst-quenching liquid.

Waves of emotion wash over me as I drink and drink. Love, hate, hope fear, and sweet, sweet ecstasy. This is the milk of the gods, the wine of Inanna. I drink until I can drink no more, until there is no more left to take, and then—I am awake. I am myself again.

And I am changed.

I am on my knees in a vast chamber hung with gilded tapestries and furnished as richly as the house of the King. The walls are inlaid with lapis and bronze, with silver and gold and many other stones that I do not recognise. Oil lamps hang from glittering chains along the walls and in their

31

flickering light the tapestries shimmer and dance their embroidered tales, woven in sparkling thread and glistening jewels. Everything shines like the river in the midday sun; impossibly bright. I am astonished at the colours, entranced by the beauty. It is as if I am newly born.

A shadow drops away from me to the floor, and I look down to see that it is a man. One of my tormentors, in fact—I remember him as one of those who attacked and robbed me—now dead and staring upwards with empty eyes. He is bleeding, slightly, from two neat puncture wounds in his throat, and the sight makes me lick my lips. As I do, I taste the remnants of blood. I know then what I was drinking.

And I want more.

There is motion above me, like a fluttering of silk at the edge of my vision, and I look up, into the incandescent eyes of the speaker, as he takes my hand and helps me to stand. His skin is marble white and cool against my own, and he is beautiful. There is no better word to describe him. Tall and slender, with a gaze like moonlight, and hair the colour of darkest night. He is the most beautiful creature I have ever seen, and I cannot help but stare in abject admiration as he smiles.

"Rise, Daughter. Rise and join us."

There is more movement around the chamber, and I see the others for the first time. There are five of them. Two women and three men. But women and men as I have never seen. They are all pale, some more than others. Their eyes glitter like jewels, and their teeth, as they smile at me, are subtly pointed, sharp as knives. I gape, my mouth open in awe, my heart pounding so hard I can feel my lips tremble with each beat. I feel I am in a dream, for surely this cannot be reality.

The speaker takes my arm, gently, slowly—like a parent to a child—and guides me toward the centre of the chamber, gesturing to the others as they step forth to encircle us.

"Meet your brethren, daughter, for you are now as they are. One of the Children of Alu."

I know these beings. I am a Priestess, a child of the Temple, of course I know. They are messengers, protectors, dealers of vengeance. I am so filled with reverence at their presence I can hardly speak, and must swallow and try twice before I murmur their collective name, my own voice melodic and strange to my ears.

"Utukku."

These are sacred beings. Inhuman and Holy.

And I have become one of them.

Chapter 5

Who and What

I wake to the crunch of three pairs of boots on the gravel rooftop. There are voices to go with the boots. Male voices, arguing. I lay still, face down, eyes closed; hunger snarling in my gut as my blood pools out beneath me. Better let them think I'm still out, at least until I can figure who and what they are.

The voice belonging to the boots nearest me speaks, interrupting the argument. "What about the half-breed?"

A second voice, further away and to my right. "Leave her. She was just bait. She'll come around, eventually. If the sun doesn't get her first."

The owner of the first voice chuckles and pokes me with what is most certainly the barrel of a gun, then hammers a hard kick into my side. My rib cage cracks at the blow, and it hurts like hell, but I still play dead, my mind working fast.

Shotgun Boy said, 'half-breed', a derisive term for those like me, used by those who think they're better. That phrase and a certain smell above and beyond that of my blood—the sickening scent of sulphurous decay— add up to something that doesn't make me happy. Not one bit. These boys are demons. Fuck.

I hate demons.

I'm still bleeding, and although I've started to heal, there's not enough blood left in me to complete the task. Hunger wrenches hard in my gut and pounds in my head, along with a high, needful whine. I'm going to lose it. Soon. This is not good.

A third voice pipes up. "I still say we drain the bitch now. All he needs is her blood anyway, right? Save us the trouble of carting her all the way back down."

The hell they will 'drain' me! Over my dead body! I tense up, ever so slightly. It's been a long time since I've fought one of the Truly Damned. Never mind more than one. And it's never gone that well. This just isn't my night.

The second voice speaks again. "No. We take her to him as planned. Alive." His voice changes, a cruel pleasure colouring his words. "He didn't say we couldn't play with her first, though."

From somewhere beside him, I hear muffled sobs and a scuffling sound. The girl. They're not talking about me. They're talking about her.

I lie there a few more moments, as the sounds of struggle get louder, accompanied by lewd taunts and sadistic laughter. The boots beside me move away, and I'm left to make my decision. I could make a break for it while they're otherwise occupied. They probably won't even notice. Okay. So. I should go. They don't want me. Don't give a shit about me, from the sounds of it. So why am I not going? Shit.

Shit, shit, shit.

I can't leave her to them. Never mind she was trying to kill me not all that long ago. I like her, for some reason. God damn it.

Biting back a groan, I get to my feet and assess the situation. About fifteen feet away from me, three mouldering demons huddle around the girl, two pinning her to the gravel rooftop and one in the process of pulling his trousers down. She's crying as she struggles against them, her glasses are gone, and she's bleeding from a few nasty cuts and scrapes, but she seems otherwise unharmed. So far. And I was right. The demons don't notice me.

Until I clear my throat. Loudly.

They freeze and all turn to gape me at the same time. It would be comical if I weren't about to get my ass kicked. They're all great big thugs of men, the human bodies they're wearing decayed by their lengthy possession.

I give them a little wave.

"Sorry to interrupt your little party, fellas, but I believe I got here first."

The one with his trousers partway down yanks them back up and looks to the other two, then back at me, initial surprise giving way to leering disdain.

"Well, well, well...looks like the leech woke up boys!"

He walks toward me, an arrogant sneer curling his blackened lips as one of his cohorts yank the girl to her feet, a hunting knife to her throat, while the other lifts the shotgun and aims it at my head.

Lovely.

I take them all in, and then look back to Mr Cocky-Pants as he saunters up, solid black eyes filled with disdain. "I think you'd better leave, half-breed. This isn't any of your business."

I shoot him a toothy grin, buying time, calculating the distance between us, and between the girl and the other two as I speak.

"On the contrary, this is precisely my business. In fact, I was in the midst of conducting this bit of business when you and your friends so rudely interrupted with that shotgun of yours. And don't call me 'half-breed'. It's rude."

He raises an eyebrow and tosses an incredulous look back over his shoulder to his mates. Which is exactly what I hoped he'd do. In that split second, I move as fast as I can, thrusting my arm forward, the heel of my hand hitting the base of his jaw with a resounding crack. He flies backwards with the force of the blow, skidding to a stop a few feet away.

Without looking to see if he stays down, I leap over him and run right for Shotgun Boy. The gun goes off as I reach him, ripping a hole in my shoulder. But at least it misses my head. It hurts like bloody hell, though, and the hungry thing inside starts to roar. There's a sweet familiar pull in my jaw and I feel my fangs press sharp against my lips.

Snarling, I grab the gun by the barrel, ripping it away from shotgun boy and breaking his arm in the process. He stumbles back, and I swing the gun around like a club against the head of the demon holding the girl.

He crumples to the rooftop, dropping both the knife and the girl—who scrambles backwards, screaming.

I grab the knife and swing back to Shotgun Boy as he leaps for me, his arm sticking out at a disturbing angle, a splintered bit of bone poking through the flesh. Shit. It's the human body that's hurt, not the demon inside.

He hits me with a blow that knocks me halfway across the roof. Somehow, I manage to hang on to the knife with one hand, and the gun with the other. Rolling to my feet, I bring up the barrel and aim for his head as he lunges for me.

The blast echoes around the surrounding buildings as he falls and doesn't get up, his head torn half off by the spread of shot at close range. There's a hot rush of air as the demon quits the body.

One down, two to go.

I hear a growl like a very angry and very big cat from behind me and turn to greet Mr Cocky-Pants mid-stride; his black teeth glistening in grinning, rotting, bloodied gums. Spinning the knife around, I let fly into his chest, and he crumples to the rooftop in a heap.

That was easy.

I follow in for the kill—but then I hear a scream from behind and turn around to see demon-boy number three dragging the struggling girl back toward the stairs. Changing direction, I leap across the roof and cut him off with a full-fanged snarl.

Unfortunately, demons don't scare easily. He tosses the girl to one side, meets my snarl and raises me an ear-piercing screech as the skin on his arms, face and chest warps and stretches impossibly—the demon beneath bending the bones in ways they weren't meant to bend—then splits open with a grisly tearing sound, splashing the rooftop with rancid flesh and blood. I cover my ears at the painful wailing, wincing back as he clenches and thrashes his stolen body; muscles and tendons distending. There is a sound like someone snapping kindling, and a hundred jagged shards of broken bone erupt from his hands and arms.

This is why it's never a good idea to pick a fight with a demon. They always cheat.

Before I can do much more than stare, he backhands me, and I go skidding across the roof yet again, a few slivers of bone embedded in my face and neck. Blinding pain rockets through my body and blood fills my vision as the control I have over myself slips away like ice on a stovetop. I hang on to the last shred of my sanity and claw the bits of bone out of my face as he roars toward me—then realise I still have the shotgun. I lift the barrel to his forehead as he pounds his fist into my gut. It's reflex more than anything like skill on my part that pulls the trigger. Another whoosh of air, and the streetlights around the site flicker and spark.

That's two.

But it's cost me. One of the bones has punctured an artery, and I feel my limbs rapidly cool as whatever blood I've left in me oozes thickly from my throat, joining the slowing flow from my shoulder and a half-dozen other wounds, all of it making me weak. Too weak. I blink blood from my eyes as everything goes foggy and off-kilter. I try to turn back to check on the girl, but my legs won't hold me up anymore and I fall to one side as the world becomes a hazy wash of red.

I watch as if from a great distance as Mr Cocky-Pants gets up from where I left him with that knife sticking out of his chest. Shit. I knew that was too easy. His stolen skin stretches impossibly as the demon swells beneath. Noxious steam erupts from his pores, and a horrid, putrid stench fills the air. I gag and choke, struggling to stay conscious as he strides across the roof towards me.

Numbly, I reach out, grasping for anything at all, and my hand brushes against the warm barrel of the shotgun. I manage to grab it, but can't get my hands to work well enough to use it before he's on me. Yanking me up by my hair, he slams me back down face-first into the gravel rooftop. The leftover bone bits from Porcupine-Boy drive deeper into my face. But he's not done. Dragging me back across the roof, he bashes my head into a half-finished wall again and again, until I see stars, then whole galaxies, then nothing but blood and a growing darkness.

He picks me up, holding me by the throat in one hand, dangling me over the edge of the roof as he sneers at me.

"Traitor."

He spits in my face, his festering breath sour and stinging. Then he lets go, and I go falling ten stories to the pavement below.

This is really going to hurt.

Chapter 6

Death

Laughter echoes around the chamber, rippling like water over stones. The speaker smiles down at me and places a cool hand on my shoulder.

"We are named Utukku by your people, that is true. But we have had a hundred names before that, and will have a hundred more before time will end." He draws me closer, holding my gaze to his own. "What is your name, Daughter?"

I answer, in an awed whisper, "Asharru."

He nods, then motions the others forward, keeping that possessive hand on my shoulder. "Come and greet your sister, my children."

One by one they step forth to meet me. To my dazzled mind, each is more beautiful than the last. Their shining eyes greet me with amusement, indulgence, indifference and affection in turns; and their lips, as each one kisses me in formal greeting, send cascading shivers down my spine.

They tell me their names, both foreign and familiar: Bion, a young man of a far northern people, with hair the colour of sand and eyes like the sea near the shore. Eshe, from the great desert empire to the West, with ebony tresses, smooth as silk, and eyes that glint lion-gold in the lamplight. Iyar and Makhir, hardly old enough to be called men; they look as if they are brothers, and are by turns amused and annoyed by my presence.

And finally, there is Lilitu.

She is pale as well; more even than the speaker, and is of smaller stature than I. Her eyes are the green of mountain forests, and they shimmer in the light like polished glass. Her hair is the colour of red ochre, and as she greets me, I see that I was wrong about the rest. They are beautiful, to be sure, but their allure pales in comparison with her own. She is exquisite, and I stare open-mouthed as she takes my hand and tells me her name.

I know the name. But she who stands before me, she cannot be the same? Lilitu, Lilu, Lilith; she is known by a hundred names to all peoples. Cursed as demon by some, revered as goddess by others, her songs and poems are recited by the king's own musicians. They are my favourite of all the stories I learned as a child.

I am so astonished I do not hear her next words. I cannot comprehend what is happening. My emotions rage within my breast. I feel I have been spinning in circles. The shining beauty of the Utukku, their alabaster skin and musical voices, the glistening tiles, jewels and tapestries of the chamber, the moonlight shimmering from above, everything becomes a storm of sensation. It is too much to bear.

Lilitu makes a soft sound of sympathy and turns to the speaker. "Look at the child, Alu. She is overwhelmed. Have you forgotten what it is like to be newly made? I will take her now, to bathe and dress her. All of you go, as you will. But bring more back with you. She will hunger again soon enough."

Alu nods at me, and bows to Lilitu. Then he gestures to the rest, and they leave, swift and silent as they came.

Lilitu takes my hand, leading me across the chamber into a long hall lit with the shimmering light of a few alcoved lamps, and hung with golden-threaded tapestries. There are figures woven into the glistening cloth, and I am dazzled, entranced by each intertwined thread. Every stitch shimmers like the sun on water, and I gasp aloud, distracted as any child, as each form seems to move along the fabric. Their embroidered gazes glint and follow as Lilitu leads me further, down curving steps carved deep into the earth and on into a smaller room, where a bath has been poured.

Candles light the room in shades of red and gold, casting dancing shadows upon the tiled walls. I am silent, staring in awe as Lilitu picks up a small clay jar and pours scented oil into the steaming water. I am so silent that she moves to me, her cool hand cradling my cheek, those deep green eyes filled with concern.

"Have you lost the will to speak, child?"

I shake my head and draw a breath. Even that feels new. The air is cool and thick in my lungs, as if I have never taken breath before. I can hear my own heartbeat, loud as thunder in my ears, and hers as well, strong and steady. I feel the flow of my blood as it circuits my body; feel it pulse through every vein, to the boundaries of my flesh and back again, in a constant rhythmic journey. I try to form the words a few times before I find my voice. When I do, it does not sound like my own. It is richer, sweeter; its timbre melodic and strange to my ears.

"I am sorry. I had thought I was dead. And now I have become...I...I am..."

I do not have the words. I do not know what I have become. I know the name, but it is a word only. It does not describe what is happening to me. It does not describe this woman who stands, pale and beautiful before me. I look to her and swallow hard against the tears stinging my eyes.

"Oh daughter." She takes me in her arms and holds me tightly as the tears spill down my cheeks.

After a moment, she lets me go, then guides me into the bath. Sitting me down like the smallest of children, she smiles and leans gently in, kissing my tears away. Then leaning back and licking her lips, she takes up a cloth, wets it, and gently washes my face.

"You have become as I am, as we all are. You said a name, and that describes us well enough. As Alu said, it is but one out of many, but it suits. Like unto your Utukku we deal out judgement; whether by our own will or by the will of the gods, it matters not, for the result is the same."

She wrings the cloth out into another smaller basin, the water pooling crimson into the hollowed stone.

"From this night on you will live as one of us. You will not change from the way you are now. You will never grow old, and you will never die. You have become immortal as the gods. This is a gift we do not give easily." She washes my neck and shoulders, then wrings the cloth again, and smiles down at me. "You are to be the last of seven. The youngest of us."

I nod. We have tales of men who would become as immortal as the gods, but they always must endure many trials, and journey far into the underworld in their search for such a gift. I have endured no trial, other than my trials for the Priesthood which seem so long ago now. I never even left my beloved city. A shadow of grief and loss shudders across my soul. My city. My fate. What has become of me?

I voice my question to Lilitu, my voice trembling. "But why? Why was I chosen?"

She continues to wash me, cleaning the rest of the blood and mud from my skin as she answers.

"You called out for the aid and vengeance of the gods, remember? We heard you and made our choice. Few can endure being what we are. When you sought to take your own life, rather than give it up to your attackers, we knew you had the will to bear our gift. So Alu came to you and then brought you to us."

A shiver passes over me as my thoughts return to the moments before what I thought was my death. Images shadow my memory, of the men who robbed and raped me, of the dagger in my hand, the arrow in my gut. With a gasp I search for the wound, to find my skin whole and smooth. The wound in my breast, where I tried to take my life, is also gone, the skin like new. I touch it in disbelief and look to Lilitu in utter amazement.

She laughs, softly. "You were healed even before you were changed."

I shake my head, still searching my skin for any sign of a wound. "How is this possible?"

She smiles again. "Our blood has a healing gift. It works in everyone differently. In some, it does not work at all. But it worked in you as we hoped it would. You were sorely wounded; you needed to be made whole again before you were changed. And so we took your blood from you and gave you ours, thrice over. The first time our blood healed you, the second time it cleansed you. The final time, it changed you. Forever."

She lifts my chin and holds my gaze to her own. Her eyes shimmer with unfathomable wisdom and power. "You did well, daughter. Not many can endure the making."

I nod again, still lost in memory. Then I recall the moment I woke as I am now, and the man falling dead away from me. I remember the taste of his blood and am ravenous. Deep within me, need uncoils, like a snake. It is the hollowest hunger and driest thirst at once. I turn to Lilitu in confusion and need, and she nods.

"You are hungry. You will hunger more for a while yet, for you are newly made, and need to feed more often. As you age, your hunger may ease. Some. But you will always need blood. Do not worry, the others will bring more to you. Soon."

She finishes bathing me, washing and oiling my hair, and then stands me up, rinsing me off with scented water, helping me out of the bath and wiping me dry with a fresh cloth. There are soft new linens of indigo and white, laid out on a table nearby. She dresses me in these with great care, and then brushes out my hair, leaving it to fall loose and curling to my hips. Then she turns me to face a gleaming mirror of polished copper.

"Now, child, look; look and see what you have become."

Lifting my head to gaze upon my reflection, I gasp. My skin is pure and soft and without blemish. My hair is black as a moonless night, falling about my shoulders in shining waves, smooth as silk. And my eyes—I take a step closer to the mirror, touching my cheek and staring in disbelief, for their usual blue has now become a shimmering silver incandescence, as if something other is radiating from within.

I turn to Lilitu, and she nods again. "That is your hunger and emotion raging within you. Your eyes will always betray what you are, what you feel. Their light will calm when you do. In time you will learn control."

I gaze again at my reflection, amazed. Lilitu lets me stare for a few more moments, and then she takes my hand, pulling me away.

"Come. You will become used to yourself. The others will return soon."

She guides me back up, through yet another painted corridor, and up again through a maze of stairs and passages to a chamber that is nearer to the earth above. This one, however, is bare, unlike those more richly decorated below. There are several openings in the ceiling through which moonlight streams down, lighting my surroundings as clearly as if it were day. I stare at the patterns in the stone, at the glistening grains of sand on the ground, amazed at each intricate detail, at the scope of all I can now behold.

Soon enough I hear a sound from above, and upon its heels, I catch a scent that makes the hunger inside wake and ache with need. All distraction at the beauty of my surroundings flies away, as unbidden, I feel a pang again in my jaw, and an echo of it ripple within my gut, so sharp I gasp and clutch at my abdomen.

Then two of the others—Iyar and Makhir—return, dragging with them two struggling prisoners. Men of the enemy. The scent of their blood and fear is overwhelming. The thirst within rises and turns outwards as the others let the men go in the centre of the room.

Snarling, I leap upon the first of them, crushing him down against the floor. He screams and keeps on screaming as I yank his head back by his braided hair. He thrashes beneath me, but it is the impotent struggling of a small child. I can clearly mark the map of his blood beneath his skin, and without hesitation, I sink my fangs into his throat, into the place where the flow is the strongest. His screams become a wet gurgle, then ragged gasps, then silence, as his life's blood spills into my mouth like the darkest, sweetest wine.

I moan with the pleasure of desperate need quenched, pulling him close as I drink in great, near choking draughts. Someone else is screaming and crying nearby, and I am vaguely aware that the others have gone, leaving me alone with my prey, but I do not care. All I know is this: hunger, thirst, and release. Again, a flood of sensation spills into me as I drink; and this time I recognise it for what it is: my prey's dying emotions. I shudder with each wave and drink until there is no more to drink. Then I lift my head, licking my lips as I let his rapidly cooling body drop to the floor.

Standing up, I look across the chamber at the other man. He has stopped screaming, and now is breathing raggedly, his eyes wide and staring into the darkness. He is clutching a small silver amulet tight to his chest, and whimpering a prayer over and over. I move closer to him, the hunger within me easing enough to let me consider him for a moment, and to note him for what he is; a man-boy, old enough to fight, but not yet old enough to grow a beard.

I step even closer, close enough to let him see me, and his prayers become gasping sobs. Falling to his knees in terror, he begs, in his own rough tongue, for his life. He calls upon his gods, and then, when they do not answer, he calls upon me, naming me goddess, begging for my mercy.

Tipping my head to one side, I lean down and lift him up. His weight is nothing to me. He meets my eyes and his own widen in horror, his sobs and pleas growing louder. His terror drives his heart, and it beats like a drum in his chest. That sweet sound sends a thrill of want through my body. I put my finger to his lips, smiling to comfort him.

"Shhh..."

I pull him into my arms, where he clings to me, sobbing like a babe. I brush his hair back with my hand as I hold him to my breast, and then I lean in and sink my fangs deep into his throat. He gasps, tenses, and then goes limp with a quivering sigh. Slowly, more sweetly this time, I drink his life; the sanguine flood flowing into me as I sink to my knees with him in my arms. This time I pay attention to the feelings borne in his blood. Fleeting phantoms of fear and hope, love and loss, and finally of bliss. After a few minutes, his heart shudders in his breast, its frantic beating fading and failing until my own heartbeat is all I can hear. Only then do I pull away, gently laying him on the floor of the chamber.

I watch as he dies. Then I take his amulet from him, balancing the cold silver in my now warm hand as I look to see what god it was the boy prayed to in vain.

A shudder passes over me then, as I recognise the seal of Enki. God of life. Giver of gifts. The first conduit between the gods and men. The first to give their word to the Priesthood. To men and women like me. Only not like me. For I am no longer me. I will no longer give to my people anything.

Tears spill down my cheeks and a sob escapes my lips, followed by another, and another, until I choke on the rushing flood of grief. I look again to the young man, his form seeming to shrink as his soul sinks into the land of the winged dead. Dead. By my hand. Dead like my mother, murdered. Her life torn from her as mine has been torn from me. As I have taken the young man's life from him.

Is this then what I have become? No longer one who gives, but one who takes? I shudder, sobs ripping through me, anguish rising like a tide in my mind so that I cannot think for sorrow; until I can no longer hold it within, and so lift my head and release a cry that rebounds around the chamber, echoing around me, as I clutch the amulet so hard in my hand it hurts.

The god of life will hear no prayers for or against me.

For I have become death.

Chapter 7

Weak and Wounded

Consciousness returns, accompanied by raging thirst and shooting pain. I don't know how much time has passed, but I'm not burning, so the sun isn't up yet. I try to get to my knees, but most of my bones are broken, and the effort only wakes the thing inside. It screams in my head, a high, piercing wail; hunger pounding through every pore. I'm starving, and too weak and wounded to move.

I fight to open my eyes. It's a struggle, but I manage to get one blood-caked eye open. First the pavement comes into focus, then the fenced-off lot beyond. I've landed face down on the ground a few feet from a parked car, and I can hear, past the pounding in my head, the sounds of a struggle just out of my line of vision; a male voice cursing, gravel crunching, metal creaking, and a desperate, muffled female sobbing.

The girl. Shit. The demon is shoving her into the boot of his car. He's going to get away, going to take the girl and leave me here. No. This isn't how it ends.

I push past pain and try to move. Nothing happens. Gritting my teeth, I try again. This time I manage to move my hand. It's heavy. And my fist is clenched around something hard and cold.

The gun.

I still have the shotgun, and it's not broken. Jesus, that was lucky. Only I can't move. Everything else is broken. Not so lucky.

Fuck.

I hear the slam of a car door, then steps on gravel. Coming toward me. I was wrong. He isn't done with me yet. In desperation, I will my body to move. Move or I will die here tonight. Move. Move. Move!

After what feels like forever, I manage to roll over to one side, balancing on one broken arm—and drag the gun slowly up with the other hand. I can't see. Everything's blurry and red-tinged—but there's a dark shape looming toward me, and by the smell of it, it's Mr Cocky Pants. With the last bit of strength I have in me, I aim for where I think his head is, and pull the trigger. The blast ricochets around the surrounding buildings, and, with an explosion of streetlights and one final whoosh of air, the last demon is gone.

Dropping the gun, I fall backwards; face up to the fading stars. With my one good eye I watch the eastern half of the sky grow pale. I no longer have the blood to heal, and I can't get my body to move anymore. The thing inside is already turning inwards, clawing in desperation at my soul, and although that won't kill me, the rising sun certainly will.

So this is how it ends. Dying from trying to save a girl who was trying to kill me. I'd laugh if I had any breath left.

Sight goes first, everything fading from fuzzy red to a milky fog, then grey, then black. Although I can't see it, I know the first rays of the sun are terribly close to the horizon, as day-drain leeches into my limbs, and all strength abandons me. Not long now. I fight for each remaining breath, broken ribs stabbing as my veins wither away. I feel my heartbeat slow and falter and wonder idly if I will lose consciousness before the sun takes me. I hope so. Burning hurts so much.

My dying senses get a jolt when I hear a thump, then a click, then the creaking of metal on metal, and the girl's scuffing footsteps as she stumbles out of the boot. She's breathing fast. Crying. I smell her tears, her sweat, her blood. So close. And coming closer. I'm confused as I hear her steps on the gravel walking toward me.

Why isn't she running away?

Then she grabs me by what's left of my jacket, dragging me...somewhere. The air gets cooler and I realise she's pulled me under the shadow of the building. Out of the threat of the sun. Heat rises from her skin in waves I can feel. She's so brilliantly alive. And before I can question why she's helping me, something soft and warm presses against my broken lips. Logic and thought slip from my grasp in a split second as the thing inside me turns outward in a surge of need.

Everything goes all disjointed, like a film with most of the stills missing, but the reel still spinning like mad. In that burst of need I can move again, and I grasp the warm soft thing in both hands and sink my fangs into flesh and the quickening surge of warm, sweet blood.

She gives a little cry as I bite down, but I'm too far gone to care. I sink into the fire of the thing inside, revelling in the freedom of it. It's perfect. Pure animal. All I know is hunger, relief, and aching release as I drink my fill. She gasps, then sighs, her body going limp as her blood, hot and sweet, spills into me. So strong.

I moan and pull her in, drinking deep, as thought fades away into ecstasy. I need this. I need this more than anything. My heart begins to beat in time with her own, my ears ringing with the thrill as I sink into the high, dragging her down with me into blessed oblivion. Her life pours through my waiting body like a flash flood through a long dry desert. I'm in Heaven, and I don't want it to end. I reel under wave after wave of emotion, so strong; fear, hope, grief, bliss—they are never-ending. Her heart flutters, once, twice—and still I keep drinking, chasing her heartbeat; nursing the push of every pulse. More. I need more.

Then I get a wave of deeper feeling. Ancient and overwhelming. An abiding love that makes me shudder beneath the weight of it—and what I can only describe as a sharp mental smack blasts through my head, knocking me back to reality. With a cry, I shove her hard away as the rush surges through me. Her blood is so powerful. Too powerful.

I struggle to my knees, grasping the nearest steel beam for something solid to hang on to as the sky and ground change places. Waves of pleasure wash over me as my body begins to heal like it never normally could under the sun. Day-drain disappears and strength returns, my wounds closing in a matter of minutes. And all the while that heavenly high slingshots through me. I don't know how long I'm lost in it, but as I come to, I realise why she's so familiar to me.

This girl has angel blood.

Slowly, I roll to my knees, one hand still gripping the beam as I look around to find her lying on the gravel a few feet away, pale and still.

"No."

Cold shame crashes as I stumble over. She's alive, but barely. She's covered in scrapes and bruises, and her right wrist is oozing blood from two neat puncture wounds. An ache burns in me at the sight. I want more. I always want more. But no. I'm not a killer.

Not anymore.

Tears rise, burning my eyes, but I blink them back as I get a grip on myself, rip off the cleanest bit of my shirt and bandage her wrist as best I can. It won't help. I've taken too much. I know it even as I try to help her. I slam my fist into the ground, sending small bits of concrete flying.

No.

I have to save her. It mightn't work, but I've got to try. Sitting up, I pull her into my arms and bite into my wrist, placing the wound over her lips. Just a bit. A bit will do no harm, and it might keep her alive. If her body accepts it. It's not like in the movies. It's never that easy.

"Come on, come on..."

I do something pretty close to praying, willing her to take it with everything I have in me—until her mouth closes around the wound, and she begins to drink.

I let out a long breath, and sink back against the beam with her in my arms. Hallelujah. She'll live. Okay. But I still need to get her somewhere safe.

I wait until she takes a few deep mouthfuls, then pull away. She moans and mouths for more, but I can't risk it. I have to finish healing my own wounds, and too much of my blood can cause strong reactions in humans. Not that this girl's all human. Still.

Laying her back down on the ground for a moment, I do a quick search around for my mobile. I don't have much time. After a few minutes I find it. In several pieces. It must've shattered when I landed. Okay, so I can't call Jude. New plan. I pocket the pieces of phone and risk a wincing glance up at the sky, which is worryingly near blue.

Damn it. Looks like it'll be a sunny day. Not good. I'm still reeling with the blood-high, but it's calming down enough to let me think. I really screwed up. There's a huge mess up on the rooftop. A mess I can't get to right now. My blood is everywhere up there, and although it'll burn up in the sunlight, the corpses won't. Plus, the demons that were in them aren't dead. They'll take a while to come back. But they will come back. And when they do, they'll be angry.

Shit.

Hunching my shoulders against the ever-brightening sky, I dash over to the body of Mr Cocky Pants, scrambling through his pockets. It's not long before I come up with a pretty damn big wad of cash, a handgun, a substantial bag of various illegal substances, and his car keys.

Brilliant.

Hurrying, I lift the still-unconscious girl to the car, slide her into the passenger seat and buckle her in. There's more colour in her cheeks now, and her wrist has stopped bleeding, which is good. For both of us. I cover her with my shredded jacket, grab the shotgun and the handgun, toss them, the cash and the drugs in the backseat, and rush to the driver's side; slamming the door, jamming the key into the ignition and gunning the engine.

The car goes skidding out of the lot, spitting gravel and burning rubber as I head for home, away from the sunrise; thanking the gods it's early in the AM on a Sunday and there's no traffic.

I don't live all that far away. Especially not at this speed. Not ten minutes later I slow the car down as I turn onto the quays. No need to call unnecessary attention to myself.

The sun is above the horizon now, but the entrance to my garage is in shade. Ducking out of the car, I punch the security code into the little box by the door. It rumbles open, and I get back in the car and drive down into cool, blessed darkness. Getting out, I hit the keypad to shut and lock the door, then gather the girl into my arms, and head up the stairs.

She's warm, warmer than I ever am. And even over the sweet metallic scent of her blood, over the deeper iron scent of my own, and the sour stench of demon, there is the subtle scent of her. She smells so good. I take a deep breath before laying her down on the bed, then get a firm grip on myself before leaning in, my fingers at her throat, to check her pulse. It's there, faint, but steady. She'll be okay.

The desire to taste her again rises, and I jerk my hand back, clenching my fists as I push it away. After a moment, it subsides enough for me to carry on. Her clothes are torn and covered with blood, most of it mine. I carefully undress her, gently tuck her under the duvet, then move across to the kitchen.

Dumping her clothes and shoes on a chair, I think for a second, then go back down to the demon's car. I find two more clips for the gun and another bundle of drugs in the glove box, but nothing else except rubbish. Grabbing the gear, I come back up and toss everything on the table—money, drugs, guns, keys and my own broken mobile from my pocket. Then I remember Jude. He'll be on his way by now.

Shit.

I run a hand through my hair, shedding flakes of dried blood on the table and floor as I think. I look across to the sleeping girl. She might have a phone I can use.

Picking up her jacket from the pile of clothes, I go through the pockets and remove a folded sheet of paper, two candy bars, a glasses case with a spare pair, a small amount of cash, a couple of credit cards, and a student ID for Trinity. Her name is printed in neat computer lettering next to a small photograph of her wearing glasses and looking studious. Grace Carroll. Grace. I say it, under my breath. A good name.

I also find three small vials labelled 'Holy Water', and bingo: an intact mobile. Locked of course.

Walking softly back over to the bed, I gently take the girl's—Grace's—hand and, recalling how she held the crossbow, press her right index finger to the phone. It unlocks with a click. I let out a sigh, tuck her hand gently back under the duvet, move back to the kitchen and punch in Jude's number. After a few rings he answers cautiously.

"Hello?"

"It's me. Listen, are you close?"

"Rue, what's going on?"

I shake my head. "I'll explain when you get here."

"I'm on my way now. It took longer than I thought."

He sounds irritated. I close my eyes, feeling the last of my wounds heal, leaving only bruises, the blood-high fading incrementally as a result. I can only imagine how sweet and strong it would be were I not wounded at all.

I catch myself licking my lips and shake myself out of it. "Look, my phone's broken. Call me on this number when you get here and I'll buzz you in."

"Is everything okay?"

"Everything's fine." I lie and end the call.

For a minute I stare at the little glowing screen, lost in thought. Everything is so not fine I hardly know where to begin. I put the phone down and stare at the pile of stuff on the table as I try to work everything out. I need to calm down. Things have been this screwed up before, just not for a long time, and not in this way. Methodically, I go back over what happened tonight.

Those demons came out of nowhere. Which means they probably had help. They were weaker than usual, or I never would've been able to defeat them. And they were obviously sent after the girl. But by whom? They said 'he'. Another demon? Maybe. Maybe not.

They were talking about draining her, saying all 'he' wanted was her blood. Understandable. Her blood is incredibly powerful. But what the hell would demons want with angelic blood? They aren't going to drink it. At least I don't think they are. There's so much I still don't know about the Truly Damned. Frowning, I reach over, going through the pile of demon things. The shotgun is no longer loaded, but Mr Cocky Pants' gun is, and it's fully automatic. With a full magazine. Don't know why he didn't just shoot me.

I tug open the plastic-wrapped bundles of what turn out to be heroin, cocaine, and various pills and powders, all bagged and ready for street sale from the looks of it. Each little baggie is stamped with a black mark.

Frowning, I pick one up and look closer. It's a chaos symbol. Lovely. I toss the baggie back with the rest and count the cash. Three grand and change. All mine now.

I look over to the bed, watching the girl sleep. My blood's still healing her, even as hers is healing me. The colour has returned to her face, and her heartbeat is strong enough now for me to hear it from across the room. Jesus. I've never met an angel baby before. But that's what she is. They are rare, the offspring of angels. Rarer even than my kind. And we're rare enough.

I wonder if she knows what she is.

I know the rumours, but I also know from experience they are just that. Rumours. Supposedly, if a thing like me drinks from a thing like her, it will cure the demonic disease within us. Presto. Instant fix.

But it's not true. Angel blood only makes us stronger, able to withstand the drain of daylight, able to heal faster, and to go longer without feeding. It can also silence the thing inside for a while. Which is nice.

It's also highly addictive. Most of my kind have never had the chance to drink it, and so the rumours persist. Now I've had it twice. And, truth be told, I'm already craving more. Last time it took months for the desire to wear off.

I put my head in my hands and think back, recalling everything I know about angels and their offspring. Not that they were always called angels.

Not that I was always called a vampire.

Chapter 8

Dark

I wake to silence and a raw and gnawing hunger. My limbs are heavy and weak, and for a moment I do not know where I am. Then it comes back in a flood. I am beneath the earth, in cool carved stone chambers that are to be my home for eternity. Lilitu brought me here after I fed. A shudder passes over me as I remember. I was crying, sobbing. I grieved the death of the young man I killed, the murder of my mother, the loss of my city, the loss of my gods, and most of all the loss of myself. All I had thought I would become.

Lilitu comforted me through the night as I wept until I could weep no more, kissing the tears from my face, soothing my sorrow with soft words of comfort. She led me here, at some point in the early hours before dawn, to these rooms, to this bed, where she laid me down and held me as I cried. Even as my own mother used to, when I was small. I do not remember when I gave in to sleep, but my dreams were black and empty.

Forcing my leaden limbs to move, and fighting a terrible light-headedness, I stand and survey my room. It is as richly appointed as the caverns above. The bed is soft and piled high with furs and fine linens; the pillows stained with blood. I am at first shocked to see it—and feel my face and head for a wound. Then I look to my hands to find my fingers also stained, and remember. The taste of blood as I wept. The blood of my own tears upon my lips, Lilitu drinking them softly, as I cried and cried.

I shudder involuntarily, then walk to the adjoining room, where there is a large basin for bathing under a carved nook filled with soft soaps and scented oils, combs and brushes. Next to the basin is a polished copper mirror, and beside that, a long narrow couch piled high with the finest clothes. There are candles and lamps set about the chamber at intervals. Only one of the oil lamps is lit, yet I can see quite clearly.

Avoiding the mirror, I walk back into my bedchamber. Like the rest of the rooms in this place, it is circular, with a low curving ceiling; a ceiling that has dark squares of heavy cloth hung at intervals along its lowest points, where it meets the wall. Curious, I walk to the one nearest and tug the cloth aside—only to be blinded by searing light. I scream, throwing my hand in front of my face and hurling myself backwards as the cloth falls back to cover what I now know to be a shaft like those in the chamber above. The smell of burning flesh fills the room, and I gape in horror at my hand and arm. They are scorched, the skin red and blistered, like that of an animal on a spit. I can feel the skin on my face is the same where the light fell upon me first.

The pain is terrible, and I crouch down against the wall, sobbing, shaking, and too terrified to move.

Lilitu finds me there, some time later, shivering and petrified. Kneeling beside me, she reaches out to brush my hair from my face with a cool hand.

"What is it, daughter?"

Shaking my head, I look up to meet her eyes. "I woke, earlier, and all was silent. I went to pull aside the curtain, and the light..." I cannot finish, still not understanding.

"I am sorry, child." She shakes her head, her eyes soft with sympathy. "I should have told you, but I did not expect you to wake before me." She sighs. "It happens sometimes, that the newly made wake well before nightfall." She takes my hand in her own as she continues.

"You will no longer be able to walk in daylight, for you have become a creature of night, and of darkness. The shafts provide us with fresh air, and are fitted with copper mirrors, so that they reflect the light of the moon and stars into our dwelling. Of course, by day, they reflect sunlight, and as you have seen, the light of the sun will harm you, and will kill you if you remain in it for long. Because you are young it will burn you swiftly, and severely."

She smiles, giving my hand a gentle squeeze. "When you are older, it may not be so. You will be stronger, and able to stand in shadows or move about when the sun is veiled behind layers of cloud. But its light will always tax you, take your strength and leave only weakness. This is why we sleep when the sun wakes. In time you will not rise so early, for the longer we live the more the light of day makes us weary, even when we hide from it."

Cupping my chin, she leans in to plant a soft kiss on my forehead, then she stands and pulls me to my feet. "But it is day no more. Night has fallen, and you are healed."

Startled at the revelation, and disbelieving, I look down at my hand to find it whole and unblemished once more. I touch my face, to find the same. The pain too is gone, and in its place, a growing, ravenous hunger.

Lilitu smiles again, but this time the smile is that of a predator, her eyes alight like a lion's. "Come. Alu waits to take you into the city. Tonight, you hunt with us."

My own hunger stirs once more at her words, and at the memory of the night before. A hollow ache grows within as she leads me out of my rooms and up through the maze of corridors, to the central chamber where Alu is waiting. He nods to Lilitu, and to me as I step to his side.

"I see your hunger moves within you, daughter. This is good. But do not rush to feed. You must learn to walk among your prey; to choose the right moment. Tonight, we will show you."

With that, he and Lilitu walk out of the chamber, and up a winding stair. They move like the wind, but it is not difficult for me to follow. In moments only, we reach the surface; the night sky stretching out above us like a coverlet.

We stand on an outcropping of rock only a few miles north of my city. Below us, I recognise the looming outline of the temple, and the curving silver of the great river as it flows past the walls that surround my home. At first, I feel a surge of joy, thinking perhaps my city was not ruined after all, perhaps my people survived—but the starry night is bright as day to my new eyes, and when I look closer, I can see smoke curling up in places, crops burnt and livestock slaughtered. A shudder passes over me, which has nothing to do with fear, as fury builds in my breast. I turn to find Alu and Lilitu watching, and nod.

"I am ready."

We three descend like a silent storm. I am amazed at how quickly the distance is covered. I can run faster than the swiftest chariot and not be short of breath. I delight in this newfound speed and strength. As we approach the city, I see that the gates no longer stand. No one guards the northern entrance. The stench of death lies heavy in the air. Beyond the crumbled walls, and into the city proper, past ghosts of houses, no one moves. This is a city defeated. A city ruined.

Grief and anger clench around my heart as we move silently between the buildings. This was my city. These were my people. The pain in my jaw stabs anew, and I feel the unfamiliar sharpness of my new teeth against my lips. A furious hunger stirs within, and I snarl as we round the corner into the temple complex to find a small encampment of the enemy. Ravagers. Murderers. Rage builds to a tempest in my breast, and without thought, I move to attack, vengeance and hunger screaming to be satisfied in equal measure. I do not get more than two steps out of the shadows, however, before I am stopped mid-stride by a hand on my arm. Lilitu. Her strength is unfathomable. Although her hand presses only softly upon my arm, still, I cannot move. She shakes her head and gestures me to stay and watch. I obey, stepping back as Alu moves alone into the camp.

There are not many of the enemy here. These few seem to be what was left to hold the defeated city, and they are drunk, quarrelling and shouting over their fires. I watch my maker walk among the men unseen, drifting through the camp like so much smoke, until he finds one who has moved a little away from the others to relieve himself. Alu strikes like lightning, giving the man no time to scream as he drags him back into the gloom to finish him. My hunger twists within me like a knife as I watch, but still Lilitu will not let me go. This time she leans in and whispers in my ear.

"Wait, daughter. Hold tight your hunger, but for another moment. Then when you feed, it will be all the sweeter."

And with that she is gone, so swiftly I gasp, startled. I peer into the camp, to find her already there. Unlike Alu, however, she lets herself be seen, walking amongst the men like the priestesses at the New Year. She is all too soon noticed by not one, but two of them. They follow her out into the darkness. Willingly.

I know they will not live to see the morning.

It is my turn. I wait another moment, watching the men as they celebrate, ignorant of the fact that their deaths walk among them—and then I too move into the camp, skirting the edges, the men oblivious to my presence.

I see the warmth rising from their bodies in ripples, like heat from noonday sand. My hunger pulses in me, driving me nearer, and nearer still. I smell their blood, their life. It is intoxicating. I move further into the camp, wondering which one I will choose, when the choice is made for me. One man, drunk and half asleep, stumbles up from beside a fire, and right into my path. He starts back, cursing, then gasps as he sees my eyes, grabbing for his dagger. Too late. With a snarl I am upon him, one hand over his mouth so he cannot scream. I drag him back into the shadows and sink my fangs into his throat.

His struggles stop as I bite down, and I thrill to the surge of his blood, his hope and fear echoed in the pulsing stream. Gods. This is bliss. And over far too soon. In minutes I have taken my fill, and I let him drop to the earth as his life's blood moves within me, warming me, making the ache within a little less so. I watch him die and feel a stabbing of grief. But it is short-lived, my sorrow. For tonight I am vengeance.

I move back through the camp, taking two more men to their deaths, striking like an arrow from a bow, knowing less sorrow with each. And then Lilitu is there, at my side, drawing me back.

Drunk with blood now, and wanting more, I do not wish to go, but she pulls me away. Away from the hunt, and the men still blind to the death all around them. She takes my hand, like a mother to a child, and together we move like ghosts through the deserted city, then out beyond the walls.

I turn to ask where she is leading me, when she stops, drawing my attention to a crowd that has gathered around a rectangular pit in the ground, a little way from the city. I stare, uncomprehendingly at first, at a group of people—my people—as they loosely wrap body after body in smoke and blood-stained cloth, and throw them into the mass grave.

I cannot believe it. There are so many dead. And such a burial, without ceremony, without carefully cleaned and blessed linens—without even a priest—is sacrilege. These dead will not be remembered. I choke back a sob as images of the attack, of the screams of my people, of the smoking body of my mother cascade over me again. No. I will not allow this. With a cry, I run forward before Lilitu can stop me.

Stumbling down into the crowd below, I head straight for the bodies, weeping as I rip the cloth away from the face of each one, past caring if I am seen. I must find my mother. She cannot be buried this way. She will not be forgotten.

The people start and run from me as I stumble amongst them. Desperate, I turn to face one of them; a middle-aged woman with grim lines in her face. I reach out to her in supplication, whimpering my mother's name, but she backs away, her fingers splayed in a sign of banishment as she shouts at me, "Gidim...Edimmu!"

Screaming my frustration, I move away, searching frantically through the dead, calling out my mother's name, tearing at face after face of the soon-to-be-forgotten. But I do not find her. I do not find my mother. I look to the crowd once more, and they stumble over each other as they back away, muttering prayers of protection and making holy signs against me.

Against *me*.

I stop, my heart breaking, and reach to them, pleading—but meet only faces filled with fear. Crying out once more, I sob my mother's name in a desperate question, but they shake their heads and turn away. None will help me. None will even meet my gaze. My people.

They are terrified of me.

Suddenly, Lilitu is there, and Alu with her. My maker draws himself up, beautiful and terrible, his fangs bared, his eyes like silver fire, letting everyone see him, before turning to lift me up and carry me away. The three of us speed south toward the gulf, where we finally slow, and stop.

There Alu lets me go, and I fall to my knees on the sand, screaming my sorrow to the sea. Again, and again I cry, beating my rage and grief into the waves, until it seems all the oceans are filled with my loss, and I am left an empty shell.

Alu stands a little way away, watching silently. After a while, he leaves without a word. Lilitu, however, stays with me until the eastern sky fades to a line of bitter blue, and I feel my limbs grow weak. Then she draws me up into her arms, speeding us both back to the North, back into the maze of chambers under the earth, back into my own rooms, where I numbly let her guide me to sit.

Once more she takes up basin and cloth, once more she kisses away my tears; once more she washes my face, then gently washes my hands, softly wiping the mud and blood from each finger. I do not speak, even as she removes my sandals and bathes my feet like a servant. I am death, and death is silent, cold and empty. She watches me for a long while, then finally speaks.

"I know how it is with you, Asharru."

It is the first time she has used my name, and I lift my eyes to her own, startled to hear it. She holds my gaze as she continues. "I too felt as you do, when I was newly made. Grief stormed within my breast like a tempest until I felt my rage and sorrow would drown the world."

She pauses as she dries my feet and guides me to my bed, where she lays me down with my head in her lap, smoothing my hair as she speaks.

"All that I had, all that I thought I was and ever would be, was stolen from me in an instant. I thought the pain would never end." She sighs, resting her hand on my cheek.

"But it did end. As yours will end. I promise you."

I shake my head at her words. I do not believe this suffering shall ever cease. Why should it? I am a drowning soul, damned to darkness and dust.

Forever.

A shudder passes over me, and I close my eyes, hoping that this is all a nightmare, a vision only; that I am still in the chamber beneath the temple of Inanna, and that I will wake to the sun shining over my beloved, peaceful city.

But this is not a dream, and never again will I wake to sunlight. Never again will I have the love and adoration of my people, never again will they turn to me for guidance. They are no longer my people, for I am no longer one of them. The truth of it cuts me like a knife, and I cling to Lilitu as she holds me, weeping until I have no more tears; and the dawn draws me away into empty, aching dreams.

Chapter 9

Demon and Angel

Grace's mobile rings, startling me out of my reverie. It's Jude. He starts talking as soon as I hit accept. "I'm here."

I buzz him in and hear him rushing up the stairs. He bursts through the door, carrying an insulated cooler bag, and gasps when he sees me. "Christ, Rue, what the—!"

His eyes go wide as he takes in my shredded and blood-stained clothes, my face and its remaining bruises; then his gaze trails to the unconscious girl in my bed. He looks to me, back to her, me again. I shake my head and put a finger to my lips, motioning him over to the kitchen.

His lips tighten, but he stays quiet as he puts the bag on the table and sits down. His eyes flick to the girl, down to the paraphernalia on the table, then back. He leans in to whisper, although that's silly. I could hear him whisper a hundred feet away if I wanted to.

"What happened to you? And who is she?"

I tell him everything, the whole night's events, starting with the nightmare. I only leave out the fact that it was demons that attacked us, not just men, and the bit about the girl's—Grace's—angelic blood. That's her secret to keep, not mine to give away. Besides, Jude's a priest. He knows what I am, and believes, as he's seen enough proof in the past, but I don't know about the whole demon and angel thing. I'm not sure how he'll react to the truth behind his faith. So, I leave it. For now.

He listens without interruption then frowns as I finish.

"So these guys—what did they want with her?"

"I don't know. Anyway, I got in the way."

He glances over to the girl again, frowning. "Will she be okay?"

"She'll be fine. My blood's healing her, her body's just making her sleep while it works. It affects some people that way. She'll wake up soon enough."

He meets my eyes, his own full of worry. "And when she does, what then?"

I shrug. "Then...we'll talk."

He sighs, rubbing his eyes with thumb and forefinger. "Are you sure that's a good idea? I mean, you don't know anything about her."

"Not true. Her name is Grace, she's enrolled at Trinity, and she's not a very good vampire hunter. Somehow, she found me. And then those men found her. Then she saved my life, and then I saved hers. That's more than enough to start a conversation."

He glares at me. "I only want you to be careful."

I smile. He's a good friend. And the only real friend I have. "I'm always careful."

He frowns, not happy. "Right. I'm worried about you. Why do you think you dumped all the blood out earlier? And you don't even remember doing it?"

I change the subject. I don't want to think about it right now. "I don't know. Anyway, I need to clean up. And get some rest."

He nods, a puzzled look on his face. "I was gonna say, you're very awake for seven AM."

I look to the microwave display again, surprised. Two hours past sunrise and I'm still way more alert than I would normally be. No day-drain at all. I was so intent on getting away from the sun, getting Grace back here, that I didn't notice. No weakness. No vertigo. It's her blood.

Gods, I want more.

"Must be all the excitement." I lie and give Jude a reassuring grin. "You go on. It's Sunday, after all. And thanks for getting more blood for me."

He stands, still looking at me with that worried expression. "Are you sure you'll be okay?"

"Who're you talking to?"

"What if she tries to hurt you?"

"She won't. Not after everything that's happened."

"Are you sure?"

"I'm sure."

I don't remind him why I'm sure. When humans drink my blood, it makes them very attached to me, and unwilling—even unable—to do me any harm. It's an effect that wears off, after a while. Jude drank my blood once. He should remember, and after a moment, I see that he does.

He sighs again. "Okay. Listen, I have to get back for early mass. After-wards, I'll go to the building site and see what's happening, if anything. I'll come back by tonight." He looks me over again. "And I'll burn those." He gestures to my clothes and brings me the bin.

I acquiesce; removing my now ruined jeans, t-shirt, boots—everything's past saving—and tossing them in one by one. I'm way beyond being modest. Jude frowns again at the rest of my nearly healed wounds, his lips a tight line as he picks up the bin.

"You'll deal with the stuff on the table?"

I nod, heading for the shower as he heads for the door.

"Rue?"

I stop, looking over at him. "Yeah?"

He looks uncomfortable, worried, and guilty for some reason. "Just ... be careful, okay?"

"I will. I promise. You too."

He nods and heads out. The door bangs shut behind him, and, with a last check on Grace, I head for the shower.

I'm in there for a while, enjoying the feeling of the water against my skin. It's amazing what angelic blood does to my senses. Everything is clearer, brighter, better. Taste, touch, smell, sound, sight; it's like I haven't been truly alive in years. Fresh human blood gives me a great buzz too, don't get me wrong, but compared to this, it's nothing. And stored blood—what I've been living on lately—is sustenance, nothing more.

I'm so lost to the sensations I don't hear her until she jerks open the shower door. I open my eyes to her standing there, the demon's gun in her hands, aimed point-blank at my head.

It's been a long time since I've been this surprised.

I stand there a moment, blinking as water runs over me and splashes out onto the floor. She shouldn't be able to try and harm me at all. Intriguing. I hold her gaze, watching her watch me. Her heart pounds in my ears. She takes a step closer until the nose of the gun is millimetres away from my head. We stand that way for the better part of a minute.

Of course, I could grab the gun and kill her in a split second. Then again, she could shoot me in that same split second. And at this range, with that gun, I'm pretty sure she wouldn't miss. That gun could take most of my head off. And that could kill me.

After that first minute her arms begin to tremble, and she licks her lips as her gaze drifts over my body, lingering for a millisecond on my breasts, my hips—then darting quickly back to mine. So the effects of my blood aren't entirely dampened.

Okay.

Keeping my eyes on hers, I open myself up to her emotions. I sense her fear and anger, and a rising desire, which makes her confused and afraid. Those raging emotions fire my own. She smells so damn good, the trace of vanilla mixing with a spicier, very human aroma. And underneath all of that, the sweet smell of her blood. I feel the heat rising from her skin, and I want her. Badly. I watch her eyes widen as mine go incandescent.

She licks her lips again, and finally speaks, her voice a husky whisper. "What did you do to me?"

In this situation, I figure honesty is the best policy. "I fed you some of my blood."

The gun in her hands is trembling more and more. She can't keep this up for long. "Why?"

I keep my gaze locked to hers. "Because I nearly killed you when you fed me. My blood can heal. Sometimes."

Her eyes well with tears now, her emotions spinning to a breaking point. But she keeps the gun to my head. "Did it...did you...make me like you?"

I shake my head, slowly. "No."

Relief floods through her and her resistance to the effects of my blood gives way a bit more. Her pupils widen and her breath quickens. But she has some willpower.

Catching herself up as her gaze drifts down my body again, she grips the gun with renewed intention, clenching her jaw.

"Why am I naked?"

"Your clothes were ruined." I meet her gaze with growing difficulty as desire arcs through me, sudden and strong.

Tiny droplets of water gather on her eyelashes, and she blinks them away, licking her lips yet again.

"I know you killed them."

"Who—the demons?"

She shakes her head, ever so slightly. The steam from the pouring water is making her hair damp. Little rivulets drip down her face, her neck, in between the curve of her breasts. My desire is now outpacing hers; I want to take her, drink her, make her mine. It's driving me mad.

This time it's me fighting to keep my eyes from straying as I answer her honestly, my voice heavy with need. "I haven't killed anyone in a hundred years."

She blinks, a few times, the gun trembling violently now, along with her lips, as she whispers a single word.

"Oh."

With that, her resolve collapses. As does mine.

The gun clatters to the floor as I reach out and pull her roughly to me. I can't help myself. She moans as I lean in and kiss her deeply, curving her body into mine as she kisses me back. I know her desire is fuelled by my blood as mine is by hers. But I don't give a damn. I barely remember to hold back my strength as I turn and shove her against the shower wall. I don't want to kill her. I just want her.

She responds with a need that matches my own, moaning as I kiss her deeply again, gasping as I run my hands over her body. Her skin is hot, even under the now lukewarm water. After a few minutes, I pull away from the kiss, licking her blood from my lips. She gasps as I hold her up against the wall with one hand, caressing her with the other.

I breathe her in as I move my lips along her flesh, now kissing, now nipping at her flushed skin, drawing blood a few times, but never more than a tiny amount, until it's me that's trembling. Still, I hold myself back, waiting for her moment as well as my own. She clenches her hands in my hair as I move my kisses slowly down, softly at first and then with intent, listening to her breathing change, reading her want.

At some point, her legs give out, and I catch her, sinking into the bath with her beneath me, the water splashing down around us as I kiss the core of her craving; lingering there, teasing and tantalising, until she is whimpering and shuddering with need. Caressing her breasts with my left hand, I move my right down to meet the place where my lips remain, then gently move inside. She cries out, arching her hips up to meet me, and so I close my eyes and bend my body across her own, my movements soft and slow at first; then faster and harder; harder and faster until the bath shakes with our rocking.

At the last moment, as she reaches that point of no return, I sink my fangs into the smooth curve of her throat, drinking deeply, waves of pleasure washing over me as she cries out and shudders once, twice, again—then falls limp against the bath.

Somehow, I manage to keep control, taking only the one delirious drink, then pulling away before I'm lost completely.

My heart pounds with the power of her blood as I get to my knees, then stand up slowly, reeling with the rush. Again. Gods, yes. Lifting her up, I slam off the now freezing flow of water and manage, somehow, in my blood-drunk state, to get us both across the flat to the bed. She's still shuddering, and I tug the covers up over us and wrap her in my arms.

Her blood spins in my veins, making me deliciously warm and dizzy. I love it, and don't give a damn about anything else in that moment, as I drift away into heavenly sleep.

Chapter 10

Silence

L ilitu was right. Tonight, I am two hundred and fifty years in this place, and, in the centuries that have passed since the night of my making, the pain and loss have faded. Some. I still grieve for every life I take. But I no longer grieve for myself, nor try to deny what I am.

I have changed, even as I have not. My skin has grown pale, my eyes shine in the lamplight, like jewels, and my teeth are moon-white, and wickedly sharp. I am a deadly thing, inhuman. A creature of darkness, of silence, and of shadow.

My city has also changed. Ur, once-great city of more than sixty thousand people, once the capital of a vast and powerful empire, is now little more than a shepherd's village, never recovered from the slaughter two and a half centuries past. My people are fading like mist in the spring wind, their once great empire no more.

Another people have taken their place, calling their new domain Babylon, and their capital city to the North the same. These new rulers use my people's language in sacred writings, and the stories and songs of my people are still remembered, but not in the language I knew. My tongue is no longer spoken by the common man. I no longer hear it in the streets as I walk the night. Everything has changed around me; even the land itself, as if the very earth is mourning my people's passing. The soil has grown harsh and unforgiving, and the river's course has moved eastwards over the years, bending far from the walls of Ur. The irrigation ditches surrounding my city are dry as old bone; the fields and orchards they once fed now bloom only dust, their trees skeletal, dead and broken.

Over years that have transpired as moments, I have learned much. Some things I have learned from the others, some on my own; for time is mine to be spent on whatever I should wish.

I now know more of the history of the world and its many peoples than I thought existed, and have learned how to speak, read and write in the varied languages of my brethren. I have studied the physical disciplines of their myriad cultures, training nightly in the arts of fighting with sword and dagger, with spear and bow, and with my bare hands; for my brethren tell me that keeping my body prepared and strong is of vital importance, to be able to withstand—for a short time at least—the debilitating effects of daylight should ever I need to fight for survival while the sun stalks the sky.

I have as well learned the techniques of the finer arts; of music and dance, of writing, and drawing, and although I cannot sing or create music like Eshe, paint beautiful images like Lilitu, or carve graceful forms from stone like Bion, I have discovered gifts I would have never known had I not time to cultivate them.

I have taken up reed and tablet, have copied down all the stories and myths of my people I can recall, and have even composed verses of my own. I am told I have some skill with the written word. My lament for the loss of my city brought tears to the eyes of my brethren when I recited it to them, and although my writings may never be read by mortal men, it is a gift I am glad to have.

The hunt, however, is the most important aspect of all my learning, and in this, I have become terribly skilled. I have learnt to walk with ease amongst men; to strike in the night with the swiftness of the adder, and leave none to tell the tale. I have learned also to disguise my kills; to conceal the marks left by my bite, and make my prey's death seem natural, or self-inflicted. No longer do I let myself be seen for what I am. Although as I walk dark streets, I often hear whispered rumours of creatures, demons they say; monsters that stalk the night, seeking to steal the life from the unwary. The truth of the past, when I stormed my grief for all to see, has become legend, and we are none of us entirely unknown.

In the alcoves above their doorways, the people place sacred images of their gods, meant to keep us away. It is unnecessary. Early on I learned that we cannot enter any home unless we are granted permission. To enter without invitation brings us terrible pain, as it causes the stolen blood to boil within our bodies. None of the others know the reason why. Even Lilitu says she does not know. I have only experienced it once, in the early nights, when I tried to return to the house where I was raised. Never again will I risk it.

Instead, I hunt the dark streets for those who would also make the night their home: the thief, the rapist, the murderer, the vandal, the drunkard. Even in the smaller cities, there are always those who would hide misdeeds in darkness. These are for me.

Sometimes, when the night is at its most silent, I climb the steps of the Ziggurat, watching the priests at their work in the Temples. These places are not private, and I could enter freely if I wished. But I cannot bring myself to go within. The memories within those walls are still too strong, the longing and loss still too great to bear.

To distract myself from grief, I have taken to walking out into the desert alone after a hunt, watching the movement of the ever-shifting sands, the whispering river, and the dark unchanging sea. I have grown to love the deep stillness there. It is a comfort. I have even collected small vials of earth, from the streets of my city, from the desert beyond, from the bank of the river. These I keep safe, wrapped in silk and stored within a small silver box, along with a few mementoes of my life before.

Although we dwell in the same caverns together, as we have always done, although we are all the Children of Alu, and we talk and pass the time together, we do not take comfort from one another as humans do. I do not mean to say we do not care for each other—we do—but it is not the same love I knew as a mortal. We do not have fear of death or darkness to bind us together. We are darkness. We are death. And each of us must bear this knowledge alone.

I think I feel the burden more than the others do. Perhaps it is because I am still young, by the reckoning of the gods, whose creatures we are said to be. Perhaps one night I will no longer grieve for the lives I must take to feed the raging hunger within. Lilitu tells me this will be so. But I am beginning to wonder if I am like her. Or any of them. I have seen the ease and even enjoyment with which they kill. Iyar and Makhir especially seem to love tormenting their prey. They are cruel and without mercy, and do not care if the lives they take are those of the evil or innocent, young or old, man, woman or child.

I have never killed a child. I do not see how I could do so. In those first nights I killed many men, and in the nights since I have killed both men and women. But never, ever a child.

The Utukku, I was taught, were judges of men, working for the gods, carrying the blood of the animal sacrifice to the underworld. That is our purpose, according to the beliefs of my people. I tell myself that in this I am still a keeper of justice. That at least I do not take the life of the innocent. And yet in my heart of hearts, I fear that I tell myself lies. I have yet to meet a god, or journey to the underworld. Never have I carried a sacrifice anywhere. And animal blood gives me no sustenance. No. I must kill men to survive.

Which means my people were right, that night so long ago, when I searched madly for my mother's body, lost to my grief. They named me 'Edimmu', and so I am. Like those hungry ghosts of legend, I walk the night alone. Like them, I too was torn away from my life, refused entrance into the Underworld, and like them, I too must terrorise the living. Only I am not dead. Perhaps if I were, I would not feel this way. And that thought—that one thought—is enough to give me hope. It is my pain that reminds me of who I am. Therefore, I cling to my grief like a lover, needing to feel sorrow to feel that I yet live.

Alu is my maker, yet he and I are not close. I love him, but it is no greater love than I feel for any of my brethren. Save Lilitu. I do not know why this is. I never had a father. Temple born children do not have fathers. It is understood that we are the seed of the god Enki, in the guise of a man, brought to fruit within and born of our mothers, the priestesses who embody the goddess. Perhaps the love I bear for Alu is like the love of a daughter for a father. I do not know. All I know is that I do not feel any closeness to him, not the way I do toward Lilitu.

Lilitu I love above all the rest.

In the early nights, she often stayed with me until I fell asleep, and even now is often there when I wake. She has become both mother and lover to me. At times I feel that perhaps she also loves me more than the others. And that gives me some small comfort.

Tonight, I rise early, as I always do, and, after dressing, make my way up through the dark passages of stone toward the surface. I am hungry— as always when I wake—but I have more control now. No longer do I need to take two or three lives a night. Sometimes of late I have gone a night without feeding at all. That is dangerous, however, for the longer I go without, the less control I have over the beast inside.

As I walk the corridors, I look at the tapestries, tracing the stories woven into the cloth with a pale hand. I know them all by heart. Old stories. Some so old as to have been forgotten by men, some that I learned as a young girl, some that I never knew until I came here, and Lilitu showed them to me.

She told me that these catacombs were carved into the cliffs in ages past to hold the bodies of the mythical kings of old, before my people rose up and became a great nation; before the deluge. Before men lived such brief lives. In some rooms, there are still mummified bodies buried with all their earthly treasures, but most have long since crumbled into dust. These tombs were forgotten long before I was born, and the Utukku have had possession of them long before I was made. But the tapestries still survive, mended by the skilled hands of immortals.

There is the tale of the beginning of all things woven into the cloth. First an endless, sapphire sea; then that sea is shown broken by a flat disc of green earth and blue sky formed from its waters, in beads of agate and lapis lazuli. The sun, moon and stars are then stitched in their places with glittering silver and gold thread, and each of these sections, Sea, Sky,

Heaven and Earth, has its own god, embroidered in gleaming thread and precious stone.

There is the tale of the Annunaki, first children of the gods, come to earth from the far heavens, and, acting as gods themselves, creating mankind to serve them, to care for the earth and all its creatures in their name.

Also woven along the winding walls is the tale of the Deluge; when Enlil, King of the gods, drowned the earth to destroy humanity because they had grown too noisy. Enki warned one good man—Utnapishtim—of what was to come, instructing him to build a boat and bring all the beasts of the field on board thereby saving humanity and animals alike.

With cool fingers, I trace the embroidered form of Enki. God of water, god of life. The image reminds me of that first night, and I reach under the collar of my linen shirt to grasp the amulet I took from the boy, so long ago. I do not even know if I believe in the gods anymore. If they were ever real, they seem now to have abandoned their creation.

A stabbing of sorrow stings my heart at the loss of my belief, and I turn away from the wall of stories to find Lilitu standing there, watching me, her green eyes glittering in the flickering lamplight.

"Are you still praying to your gods, Daughter?"

Startled that her words so closely echo my thoughts, I blink back blood tears, and shake my head. "No. I do not think they would hear."

She gives a soft laugh, that dark wisdom shining in her eyes. "Perhaps not. Or perhaps they would hear you more clearly than ever before. For are you not much nearer to gods than mortals now?"

I shrug in answer. I do not feel like a god. Seeing my sorrow on this subject, she does not pursue it further, but instead takes my arm and leads me away. "Come. Walk with me a while."

I acquiesce, strolling beside her through the winding stone corridors up to the surface, and the hidden opening of the catacombs. She shoves aside the heavy stone that blocks the entrance with little effort; a stone that would take several strong men to move. I could not push it so far, nor so easily. But I am used to her unfathomable strength and speed. I have often wondered how old she is, but have never dared ask. It is an unspoken rule. We do not inquire after the age or history of another. And yet the others know mine as I am the youngest of us. Which is rather unjust.

I stay silent as we move out into the desert night, thinking on this; that after all this time I still know so little of the others while they know much of me. We walk down the rocky mountainside toward the river, coming out of the shadow of the cliffs, and the stars above draw my attention away from my own concerns. What I have become has not dulled my appreciation of the beauty of the world. In fact, with time, it has only grown. I can see so clearly now, the sparkling beauty of the night, the singing multi-coloured shimmer of the stars, home of the gods, calling to me as they have always done, reminding me of who I once was.

Under my breath, I recite the names of each constellation as we walk across stone and sand, and Lilitu tilts her head to the sky as well. "We called them by different names, when I was young."

Surprised, I turn to look at her, wanting so much to ask when that was, burning to know how long it has been since the creature beside me walked in the light of day. Surely, she must have, at one time. But I hold my tongue. I dare not ask. Then she smiles at me, and I realise that once again she has read my thoughts.

"You may ask, Asharru. You, and only you, may know the truth."

Chapter 11

Dead or Undead

For the first time in a long time I wake up gently, instead of starting up out of the horror of the nightmare. I'm also not hungry. Which is strange. And pleasant.

Grace.

I turn to find she's not there beside me and get a little ache inside at the thought of her. I've got o be careful. I'm already feeling a little addicted. And I'm still a little high. Taking a deep breath, I run my hands through my hair. Get a grip.

After a few seconds I hear her, downstairs. Getting up, I tug on a t-shirt and jeans and head down. She's there, on one side of the couch, cocooned in one of my blankets, her arms around her knees. Curled into a little ball and quietly sobbing. A couple of candy-bar wrappers are crumpled on the table beside the couch, and she's switched on the lamp on the other side. The heavy curtains over all the windows down here are open, but the security shutters are all down; the remote that controls them sitting in front of her on the coffee table.

I watch her for a moment, wondering what I should do. It's been a long time since I've had a human spend the night, and I've never woken up with one alive and crying on my couch. She looks so lost. My heart gives another twinge. I have to admit to myself that I care about this girl. And I'm to blame, at least in part, for her pain. Last night was wrong. I took advantage, and I knew what I was doing, even in the middle of it all. I gave in to temptation, with little thought of consequence.

Fuck.

I cross the room toward her, stopping a couple feet away, and then speaking softly. "Hiya."

She starts, and looks up at me, her face stained with tears old and new. She gives a little shudder and wipes at her nose with the back of her hand. "Hi."

I move to the opposite side of the couch and sit down, curling my legs up under me and giving her a little smile, showing I'm not going to hurt her. "Listen—"

She interrupts in a storm of words. "I tried to leave. I... I couldn't. I'd get to the door and have to stop. Then I tried the windows. I even got them open." She gestures to the shutters. "But I had to shut them again." She stops, sniffs. "Every time. I tried. But I couldn't leave. I couldn't leave you. What's happening to me?"

Her tone veers wildly between suspicion and helpless trust, and that makes me wince. I hate the influence of my blood. It's why I stay away when I've had to feed someone for one reason or another. Of course, most vampires keep feeding them small amounts until they have loyal little pets. Or slaves, depending on the vampire. Some even keep them as lovers; fooling themselves into thinking they have a relationship. But there's nothing real about it. Repeated ingestion of our blood also tends to make humans go a bit mad after a while. Just like Renfield. Stoker got that much right, at least.

At any rate, I have to tell her the truth. And later, when my blood wears off, she'll hate me for it.

I sigh and meet her eyes, realising for the first time they are a lovely shade of hazel, and filled with such innocence.

"It's my blood. When humans drink it—it depends on each person—but it can heal you, make you stronger, faster; make all your senses keener. And it can make you want—*need*—to be around me. A lot."

She stares at me for a few long moments, searching my face. Her pupils still dilate at the sight of me. Her breath comes quicker, her heart beats faster, and she's oh-so-imperceptibly leaning toward me. All of which means the effects of my blood haven't even begun to wear off yet.

But she's fighting it for all she's worth. Which is admirable. She gives another little shudder and looks down at her hands.

"So this morning, in the shower, everything..."

Guilt washes over me in a bitter torrent. "An effect of my blood in you. I'm sorry. I shouldn't have. I just...wanted you. It was in the moment, and after everything that'd happened..."

I trail off as her eyes well up, and although I can tell she's fighting against crying in front of me, tears spill down her cheeks.

Her next question comes in a ragged whisper. "Is it...will it...will these feelings...last...very long?"

I shake my head. "No. Without you taking more blood from me, a week or so at most." I hold her gaze; doing everything I can to reassure her. And myself. "It won't happen again."

And I mean it. I can resist temptation. I have to. For both our sakes.

She stares at me for another minute during which I wish I could read minds like vampires in the movies. I can only read her emotions, and they are boiling under the surface; fear, shock, sadness, shame, and desire. My own emotions begin to respond in kind and I pull my mind away. No.

Closing my eyes, I rub my temples with one hand as I shove down the desire to taste her. Again. I realise, and not for the first time, how close I always am to simply taking what I want. Like I did last night.

Jesus. I am still the monster in the fairy tale.

Tears sting my own eyes as sorrow wells up inside at the cold confrontation of the thing I am, no matter how hard I try not to be. I look down, trying to blink them away before she sees.

Then, to my utter surprise, I feel her warm hand cover my own.

Startled, I look back up to meet her gaze; to find it neither accusing nor hateful, but soft and forgiving. I stare at her, my turn to be confused. Is this the influence of my blood? Or is it more? For a moment I am lost in her gaze, wondering. For a moment I dare to hope. Then her eyes widen at the sight of my blood tears, and I stand up, brushing them away with the heel of my hand.

"We should get you some food."

I move toward the stairs, wiping the blood off my face as best I can, then licking it from my hand before I turn and give her the best smile I can manage at the moment, which is a pretty poor one, I'll admit.

She sits there, staring—but then she gives herself a little shake and stands to follow me upstairs, still wrapped in the blanket. Gods, I can be stupid. She's probably in shock, and here I am feeling sorry for myself. I turn the conversation to small, practical things, keeping her occupied.

"You can wear some of my clothes, I think we're the same size. And I'll put the water on. You can have a wash if you want."

Her eyes darken at the reminder of the shower. Back up in the kitchen, I switch on the light and nod to a chair at the table, clearing off the shotgun and demon gear to another chair.

She sits down, shivering. Fuck. I grab another blanket off the bed, gently tuck it around her, then get her a glass of water. While I'm in the kitchen, I grab a pile of restaurant delivery menus from a drawer and set them down in front of her, along with the water and her mobile. She looks up at me in confusion.

I shrug. "They're always coming in the door. I figured they'd come in handy some time."

She smiles, slowly. So beautiful. Jesus. Desire rises again and I move away, to the loo, wanting to clean up any reminders of last night. I keep talking as I do.

"Order whatever you want. I'll get it. No worries."

She doesn't answer, but she does start thumbing through the menus.

Good.

Twisting my hair up out of the way, I grab a towel and head to the loo to clean up the water and remnants of blood from the tiles. The gun's still lying there on the floor. I dry it off and tuck it into the back of my jeans. She doesn't need to see it right now. Once everything's clean, I switch the water on to heat up and walk back into the kitchen.

She fidgets with the menu she's holding. "I'm not really hungry."

I nod, moving to sit across from her. "That's another effect of my blood. You won't be hungry for a little while. But you still need food."

She glances down at the menu, then back up at me. "Is Indian okay?"

I smile. "Whatever you want is fine. I don't exactly eat."

She nods. "Okay."

Picking up the phone, she dials the number on the menu and then runs a hand through her hair. I follow the movement with my eyes. I can't help it. I love watching her. She glances up at me as she waits for an answer and catches me staring. I get up, grabbing the cooler bag Jude brought last night, opening it up and walking to the fridge as she places the order. I'm not hungry either, but I should feed anyway. It'll help stave off the cravings for her blood and make things slightly less dangerous.

With a sigh, I unpack the cooler. Six bags. That'll barely last me the week. Shit. I'll have to have Jude get more. I just hope I don't go dumping it all out in my sleep again. Anxiety blooms at the thought. I hate not being in control, not knowing why I do what I do. Tossing five of the bags into the fridge, I open the sixth, and then I realise she's stopped talking to the restaurant and is being very quiet. I turn around, IV bag in hand. She stares at me—at the blood—then clears her throat.

"They want the address."

Of course they do. I give it to her, then grab a pint glass and pour the blood in, popping it into the microwave for a few seconds. Cold blood is horrid. So is stored blood, really; empty of the spice of living sensation, it's like drinking cardboard. But at least heating it makes it a tad more palatable.

I grab the glass out of the microwave before it beeps, and, wincing at the flat and sterile taste of it—especially after the taste of her—drink it down in one go. The thing inside wakes, but only to stir and then sleep again. I close my eyes for a minute as the blood settles. It's nothing like the rush hers gives me. But I can't have her. Opening my eyes, I find her watching me. She follows my every movement as I put the glass and now empty bag in the sink, lick the blood from my lips, then move back to sit down across from her at the table.

"So..."

I make the word an open-ended question, in an attempt at moving the conversation onwards. She blinks and lets out a long breath and looks at the stuff on the table. Reaching out, she sorts through the pile of her own things. I wait for her to ask the questions I can feel she wants to. It takes a few minutes, during which I watch her take impressive control of herself, considering the situation she's in. She takes a few breaths, and makes a couple of false starts, but finally speaks, looking up to meet my eyes.

"What's your name?"

That's a start. I smile. "Rue."

She repeats my name, then meets my smile with a shy one of her own.

"I'm Grace."

I nod. "I know."

She looks surprised, and tenses, but I reach out and tap her student ID where it sits on the table, and she relaxes.

"Oh."

I wait a few moments, but when she says nothing more, I figure it's my turn. "What're you studying?"

She relaxes further as I turn the conversation toward familiar ground. Picking up her ID card, she turns it round and round in her hand.

"Comparative Religions. I'm working on my masters now."

That's impressive. And unusual. She watches me for a few minutes. Then she surprises me again.

"You breathe."

I laugh. "Yes. I'm not dead. Or undead. Whatever that means." I grin, joking to put her more at ease, and she smiles in return and goes back to watching me. I don't mind.

Those hazel eyes consider me completely, taking in my worn t-shirt and jeans, my bare feet; wandering up to my arms where they rest on the table, down to the layered black leather bracelets I always wear, to the rings on my fingers I've worn for centuries.

Her eyes widen a bit at my tattoos. I can tell she's curious, but she doesn't say anything. Instead she looks around the flat; her glance moving over the kitchen, the microwave, then drifting to the table; the laptop, the telly, the tidy piles of paperwork, journals and manuscripts everywhere; then across to the sitting room, to the comfy chairs and small tables covered in more paperwork and books; over to the heavy curtains drawn across every window, the half-burnt candles on every surface, the Persian rugs layered over the floor, and lingering on the bed on the far side of the flat.

She blushes then, and looks away for a moment—then shyly back.

"What do you do?"

I smile. Such a very human question. "For a living, you mean?"

She nods, and I shrug.

"Right now, I translate manuscripts. Fiction, non-fiction, old, new. The work comes in online, and it's easy enough. Although it's more to pass the time than anything else."

"Oh."

I watch her mind work away again, as her gaze trails over me then, pausing at the silver amulet on its chain around my neck, and then moving across my body and back down to my arms. I turn them upwards and look down at the simple tattoos that once marked me as a chosen servant of a goddess few people think about anymore.

She tips her head to one side, studying the curving black lines up my forearms. "Snakes. Signifying secrets, knowledge, wisdom, rebirth..."

I raise a brow. "Among other things."

She nods, considering in silence. Again, I wish I could tell what she's thinking.

I let the silence settle for a moment, then feel it's time to turn the conversation to the real question. "So. Why were you hunting me?"

She pauses, holding my gaze like she's searching for something. I watch the battle rage inside her; a large part of her not trusting me at all, and rightly so, while at the same time my blood sings in her veins, telling her I am the only one she should trust. I hate myself as I do it, but I have to tip the scales in my favour. I need to know how she knew about me. I lean forward and take one of her hands in both my own. Mine are warm now, freshly fed as I am, and as I knew it would, my touch fires her desire again, her need to be near me, which makes it that much easier for her to trust me. I watch it happen, behind her eyes, and keep hold of her hand as she speaks.

"I thought you had killed my friends."

I frown. "What made you think that?"

She reaches out with her other hand and grabs the folded-up paper I'd taken from her jacket pocket earlier, handing it to me. "This did."

I have to take one of my hands back to take the paper and unfold it— and then I nearly drop it. It's a fuzzy photograph. Of me. It looks like it was shot from above, with a zoom lens most likely, and from what I can tell it was taken a couple of months back, while I was out walking. Along the bottom of the page is a typewritten description. It reads like a police blotter: Female, late-twenties, 5'6, long dark hair, slender build. All around the edge of the photo are smudges of blood. Human blood. A couple of nights old, by the smell of it.

I look across to meet her eyes. "You'd better tell me everything. From the beginning."

Putting down the paper, I gently squeeze her hand to calm her. It works. She takes another shaky breath and begins.

"I'm at Trinity. I mean—you know that already." She clears her throat, takes another breath and starts again. "Anyway, um...I'm not from here. Ireland, I mean."

I nod encouragement. I'm not exactly from here either. I give her a soft smile, and she continues.

"I was born in the States, but I grew up everywhere. My Dad's an ambassador and my Mom specialised in International Law. So I moved a lot, growing up. It's hard to make new friends, every time. After a while, I stopped trying." She gives a little shrug. "I didn't mind so much. I just buried myself in books. Reading everything. Anyway, after my mom died, I moved back here. She was Irish, and so I got my citizenship and started college. I love my studies, my department, everything about it. But I never really fit in. Never felt like I belonged, no matter how many parties I went to or how many groups I joined."

She tosses me a shy little smile. "But then last year I started seeing Thomas. Professor Richardson. He was sweet, cute, and so smart."

Her eyes grow sad again, and she sighs. "I fell for him. I knew it wasn't bright, or even right, but he wanted me. He told me I was special. And with him I felt special. It was good. Really good."

She reaches up, brushing a stray curl of honey blonde hair away from her face. "It was a few months in, I guess, that I told him about my dreams and the way I see things sometimes."

I interrupt her. "What dreams? What do you see?"

She meets my eyes again, her own shadowed with emotion. "I sometimes dream of things that are about to happen. They aren't always right, but often enough. Also, I can feel what others are feeling, sometimes. Sometimes a lot. And I can tell when people are...different. I've always been able to, even when I was a kid. I didn't always know how they were different, but I knew they were."

That's not unusual. Hunters tend to recruit those with second sight. Still, I need to know how hers works.

"How can you tell?"

She shrugs. "I can see it. Like you. It's all around you. A sort of glow. Yours is dark, but with bits of light..." She trails off, seeming to stare right through me for a moment; then she shakes herself out of it. "I just know. That's all."

I nod. Everyone's sight is different. I won't press her on it now. I keep hold of her hand as she goes on.

"Thomas wasn't surprised at all. He told me he already knew, that he had the same gifts, just not as strong, and could tell that I was like him. He said he'd been waiting for me to trust him enough to tell him." She stares at our hands on the table, lost in the memory. "He told me I was right; some people were different. Some weren't people at all."

She glances up at me as she says the last, and quickly back down. "Then he told me about this group he led. He said they were people like me. Some were students of his, some weren't, but all of them were helping people with their gifts. At first, I didn't want to meet them. I've always kept this stuff secret. I mean, if I ever told anyone, they'd think I was crazy, you know? Before Thomas, only my mom knew, and she died five years ago."

A shadow of loss drifts across her face, and I feel an echo of my own, so long ago. But I stay quiet, letting her continue.

"Thomas convinced me, finally. He was so enthused. Anyway, about six months back, I went to one of their meetings, in an old house in Upper Baggot Street, where they all lived. There were only four of them. Three guys and a girl. I was expecting more. I don't know why. They were nice though—and after a couple of meetings, they told me what they really did. They called themselves 'demon hunters'. And Thomas explained he was their leader."

She smiles at me, sadly. "I thought the whole thing was daft, at first. I mean I thought they were joking. Then, when I realised they were serious, I thought they were crazy. But after a month or so, they took me out with them. Hunting."

She casts a sideways glance in my direction, but I don't react, so she goes on.

"There were two of them who could see things like me, just not as clearly. And one of them had seen a vampire at a club in Temple Bar. They'd been tracking him for two weeks. This night they took me along, saying with me they could be certain what they'd found."

She frowns. "I spotted him right away. This time I had the guys to explain it, the meaning behind the dark glow around him. They said it indicated a vampire, and it meant he was undead, damned, and...without a soul."

She winces as she says it, but I smile, showing her I'm not offended, and she gives me a shy smile back, then carries on.

"Anyway, we all followed him as he went to the club, watched as he picked up a woman. He walked her out, and we trailed them to a laneway. Then Thomas said enough, we had to save the girl from this evil."

Her gaze grows distant. "He and one of the others went into the lane, while the rest of us kept watch, and then—it all happened so fast—we heard a scream, and something dark and cold seemed to fly right by me."

She shudders and grips my hands tight. "The rest of us ran to see. The woman was there, on the ground, bleeding from a wound in her neck, and David was hurt pretty bad. The vampire was on the ground too. Dead. Thomas had chopped its head off."

I frown. That doesn't sound like the death of any vampire. In fact, it sounds a hell of a lot more like a demon quitting a body. Which any experienced hunter would have known. I mull this over as she goes on.

"They were thrilled they'd saved someone. They took David and the woman to a hospital and said it was because of me she was alive. After that, I guess I just...I don't know. I felt I'd found a place for myself. Like the world finally made sense, like I could finally do something useful. I started hanging out with them a lot, helping out. I moved in three months ago. I liked them. They made me feel like I belonged. It was nice."

She smiles. "They all really believed in what they were doing, you know? So did Thomas. Maybe even more than the rest of them." She shrugs. "We didn't do much actual hunting. Mainly it was research and reconnaissance, some weapons training. A lot of reading, collecting information and gathering 'tools of the trade', as Thomas called it. He stayed away from fieldwork and spent most of his time working. In his office. He was very involved with some project. We knew he was working on something major, but he wouldn't tell us what it was. Not even me."

She sighs. "Anyway, because of my particular gifts, it became my job to track suspected non-humans. Especially vampires. From a distance, I mean. I didn't find many."

She glances up at me again. "I did find you though."

Jesus. I must have gotten sloppy over the past few weeks. I shake my head at my own incompetence as she carries on.

"I'm the one who took the picture. A month or so ago. I wasn't absolutely sure. You were different. Something about you..."

She trails off, staring at me for a long moment, her eyes going soft. I wait, and again the inkling that I've known her before haunts the back of my mind. It's unsettling; so unsettling that I have to mentally shake myself back to the moment as she continues.

"I waited a bit before I told the others about you. I mean, you were always alone, you didn't go to clubs, I never saw you hunt, or whatever. You just took a lot of long walks, or went to the movies. Alone. Sometimes you even went into a church, which really confused me. I thought maybe I was wrong about you. Maybe you were something else altogether."

Okay. I've got to be more careful. She learned all that about me in a month. And I never sensed her following me, not until last night. Not once. That's worrying. But she's watching me, close, so I give her a reassuring smile—although I'm feeling anything but assured right now—and she goes on.

"I told Thomas about you first." Her eyes grow dark. "He said I'd done well, and that I mustn't be fooled by your seeming difference. He said I was too good, too trusting; that I naturally thought too well of others."

She glances to me again, a shadow of doubt colouring her gaze. I give her hand a gentle squeeze, and the doubt fades away immediately under my influence. I can't help but think Thomas was right, she is far too trusting. Especially of things like me.

She looks back down at our entwined hands. "Anyway, he said we'd focus on you right away, getting research, tracking you to your 'lair' as he called it."

I resist the urge to roll my eyes. 'Lair'. Jesus Christ. Who talks like that? I shake my head, but stay silent as she keeps talking.

"They were pretty obsessed. I don't know how I felt. I tried not to think about it too much. Anyway, a week ago, I followed you home. Here... I guess?" She looks around again, fear shadowing her face. "I messed up though. I came around a corner too fast, just as you were heading inside, and I thought you saw me. I mean, you looked right at me." She searches my face, eyes questioning.

I shake my head. "I never saw you before last night."

"I was so sure you had..."

She pauses, and I go over my own memories, trying to recall seeing her, sensing her. Nothing. Dammit. If she found out where I live, who knows how many others could have? How did I not notice her? I've been so out of it over the summer, so exhausted, so stressed by that damn dream, but this isn't like me. I don't understand.

I look up to find her watching me again, her expression a tangle of emotion, and she quickly looks away.

"Anyway, I ran, and when I got home, I told Thomas right away. He said this was it—we had to go after you as soon as possible, before you came after us. We spent the past few days getting ready, buying more supplies, doing more research. I wanted to look for you again, but Thomas said it was too risky. He had the others watch your place, but they never saw you. I thought maybe you'd seen me and had gone. Honestly..." She pauses, her eyes searching my own again. "Honestly I hoped you had. I didn't think it was right. Hunting you. You didn't seem..."

She doesn't finish her sentence. So I finish it for her.

"Evil?"

She nods, and gives me a soft, sad smile. Once again shame washes over me, and once again I blink back blood tears, bowing my head and clearing my throat to hide the sudden surge of emotion.

I shrug. "Yeah...well."

What can I say? That I'm not evil? That would be a lie. It doesn't matter that I'm trying not to be. In fact, that proves my point. Good people don't have to work at it.

I stare at our hands, mine pale, hers pink; wishing I was as half as good as she thinks I am, as she goes on.

"Anyway, it didn't matter. Thomas said we'd make a daylight raid. This was the day before yesterday. We had everything ready, except the Holy Water. It has to be fresh. So they sent me out for some."

She stops, looking so sad it's all I can do not to move and take her in my arms. But I know that would scare her. So I just keep holding her hand, and wait for her to go on, which she does.

"It took me a while. Thomas knows this one priest, and I had to wait for him to meet me. I was away for a few hours, and when I got back..."

Tears spill down her face again, and she wipes them away, her voice shaking. "They were all dead. Murdered. And Thomas...was just gone."

Her voice breaks as she begins to cry, and I can't stop myself. I move across and take her into my arms. She clings to me and sobs for a long time. I let her. Tears can be healing, and she's been through more than her fair share of trauma. Eventually, she calms down and I go and get her a damp cloth for her face.

She takes it, with a weak smile. "Thanks."

"Sure." I move back across the table, taking her hand in my own again. I like it there.

She shrugs. "There isn't much left to tell. I tried to call him. A few times. But his phone was off. I didn't know what to do. I knew I couldn't call the police. What would I say?"

She stops and looks down at the photo of me, there on the table. "That was in David's hand. I thought it meant something. That you had fooled me, that you really were evil. That you had followed me, and killed all of them. And it was my fault."

She closes her eyes, and fury stirs deep inside me at whoever really killed her friends. I wait as she gains control again and continues.

"So I took the picture and some of the weapons, and I just left. I didn't think. I just...I had to find you. I was so sure you'd killed them. I thought if I found you, I don't know. I wanted..."

I say it for her. "You wanted vengeance."

She meets my eyes, her own so lost. There's no anger left in them now, only a deep-seated sadness that breaks my heart. "Yes."

I understand all too well. "So you went to find me."

She nods. "I waited for you. Followed you. I figured you'd take a walk along the quays. You do it so often. Go walking alone. I thought if I could at least hurt you." She meets my gaze directly. "I was so angry."

I nod. "I know."

She shakes her head, her expression unreadable.

"I thought you'd probably kill me."

"I nearly did."

"But only because you got hurt saving me." As if she's just remembered then, she grips my hand tightly, and leans across the table, fear in her eyes. "Those things. What were they? Some kind of...zombies?"

I meet her gaze. "No. Not zombies. Demons. Demons in dead bodies."

She stares. "Dead bodies?"

"They have to steal bodies to do anything. Possess them. It's complicated. But the bodies die when they're in them and start to rot. They look like zombies. But they're way worse."

"Oh." She lets out a shaky breath and swallows hard. "They nearly killed you."

I nod, and she shudders.

"What did they want with me?"

I close my eyes. I knew she'd ask that. As far as I can tell, she has no idea what she is. I'm left with a quick decision to make, and decide that telling her now, before I know anything, will do more harm than good. She's been through enough. So I open my eyes to her own and lie.

"I don't know."

It's more of a half-truth. When I know more, I'll tell her. I change the subject, asking something else I really need to know.

"Why did you save me?"

"You saved me first, remember?"

I give a humourless laugh. "If you can call it that. I call it getting my ass kicked."

She smiles, then grows serious. "Yeah. Well. I couldn't just let you die. I thought about it. I did. I almost ran away when I got out of the car. But I saw you, lying there, after you killed that last one. And I couldn't leave you."

I hold her gaze. "But you still didn't have to feed me. How did you even know to do that, anyway?"

She gives me a crooked smile that melts my heart. "The movies?"

I raise an eyebrow. "Okay..."

She shrugs. "I don't know. I wasn't sure it would work at all. And then when it did..." She stops, and blushes again, looking away.

I sometimes forget the intense pleasure humans experience when bitten. After a hundred-odd years of trying to stick to bottled blood, it's easier to forget things like that. We are after all the perfect predator. Something in our bite releases a chemical that overwhelms the pleasure centre in the human brain. Some few are immune to it, but for most humans it's a very good sensation. They don't tend to struggle once it hits. The memory of drinking her blood floods back again and with it the desire to taste her rises up so strong I feel my fangs push against my lips.

I clear my throat and let go of her hand, getting up, walking to the sink and turning the tap on, needing to find an excuse to turn away from her.

"The water's hot now, why don't you have a wash? There are towels and everything in there. My clothes are in the wardrobe." I point across to it. "Borrow whatever you want. I'll get the food when it comes."

She stands up, still blushing, holding the blankets around her and looking both disappointed and relieved at my sudden move away. I pretend not to notice, wiping the sink clean. Again. After a moment, she turns and heads to the shower, shutting the loo door behind her.

I let out a long breath I didn't realise I was holding, and head back to the table. Frowning, I pick up the fuzzy photograph and stare at it, my mind racing.

Someone framed me. That much is certain. But who, and why? The demons that were after Grace? That doesn't seem likely. Why would they bother? No. But then again, they referred to me as "bait". That must mean they knew I would be there. How I don't know. Nor do I know how they managed to sneak up on me like they did. There's a hell of a lot I'm not seeing here. I've got to get to Grace's house. Maybe I'll find something there.

The buzzer goes off from the intercom downstairs. I punch the answer key.

"One sec."

The Indian food. Grabbing a couple bills off the table, I take the stairs two at a time down to the front door. Lost in thought, I pull it open and stop short—face to face with a sneering black-eyed demon, holding a long red-bladed dagger; a dagger that he stabs deep into my chest, and right through my heart.

Chapter 12

Questions

On the Banks of the Euphrates, Babylonia,
1754 BCE

So startled am I, by Lilitu's permission to ask the forbidden, that for a
moment I cannot speak at all, but instead stand, simply staring.
She laughs aloud, a teasing light in those ancient eyes.

"Do you not wish to know? Asharru, if you have nothing to ask, then I
have nothing to tell you." She tips her head to one side, considering. "Although perhaps it is better if you do not know. The knowledge might be too
great for your young mind."

I bristle, anger building in my breast. "I was privy to the wisdom of the
temple and the gods when I was but a mortal child! I was deemed worthy
to be the keeper of the most sacred of secrets before my third decade! Had
I been made High Priestess I would have been the voice of the gods, and
my word would have been law! And now, as Utukku, I have been walking
this earth for over two centuries! Yet you say I am not ready? I am not a
child to be coddled and lied to! I wish to know the truth! When did you
last walk in the light of day? Is Alu your maker? If he is not, who is, and
who made him? What are we, truly? Are we gods? You say we are as gods,
what does that mean? Who was the first of us? Tell me!"

My furious words only make her laugh, and I realise belatedly that it
was her intention to anger me so.

She nods her approval. "Good. I wondered when you would find your
voice again. You have of late grown quiet as Eshe. But I know that is not

your nature, Asharru. You were always strong-willed and quick to argue, even as a child."

That shocks me out of my anger, and an icy confusion blooms in my heart. "You did not know me as a child."

She does not answer. Instead, she leads me along the winding path to the banks of the river, where she sits, beckoning me to do the same. I sit down cross-legged beside her, watching as she gazes out over the moonlit water, and then back at me.

"Did you think the night of your making was the first time we ever saw you? We who dwell mere moments from the city of your birth, we who have walked among your people, night after night, for millennia?"

I stare into eyes that hold a swirling and ancient power I cannot comprehend.

Millennia. She said millennia.

I shake my head, the beginnings of dark understanding trembling within. "Do you mean to say—?"

"That you were chosen long before the night you tried to end your life rather than give it to your enemies? Yes, Daughter." She smiles, her eyes glittering with a dark light.

"It was only a matter of when we would take you, not if. The events of that night conspired to bring you to us sooner than we had planned, yes— but you are not a fool, Asharru. I am surprised that you have not thought of this before now."

I am still shaking my head. The implications of what she is telling me are too great. I was never then, to have a mortal life. My making was not an accident of fortune. It was planned. Denial and confusion crash over me in waves, as once again truths I had thought to cling to are blown away like sand in a storm. I feel the sharp sting of tears, but refuse to let them fall, as bright anger builds within my breast.

"Who was it that chose me? You said 'we'. Was it Alu? Who saw me first as a child? Who thought to take my life from me when it had hardly begun? Tell me!"

She does not flinch from my anger, nor respond in kind. Rather, her smile grows fonder as she gazes at me with love and possession.

"I chose you."

The cold sting of truth surges through me. "You..."

She nods. "I saw you first. One night as you played in the courtyard of your mother's house. You were very young, barely able to walk; but even then, I knew you were the one. You shone like the moon on water. Bright and resilient. And so strong-willed. After that first night, I watched over you as you lived and learned and loved. As you became a woman."

She smiles at the memory, heedless of the storm of fury building within me. I am trembling with it. I feel my fangs press sharp against my lip, and I stand abruptly, realisation upon realisation dawning over me.

But it is the worst of them I speak.

"That night! You could have saved me! You could have saved all of us! My mother, my sisters! My city was destroyed, and you did nothing. Nothing! None of you! You let the marauders have them, let them rape and murder and destroy! You let them have me! I did not have to die! This did not have to be!"

In that moment of rage, I raise my fist to strike her, snarling my wrath. But my hand never falls, for in the next instant she hits me with unfathomable strength, and I go flying backwards through the air, to fall with a stinging splash into the centre of the cool deep river.

Instinctively, I hold my breath as the water covers my head with a hollow roar. As I sink beneath the current, down among the reeds, the shimmer of moonlight fades above me. My heart beats like a drum in my ears as it struggles, my thoughts spinning in a thousand directions. I am immortal. Save for sunlight, nothing can harm me. I cannot die. But can I drown? I never learned to swim.

My lungs burn, and panic sets in. I thrash and struggle to reach the surface—too late. Finally, I can no longer hold my breath, and dark, cold water rushes into my lungs. Stabbing pain wracks me from limb to limb, and my body spasms and jerks as I suffocate. My heart gives a last strangled stutter, and blinding light bursts all around me, a thousand stars that fall, sputter and fade to darkness. Silence.

Nothing.

Then, out of nothingness, I return to agony. A hand hits me, hard against my back, over and over again. I try to scream, but instead of sound, a flood of blood and water spills from my lips, my throat on fire as I struggle once more to breathe. The water burns as it leaves my lungs, and when I finally find my voice, all I can do is sob. I am alive. Alive. And I never want to drown again.

I am shaking, cold, and weak, as Lilitu gently lifts me from the muddy riverbank into her arms. She says not a word, only presses her wrist firmly against my lips. Without thought, I bite and drink, clinging to her like a starving babe.

I hear her sigh above me as her blood flows into me with such force it sends me reeling. It is dark, sweet, and heady, yet is also wholly without the tangled web of fleeting feelings that are carried on mortal blood. No, this is a swift, emotionless torrent, and I am lost to it; drinking desperately, deeply, until she takes her wrist away. New strength courses through my veins, and with it, a shuddering and ancient power. I stumble to my feet, the world shimmering around me, the moonlit night bright as midday. It is as if I am newly made all over again.

She smiles at me, and I feel such a surge of deepest love. Blood tears escape my eyes to mingle with the water and mud on my face, and I do not even try to catch them as shame fills my heart at what was done and said.

She takes me in her arms then, as she has so often done, and I realise that I ache so to be near her. She is the mother I lost so long ago. Closer even, than my own mother ever was to me.

Pulling away slightly, she cups my chin in her cool strong hand and lifts my eyes to meet her own.

"Now. Do you still wish you had not been chosen? Understand me, Asharru; the attack on your city was not our doing. We do not control the movements of men. Surely you know this by now. If I had not come with Alu that evening, if I had not already chosen you, if we had not been waiting for you, you would have died with that knife in your breast. And have you forgotten, so soon, that the sun had only just set when you called out for us? We could not have come any sooner. We could not have saved anyone. Only you."

Sorrow fills me then, and more tears spill down my face as I nod, too filled with shame to speak. A shudder quakes over me, and Lilitu kisses the tears from my face as she has so often done before, then leads me again to sit beside her, a little further down the riverbank, where she takes my hand in her own, smiling softly.

"I am sorry for striking you, Asharru. I had to make you see. I love you."

I nod, my eyes searching her own for forgiveness and approval. "I am sorry as well. You are right, I had forgotten."

She smiles her acceptance of my apology, and again I bow my head, my thoughts swirling in on themselves.

A small voice inside whispers it was to my gods I cried, not the Utukku. And then, on its heels, another: are they not also gods? Is not this creature sitting before me, whose cool hand still grasps my own, a goddess out of myth and time? Many people see her so, and have for millennia. And what then, of me? Am I also a goddess?

I think back, to the young man I killed, that first night. He named me so without hesitation. I look up to meet Lilitu's waiting gaze and ask again the questions that haunt me.

"What are we? Are we gods? If we are not, then what? Who was the first of us, and when were they made? And why?"

She smiles warmly, taking up my other hand to hold in both her own, and giving them a gentle squeeze as she speaks.

"Very well, Daughter. Listen, and I will tell you the truth, as I know it better than all the rest. For I am the first of us. There is no other before me."

Chapter 13

Ash and Blood

Pain erupts from the wound, a soul-searing agony like I have never felt. It rips through me like molten fire, as the demon shoves me back through the doorway. My heels catch against the bottom step and I fall back with him on top of me, his solid black eyes inches from my own.

"The magician said to give this to you, bitch."

Pressing his full weight against me, he pins me to the stairs and twists the dagger. Hard. I try to shove him off, but it's like he's made of stone. Blood wells in my throat, and I choke, gasping for breath. The demon laughs and twists the knife again.

"Where's the girl, leech?"

Can't breathe. Can't move. Panic sets in as images from the nightmare fill my mind. Flashes of blood, smoke and sand. The smell of burning flesh fills the air, but I can't tell where it's coming from. My mind reels away from what's happening, and the demon twists the knife a third time.

"Where's the girl?"

I open my eyes to his own, and manage to draw a ragged, burning breath.

"What girl?"

He twists the knife again and then rips it up toward my throat. I grit my teeth against the pain. I won't give him the satisfaction. I push and claw at him, trying to get him off me, but he only laughs and wrenches the knife out, then stabs it back down again, into my left shoulder.

"You like my knife, you half-breed bitch? I'm gonna slice you up like a piece of meat, then leave you to burn. Now tell me, and maybe I'll stop. Where's the girl?"

I feel the blade scrape bone, pain reverberating to my teeth. Baring fangs, I snarl at him. "Fuck you!"

He sneers, tearing the knife through my flesh again, slicing left and right. Smoke curls up from where he cuts me, and the smell of burning flesh grows stronger. It's me. I'm burning.

This time I do scream.

His grins. "I'm gonna ask you one more time, leech ..." This time he punctuates each word with a twist of the knife. "Where. Is. The. Girl?"

Gasping, fighting the blackness that stalks the edges of my vision, I try to pull away. Then as I press back against the steps, I feel something cold and hard pushing into my back.

The gun.

Wrenching my shoulders around, I twist to reach one arm behind me, while the demon drags the knife down to my stomach. No good. Not enough space. Try again. Fighting the instinct to pull away, I close my eyes and arch my belly toward the blade. The demon laughs, spinning the burning point into me like a slow drill. Fighting to stay conscious, I manage to curl my right hand around the grip where it still sticks out of my jeans, just as he drives the blazing knife deep into my gut. My vision reels and shudders, as I scream, then choke on a flood of burning blood. More smoke rises as my skin blackens and chars, and the thing inside begins to howl and turn inwards.

No. Stay awake. Setting my jaw, I twist the gun around in my hand. There is just enough space between me and the step behind to turn the nose of the gun face out, aiming through my own back. Gasping with the effort, I meet the demon's eyes, and spit a mouthful of hot blood into his face.

"Fuck you. I killed her, you fuck."

With a snarl, he rips the knife out of my chest and presses himself against me perversely, shoving the edge of the burning blade against my throat.

"That's too bad for you, bitch. Because now you're gonna die."

Black eyes full of sadistic pleasure, he pushes down, letting the knife sear its way through my skin. Now. I close my eyes and clench my finger against the trigger. The gun goes off, and a spray of bullets rip out through my body and into his own. He grunts in surprise and tumbles off me to fall back against the open door.

Blood gushes out of me, flooding the steps as the demon drags his stolen body to its feet, rotting entrails dripping from his gut, knife in hand. I slowed him down, but I didn't stop him. At this point I don't think I can. The gun slips from my grasp as my fingers turn to lead. I'm losing consciousness. Then I hear running footsteps, and a shout.

The demon turns his head at the sound, and with a bellow of rage, leaps on me, stabbing the dagger down with such force it drives right through my chest and into the stone underneath, impaling me there. Flames erupt around the blade and a horrible roaring fills my head. All I can see are the demon's glistening black eyes, reflecting orange fire. A monster from my nightmare, face bathed in ash and blood.

"Rue!"

Jude. No. He'll be killed.

Baring fangs against the pain, I wrench my arm from behind me and clench the demon's head in both hands, gouging my thumbs into his eyes and pushing with all the strength I have left. He tries to pull away, but I roar and hang on, digging my nails in, as far as I can, then ripping them out again, clawing his eyes from his sockets. He screams and falls to one side, eyeballs dangling as he stumbles to his feet, crashes against the open door, then staggers out of sight as Jude's horrified face appears through the smoke.

"My God! Rue—Rue!"

I shake my head, trying to warn him, trying to find where the demon is, but I can't see, can't speak. Smoke rises from my chest in thick clouds.

I've got to get the knife out. Grasping the hilt in both hands, I pull with all my might. My hands smoulder where they touch it, smoke and heat searing my eyes. Then Jude grasps the hilt as well—and I'm free, the blade clattering down to the bottom step. The door above opens, and Grace runs down the stairs, soaking wet and wrapped in a towel.

"What's happening?"

Jude shouts something I can't hear, because I'm still burning. I grasp at him—where's the demon gone? I crane around, but all I see is Jude, swearing and choking on the smoke billowing from my wounds, eyes full of love and fear as they burn away. No. Not Jude. Me. I'm fading. The wailing in my head builds to a deafening howl, and everything goes red, then black. Nightmare images flash behind my eyes: searing knives, scorching fire; smouldering to ash—

"Rue!" Jude screams my name, and I hear him, try to find him—and blood, cold and thick pours down my throat. For a second I gain relief. But it lasts a moment only, then it begins to boil, searing through every vein. Pain and horror shudder through me in equal amounts, and I just want it to end soon, to please, please be over.

Grace is there, then, through the fire, shaking me, bringing me back one more time. I look up to meet those sweet eyes, noticing for the first time tiny flecks of gold amongst the green-blue. She is speaking, but I can't hear her past the roaring of the nightmare sun.

Then something warm and yet cooling pours over my lips, into my mouth and down my blistered throat. The pain is soothed in an instant, and the sun sputters and turns from searing light to healing, harmless night. The nightmare images fade away, and everything goes a lovely shade of moonlit blue. Slowly I become aware that I am drinking, and that it is blood. Sweet, healing blood. The power of it rebounds through me as it quenches the fire. I am lost in it. It feels so good. So very good. I want to stay in this bliss forever. I drink deeply, again and again. And then someone's shaking me, shouting, over and over.

"Stop! Rue, stop! You have to stop! You'll kill her!"

I gasp awake, pulling away, then falling backwards as the room tilts sideways. The sweet-swinging high takes me up and spins me around until I'm lost, floating on its gentle tide. Gods, yes. I love it, need it, crave it as it pounds through me once more, healing me in waves of pleasure, pain and pleasure again. It takes ages for me to come down, and when I do I find I'm on the kitchen floor, near the table, and beside me Jude is kneeling over a prone and very pale Grace, clasping a blood-soaked towel around her wrist, which is bleeding swiftly out from one jagged cut and two neat puncture wounds.

No. Not again.

Shoving Jude drunkenly out of the way, I drag Grace into my arms, clasp my fingers hard around her wrist to staunch the blood as I bite down hard into my own.

I let my blood pool a moment, then press the wound to her lips. This time she starts to drink instantly. I let her take few deep gulps, then pull away as colour slowly returns to her face.

I nod across to Jude, my voice rough and broken.

"She's okay."

He lets out a long breath, watching as Grace shudders and opens her eyes, looking up at me with blood-addled trust. A wave of guilt washes over me, but I bury it and give her a smile. "Hey."

"Hey." She smiles woozily back and sits up. I help her prop herself against the wall, pulling myself up to sit beside her. Only then do I take stock of the damage done.

I'm covered in my own blood, and the demon's. My t-shirt is in charred threads. Underneath, my skin is burnt to a crisp, but is healing quickly. The deep lacerations across my chest are closing, burnt scraps of skin falling away. My heart beats again, slow and strong. I'm alive. Not burning. There are empty IV bags scattered all around, and the floor is covered with water, soot, and blood, as are both Grace and Jude.

Shit.

I take a long breath, and give each a nod in the other's direction.

"Grace, meet Jude. Jude—Grace."

Jude smiles tightly, his dark eyes full of worry, and not a small amount of suspicion.

"Hi."

She nods to him, warily, tugging the blood and soot-covered towel around her, her gaze darting from him to me and back, uncertain.

"Jude's my friend." I reach out and give her hand a light squeeze, counting on the influence of my blood to help her trust me. "My best friend."

Jude's eyes dart to mine in surprise, but I'm more focused on hers; watching as they soften, her shoulders relaxing.

"Oh. Okay."

I give her a smile, and look to Jude again, seeing him in that moment as she must; a greying yet still handsome man in his fifties, dressed in black as always; bespectacled, with the white strip of his priests' collar standing out at his throat, and his ever-present rosary beads hanging around his neck. I smile, remembering the young, nervous priest I first met, more than 30 years ago now. Remembering how I instantly liked him. Trusted him. He really is my best friend.

One who just saved my life.

"What happened?"

Jude watches me for a second before he answers, his gaze darting back and forth between myself and Grace, worry colouring every word.

"I was coming to meet you when I heard gunshots and saw someone—something—attacking you at your door. I shouted, I didn't think, and he—it—ran away. But you were bleeding and burning, and there was this knife sticking out of you. You were on fire, trying to pull it out..."

His eyes darken with fear, and he stares down at the blood on the floor. "Anyway, we got it out. But you were still burning. I brought you up here, and we tried to put the fire out, but water didn't work. Then I thought of blood, the bags. I fed them to you, and that worked for a second, but then you kept burning, and you were screaming and screaming..."

He looks up at me again, blinking back tears. "I didn't know what to do. I thought I would lose you." He nods over to Grace. "Then she...she just pushed me out of the way. She had a knife from your drawer, and before I knew what she was doing, she'd cut her wrist and was pressing it to your lips. She kept telling you to drink, over and over. It took a few seconds... but then you did."

He stops, his gaze growing distant. I realise he's never seen me feed before, never seen the effect of my drinking from a human being. We sit in silence for a minute, then he shakes himself out of it. "You stopped burning. But then you wouldn't stop drinking, and I thought..."

He doesn't finish.

I close my eyes and take a centring breath before opening them again and giving them each a nod. "Thanks. Both of you. Really."

Grace smiles, entirely focused on my face. Crushing on the blood. "No problem."

I want to tell her it is a problem. Having a demon at my door is a problem, almost killing her—twice—is a pretty big problem and doing what I've done to her now is an even bigger problem. But then Jude interrupts, looking across to Grace again then back at me in confusion and growing impatience.

"Rue, what's going on? Why did her blood heal you when nothing else worked? What was that...thing...at the door? And what the hell was that knife? Why was it burning you?"

"The thing at the door was a demon." I get up with a groan, leaning on the nearby counter for support. "And the rest, I don't know. Let's have a look at the knife, though. Is it still on the stairs?"

Jude nods, and I take a step toward the door, but he stops me.

"Wait—don't. I'll get it."

He thumps down the stairs and I lean back against the wall, closing my eyes again; trying to ease the swinging high that still sings in my veins. I want more. Jesus. I'm hooked. Fuck. I glance over to Grace, who is still looking up at me with that horrible blood-driven trust. Shit. I want nothing more than to take her in my arms. But I can't. I won't. Instead, I lean down and offer her my hand.

"Can you stand?"

She nods, reaching out her hand for mine. I pull her gently up from the floor, then sit her down at the kitchen table again.

"I'm sorry."

She looks up at me, searching my face.

"For what?"

"I almost killed you. Again."

She shrugs, giving me that soft smile. "But you didn't."

"No."

But I would have. If Jude hadn't been here.

Tears sting my eyes, and I have to look away as Jude comes back up the stairs, the blood-covered gun in one hand, and that hellish red dagger in the other.

"It doesn't burn me." He walks to the table, putting the knife down and staring at it.

I move to stand beside him, and, without looking up, he hands me the gun. I shove it in the back of my jeans and follow his gaze to the knife, which Grace is also frowning at. Now that it's not burning me, it looks relatively normal. Well, the blade is dark red, edged with black, and the hilt is so dark it seems to drink in light—but other than that it looks like any other dagger. I remember the searing pain of it inside me, and wince.

Then Grace speaks up. "I know it."

Jude and I turn to her in unison.

"What?"

She looks up at me.

"The knife. I know it. I mean—I've seen it. In Thomas' study."

Jude frowns. "Who's Thomas?"

"Her teacher." I look from Grace to the knife and back. "Are you sure?"

She nods.

Jude looks at Grace for a minute, then down at the knife, then back up at me. "There's some kind of writing on it."

Leaning closer, and being careful not to touch it, I can see that there are black symbols etched into the blade. I frown at lettering I haven't seen in a very long time.

"It's Aramaic."

"The language of Christ?"

"And a whole hell of a lot of other people." I sigh. "But yeah."

As I stare down at the thing that nearly ended me, my vision swims, and the letters on the knife turn and spin, rearranging themselves into symbols far older, and familiar. Cuneiform. Sumerian. But it can't be. I close my eyes, rubbing at them, and then blinking them open again—and the writing has gone back to Aramaic. I let out a long breath, and realise Jude's asked me a question.

"What?"

He frowns. "I said, can you read it?"

"Oh. Yeah."

It's been a while, and the letters are covered with soot and blood. But I can just make out what it says. I read it aloud.

"Should you wield with will this blade, all that are named shall be unmade."

I look up at the two of them, glad to look away from the knife for a second. "How cute. It rhymes."

Jude glares at me. "Very funny. What does it mean?"

I shrug. "It's pretty self-explanatory. The writing's a spell. You have to know the name of the thing you want it to kill, say it to the knife, and it will kill them. Simple." I wince. "And very painful."

Jude rubs the back of his neck, staring down at the knife for a moment. Then he looks back at me. "So...it's magic."

I've told him about the existence of magic—real magic—before, but I'm pretty sure this is the first time he's seen it in action.

"Yes. Simple, but powerful, black magic."

"So the thing at the door...the..." He pauses and swallows hard, his eyes full of fear and confusion.

"The Demon." I say it for him.

"Yeah. He...it...used magic."

"No." I shake my head. "They can't. Demons. Like I've told you before, humans tend to call anything they don't understand 'magic'. But at the same time, you are the only ones that can use magic. The rest of us, whatever Other, we are magic. But we can't use it. Can't manipulate it. We can only work with what we are."

He still looks confused. "So how was the demon able to use the knife?"

I explain. "The knife's a pre-magicked thing. Anyone can use it. The spell is in the knife itself."

"But the demon couldn't have made—magicked—the knife."

"Right. He'd have to use a human to do it for him."

"So...someone made this knife to kill you?"

"It mightn't be specific to me. The spell seems generic." I frown, remembering. "That demon said something. He said, 'The magician said to give this to you'. Right after he stabbed me the first time."

Grace frowns. "I don't understand. Why did the demon have Thomas' knife?" Her eyes brim with tears as her uncertain gaze flits from the knife to me and back; my blood making her trust whatever I say or do, while recent experience is making her doubt and fear—well, pretty much everything.

I pull out a chair, take a deep breath, and sit down across from her. I have to be careful here. Her emotions are on overdrive. I can feel them, a storm just beneath the surface. However obvious it may be to me that her Thomas very likely has something to do with all of this, it doesn't seem to have occurred to her.

"It's possible the demons stole the knife. If they took Thomas, they could've taken other things. Or..."

I pause, and her eyes search my own. Questioning. Lost. Beautiful. I don't want to say it. But I have to.

"Or it could be that Thomas is involved in all of this. With the demons. Somehow."

She stares at me for a long moment, eyes dark, then she shakes her head.

"No. No. Thomas has...he's got...a lot of stuff going on. But he wouldn't. He couldn't. He hates demons. Hunts them. He always has..." She trails off, searching my face for assurance. But I can't give her any, and after a moment her eyes fill with tears, and she looks away.

I let out another breath, watching her for a moment, then watching Jude watch her. I need to tell him everything. Without upsetting her more.

"Hey, Grace?"

"Mmmm?" She looks up, expectant, and my heart clenches a little as those lovely eyes meet mine. I smile.

"Why don't you go get dressed? I'm fine now. Jude and I will clean up here."

She hesitates—which, along with being able to argue with me about Thomas, is admirable, against the effects of my blood. She must have some willpower, under that gentle surface. But I need her out of earshot. Leaning forward, I place my hand over hers, and smile, tipping the scales again with my touch.

"It's okay. I'll get you something to wear." I give her hand a gentle squeeze, then go over to the wardrobe and get out jeans, a t-shirt, knickers, bra, socks and runners, and hand them to her with a nod to the bathroom.

With the influence of my blood heightened by my touch, she smiles, tugs the towel around her, and obeys. I wait until she shuts the loo door, then I grab some kitchen roll and start cleaning up. Jude stands there, just staring. He's shaking, and breathing hard, his heart is pounding in my ears. Shit. I forget sometimes, that humans are so easily overwhelmed. And I guess this is a lot for him to digest. I look up at him, raising a brow.

"Are you just going to watch me?"

"Shit. Sorry."

It works. He snaps out of it, grabs some more kitchen roll and the bin, and starts helping. We clean in silence for a few moments, then he takes a shaky breath and speaks.

"So...who's 'the magician'? Is it this Thomas guy?"

I toss a bloodied clump of towel into the bin. "Maybe. I've no idea."

He stares up at me a second, then nods across toward the bathroom, repeating his earlier questions.

"So how...why was there a demon at the door? Why did it attack you? Why did her blood heal you, when nothing else worked? What are you not telling me, Rue?"

I sigh and rub at my eyes, still feeling pretty high from Grace's blood. Christ, it's powerful stuff. I grab another bundle of towels and some spray cleaner, scrubbing at a stubborn patch of burnt blood.

"I lied to you this morning. The men on the rooftop earlier? They weren't exactly men."

He stops scrubbing and stares at me.

I sigh. "They were demons. Hunting her. And like I said, I got in the way."

He shakes his head and starts cleaning in silence again for a few moments. I wait. After a while he tosses a blood-soaked pile of towels into the bin and looks at me again. "But...why are demons hunting her?"

Here goes.

"She has angel blood."

He stops cleaning, sits back and gapes. "What?"

"Angel blood. She's Nephilim. An angel baby."

He keeps staring, with his mouth open.

I smirk. "Jude. You look like a fish."

Snapping his mouth shut, he stares, licks his lips, starts to speak, fails, then tries again, fails, clears his throat and finally succeeds.

"Angels don't have children."

I raise a brow. "Who says?"

"The Bible—" He starts, but I interrupt him, tossing away another ball of towels and ripping off a new bunch.

"Not true. In the first book of your Bible it states quite clearly that angels mated with women, once upon a time. There are other writings as well. Some far older..."

I stop myself. I've never told him the truth about how old I really am. I honestly don't think he could handle it. Especially not right now. So I gloss over, wiping up more blood as I do.

"I don't know all the details, but it's my understanding that there is what you could call an angelic bloodline. It comes with certain gifts. Like second sight. Sometimes it comes with other abilities. The blood of the line is incredibly powerful."

I don't tell him it's also incredibly addictive. Or that I'm well on my way to being addicted.

He frowns, glancing over at the closed bathroom door again, then back at me. "But how do you know?"

I stop cleaning and meet his gaze. This much I can tell him. "Because I've fed from her. And I've fed from an angel once before. A long time ago."

He stares at me again for the longest time. I watch his face change, watch his thoughts and emotions move across his features as he considers the implications and possibilities. But I don't have time to explain any more right now. I wipe up the last bit of blood and soot, moving quickly, then standing up.

"I want you to get her out of here."

Grabbing a spare backpack from under the bed, I head to the wardrobe, shoving some more of my clothes into the bag.

"Someone will have heard those gunshots, and even if they didn't, this place isn't safe anymore. Those demons know where I live now, and although I might have bought us some time, they'll be back, and next time there'll be more of them."

As I pack, I tell him everything Grace told me earlier, including the part about someone framing me for the murder of her friends. He stands up, watching me and looking lost. I've got to snap him out of it.

"Jude!"

He blinks, and I shove the backpack at him and head to the safe. He grabs the bag, watching as I move the microwave, punch in the code, open the safe underneath, pull out a few stacks of cash, and hand them to him. He numbly puts them into the bag, not even looking at them. I grab him by the shoulders and give him a little shake.

"Jude, I need you right now. Please."

He blinks again, and comes back to the present. "Sorry."

"It's fine. Listen, that's a couple grand. Take her and get you both somewhere safe. Any private residence. No churches. No shared spaces. A hotel room is good, because it's yours for the duration, but if you do that, get a decent one. Get both of you cleaned up; get some food and whatever else you need. Okay?"

He nods, then he frowns at me again. "Why does it have to be private?"

"Demons can't enter any private place unless they're invited."

"But this is a private place..." He frowns.

I shoot him a look. "They can't enter any private place, unless there's already a demonic presence there."

I let that sink in. I may have once been human, but the thing that makes me what I am is all demon.

He meets my eyes, the confusion on his face turning slowly to dark and sad realisation. "I see."

"Good."

I give him a smile I hope is reassuring, and step in close for a second, keeping my voice low. "Listen, I don't think she knows what she is. I haven't told her. Let's just leave it that way for now. Okay?"

He frowns, and takes a breath like he's about to argue, but then he sighs. "Okay."

The bathroom door opens then, and Grace steps out. I move to her side so quickly that Jude gasps. I usually try not to move as fast as I can around him, but right now I don't care. My heart aches when she lifts her eyes to meet my own. I get a firm grip on the desire to drink her again, and smile.

"Hey."

She looks a bit high from my blood, but otherwise fine. Beautiful in fact. "Hey."

"You okay?"

She nods, giving me a soft smile.

I smile in return; even though I know that look in her eyes is blood-driven. My blood. Whispering to her that she wants me, that she needs me. Loves me. And even though I know it will wear off, there's a part of me that wishes it wouldn't. That wishes that look in those sweet eyes was real.

But it's not, and I have to face it. Protect her as much as I can. From every danger.

Including me.

"Listen, it's not safe here anymore."

Her eyes grow wide. She looks across at Jude, then back, confusion and fear colouring her face. I take her gently by the shoulders, holding her gaze.

"I might have bought us some time, but I don't know how much. I want you to go with Jude. He'll get you someplace secure. Okay?"

Shaking her head, she moves to pull away. "No. I want to stay with you."

I was afraid of this. But I can't let it happen. That demon might have bought my lie about having killed her, but I doubt it. He'll be back, and he'll bring friends, and I've no idea how many, or how soon. I have to take the offensive, and that means she can't be with me. Taking her hands in both my own, I open myself up to her emotions and push my own forward. It isn't mind control, but it's pretty heavy manipulation.

I hate it.

"Grace, listen, I really need you to go with Jude. You can trust him. He'll keep you safe. And I'll find you later. I've just got to take care of a few things. Okay?" I give her hands a gentle squeeze.

She blinks a couple of times, her eyes darting back and forth between Jude and me. For a moment I think she's going to be able to argue. It's incredibly strong, that mind of hers. I watch as she struggles. Then her will shatters under the pressure, and she nods.

"Okay."

"Good." I smile, grabbing up the last few things of hers from the table, which I hand to Jude to pack. Her mobile's still there, and on instinct—and because mine's bollixed—I pick it up, holding it up to show her.

"I'm going to borrow this, okay? I'll get it back to you. Can you unlock it for me?" I give her another reassuring smile, and she nods, gets up, changes the phone's settings and hands it back to me, then goes and stands beside Jude.

I take her jacket and place it around her shoulders, noting that her eyes follow my every move. I keep talking to keep her mind on my instructions and off everything else. No matter if it's for her own good or not, I feel like such an ass.

"I've packed some more of my clothes for you. There's money enough to buy whatever else you need. Get some food, yeah?"

She nods, and stands, there, waiting. Assured she'll do what I ask, I cross back into the kitchen and fish in a drawer for my car keys, handing them over to Jude, along with the handgun and the extra clips.

"Take these. And the Merc. It's running pretty good. Stay with her. Be safe. I'll call you as soon as I can."

He nods, eyes dark as he grabs the gun with a frown, staring at it a moment, then shoving it and the clips in the bag. "Listen, I forgot to tell you, I swung by the building site on my way here. It's clean. No bodies, no cops. Nothing."

I run my hand through my hair, letting out a breath. "The demons must've cleaned up their mess. I thought they might."

"What will you do?"

"Get out of here, first off; then go and find some answers."

"Be careful."

I smile, and give him the same answer as always. "I always am."

He shakes his head and heads down the back stairs to the garage. Grace starts to follow, then turns back to me.

"Rue?"

I look up. "Yeah?"

But she doesn't say anything, just stands there, looking at me, tears welling up in her eyes. After a moment, during which I'm sure she's going to find the will to argue with me again, she clears her throat and shakes her head. "Nothing. Just ... hurry. Yeah?"

"I will." I give her a smile, and she smiles back, then turns and follows Jude down the steps, and I'm alone.

I take a long look around, a deep anger burning inside. This is my home, and has been for the past century. I really like living here. And now it's been invaded. Fucking demons.

I need to find out who's behind these attacks, what and how they know about me and what the hell they want with Grace. Then I need to make them leave both of us alone. They caught me off guard twice. It won't happen again.

I get cleaned up and changed: jeans, t-shirt, boots, scarves, fingerless gloves, hoodie, and my second favourite leather jacket. Then I quickly pack a few things I might need: sunglasses, sunblock, laptop, change of clothes; and a little silver box containing a few cherished things I've had forever. Just in case.

I shove everything into a holdall along with the remaining bags of blood in their cooler bag, the cash and drugs I took from the rooftop demons, the rest of my cash in various currencies and all my different passports from the safe, shoving a few hundred Euros into my pocket. I have credit cards, and a few bank accounts—who can live without them? But I still like to do most of my business in cash. It's safer.

Tossing the bag over my shoulder and making a final check, I realise I've forgotten the knife.

Shit.

For a moment I stand there staring at it. I don't want to touch the thing, but I can't leave it behind either. Better with me than anywhere else. Thinking about it for a second, I grab an old silk scarf from beside the bed, double it around my hand, and gingerly pick it up. No burning. Thank the gods. I quickly wrap the scarf around the blade, making sure every part of the thing is good and covered before I stick it in my inside jacket pocket. It's so damn long I have to push it through the bottom of the pocket into the lining, but at least if it begins to burn me again I'll feel it right away and get rid of the damn thing.

After one last look around the flat, I head downstairs to the garage. I've got maybe five hours before sunrise. Tossing the bag into the passenger seat, I get back into my new stolen demon car, put on my sunglasses, and head for the first place on my list.

Chapter 14

Answers

C old shock cascades over me at Lilitu's words. The first of us. No other before her. It is beyond belief. And yet beneath the initial wave of incredulity is a deep-seated knowledge, that the words she speaks are true. Even so, I cannot do more than stare at her, shivering slightly in the rising river wind that whispers over my still-damp skin.

She smiles, and I ache with a child-like need as she removes the sheepskin from her shoulders and wraps its woollen warmth around my own.

"Do not be so amazed, daughter, that I was once as you were: a mortal, human woman. More like you even, than you know, for I was also once what you would call Priestess. My people did not have that word, but I too was revered as one who could speak to the gods and the spirits that reside in all things, one who could journey into other worlds, and bring back knowledge and healing gifts to the people. I also knew the words and ways of bending the world to my will with magic, as it has come to be called. To me, it was simply a way of life."

She pauses, and I nod, understanding more the closeness I have always felt for her, even in those first nights. I smile softly, and she seems satisfied as she continues her tale, looking out across the wide river into a far distant past.

"Long ago this river and its brother to the East were just two of four great rivers that flowed into the ocean, far to the south. The smaller sea that you know so well, the one upon whose shores you played as a child, and whose saltwater we taste on the warming wind, did not exist. Instead, where that dark water now ebbs and flows, left by the deluge, there existed a great and fertile valley. An Edin, even as your people called this plain. But the word came not from your people. It came from mine."

I gape at her. I cannot imagine. To have come from a time before time. A time of legends. Before the sea was made. Before the deluge. I am amazed, and must ask.

"What is it like, to have lived so long?"

She smiles. "You will find out, Daughter. It is a life, like any other. Years pass as moments, and it is difficult to hold them. But you will get used to it, as I have. Time is not the enemy."

Those ancient eyes grow distant then, and I feel in that moment a shadow of the weight of her existence; one that I cannot even begin to fathom. I wait, watching her, wondering at this—and after a moment, she carries on.

"Those four great rivers, themselves fed by many tributaries, also fed in their turn many deep blue lakes and sweet green pastures all across the land. We had no need to guide the water to our fields as your people do. This place where we sit now was not then desert. Instead, it was a place of high cool winds, of rolling hills and hollows sheltering deep green trees; of rain and snow, and glistening blue sunlight. Below, in the warmer valleys that now lie under the sea, my people flourished. Food was plentiful; our stores were heavy with grain and fruit and our herds were fat and full."

"We were wealthy, although we did not count wealth in the same way as men do now. Still, all was good. I was young and strong, and devoted to my learning; to the study of earth and sky, and of plants and their properties. I was dedicated to my people. And to my children."

I gasp aloud, more astonished than before. Children. Lilitu had children. The thought had never occurred to me. Those deep-green eyes meet my own and as she smiles again, I know she sees my thoughts, and forgives them.

"Yes. I had three children. Two sons, and one daughter. They were beautiful. Full of love and light and everything that is good. They were my life."

Shadows move in her eyes, and I hold still as stone, transfixed, as she continues.

"We were a peaceful people. There was so much plenty, we wanted for nothing, and so had no need to make war. Still, men covet, and succumb to jealousy, and there were disagreements and violence."

"Since I was a high-ranking woman in our village, I was often called upon to decide in these cases, to be what your people would term a judge. I oversaw many disputes, and tried my best to be fair and just, and to carry out the will of the gods in all things. Sometimes I would be called to another village to settle a disagreement. I did not mind, for it was good to be so respected, and I was serving my people according to the will of the gods."

"It was during one of these journeys, when I was called upon to settle a large dispute in a village farther up the valley, closer to the mountains, that everything I thought was right, and true, and good was scattered on the wind like dry leaves."

She stops talking suddenly, as if she has come up hard against a wall of memory. I can feel the rising tide of her sorrow, carried on the backs of words to come, and I wait, holding my breath, for her to go on. Soon enough, she takes a deep breath, and speaks again.

"The village was small, and set back against the shadow of rolling green hills; and when I arrived, it was near dark. As I so often did, I had brought my young daughter with me on the journey, for she would follow in my footsteps when she came of age. She was a good girl, sweet and pure and full of joy. The messenger that had been sent for me had remained behind, hosted in our village, as was our custom; but he had said I would be greeted by villagers to guide my way, and to give me food and drink."

"Instead, I was greeted with silence. No welcome fires burned; no children ran about in the gathering dusk. All was still, and dark. And as my daughter's small hand sought my own, I knew in my heart of hearts that this was horribly wrong."

Her hand clenches mine, and I wind my fingers around her own, as she carries on.

"As we walked farther into the village, the night seemed to pull in tight around us, until I felt it was choking me. I began to be afraid, but of what I did not know. I did know, however, how to speak light into darkness. I reached out, with my mind, and my will, to pull in the power I needed for such a task—and that is when I felt it. A darkness so profound that all light fled from its presence. There was no power to aid me, for all goodness had been consumed from the place by an evil that now turned its vile attention upon me. Upon me and my precious child. And smiled."

A shiver snakes down my spine at her words. Her eyes remain clouded with memory.

"I turned then, lifted up my child, and ran. I knew, in the very centre of my being, that this evil was beyond any judgement I could give, beyond any meagre power I had. My only thought was to get away. To save my child and myself. But no matter how fast or how far I ran, I felt the evil behind me, laughing at me. Taunting me. Hunting me."

She lifts her eyes to meet mine and I shudder at her words, the night around us seeming to grow darker as she speaks.

"I ran until I could run no more. Until I fell to the ground, spent, my legs no longer able to carry me. We were somewhere in the hills above the village. There, huddled beneath an ancient tree, I sheltered my child in my arms."

"She was terrified, but brave, my daughter. She did not even cry, only buried her face in my shoulder as the evil that pursued us slowed, and came closer. Walking. And I saw that it was a man. Yet not a man, but rather a dark spirit; clothed in the body of a man. I saw him for what he was, as he knew I would. As he came near, he smiled again, and spoke, with the mouth of a man, yet with a voice that did not belong in this world."

She stops, and I seek her eyes, needing to hear what was said, yet afraid of what I might hear. She sees this, and nods.

"He said, 'I have been waiting for you.'"

"And as I looked up, into his eyes, as dark and empty as a moonless night, I knew it was true. I felt his power, his fury, his impatience, and finally his satisfaction as he looked down upon me."

She closes her eyes then, and I watch bitter memory echo across her countenance.

"He reached down, and held out his hand to lift me from the ground where I lay. I let him. I could not run any more, and I knew that no matter how hard I tried to fight him, he would win. For him it was no contest. So, I would do his bidding, and bide my time. This is what I told myself, in my deepest being. It was as if there were two of me, from that moment. One that watched, and one that acted."

"I cradled my daughter in my arms as he led us both back into the village below. She did not speak; only clung to me in silent terror. It was her fear that kept my own from overtaking me as we neared the village and more men appeared. Only they also were not men, but more evil spirits, wearing the bodies of the village men. Their eyes gave them away, for none were human, but rather were black, hollow, and filled with hate."

"As we walked back through the village, I saw more bodies, bodies of women and children and old men, on the ground, torn, bloodied and broken; and still more villagers bound and kneeling in terrified, huddled groups. I knew these spirits had done this. But to what purpose, I could not fathom."

Again, she stops, her eyes still closed. I watch her, fascinated, as she takes a calming breath before speaking again.

"Their leader—for that is what he was, of this I had no doubt—led me by the hand to the centre of the village. And there, bound by forces I could not see, on hands and knees in the centre of a circle of blood, was a being I could barely gaze upon, much less comprehend. A creature born of another world, brought over whole into our own. Tall and winged, pale and powerful as the wind. And yet he was bent. Broken. Bleeding. As I stood, staring, he lifted his head, looked at me, and knew me."

Her eyes open then, to seek my own, and in their depths is an echo of terror. "You would have named him Anunnaki, Asharru. I knew him only as a dark and powerful god."

"I gaped, in fear and disbelief, for although I was used to communing with spirits, and journeying into other worlds, never had I seen so beautiful and dreadful a being. As I stared, the one who had led me let my hand go, and swiftly lifted my child from my arms. I cried out, reaching for her, my attention drawn from the circle and the unspeakable being within by an instinct older even than time, but he took a step back, his hand around my daughter's neck. I watched in choking terror as the nails burst from each foetid finger, pushing through his rotting flesh, each one black and curving, like the talons of a vulture. He could—and would, I saw with horror—rip my daughter's life from her in an instant. So, I quieted myself, as he uttered a command."

"'Give me your name, woman.'"

"His voice was the night wind howling through mountain passes. I knew that to give him my name would be the end of me. Names are power. But his hand tightened around my daughter's fragile throat. And so I told him. How could I not?"

She pauses, again, her eyes once more dark and distant. For a moment, only the rising wind breaks the silence. Then she speaks again.

"He smiled once more, a vile grin I will never forget, and moved his hand away from my daughter's throat. As if it was never his intention to harm her."

"'Good', he said. Although from his lips the word wrenched away from its meaning. I shuddered at the sound of his voice."

"'You are one who settles disputes.'"

"It was not a question. Still watching him with my child, powerless to do anything more, I nodded, and he spoke again, gesturing, and drawing my gaze helplessly back to the circle, and the being bound within. 'You will settle this score, then. And decide a fitting punishment. For this is my brother. And he has betrayed me.'"

Chapter 15

Good and Bad

It isn't hard to find the house. I can smell it a street away. Far too faint for any human to smell, but to me it's like a beacon, a strong, clear scent of blood, decay and something else. Something dark.

Parking my stolen demon car down the street, I grab some cash out of the holdall, toss the bag in the boot, then shut everything tight.

Shoving the cash in my pocket along with Grace's phone, I do a quick check for people and cameras. There are no people on the street at the moment, but I spot three cameras; one at a club entrance, and one on each corner. All aimed at the street.

I tug the hoodie up around my face, tuck my head into its shadow and walk down the street for a bit before darting down a laneway. Taking one more careful glance around, I climb up the darkest wall and onto the roof of a building a few doors down from Grace's. I'm good at climbing. I can't spider around like Coppola's Dracula, but my fingers find grip in the smallest of cracks in red brick. Anyway, I've found it's usually best to approach a potentially dangerous situation from above. It's funny, but true—no one ever looks up.

From the roof I look out over the whole of Upper and Lower Baggot Streets, up to the Church of the Immaculate Heart of Mary and The Royal City of Dublin Hospital, and down across the Baggot Street Bridge towards Merrion Square and Stephen's Green. The buildings here are mostly Victorian and Georgian terraced houses that have been converted into offices, hotels or apartments with a few nightclubs taking up the basements. Grace's house is one of the few left in its original state.

Moving across the slanted rooftops, I reach her building in a few minutes and pause there, listening. It's half-twelve on a clear Sunday night. Quiet enough. I can feel the bass pulse of music from one of the clubs on the street below, but most of the patrons are gone home now.

Walking to a skylight, I crouch down, peering inside. No movement, no light. High ceilings, old fixtures. Bookshelves line the walls. Oriental rugs line the floor. A library then, or study. But can I even go in?

Only one way to find out.

Taking one last look around, I grip the edges of the skylight and give it a quick tug, keeping a firm grip on one side of the frame. It pops out easily in my grasp, with a tiny rattle and thump from the latch as it breaks off and falls to the floor. Setting the framed glass to one side, I wait a moment, take a deep breath against the distinct possibility that this will be intensely painful, as I'm not exactly invited—then shove my hand inside.

Nothing.

Good. And also bad.

Taking one last look around to make doubly sure no one's watching, I take a deep breath, fold my arms into my chest and jump in, landing lightly on my feet a few meters below.

The house is dark, silent, and filled with the overpowering scent of death and demons. Tensing up, I stand perfectly still for a few minutes, listening to the dark house around me. Although I've made very little sound; so little that humans wouldn't have heard me, other things could have. But I don't hear a thing. Relieved, I let out a long, slow breath. Demons have been here, that's for certain, but they seem to be gone.

I survey my surroundings. Although the windows here are covered with dark, heavy curtains, I can see well enough by the dim light coming through the opening above. It's a library, like I thought, and a nice one. Every wall is floor-to-ceiling bookcases, and every shelf overflowing.

The collection is impressive, even by my standards. I scan the titles and raise a brow: ancient history, culture, mythology, theology, magic, mysticism, sorcery, and demonology. All the books are old and most are rare.

Guessing this must be Thomas' study, I make a slow circuit of the room, taking everything in.

Upon closer inspection, it seems a few books are missing. There are several conspicuous gaps along the shelves. Unfortunately, there's no real way of telling what the missing books are. On the far wall there is a glass-fronted display case with nothing in it. Where the knife came from? Maybe, maybe not. Frowning, I make my way across the room to a large old oak desk. There's nothing on top but an old paperweight and a few biros. No notebooks, no paperwork. No evidence of an evening interrupted.

I try the drawers, and as I suspected, they're locked. No matter. I give the first one a little extra tug, and it pops out in my hand. Pens, paper, notebooks. The next drawer is more of the same, but the last and largest one is empty, except for a few scraps of paper and a tube of bookbinding glue. The whole desk looks recently cleared out. Shutting the drawers, I move across to the door. It's locked from the outside. Okay. I snap the lock with another sharp tug, and wait a moment before moving into a dark hall beyond.

The smell of death gets stronger, but there are no bodies yet, and no blood. I move down the hall, a couple more skylights in the ceiling above lending enough light to let me see. There are few furnishings here, only a couple of side tables, and some art prints on the walls. There's only one more door on this floor, and it's locked. Again, I give it a little push, and again the lock snaps, the door swinging open into what must be the master bedroom.

I figure again that it belongs to Thomas, and know it when I walk in and get a faint and now sweetly familiar scent of vanilla. Grace. Desire rises in me, but I quash it immediately. I can't have her, that's just the way it is. I've got to break this addiction before I'm lost to it, and something bad happens. Trying to distract myself, I move around the room. It's fairly Spartan. A few books, some clothes, the usual things. On one side a door leads to a sparkling clean master bath. I check behind the shower curtain and door like any good movie cop, but find nothing out of the ordinary.

Moving back into the bedroom, I find a framed photo on the bedside table. It's a picture of Grace, posing and smiling with a man that must be Thomas. Lifting the frame, I study the image. He's a good bit older than her, maybe late-40's. Bright, intelligent eyes that aren't quite smiling stare out at me. There is a cunning look about his face, and something very possessive about the way his arm is wrapped around Grace's waist. Frowning, I put the picture down, and go back to my circuit of the room.

The faint sweet scent is coming more from one side of the bed than the other. I tug open the drawer of the bedside locker. Grace's things. Not many of them. A couple of books, some toiletries, a change of clothes, that's it. I kneel down, peering under the bed. Boxes. Boxes that smell like Grace. I pull one out to find more clothes, more books, some knick-knacks. Still not unpacked after three months? Frowning, I shove the box back and head out of the bedroom and down the stairs to the next floor.

There are four doors here, three on one side, and a fourth near where the hall ends at a landing and staircase. The smell of demon is stronger nearer the stairs, but I'm not going down there just yet. Instead I try the first door to my left. Unlike the rooms upstairs, it's unlocked.

It's a bedroom. Two single beds, a desk, clothes, some books, a computer. This must belong to two of the hunters. Lads, by the look of things. There are rumpled clothes on the beds and floor, video game posters featuring scantily-clad-impossibly-giant-sword-wielding women on the walls and an open laptop on the desk—password protected. I scan the room, and move on to the next, but they're both the same dorm-like bedrooms, nothing remarkable.

Moving on down the hall, I try the third door on that side. Again, it's unlocked, and again it's a library; but nothing like the one above. This one is stacked full of books that are mostly new, although a few have been made to look old. There are hundreds of books, fiction and non; on vampires, demons, myths, legends, and magic. Or rather, 'Magick'. Magick with a "k". It's like the play-pretend version of the real library upstairs.

I don't understand it. The library above is filled with priceless books, most containing actual knowledge of one sort or another. This library is rubbish. Entertaining rubbish, to be sure, but rubbish nonetheless. I should know, I've read most of the books in both.

Leaving the second library, I move toward the stairs, and try the last door. Unlocked again. I turn the latch and let it swing open. For a minute I just stand there, not quite believing my eyes. It's a weapons room. Specifically, a weapons-to-use-against-things-like-me-room. Jesus Christ. It's unbelievable. Like a prop closet for a bad horror film.

Long strands of garlic hang from the ceiling, and there are piles of sharpened wooden stakes, sorted by size and stacked on tables next to different kinds of crossbows. Hundreds of crosses and crucifixes on silver chains hang from hooks on the walls, and there are even tins of mustard and sunflower seeds.

The whole back wall is covered with replica swords, spears, katanas, sabres and battle-axes. It's like someone took to heart everything they read in every vampire book or saw in any horror movie, thinking it was true. It'd be funny if it weren't so frightening, what psychotic people like this are capable of. Then I think of Grace as one of these people, and it doesn't fit. Even after what she told me I still don't understand how she was convinced to join them.

Wandering through the room, I pick up a stake and weigh it in my hand, then run a finger over the crucifixes, setting them swinging against each other. None of this stuff—except for the sharp things, if someone was strong enough to take off my head with one—has any effect on me; or on any other vampire, as far as I know. It's all a lie, propagated by Hollywood, based on a story, based on an age-old myth; which is itself based on a reality I know all too well. And any real hunter would know as least some of that reality. Which is what makes real hunters so dangerous. From the looks of things, these kids weren't real hunters at all.

No wonder Grace came at me armed with a wooden stake and some holy water. Someone's been playing dangerous games. Shaking my head, I leave the weapons room and move downstairs, to the ground floor.

The scent of blood and decay becomes overpowering as I descend the stairs into the front hall. It's darker here. There's no light except for a faint glimmer from the streetlamp outside that spills in from two small cut glass windows on either side of the front door, but I can see well enough. The front door is latched, from the inside, with the key in the lock—which strikes me as odd. If Grace was the last one here, and presumably she locked the door behind her, then why is it locked from within?

Because someone else has been here since that's why.

A cold chill runs down my spine as I turn to face another door straight ahead. It's ajar, the room so inky black beyond even I can't tell what's there. Taking a slow breath, I inch forward and give it a push; letting it swing open before moving through. It opens smoothly, not even a creak. I walk slowly into the room, expecting the worst—but there's nothing.

The streetlight spilling in from behind allows me to see that it's an average, everyday kitchen. Kettle, hob, oven, presses, microwave, tiled walls and a chequered floor with a couple of faded rugs. There are four cushion-covered chairs around a wooden table, which is itself covered with cups, empty beer and soda cans and piles of paperwork.

Letting out a slow breath, I move through the room. There's a back door here with a dark-curtained window. I draw the cloth aside, peering out at the small, gated back lane behind the house. Also average. And also empty except for a few half-dead plants and some bins. Compost, Rubbish, Recycling.

Shaking my head, I turn away from the window to face one last door. It seems to lead back toward the front of the house again, turning me in a circle into the last remaining room. It's made of oak and painted red, with an old-fashioned curved handle, which I try, to find it locked tight. I really don't want to open this door. But I've come this far.

Wincing with the expectation of—well, anything bad, really—I grasp the doorknob in one hand, yanking it back towards me with all my strength. The door explodes out of its frame; the locks and hinges snapping and clattering to the floor. Okay. Not quiet. A warm breeze wafts from the dark opening, along with that nauseating smell. Again I freeze, listening.

Nothing.

Leaning the door against the wall, I move through the doorway. I'm not more than half a step in when the thing inside wakes and starts screaming. Behind the wailing is an alien rush of rage. Not mine. Reeling, I catch myself against the doorframe and fight back, baring my fangs with the effort. It takes a minute, and gives me an instant migraine, but the screaming fades to a whining whisper, and the pounding wrath to a seething hum.

Able to think again, I continue into the room, gritting my teeth against the internal frenzy. The thing inside does not like it here, that much is clear. It takes all my effort to move on. Thankfully I don't have to go much further.

The first thing I see is the blood. It's everywhere. Floor, walls, ceiling—everything is covered in blood. The second thing I see are the bodies, lying face-up on the hardwood floor. There are four of them. One woman, three men. They have been placed so that their heads are together in the centre, their arms stretched out to touch each other at their sides, their feet pointing in four directions, like some sick imitation of a Busby Berkeley number.

The third thing I see, as the pain recedes and my vision clears, is a complex series of patterns, drawn in the blood, around and upon the bodies. Inside a clearly marked circle are hundreds of symbols, letters, and lines, all crossing one another with a dark purpose that bends in my mind and burns in my vision, making me dizzy. It's a pattern some part of me recognises. A pattern designed to draw something vile and powerful into its web. I can feel the remnants of its presence echo around the room, pushing and pulling at me, giving me vertigo. My vision blurs as the room spins and I stumble backwards, retching old blood against the doorframe.

This was no murder. This was a sacrifice.

Chapter 16

Betrayal

Lilitu lifts her eyes to mine, as she recounts the words the evil spirit said to her, so long ago. "What could I do, Asharru? What could I say? He had my name. He had my child. I had no choice."

She pauses and turns away to stare out at the ever-moving waters of the river, her eyes holding an ageless sorrow.

"And so, love and terror bound, I agreed. Keeping my eyes fastened to his own, as he yet held my daughter in his cruel arms, I bade him tell me the nature of his brother's betrayal. I reminded him that to deliver just punishment, I needed to know the truth. I made him swear upon whichever thing he most loved that he would tell no lies. He chose to swear upon his brother's life, a vow I did not then comprehend, although now, these many years later, I think I understand."

She stops, and squeezes my hands, as if to make certain I am listening. I nod, taking to my heart what knowledge she gives me, she who is so much older than I ever imagined possible. After a moment, she seems satisfied, and carries on.

"He told me how it came to be—the betrayal, as he called it—that had led them to this place. Before time began, he said, before the birth of humanity, they had existed. The earth was once theirs, not ours. It belonged to his kind, the domain of dark gods, given to them as a gift."

"I asked by whom was it given, but he said it did not matter. What mattered was that it was taken away, he said. Taken away and given instead to Mankind. While he and all his ilk were banished, driven from this world into another. I asked him why this had come to pass, why was this earth taken from his kind, if it had ever truly been theirs—but the question angered him. Once more his hand closed around my child's throat, and I begged his forgiveness for my impudence. He relented, and I did not interrupt him again."

"He said they had been banished to a world without light, without hope, without change. A dead world, he called it. A world that did not feed them, did not shelter them. A world he hated. He said he and his brother had searched for millennia for a way to return to this world. Our world. And yet they had found none. Until his brother came to him, saying he had found a way for all of them to return. They had triumphed. He did not think to question his brother. Why would he think of betrayal? He loved him. His twin. Closer than skin to blood they were."

"As he told me this, he looked upon the being bound in the circle, and I saw no love in his black eyes, nothing but pure and vile hatred. If there had ever been love in this creature standing before me, I could not see it. But I dared not speak again until he finished. So I stayed silent as he continued his tale."

"He said that upon hearing his brother's news, he gathered half their legions, leaving the other half to wait and guard the way, for they were not the only ones who wished to return to this world. Countless others of his kind had been seeking a way back, and would fight to their unmaking to stake their claim. He and his brother would have it first, he said. The earth would be theirs to rule."

She glances to me again, her eyes glinting starlight as she speaks.

"They gathered to the place where his brother had found a way into our world. They commanded their servants to go before them, and it was not until his brother sent him through, promising to follow, that he knew the way was wrong. For although it did carry them into our world—that much was true—it did not bring them over whole. Rather, it tore their spirits from their bodies, leaving them without form. More, the journey was too much for some, and many hundreds of them were torn asunder by the winds between the worlds. Unmade. Lost forever."

"At first, he said, when he realised what had happened, he thought it a mistake. Never did he think of betrayal. That was until his brother did not follow them through. Until he tried to turn back, to find the way was shut. That was when he understood the supposed triumphant return to be a ruse. Only then did he realise that he had been betrayed by his own flesh and blood."

She pauses in her telling, and a shiver passes over me. I look around the ageing night. The reeds along the river hold new shadows; shadows that seem to move against the wind. Feeling afraid of the dark for the first time in a long time, I lean in as she continues.

"He vowed to have his vengeance, no matter the cost. And thus, he began to plot his revenge. He found that in spirit form he could influence the minds of men, and that men, simple as they were, were easy targets for his manipulations."

"Gradually, over hundreds of years, he learned that not only could he influence and manipulate mankind, but that he could possess their bodies, moving through the world in their physical forms. Over time, he gathered what he could of his legions to him, and taught them all this newfound skill. And all the while he searched for the means to exact his vengeance upon his brother."

"Finally, after thousands of years, he found a way. He had watched humans develop language and a primitive magic, as he called it, over the centuries, and he realised that he could use it to his benefit. And so, he found a suitable human. In that very village. A man who could see the energies that make up all things, and who could bend these energies to his will."

She stops again, and I watch her close, a prisoner to her tale. After a moment, she carries on.

"He offered himself as a spirit guide to the village man, teaching him many things, and the man became powerful, trusting, and grateful to him.

It was then that he taught the village man a way to call beings from other worlds into our own."

"It was dark magic, and at first it did not work. Those they called forth perished, or they called forth beings he did not care for. Still, he tried for years, perfecting the spell, adding power to the ritual. And then, seven days before that day, they called forth his own brother. Whole into our world. And bound him into the circle. Trapped in blood."

Lilitu looks to me, coming back to the present, if only for a moment.

"If you could have seen his eyes, Asharru, as he told me his tale. I began then, I think, to understand evil. And I was afraid. But I was more afraid for my child. So I bade him continue."

"He told me he had no more need then, for the village man, and so took his body. Then he called forth his legions, and they came, taking the forms of the rest of the village men, and killing most of the women and children."

"He then turned upon the dark god, his brother, intending to have his revenge. But he soon realised that he could not enter the circle, for within it was a way back into his own world, and, having found great power in our own, he did not wish to return. Nor could he do his brother any kind of harm, for although he was in human form, he was not human, and so could not work human magic. He would need another to do it for him. A human. It was then he sent for me."

She takes a steadying breath, closing her eyes.

"My thoughts went to the messenger that had come to my village, knowing then that he had been a messenger for the dark gods, and wondering what had become of my village, my family. As if he read the thought, the vile spirit grinned at me, blackened lips cracking as they split the face of his stolen body. My daughter shuddered in his arms, but still did not cry; only stared at me with the true faith of a child in her mother, and that gave me strength."

"Walking to the circle where the dark god still bent in silence, I bade him rise, and speak to me, to tell me in his own words what had happened, if all that his brother had told me was true."

Again she stops, and I notice her hand is shaking where it rests in mine. I say nothing, only wait. It is a long moment before she speaks again, and when she does, her voice trembles.

"For a moment I thought he would not rise, would not answer. But then he lifted those shining silver eyes to meet my own. Again, I felt he knew me. That all my secrets were laid bare before him. I knew if he were not trapped within that circle, he would reach down and pluck my heart from my chest as easily as a child plucks a flower from the ground. And for much the same reason. Killing me not out of hatred, but out of ability. He simply did not care for me. For us."

"He bent his head to me, in acquiescence. Then he turned away, gazing at his brother as he answered my question, his voice causing my bones to ache with its resonance."

"'All that was said is true,' he said. 'Pass your strictest judgement, mortal. I will abide.'"

"I was shocked. At a loss. I had expected the dark god to deny his brother's tale, to defend himself. Not this. I looked back to his brother, uncertain of what to do next. What judgement could I even pass on creatures such as these? How could any punishment suffice?"

"But the evil spirit only smiled. 'Do then, what my brother commands, witch. Use your magic, take his power, weave his punishment, and show no mercy. For if I do not find it a fitting retribution, neither you nor your whelp shall live to see the morning.'"

She closes her eyes, loosing a trembling breath as she continues her tale.

"The evil spirit grinned to me, and then to his brother, sneering with dark delight. I knew I must do as he commanded, or my child would lose her life. So, I took a step toward the circle wherein the dark god still knelt. My voice shook as I bade him tell me his name."

"'Elathan', He said, his voice little more than a whisper."

"I looked back to his brother, to gauge the truth of his answer, and he nodded. 'Begin, woman', he said, his claws ever threatening my daughter's throat."

"I stepped to the edge of the blood-drawn circle. The dark god struggled to his feet as I approached, and I met and held his gaze. Speaking his name aloud, I raised my hands, commanding the spirits to come, to bear witness, and to lend me their strength. Calling out to the elements: earth, water, sea, sky and spirit, I raised up all the power I knew to raise. Still, I did not think it would be enough—what could my human power do against creatures such as these?"

"And yet, when the fullness of my power was raised, when I shook with the holding of it, I felt another power near, and instinctively reached out with my mind, taking it and adding it to my own. This new power surged through me, dark and strong as the sea. And with it came words. Old words. Words of truth. Words of power. Words to weave a spell so strong even the gods could not stand against it."

"I do not know where they came from, the dark god before me, or the demon behind. Perhaps they lay hidden in my mind, but whencesoever they came, they rose in a flood, from my mind to my mouth as if pulled by a thread, each one burning my lips as it left. Each one etched into my memory."

She stops and opens her eyes, meeting and holding my own; and I tremble at what I see there. A recollection of a dark power so strong I do not know how she can stand beneath the shadow of it. When she speaks again, her voice is sharp with warning.

"No one has heard these words since that night, Asharru. I tell them to you now knowing that you will never speak them, never divulge the truth of what I am about to tell you to any soul, living or dead."

I nod in agreement, swallowing hard against a sudden surge of fear. "I will never. I swear it."

She holds my gaze to for a moment more—then, seeming satisfied with my oath, she continues her tale.

"I felt the dark spirits gather behind me, crowding close in their stolen bodies to witness the punishment I would bring forth. I felt their hunger, their hate and greed, but, caught up in the magic of my own making, I could not stop, could neither turn my head nor pull my gaze away as I called the power forth."

"Again, I spoke his name, calling the magic down into the blood circle that held him fast. A third time I spoke his name, and then the words that would spell his doom—and my own—fell fast from my lips."

'You who stand before me, who hath betrayed your brethren, behold!
Bear witness to this, your penance for all eternity:
You shall be unmade, spirit from flesh, body from bone, mind from meat.
Even as you have unmade thousands.
And yet you shall not be lost in this unmaking.
Rather, will you know eternal suffering
as you are severed into countless divisions.
More than there are stars in all the heavens,
More even than all the grains of sand on earth, so shall you be riven.
And when you are thus dissevered, then shall you be bound,
forever unchanging, to the flesh of another.
From this retribution you shall find neither release, nor relief.
Their soul will not feed you, nor their mind free you.
Thus, imprisoned in flesh will you hunger and thirst beyond all understanding,
And yet all sustenance for you shall be blood.
The blood of men shall be your water, your wheat and your wine.
You shall seek it for all eternity,
No more will you walk beneath the sun,
for its light will wither and weaken you;
its sacred arms burn you as the hottest flame.
Thus, shall you ever dwell in darkness.
From this punishment there shall be no escape; no dilution, nor absolution.
So shall you seek in eternal night for solace and for sustenance,
until the gods command your existence ended.
As it is said, let it be done.'"

She meets my eyes once more, and again I know she is not seeing me, but a far distant place and time.

"As soon as the last word left my lips, I felt the power leave me, and surge into the circle to surround the dark god. I fell to my knees at the loss of it, but I could not yet look away. I think I had no true comprehension of the magic I brought forth until I saw its result."

She pauses, gazing across the dark water a long moment before carrying on.

"It was as if the dark god was lifted by unseen hands, holding him aloft. There grew a storm within the circle, as of all the winds in all the world come together, and yet without all was silence. I saw him lifted, saw him scream as his wings were ripped from him; as his skin was stretched and torn; as the tempest flayed his flesh."

"I watched in horror as the blood was pulled from his veins into the air, as his sinews were severed from his bones, as those bones were broken to shards before my eyes, crumbling like dry reeds in a summer storm. I watched as the unheard wind sliced and savaged him, tearing him into a hundred pieces, then thousands, then more; watched the storm of my making rip him asunder, until his flesh, blood, spirit and bone were nothing more than so much sand. Until there was nothing left in the circle but a reeling blood-black storm."

"Then from behind me came a sound. A rasping, scraping sound. At first, I did not know what it was, but then, as it grew in volume, I knew. It was laughter. The demon behind me was laughing. And all the rest laughed with him. Horrified still, and shocked at what I had just done, I struggled to my feet, and turned to face the evil one as he stepped toward me, a horrid smile on his lips."

"'Well done, witch. Even I could not have designed such a punishment.'"

"I shook my head, my eyes on my child. 'I have done what you requested. Give me my child and we will go.'"

"He laughed harder then, and stepped so close to me that I could smell the stench of decay rising from his stolen body. I craved to reach out and tear my daughter from his arms, but I knew if I did, he would kill us both. So I stood, trembling, until he stood so near his breath fell upon my face with every word."

"'Oh, but you have forgotten one thing, woman, in the making of your spell, wondrous though it is.'"

"He smiled again, and my heart sank in my chest. I think I knew then that he had never intended to keep his word. A breeze rose around us, and I could smell the sweet scent of my daughter's hair, even beyond the stench of the demon as he whispered in my ear."

"'Where is the prison of flesh to hold him?'"

"He lifted his hand, brushing a tear from my cheek—and then he struck, his jagged nail slitting my throat. Then, as I gasped and grabbed at the wound, he shoved me hard into the circle. Away from my child, away from my life. Into the very centre of that blood-black wind."

Her eyes, rimmed now with blood tears, focus again on my own, back from the distant past into the present, if only for a moment.

"I need not tell you, Asharru, how the tide of time gives up its steady flow when one of us is made. The moment of our making is an eternity, and the pain of the change seems as if it will never cease."

I nod, for that first night is etched upon my mind. Never will I forget the searing, unbearable pain. The curling, dark pleasure. Lilitu holds my gaze to her own for a few long moments, then offers a tight smile.

"You felt pain as you had never known, and yet there was pleasure in your making, and with it some release. Be grateful for that, my daughter; for in my making—the first making—there was only horror."

She looks away again, her ageless gaze moving over the dark expanse of water before us.

"As I fell into the choking darkness, clutching desperately at the gaping wound in my throat, I thought I heard my child scream—and then all sound without the circle was drowned by the tempest within. I could see nothing but suffocating blackness, hear nothing but a wailing like that from a thousand hells. And yet, I could feel."

"A blistering wind flayed my skin as the sorcerous storm turned its fury upon me. I felt a thousand unseen chains wrap themselves around every limb, lifting me up, holding me prone, imprisoned in mid-air as my own blood poured from me, to join the spinning torrent."

"The chains began to push and pull, to warp and twist my flesh. I could feel my bones crack and shatter, and opened my mouth to scream. As I did so, the dark storm turned once more around me—and then, as if it had only been waiting for that moment, it entered me, pouring into my mouth, down my throat and into my core; in a boiling blood-black surge."

She looks back at me, the storm in her eyes mirroring that in her tale.

"I cannot describe the torment. No words could. I was drowning in agony. You could take the pain of your own making and times it a hundred; more even, and still know only a fraction of my own."

"I lost my mind to it. I was no longer myself; I had become suffering. Time lost its hold on my being, as did thought. I was conscious only of never-ending pain, as I was overtaken by that spell of my own making, as the form and spirit of another was moulded to my flesh. I thought perhaps I was already among the lost, trapped forever in the underworld; that the pain would be my eternity. In my mind—for I had no more voice—I begged for mercy, for death, for an end to all things."

Again, she stops speaking, her gaze slipping past me to linger long on the dark current before us. She is quiet for so long that I once more fear she will not continue. In the silence, I can hear the soft whisper of the river water against the sand, the low murmur of the wind through the palms, and the faintest beginnings of the dawn chorus. A low fear fills me; that we will run out of night before she can finish her tale, and child-like impatience moves me. I squeeze her hand in mine, seeking out her gaze, trying to pull her back from the abyss of the past.

She looks at me then, and her eyes, now spilling forth blood tears, are filled with such immeasurable sorrow that my heart breaks. Tears rise to my own eyes as she continues.

"And then, just as I had come to believe the torment would never cease, the chains that held me let me go, the burning wind that had whipped through my soul dropped away, and the screams that had surrounded and deafened me fell silent. I fell to the ground, weak, unable to stand, but finally able to see. And yet my vision was strange. Unfamiliar. It was as if I was seeing the world through a cloth of crimson. All around me was red, blood red. Suddenly a great and unbearable thirst came upon me, and on its heels, an equally unbearable hunger. I was starving, desperate. All thought disappeared in the face of this new torment. I struggled to my knees, crawling, crying, gasping. Driven by single-minded need. And then—I felt it. Smelled it. Nearby. Alive, warm. Moving. And I needed it. It was there—just out of reach."

She does not look away from me now, and holds tight to my hand. Her tears leave carmine-crooked trails down her face, and her next words come in a ragged, broken whisper.

"I think I heard him laugh. In that moment. The evil spirit. I think he was there, watching, waiting through all my torment. I believe as much, but I cannot be certain. I tell myself my mind was broken, my soul shattered, my body not my own. And although I know all of these things are true, no reasoning will ever quench the sorrow of my heart."

Her voice breaks and she closes her eyes, sending a new stream of tears down her face to stain the white linen at her throat. My tears follow her own, and I seek for words of comfort. Before I can draw breath to speak them, however, she opens her eyes and holds them fast to my own, her voice shaking with each word.

"All I knew, all I could see, hear and feel was need. Need drove me, and as I crawled in the dust, newfound strength coursed through every limb. Instinct pushed me forward, as an unfamiliar pain shot through my jaw. Then, the warmth was there. Reaching out, I pulled it to me and found that it was soft, and smelled of heaven. Hunger and thirst stormed within as I bent over that which I needed and sunk my teeth into warm, delicate sweetness; sweetness that gave way so swiftly as I drank, achingly, urgently. Deeply."

Her hands are shaking in my own, and I grip them tightly, icy horror stirring slowly in my breast. Her eyes do not waver from my own, although each word she speaks now wells up from a chasm of grief.

"Relief came quickly, as I drank my first. I drank until there was nothing more. Until the warmth I held in my arms grew cool. And then—I could see again. I was myself; yet changed. Clarity washed over me, and with it, realisation."

"I dropped my gaze to what I held, heavy and cold against my warming flesh. Knowing, and aching not to know. And yet, horror bound I had to look—to find that what I clutched so tightly in my arms was the dead and bloodless body of my own precious child."

Chapter 17

Big and Ugly

As I stare, barely believing what I'm seeing, the blood-painted symbols waver in my vision, and the whole room seems to grow darker. Something moves in that darkness, in the centre of the room; a twisting shadow of smoke and ash.

I gasp, stepping back, and the shape turns to stare right at me, with eyes that burn into my soul. The pain in my head stabs once more, bringing tears to my eyes; and when I wipe them away and look again, the shadow is gone.

Okay. Not real. A nightmare image, taken from my mind, that's all.

Drawing a deep, slow breath, I wait for my head to clear before carefully moving further into the room, making sure not to step on any of the symbols. I can't work magic, but that doesn't mean it can't work on me. Even already-used magic like this can still be dangerous. As evidenced by what just happened.

Whatever powerful sorcery was done here reacted when I stepped into the room. Even from outside the blood circle, it clawed at me, trying to pull me in. Jesus. Who could have worked such dark and powerful magic, and more importantly, why?

I don't know as much about magic as I should. It has been used on me, and on more than one occasion, but not for a very long time, and, after the last time, I've avoided it and its bearers like the sun.

Still feeling shaky, I make a slow and careful circuit of the once formal Victorian sitting room; decorative plastered ceiling, enamelled fireplace, deep oak trim—only there's none of the usual furniture here. Instead, the room is bare to the walls, with long, heavy curtains hung to block the front-facing windows. I pull one aside, staring out at the empty street for a moment before turning back to study the symbols in the yellow street-light. Those nearest the bodies are smudged and difficult to read, but the rest are still clear enough. Some of them I don't recognise, but many of them have been in use for millennia. On their own, they're not evil, or even that powerful. But combined like this, and painted in blood?

Someone knew exactly what they were doing here. Someone willing to kill to raise the power they needed.

But this doesn't make sense. Grace said she'd come back to find her friends murdered. If she'd found them like this, she would have known this wasn't any usual murder, and she should've twigged that no vampire in their right mind would have done this. Contrary to the Hollywood portrayal, vampires don't waste blood. Not a drop. And we certainly don't paint with it. Puzzled, I move back to the bodies, stepping over the blood-drawn lines where they've already been smudged. Squatting down, I study the victims in the half-light that spills through the broken door.

In an instant, I see why Grace thought I'd killed them. They each have two deep puncture wounds in their throats. At the carotid, which, if left unattended, will always kill. Too big, too messy, too much blood flow. I've made the same mistake many times, killing my prey even when I didn't mean to. The external jugular is much easier and safer. Of course, the danger of killing someone is always there. But whoever did this didn't care about keeping their victims alive.

Shaking my head, I lean in closer, studying the wounds. I can tell right away they weren't made by anything with teeth. First, they're way too deep, easily more than two inches. I've never met a vampire with fangs that long; bad horror films notwithstanding. Mine are maybe an inch long when fully extended. Second, although they do at first glance resemble a bite mark from two fangs, these wounds are decidedly square. I've never met a vampire with square teeth. Third, the wounds are too close together. My fangs are in the same place as a human's canines, and just as far apart. These wounds look like they were left by a buck-toothed Nosferatu. If I had to guess, I'd say they were made with a large two-pronged fork.

So someone wanted to make Grace think a vampire—namely me—had killed her friends. Why? I stand and stare around the room again, running a hand through my hair as I think. The demons on the roof last night said I was bait. So someone wanted Grace to come after me, so they could come after her. But that makes no sense. Obviously, they knew where she was and what she was. Why didn't they just take her before? Why did they need me at all? And why did they do this? For that matter who the hell are 'they'?

I look down again at the sacrificial victims. The puncture wounds, however they were made, would've let out a rush of blood from each throat that had to have been caught in something. If they really wanted Grace to think a vampire had done this, they wouldn't have left much blood in the bodies or anywhere around them. So presumably, when she found them, they weren't like this at all.

Okay. Think, Rue, think.

These are the four would-be hunters Grace told me about, that much is obvious. And her professor boyfriend isn't among the dead. She said he was gone. But where? Kidnapped? Murdered elsewhere? Or is there a darker possibility?

I go over the timeline. Grace's friends were killed and drained before she found them. Then, after she left, and before I got here, someone continued with the ritual. Which would've taken hours. Squatting down, I wipe up some of the already smudged blood with a finger, bringing it to my nose, then to my mouth. It's gone off, tastes a couple of nights old, and is made up of more than one person's blood. Which makes sense. Someone needed a few people's worth of blood for this. But I've no idea why, or what specifically the ritual did. I don't know enough about the kind of magic used. Only that it was very, very bad.

Standing up again, I go back to the kitchen, grabbing a pen and a couple of pieces of paper from the pile on the table. I'll copy down some of the symbols and lettering, maybe Grace will recognise them.

Moving back into the sitting room, I begin to sketch them down. I don't get through more than three or four when I hear a car pull into the back lane. The hair on the nape of my neck stands up, and the whimpering in my head grows into a high-pitched whine. I freeze a moment, listening, as car doors open and arguing voices get out.

Darting back to the kitchen, I peer out the crack in the curtain, and a cold lump grows in my throat. Demons. I can smell them from here. Big and ugly. And four of them this time. Fucking Hell. Don't they ever travel alone?

Time to go. I shove the sketches into my pocket and dash out of the kitchen, back into the hall and up the stairs. I'm halfway to the third floor when I stop myself. I should stay. If I can find a good place to hide, I can eavesdrop, and maybe get more of an idea as to what the hell is going on. Of course, they could find me. They'll figure out someone was here, that's for sure. But maybe they'll think I've taken off, like a sane person.

Shit.

For the second time in as many nights, I decide not to run. As I turn around, I hear the kitchen doorknob rattle—then the whole door bang and shake, as it's given a good kick. Dashing back into the sitting room, I take a good look around, before spotting the perfect hiding place. If I can get up there.

Vampires have more supple bones than humans, like those of a cat. It's a part of our physiology that helps us to run, jump, and absorb shocks with relative ease; as well as enabling us to open our jaws just that little bit more—and to fit into some pretty small spaces. Even so, Dublin fireplaces are notoriously tiny. Unlike in the countryside, most of the inner-city fireplaces were designed to burn coal. Smaller fuel source, smaller fireplace, smaller chimney.

Another kick from the kitchen, and I hear the door crack. Small or not, better make it quick. Pulling aside the grate, I cram myself into the fireplace, yank the grate back in place, and just manage to wedge myself up into the narrow chimney as a third kick connects with the kitchen door, and the whole thing goes flying into the opposite wall.

At least that's what it sounds like. I can't see anything but soot-covered brick. Gritting my teeth, I squeeze myself upwards, pushing against the sides with my toes—making sure all of me is actually in the chimney—and prop my feet uncomfortably against either side to keep me there. I hold my breath as voices and heavy footsteps enter the house, one deep voice shouting over the others.

"That's how it's done. Christ, why'd you have to choose such a shitty body?"

Another voice, thinner sounding and whining, answers. "I didn't choose it. I lost the fucking bet, remember? Had to go last. Besides, I wasn't using my strength, just its. You're gonna use yours up too fast that way."

Two more voices laugh, and all of them move closer, as the first voice speaks again.

"Never mind. When the boss is done, we won't ever need these stinking skin sacks again."

There is more movement, the sound of heavy footsteps walking toward the sitting room, as the first voice—must be the one in charge—speaks again. "Wait!"

The footsteps stop. Shit. Did they see me? I tense up, holding my breath as the voice continues.

"Don't just waltz in there, unless you wanna be sucked in, you dimwit! Watch the circle. Don't step on anything until after we're done."

I let the breath out, slowly. They didn't see me. And I was right. The spell is still dangerous. More so to them than me, I bet. Another voice, nearer to me, mutters a curse—and a fourth speaks a bit farther away.

"Hell's bowels! Look at the door!"

Shit. The door I ripped from its hinges. There's the sound of more steps, some shuffling, and a movement of metal. The fourth voice speaks again.

"Could've happened with the ritual?"

There is a general muttering of agreement, and then Mr In Charge speaks again.

"Maybe..."

More silence, and then I hear someone sniffing the air, like a dog. Shit. The blood I puked up is still there on the doorframe. Shit, shit! Closing my eyes, I hold as still as I can, willing myself to become one with the bloody uncomfortable chimney. I'm not here. Never was. I hold my breath, find a mantra and cling to it, repeating it over and over in my mind. After a few seconds, Mr In Charge speaks again, apparently satisfied.

"I dunno. Doesn't matter, anyway. Let's get this done. You two head upstairs and get the books the magician wants. Third-floor library, he said. Take anything else you want. We'll get these set down here. And get the lead out!"

There is more muttering and arguing as two of the voices—Mr Whiny and Mr Gobshite, I dub them in my mind—move out into the hall and up the stairs. They are talking to and over each other, arguing about the state of the bodies they've possessed, about whose will last longer; and as they move upstairs the argument changes to one over the strength of their true forms. Closer to me, Mr In Charge directs the fourth demon to "get busy". But my attention is on the two heading upstairs. I listen as they move to the third floor, waiting for what I know they will soon discover. Sure enough, there is a sudden long pause, while I imagine they stare at the locks I so recently shattered, maybe even up at the broken skylight, and at each other. Then, as I knew he would, Mr Whiny calls out.

"Uh, lads?"

Closer, very close: Mr In Charge. "What?"

"I think you should see this."

Mr In Charge gives a disgruntled sigh and I hear a shuffling, then more heavy footsteps as he moves back through the kitchen to shout up the stairs. "See what?"

"Just get up here!"

"Shit."

Footsteps, and his voice aimed away, talking to whoever is down here with him. "Stay here and finish up with that, so we can move in here. I'll be right back."

Footsteps moving away again, up the stairs. At the same time, there's a shuffling very near to me, along with a splashing and wiping sound. Daring to breathe again, I take a soft, slow breath in, and get a whiff of something chemical. Bleach. They're cleaning up the blood. Okay. I dare to shift my weight slightly as the scrubbing sound grows more vigorous, then I focus my attention on the conversation upstairs as Mr In Charge arrives on the scene.

"What the fuck is so damned fucking important?"

He stops talking, and I imagine the broken locks and shattered door frames being pointed out to him. There is no more talking for a few minutes, and only creaking footsteps above. I imagine they are looking for me. Or whomever they think it is. The sound in the room beside me stops too, as Mr Scrubby listens in.

After a couple of minutes, the conversation starts again, with Mr Gobshite: "No one here."

"No one in here either." That was Mr Whiny.

There's another long pause, and then Mr In Charge speaks again. "Whoever it was they're gone. Must've took off when they heard us coming."

Mr Whiny: "Who do you think it was?"

"Maybe one of the others? Maybe somebody found out what the boss is up to?" That was Mr Gobshite.

It's Mr In Charge who replies. "We'd be knee-deep in shit right now if that was true. None of them knows what we're doing."

Shuffling footsteps, muttered agreement.

Then Mr In Charge again. "Let's get this over with. I've got better things to do."

Heavy footsteps again, coming downstairs, while the continued conversation and activity above moves further away. Mr Scrubby starts scrubbing away again, as Mr In Charge comes around through the kitchen.

"Aren't you done yet?"

Mr Scrubby swears under his breath, and Mr In Charge laughs and walks into the room. "The circle's broken now anyway. Let's get these set."

There is a crinkling sound, like plastic wrap, and a new chemical smell, as two sets of footsteps move around the room.

"Christ's grave they stink!" That was Mr In Charge.

Mr Scrubby finally speaks up. "Yeah. Almost as bad as you do."

There is more laughter and the sound of something liquid being sloshed around, then a wet thump against the wall, followed by a splash and a curse from Mr Scrubby. Those same heavy footsteps—Mr In Charge and his boots—move again, back into the kitchen. I hear something dragging, and then more plastic sounds. Then faster footsteps back into the sitting room. Mr In Charge. He speaks as he walks back in.

"There's one."

One what? They're working on something, and I wish I'd chosen a better hiding spot. Somewhere with a line of sight. Somewhere more comfortable. My right hip throbs where it's jammed up against the chimney wall, the rough brick pressing uncomfortably into my spine.

Then Mr Scrubby speaks again, further away this time. "You hear back from Con?"

Mr In Charge grunts in reply, and there are more heavy footsteps, slower, away into the kitchen, and another plastic sound. Then the footsteps walk back and stand for a moment.

"Not yet. The magician traced the girl to someplace on the quays, and gave him some sort of special knife, in case of trouble. That's all I know."

"Think he got the girl?"

Mr In Charge grunts again by way of an answer, and I bet I know who Con is. Knife Boy. Which means the demon that stabbed me—that nearly killed me—is with these guys, and hasn't reported back yet. Because I hurt him bad enough to put him out of play. For now.

A shrill beeping derails my train of thought. Someone's phone. Mr In Charge answers.

"Yeah?"

Silence. A tinny voice from the phone speaker.

"You what? What do you mean?"

More silence. Then, "She did what? Seriously?"

I can hear the tinny voice from the phone, complaining. Mr In Charge is not at all sympathetic. Not that demons usually are.

"Well, you're gonna have to find a new one. Too bad for you. What about the leech?"

A pause. "Are you sure?"

Pause.

"Fucking half-breed bitch." Mr In Charge's voice drips with disgust.

Another long pause.

Then, "No, I think you should go back and tell him."

Another pause, more sounds of desperation from the voice on the line, which are cut short by Mr In Charge's curt reply.

"Not my problem."

There's a plastic sounding beep as Mr In Charge hangs up, then Mr Scrubby's footsteps clunk back across the room.

"Was that Con?"

"Yeah. Says he killed the leech, but before she died she claimed to have killed the girl."

"Shit!" Mr Scrubby stops moving. I hold my breath. If they think Grace is dead—

Mr In Charge keeps rustling plastic things. "Don't be stupid. If the girl was dead we'd know. Here, take a couple of these."

Fuck. They don't.

Mr Scrubby walks across the floor. From the sound of it, both demons are back by the kitchen door again. "So why'd the leech lie?"

"Who fucking knows why these half-breeds do anything? Fucking junkies, the lot."

They both laugh, derisively. Then Mr In Charge continues.

"I think he's lying."

"What about?"

Both of them move out of the room, back into the kitchen. There is another click, like a switch being flipped on. And another smell. Gas. What the hell are they doing?

"About killing the leech. He says she blinded him, and he had to run off. Never actually saw the bitch die."

"What?"

"Yeah. I'm telling you, that boy's a psycho. He kept going on about his special knife. Seems to care more about that than losing the girl!"

"Fucks' sake!"

Suddenly I realise what the plastic sound is. It's the sound of tape being wound out, torn off and applied. What the hell are they taping? Two sets of footsteps come tromping down the stairs again, Mr Whiny and Mr Gobshite, still arguing with each other. Mr In Charge wraps up the conversation with Mr Scrubby quickly.

"Never mind. The girl's still unprotected. Let's get done here, send these two back to the site and then we'll go get her. We'll pick up where Con left off, check if the leech is dead. If she's not, we'll find her. You and me. When we find her, we find the girl. Then we'll be first in line when the boss makes the change. And after that nothing will ever get in our way again."

Both demons laugh, and I let out the breath and lean my forehead against soot-covered brick. They don't believe my lie, or Knife boy's. Which sucks, as that would've given us some advantage.

More footsteps as the other two come into the room. Someone is panting and there is a loud thump.

"Here's the books. Don't know why he didn't get them before. They're fucking heavy." That was Mr Whiny.

There's another thump, this one more metallic.

Mr In Charge shouts at someone. "What the fuck're you gonna do with those?"

Mr Gobshite replies, defensive. "You said take whatever we want. Besides, they might come in handy. Never can have too many weapons!"

I can almost see Mr In Charge roll his eyes. "Yes, you can. Especially if they're cheap replicas. Look!"

There's a scrape and clank. Then a loud clang followed by a metallic clatter.

"See? Broke. Leave it. We have guns. Don't need anything else. Put those books in the boot. Start the engine. We'll have about a minute once I set this."

More grunts, grumbling and booted footsteps, this time in a hurry— and I realise what the demons were taping, and what that second chemical smell was. Explosives. And the click. They've switched the gas on. They're going to blow the place sky high. Shit, fuck! I shift my weight as much as I can in the confined space. I've got to get out of here. From the kitchen, I hear a series of clicks and a steady beep-beeping; then a last set of hurried footsteps out the door as the car engine revs.

Time to go. Now. I shift my weight again in the chimney, ready to roll as I slide down and hit the fireplace—only I don't slide down. I hear tyres spin as the demons speed away and I realise with a horrible sinking feeling that I'm stuck.

My hips are pressed tight against the wall of the chimney, and the heel of my boot has somehow got wedged into a crack in the brick.

Shit!

I twist around as much as the chimney will allow, trying to slide loose, pushing at the bricks. But I can't move my arms more than a few centimetres, and without leverage even my considerable strength is useless. Shit, shit!

I struggle more, kicking and scraping with my feet, trying to gain any kind of grip, and manage to lift myself into the narrowing chimney a few more inches—then I hear a click, and the beeping stops. For a second I smell a tinge of sulphur in the air, and then there is a sharp sucking sound, and a sudden hush—followed by a rapid rush of hot air and a deafening roar.

My eardrums explode, and in the ringing silence that follows I taste my own blood on my lips. The walls around me warp inwards, then convulse back out as everything erupts in smoke and fire. I am jolted and thrown up into the air like a rag doll—and then I am oh-so-slowly tumbling down into a suffocating inferno. Bits of my clothes and skin burn as I fall, sending glowing ashes dancing into the night sky above. It's beautiful. A smothering blackness closes in again, and I fight to hold on to consciousness as the thing in my head starts screaming, louder, and louder, until I am deafened by the sound.

I think I hit the ground then, or maybe the ground hits me; and the last disjointed thought I have before all thought fades, is that the nightmare has me in its grip again, and this time I don't know if I'll ever wake up.

Chapter 18

Knowledge

On the Banks of the Euphrates, Babylonia,
1754 BCE

I stare at Lilitu in shock and sorrow, any words of comfort I think to speak dying before they reach my lips. How could any words suffice? She killed her own child. I cannot fathom how she must feel, how she could carry on from that moment. And more, to bear the burden, the certain knowledge that it was her own dark magic that caused her child's death; that caused her to be changed. That caused all of us to be changed.

She does not seem to see my horror, however, as she finishes her tale, her voice broken and bone-tired.

"I think I went mad then. For some time. When I finally came to myself again, it was months later. Somehow, I had survived, if only by instinct. I found myself in a mountain cave, far away from any village. And in the back of the cave were piled the bodies of those I had killed without knowing. I vowed then to take control. I would not give myself over to darkness, to madness and despair. I would survive the curse of my own making, no matter how long it took."

She stops talking—and I am on my feet before I realise what I am doing. All of what she has told me, every word, pounds in my mind, echoing and twisting round and round until I think I will go mad. It was she who created this curse. For that is what it is; a savage, brutal, unending curse. The knowledge beats down upon my soul until I feel I am crushed by the weight of it. We are not gods; neither their servants nor their creation, but rather are demon-kind; darkness twisted and imprisoned forever. We are the walking embodiment of punishment. A prison made flesh.

She looks up, wiping at her tears as she comes back to the present. "Where are you going, daughter? It is nearly dawn."

I shake my head, tears overflowing my own eyes to stream down my face. "I cannot—it is too great. I cannot bear it!"

I turn away, running to where I do not know. Only away. I hear her voice as she calls out after me, but I do not turn back, and she does not follow. I do not stop running until I reach the sea, where I sink to my knees in the cool wet sand, sobbing tears that spill in crimson drops into the foaming tide.

Too much. The knowledge I have been given is too much to bear. I do not know what to do with such a burden. The weight of my own sorrow rises up and is made even heavier by all that I now know. I realise that even after all this time, although I thought I had accepted my fate, in truth I had still hoped that the gods would hear me again, that I would eventually be given a reason for my existence. And now I have been. And all hope is dashed. We are base beings of dark magic, and made for what reason? Revenge. No higher purpose. No judges nor messengers for the gods, not sacred, but profane.

A great darkness boils up from deep within me, and with it rises a sudden scathing anger; anger that soon becomes boundless bestial rage. I scream and beat my fury into the sea, pounding the sand until my hands bleed and heal and bleed again. And still my rage is not abated. With a cry, I stand and seek thoughtlessly for an object to destroy, and spy, not a mile away, a row of shallow-bottomed boats moored where the river meets the sea.

I am among the vessels in seconds, howling my rage; smashing the dark wood and ripping to shreds the nets that were resting within the bows. In moments only, everything is ruined, the shore covered with scraps of wood, tar and netting. Breathing hard, yet still trembling with fury, I shatter one last curved plank—and hear a gasp of terror.

Turning toward the sound, I see a warm body. A mortal, come to ready the nets before dawn. He is standing only a few feet away, frozen in fear, and at the sight of him, seething anger becomes murderous hunger. I have no thought, only needful fury, and on that dark desire I act. He does not have time to cry out again.

I leap upon him, crushing him into the mud as I sink my fangs deep into his throat. I drink deeply, shuddering with clashing emotion as his blood pours through me, calming me on its flowing tide. I drink until there is no more to take. Until I drown my rage in blood. Only then do I lift my head and drop the body, dead and already cooling, to the earth. Only then do I understand what I have done. The body, slight and raggedly clothed, too thin, too small, and the eyes, large, innocent and staring from the tiny face tell all.

I have killed a child.

I stumble to my feet, backing away from his body, reeling in blood-drunk shock. Shuddering sorrow builds in me so fast I fear I will drown again from within. I am a killer of innocence. Is this how it is to be? Is this all that I am?

Spinning round to face the sea, I am suddenly blinded by the reflection of the rising sun upon the rippling water. Abject terror replaces sorrow, and I run, fast and hard, away from the searing light, stumbling in growing panic over the shifting sands. The dread leaden weakness of day shudders through my limbs, followed by a sickening light-headedness that causes me to fall hard onto the ground. Fear rises and threatens to choke me. I am too far away to reach the safety of the catacombs. I know it.

I will die here this night.

Half-blind and faint with daylight frailty, I get up, turning about, seeking any shelter, and find only a small pile of boulders, too small to hide me in their shade. The sun rages higher into the sky and I weep in pain and despair, white smoke pouring from my flesh as I fall to my knees. No. I do not wish to die. The thought floods over me and on its heels a desperate hope.

With a cry, I thrust my hands into the earth beneath the stones, and dig, as quickly as I can. In moments I have hollowed out a cave of sorts. I crawl in, crying out as the sand scrapes my singed flesh. Trembling with the effort, I pull the earth and stones back over me, leaving only a little hollow from which to breathe, safe in the small darkness. Safe.

Safe.

Fear ebbs away as I am no longer burning, leaving only sorrow once more. I am alone. Alone and buried. The last thought that crosses my mind before sleep takes me is that I am truly cursed, truly fallen, and there will be no redemption.

Some hours later, I wake in panic, unable to breathe. Sand has sifted into the hollow as I slept, slowly smothering me. I choke and gasp in panic, pushing and clawing with all my might—until I burst from the ground in an explosion of earth and stone. Alive, exhausted, hungry and filled with shuddering sorrow. The horror of what I am, what I have done, follows me as I walk slowly back toward the catacombs.

I pass by the place where I killed the child, to find that his body is gone, as are the largest scraps of the ruined boats and netting. There is a strong smell of incense on the air, and as I pass further east of the city of Ur, I see a faint glow from atop the Ziggurat. This must be a holy night. I should know which it is, but cannot recall. That realisation only adds to the emptiness within.

I am lost.

As I approach the mountains that hide the catacombs, I see the others gathered at the crest of the hill, their silhouettes black against the moonlit sky. As I ascend, they turn as one to me, their eyes glittering, accusing, their faces still as stone. None of them greet me, and I stop, confused. Lilitu is standing off to one side, looking at me with a knowing sadness, but it is Alu who steps forward to speak, his voice dark with fury.

"Gather what possessions you can carry. We are leaving this place. Tonight."

I am shocked. "What? Why?"

He snarls, fangs bared, and lunges forward, striking me across the face so hard that I am thrown backward into the mountain. I smash against the stone, ribs cracking, and fall to my knees on the rocky path. Tears spring up to burn my eyes as he leers over me with an anger like thunder.

"Why? Because of you! Because in your thoughtlessness you left the body of a boy-child, his wounds clear for all to see!" He points to the glow from the nearby city. "Because of you the people have called down hunters from the larger cities, and they are even now rallying at the temple, calling on their gods before they come to destroy us!"

I struggle to my feet, then turn and look toward the glowing temple in the distance. What I thought was celebration was really preparation. But I still do not understand, fear and denial washing over me in turns.

"Surely we could withstand them? All of us together…"

I trail off as Alu clenches his fist, stepping threateningly close, his voice low and filled with venom. "And if they come by day? What then, Asharru? Would you have us venture into the sun and fight?"

A sinking horror clasps its fist around my heart. I shake my head, tears spilling freely down my face. "I…I did not know."

I look to each of them in turn, my gaze settling finally on Lilitu. Does she hate me? Do they all hate me? She meets my gaze, but I find no comfort in her eyes.

Disheartened, I look back to Alu. "I am sorry."

He snarls and moves to strike me again, but then Lilitu is there, a hand on his arm.

"Enough."

She turns to me. "Go and get what belongings you will take, Daughter. We leave now."

I struggle to my feet, broken bones beginning to heal as I hurry to my bedchamber and gather what possessions I hold dear. They are not many. Only some clothing, and the small lapis inlaid silver box of mementoes. I bundle box and clothing together and hurry back into the corridor. All is dark, but the tapestries glint in the lamplight as I pass the wall of stories.

I stop in front of the embroidered forms of Enki and Inanna. It is heavy, this tapestry. I know it. But I cannot leave it behind. It reminds me of who I was, and could have been. Should have been. I will not leave it behind.

Setting down my bundle, I take down the tapestry from its place, roll it gently, and bind it up with the rest. Then I hurry upwards through the winding corridors to the surface where the others are waiting.

Alu turns to look at me as I return. His face is tight with anger. He hates me now; of this I am certain. The thought fills me with confused sadness. He turns without speaking, and walks away, down the rocky hillside and on into the desert. The others follow, and I move to do the same, but then I stop, my heart catching in my throat as I glimpse the glow of the city below. My city. Suffocating grief fills my soul as I gaze down upon it. Those were my people, and that temple, from which a thousand hateful torches now burn, was my rightful home. And now my people are gone, and I must leave the only place I have ever known. Again, the thought fills my mind: that I am lost. Adrift.

Alone.

I hear the scuff of a sandal on the path, and Lilitu is there, holding out her hand. "Come, Daughter. Do not lose yourself to grief. What is done is done. It is time to go."

I nod, and with a last shudder of sorrow, I place my hand in hers, turn my back on the city of Ur, and walk away over shifting midnight sands.

Chapter 19

Bruised and Broken

Sound. Muffled, then ringing and echoing, rushing up from under. Like coming up for air. Louder. Sirens, squealing brakes, far away. Closer. Am I awake? I'm awake. Someone is shouting.

"Over here!"

Snatches of conversation, crackling radio. Then everything is suddenly, deafeningly loud. More sirens, more shouting. Right next to me. I try to move and realise with a stabbing jolt that comes from everywhere that things are broken. Lots of things. I smell smoke, and burning flesh.

The nightmare taunts the edges of my consciousness.

"Miss? Miss?"

Sound melts away again, rolls and bubbles like water, comes back. Someone is speaking. Someone who leans in close, wraps something tight around my neck, rolls me over, lifts me up. Someone warm and full of pulsing blood. Hungry. The thing inside snarls need as I fight my way out of a pain-filled fog.

Something rattles, jolts. I'm moving. Being moved.

"Up. Okay. Let's go."

A male voice. Another jolt, and pain rockets through every limb. Moving again. Metal slams against metal. A car? An engine revs, and sirens wail again. Louder. Moving with me. Not a car. An ambulance. Paramedics. Shit. Shit shit!

I'm awake.

Someone leans in again, and a latex encased thumb and forefinger part my left eyelid—none too gently. Bright light. Not good. I jerk my face away. Pain. I bite back a groan. Grace's blood is still spinning through me, healing me quickly, but there's not enough of it. Which means I'm going to be very hungry, very soon. Have to think fast. Have to get out of here.

"Hey take it easy. You're gonna be okay."

Paramedic training: how to talk to injured persons 101. Good. He must not have seen my hunger-blazed eyes. I let out another moan—not really faking—and dare to open them, just a bit, feigning semi-consciousness.

I'm in an ambulance. On a trolley, a paramedic frowning above me, concerned, professional and readying an IV bag full of fluid. A neck brace is velcroed tight around my neck, and I'm firmly strapped to a gurney. Shit. This just isn't my night. I look around as much as I can, taking in the rest of the inside of the speeding vehicle. Cabinets, shelves, bandages, equipment. Doors. Tensing up, I wait for the right moment.

Fuck it. There's never going to be a right moment.

Pressing back and down against the gurney, I shove myself forward, snapping the straps buckled around me like so much thread. The just-healed bones in my wrists twist and jab but I bare fangs against pain. Keep going. The paramedic turns, hollers and lunges for me, but he's too late. Knocking him back against the wall with an outstretched hand, I get one foot on the floor, aim for the doors, and, using all my strength, duck my head and throw myself through, shoulder first. The corrugated metal screams as the double-doors burst outwards, one of them breaking half off its hinges—and I hit the ground with a teeth-shattering crunch.

Bones break as I tumble across the tarmac, and shooting pain stabs through every joint but I can't stop now. Tyres screech to a stop behind me, and the paramedic yells again, but I'm already on my feet and running, with all the speed I can muster as injured as I am, as fast and far away as I can.

I finally stumble to a stop halfway down a narrow laneway, ripping the neck brace off and vomiting up soot and blood behind a pile of boxes. My throat is raw, my lungs feel like they've been sandpapered, and my mouth tastes like I've swallowed a coal bunker. Have to rest. Sliding down to sit against a grimy wall, I wrap my arms around my heaving chest. Everything hurts. The thing inside my head is awake and whining, but I snarl and shove it away. Have to think. Take stock.

Wincing up at the rectangle of sky above me, I try and gauge how much night I have left. The sky is clear and indigo, fading fast to violet in the east. No stars left. Not much then. An hour, maybe. Grimacing, I stretch out my bruised and broken limbs, one at a time, inspecting the damage, trying to calm myself down.

Shit.

It's a good thing I was wearing layers. It's bad, but it could've been worse. My jacket and hoodie are burnt through, but they saved most of the skin on my arms. My hands are scorched, mostly on the back, the gloves completely burnt away. I think I remember shielding my face, in the seconds before the explosion, but from the feel of it, I'm singed there as well. My lips are cracked and bleeding and my hair is burnt away to a far shorter length than it was, but that's the least of my worries. More worrying is the fact that my legs are badly burnt, the left more than the right; my jeans fused to my skin in several places. Most of my ribs are cracked or broken, as is my left arm, by the feel of it. And worst of all sound and vision keep fading in and out. Which means I have a head injury. Probably a bad one.

All my wounds are healing, causing waves of shooting pain as they do—which is good—but the process is slowing down. Which is bad.

Letting out another ragged moan, I lean back against the wall, resting for a few more minutes while I try to think. Hunger twists inside, and I clench a fist against my gut. I have to feed. Soon. I also have to get out of the threat of the rising sun. The way I look, there's no way I'll be able to check in to a hotel. Too risky. The very un-subtle way I left that ambulance will have called no small amount of attention to myself. And I'm sure I'll be suspect number one in the bombing of Grace's house. I would suspect me if I were a cop. Innocent people don't jump out of speeding ambulances.

Shit.

I could find Jude and Grace. My heart gives a little tug in my chest at the thought. I so want to be with Grace right now. But that's just selfish need and probably the addiction talking. It's too dangerous for me to be around her. I should call though. I said I would. Biting back a groan, I reach a still-healing arm into the pocket where I put Grace's phone—to find it empty.

I do a quick check of all my pockets. The cash I had on me is burnt to a crisp. The car keys are gone, sunglasses are gone, and all my credit cards are melted. Fighting a rising tide of panic, I feel for the knife in my inside pocket. Still there. I let out a sigh of relief. I hate the thing, but if it fell into someone else's hands—well, I wouldn't want to be the one responsible.

So, no calling Grace. No going to a hotel. No going home, as it's probably overrun with demons by now. And the car with the backpack and bagged blood, not to mention the rest of my cash, is back the way I came. On a street quite possibly crawling with police who are quite probably looking for me.

I really know how to fuck things up. Letting my head thump back against the wall, I cry out as new pain rockets down my spine. Shit. I clamp my jaw against the pain, biting my lip in the process. My blood tastes weak and thin. I don't have much time left. There's only one place I can go.

Although vampires are loners by nature, and don't usually hang out in big goth-filled clubs or covens or nests or whatever the latest films call it, there are, and always have been, safe havens. Just a few, and only we know what and where they are.

In larger cities, there are usually two or three, but in Dublin there's only one, and it has recently been taken over by a vampire I know very well. He doesn't like me much. But it's the only place I can think to go. They'll have everything I need, and I can rest and heal and call Grace and make sure she's okay. If I can even get there from here, in my current state.

Where the hell am I anyway? I ran away so fast, I've no idea where I ended up.

Grunting with the effort, I drag myself to my feet, and stumble to the end of the lane, using the wall for support. The street is deserted, a low, pre-dawn mist curling around the edges of lampposts and rubbish bins. From the look of things, I'm near Merrion Square. Which means I ran farther than I'd thought, but I'm also still pretty far away from where I need to be. Leaning back against the wall again, I mentally map out the best route. I can move very fast, when I want to, and when I'm well fed. But such quick movement now will drain the blood from me even faster than it's already going. Plus the rising sun will make me steadily slower and weaker, the higher it gets. Leaning out again, I take a look at the eastern sky, above the buildings. Light purple. It's now or never.

Baring fangs against the screaming resistance of my broken body, I move. One short dash to another. Laneway to shadow of building, shadow to skip to street, and then up and over a low wall into the lovely darkness of Merrion Square. Stopping to rest under an old oak, I get my bearings before setting out again, moving slowly through the shelter of the park.

Just shy of the opposite side, I have to stop, head spinning, lungs burning. The birds are singing like crazy in the trees above me. The Dawn Chorus. It's amazing; something I never get to hear. Leaning back against the rough bark of another tree, I close my eyes, resting again, taking the moment in.

"You shouldn't be here, vampire."

Startled, I open my eyes—to meet those of something I've rarely seen. At first glance, it's an exquisite young man, tall, pale and casually graceful; a vision in blue jeans and white t-shirt. Dark hair spills over feral green eyes that meet my own in clear challenge. He has his arm around the waist of a nearly as pretty and very intoxicated-looking boy. Maybe late teens. The drunk boy is human. Green eyes, however, is not.

Power moves in and around him, a power I can clearly feel. The birds above stop singing, and the light wind that had earlier stirred the leaves above drops to absolute stillness. The air grows warmer, thicker; sweeter. And all the life around me—the tree at my back, the grass at my feet, the moss beneath my fingertips—leans almost imperceptibly towards him. As if he is the epicentre of everything green and growing.

The thing inside me responds to that flowing river of life and wants to take it. My gut snarls and burns and I clench my fists so hard my nails cut into my palms. Not him. Jesus, not him.

The human word for what these beings are doesn't do them justice. And I know enough to know there are hundreds, even thousands of them in this country. More than anywhere else in the world. So many, in fact, that many mortals here still readily believe in them, even fear them, when they don't believe in anything else. Many don't even call them by any name other than 'Good', for fear of offending one of them. Which I seem to have just done. Shaking my head, I manage to find my voice, broken and burnt as it is; wincing as I lift my arms in front of me in the universal gesture of surrender, and nodding in the direction I'm heading.

"I'm just cutting through."

He stays very still, watching me. I don't move. I don't have the strength to fight him right now, and no desire to. Don't know if he knows that, though. His kind and my kind don't hate each other—or at least I don't hate them. But we're generally not friends either. Competition for the same resource, I think. I take another look at the very out-of-it human he's holding up. Although I'm not sure how his kind need humans, I know they do. And this boy is obviously his. I go back to watching him watching me, every one of my muscles tense and trembling. He seems to be considering, taking in my burns and broken limbs. Finally, he nods.

"Then leave. You cannot hunt here."

I nod, relief winging over me as I take a breath to explain, and apologise—but then there is a huge rush of air around me, and I land on my back on the pavement outside the north boundary of the park, all the breath knocked out of me for a moment.

Well, that was impressive.

Reminding myself to never piss him off, I roll slowly to my feet with a groan. It's a damn good thing it's too early for traffic. He landed me smack in the middle of the street. But at least I'm that much closer to where I need to be. Coughing and spitting up another mouthful of blood and soot on the pavement, I dash into the nearest lane, rest a bit, then continue my zigzagging trek across town, keeping an eye on the sky above.

That sky is an unmistakable shade of impending blue by the time I reach the north side of Trinity, having cut through campus, which is blessedly deserted this early in the AM. Being here reminds me of Grace, and at the thought of her, my heart aches. Damn it. I hope she's safe.

Leaning against the campus wall, I listen to the sounds of the street without. There are a few cars around now, and I can hear lorries backing up, deliveries being made and rubbish being collected. The city is waking up. And I still have a couple of streets to go. Got to keep moving. Gauging the distance, I take a leap for the wall, throwing myself rather ungracefully over the six-or-so-metre stone and wrought-iron structure.

Misjudging both the height and the drop on the opposite side, I impale my right thigh on a sharper-than-it-seemed iron fleur de lis, and fall as I land, bleeding out what blood I have left all over the pavement. On top of all that, I'm wracked by yet another coughing fit. I hate this. I hate iron-spike-topped walls. I hate smoke. And fire. And the sun. I really, really hate the sun.

It takes me a few moments to be able to move again, much less breathe, and I struggle to stand, swaying and using the wall for support. I wince as I look around, the dawning light hurting my eyes. I've landed on Pearse Street. Right where I've intended. Right where the night bus links are. And right in front of a very shocked looking group of Roma women, preparing for their day of flower selling and fortune-telling. Shit. None of us moves for a moment. Then a younger woman in the group screams— and I run. Behind me, I hear curses and shouts in Romani. They know me for what I am. But are unlikely to give chase. I hope.

I don't slow down until I'm a street away from the haven. And then I have to. My legs are shaking so it's all I can do to put one foot in front of the other. Nothing is healing anymore. The blood's gone, and there's no shoving away the screaming thing inside my mind. Hunger and thirst rage through me as I make my way around the next corner, leaning against the building as I go. A few cars pass me by, and I tug the half-burnt hoodie over my head. I need blood, and shelter from the sun, which has just crested the horizon in blazing golden fury.

A whimper escapes my lips as I turn the last corner, to face the dawn streaming like molten bronze across the river, spilling right up against the side of the street and onto the wall of the building I'm headed to. It's like it's chasing me, hunting me down. Day-drain leeches into my limbs, and all strength seeps away like water down a drain. Throwing my hands in front of my face and hunching my shoulders, I keep my front half turned to the building as I head for the door, the exposed skin on the backs of my legs beginning to singe and smoke.

Red. I know it's a red door. Okay, there it is, and now I have to find the bell, but I can barely see. The light is blinding me and making me weak and nauseous.

Vertigo crashes, and I grasp the side of the Georgian door to keep from falling. Fuck the bell. With a desperate cry, I bang on the door, again and again, holding myself upright with my last stitch of strength, as white smoke whorls from my hands, arms, back and neck. Pain, panic and hunger roar together in my mind as my legs give out and everything begins to dissolve to madness. Then the door opens—and I am pulled by strong hands into sweet, soothing shadow.

Chapter 20

Babylon

Babylon.

Never have I seen such a place. Even my own city, the once-great city of Ur in its prime, was never so immense, its walls never so tall, its winding streets never so long, its temples so vast and towering.

Babylon sits on either side of the great river, whose floodwaters the city's builders have bound beneath towering embankments, or tamed into covered canals, those dark tunnels feeding the fertile waters into the orchards and fields that sustain the city. The flickering light of a thousand oil lamps is reflected in the rippling black water, and the bittersweet scent of incense lies heavy in the air. Another river flows southwest of the city toward a great inland sea, which is surrounded by high red stone cliffs. Narrowing my lashes against the ever more violet horizon, I can just make out the gleaming mist that blankets those deep waters. But the pre-dawn light hurts my eyes, and I turn away to stare again at the darkly sleeping city.

We are waiting on the side of a hill outside the city's southwestern gates; Bion, Iyar, Makhir and myself. Lilitu, Alu and Eshe are already within, for we must find shelter, and it must be inside the city. There exists in this land neither catacomb nor cave to hide us from the day; at least none that any of us know of.

And so, we wait in silence. Silence, which has been the rule during our two-nights journey north. Alu has not even acknowledged my presence, not even when we sought our first day's shelter in rough stone caves along the river. The others have given me glances only; not a one has spoken any word to me, neither of comfort nor of anger. Not even Lilitu—although she at least stayed with me when I fell behind the rest, in my hunger and exhaustion.

We did not hunt as we journeyed, and this, coupled with the heavy burden of the tapestry that I would not leave behind, slowed my progress greatly. Although I still move more swiftly than could any mortal, I could not keep pace with the rest. Lilitu alone walked beside me, slept beside me, and when I woke the second evening with a hollow hunger raging within, pulled me a little away from the rest and fed me from her own wrist.

Her blood, unfathomably rich, eased my hunger, and gave me strength for the remainder of the journey. I knew that she, at least, did not hate me, and all my spinning thoughts of anger and blame spun away like so much dust in the wind. I love her. How could I not? This curse is demon borne and truly no fault of her own, but rather a cruel trick. She was, and is a victim, like the rest of us. Betrayed into darkness.

Instead, I have found a new target for these stinging arrows of condemnation. For after all it was not Lilitu who killed the boy by the sea. It was me. The knowledge and the sorrow it begets build within my breast until I am certain my heart will shatter under the strain. And yet it beats on. For death cannot die.

Upon our arrival Alu commanded the four of us to wait, and thus we do. This waiting seems to have broken the code of silence, for Bion turns to me and the others, distracting me from my dark thoughts.

"They have been gone too long. Already the sun stalks the eastern sky. What will we do if they do not return in time?"

The apprehension I feel is echoed in the faces of my brethren as we all as one turn our faces east to where the crooked line of sky above the distant mountains has turned threateningly pale. Again, it hurts my eyes, and I turn away, my limbs feeling heavy, weakened by the coming dawn.

"They will come."

Iyar laughs darkly, his eyes bright with hunger. "Ah, to be young and so easily swayed by favour. Tell me, sister, how can you be certain?"

I frown at him, anger stirring in my breast. "Always you mock me, Iyar. I am certain. As you should be. Are we not their children?"

Once more my words provoke mocking laughter, this time from both Iyar and Makhir. Bion alone does not laugh at me, but instead shakes his head with a dark smile.

"We all may be Children of Alu, Asharru, but only you are favoured of Lilitu. I know they will come for us only for she would not leave you. Do not think it goes unseen, the way she dotes upon you."

My heart sinks at his condescending words. Am I always to be seen as a spoiled child? Anger boils within my breast, and, glad of the chance to strike outwards, I snarl at the three of them.

"Whoever Lilitu favours is no fault of mine! I have courted no preference from any of you!"

Bion laughs. "Indeed, you have not. Even so, you are held in favour. Yet beware, Asharru. When the serpent turns, the bite is deadly."

I frown, taken aback by his warning. I take a breath to bid him explain—but before I can speak, Eshe appears out of the dimming night, her glittering eyes bright against the coming dawn.

"We have found shelter. Come."

She turns and speeds like the wind toward the city. So swiftly she moves, and my brethren behind her, it is all I can do to follow. Yet follow I must. Down the wheat-rich slope to the fertile plain, and onwards, toward the city gates, which are shut against the night and all its dangers.

Dangers like us.

The southwestern gate is set back into the wall, and is guarded by two armed men. They stand atop two high towers, spears in hand, torches blazing nearby to help them see into the night.

Eshe leads us directly down the brick-paved path toward the gates. I am certain we will have to kill the men to make the promised shelter within, yet they never see us. Just before we reach the towering gates Eshe turns abruptly and ascends the wall at its most shadowed point, climbing with astonishing ease to disappear over the battlements above.

Startled, I turn to question the others, but Iyar and Makhir are already climbing, and Bion simply shrugs and follows, leaving me standing alone. I stay a moment more, gauging the height of the wall and the proximity of the guards. Never have I tried to climb so tall and smooth a surface. And yet the others have already disappeared over. So climb I must.

Removing my sandals and strapping the cumbersome burden of the tapestry across my shoulders, I make a leap for the wall—and fall back again, slipping down several feet as my fingers scramble for hold in the painted mud-brick. I catch myself a few feet from the ground, my finger-tips wedged in the smallest crack between two bricks. A small shower of mortar and dust rains down beneath me, and I press flat against the wall for a moment, listening. If the men have heard me, I shall have to kill them, and I do not know how I will be able to do so without causing an alarm to be raised, which would then call attention to our presence here, which would anger the others again, I know it.

I do not wish to cause another exodus.

Holding my breath, I tense against the expectation that I am discovered. But the men have not heard me. No one comes; neither from above nor below, and so I continue my climb. It is difficult. Although my fingers and toes seem to find faults in the brick with ever-evolving expertise that surprises me, even so, when I reach the top I am trembling and hungry.

I crouch down to look below. The city stretches before me; a bewildering maze of streets and buildings, clothed in smoking lamplight and fluttering banners in every colour. As I stare, astonished at the vastness, I hear a subtle sound, and look down to find my brethren waiting. Eshe motions impatiently to the East, and as I follow her gesture, the first burning arms of the sun arch over the horizon, blinding me with their intensity.

Tears rise to blur my vision, my skin tingles and begins to burn. My heart rises to my throat in panic. The sun. Rising. All power leeches from my limbs as daylight weakness overtakes me. There is neither time nor strength left in me to climb down the other side. I must jump.

Although I know it will not kill me, I am bathed in a wash of cold fear as I leap from my crouch, cool morning air rushing past my ears as for a moment I take flight—only to land with a jolting crunch of flesh and bone on the smooth stone below. I know a surprising, searing flash of terrible pain—and then nothing more, as consciousness blessedly leaves me floating painless and wondering once more if I truly am dead, and all life but a ghostly dream.

I am not left to wonder long. When I wake it is to arguing voices, and agony; as if all of my bones have been ripped from their anchorage and loose stones put in their place.

Hunger rises within me and battles for place in my torment. I try to move, but the effort only brings more pain. I scream, but can only gurgle and choke from torn lungs, and then Lilitu is there, those deep green eyes holding fast to my own as yet again she places her wrist against my lips.

"Drink, daughter. Drink and sleep. Your body is broken, but you shall heal."

She need not command me further, for I have already clasped her wrist in one hand and am drinking deeply, desperate for this relief. It is slow to come. Her blood moves through me, the familiar heady flow soothing hunger, if not pain. Even Lilitu's blood cannot mend my broken form while the sun reigns. When she pulls away, I cannot even grasp for more, weak as I am. I remember then; the wall, the rising sun, my leap of faith and fall onto stone. I try to speak, to ask her where we are, where the others are, but she shakes her head and places a cool finger against my lips.

"Be still, Asharru. It is day and we are all of us weak, yet we are safe, for now." She smiles down at me, her cool hand stroking my hair; and it seems to me, as I drift into wounded slumber, that her words slip inside my head, calming me, soothing me, bidding me obey their soft command.

"Sleep, daughter. You are safe, and will heal. I will be with you when you wake."

And try though I might, I cannot stay awake against the tumbling tide of her voice, and so slip away once more into that sea of darkness within.

Chapter 21

Black and Red

"Jesus Christ!" The exclamation bursts from the lips of the shorter of the two boys who pull me inside. I can only assume I'm the inspiration for the profanity. The other, taller one shushes him. They're young, eighteen or twenty at a push. Young and human, warm and full of life. Full of blood. Dark, sweet, pulsing blood.

I can't think, can't see anything but the river of blue flowing under their all-too-fragile flesh, can't hear anything but the pounding of their hearts. Too close. They're too close.

Hungry. Thirsty. Now.

The thing inside turns outwards, sensing opportunity, seeking release, and I can't fight it anymore. Reaching out a still-smoking hand, I grab the one nearest me, yank his head back by his bottle-blonde hair, and sink my fangs deep into his throat. He doesn't fight me, doesn't cry out or even struggle. Instead, he wraps a warm arm around my neck, like he's trying to pull me in. But I don't care. I barely even notice as I sink with him to the floor, drinking deeply, needfully. His blood spins into me in a hot arterial flood, bringing sweet, blessed relief. I gulp it down, sighing as my body takes it, turns it, and makes it mine. I drink, and keep on drinking, grasping his warm body tight, kneading his flesh, trying to wring the blood from his bones. His heart hammers against my chest as it struggles to keep him alive, his own emotions raging through me, mingling with my own, then fading. And still I keep drinking. It's so very good. His heart flutters and skips between beats, but I know he can still give me more. I need more. And that need is all I am. I give myself wholly to it, lost in blood-drenched bliss.

Then something grabs me hard around the throat, cutting off my air, and I slowly become aware of what I am doing; that there is a surprisingly strong arm wrapped around my neck, choking me, dragging me backwards, pulling me hard away from my prey, and that a polite yet urgent voice has been saying something for a little while now.

"Please, Miss. Miss. I'm sorry, Miss, but you really need to stop now. Stop. Please. He won't survive, and he is a favourite. Please."

It's enough to bring me out of it. Just. With a gasping cry, and fighting hard against the driving need to drink more, to take it all, every last drop, I let go of the now unconscious young man and fall back against the opposite wall, looking wildly around as I come to my senses.

"It's okay. You're safe."

He's squatting down, a few feet away, a hand out toward me, palm open and forward. The other boy. Cautious, but unafraid. Like he's quieting a wild animal. He nods as he sees me blinking and aware, and leans down to apply pressure to the punctured and still bleeding throat of the other, all without ever turning his back on me. After a moment, he shakes his head.

"Will you stay here a moment, Miss...?"

Still spinning from the heady high of fresh blood, I somehow manage to find my voice.

"It's Rue. Just Rue. I'll stay."

He nods again, then bends down and lifts his friend in a fireman carry, inclining his head to me before moving away, down a narrow hall and out of sight, leaving me there.

Slumping back against the wall, I take a look around. I'm sitting on the black and red-tiled floor in the grand front hall of a Victorian Gothic revival building. Everything's black and deep blood red, from the velvet curtains to the old-fashioned wallpaper. It's a practical colour scheme, if not my favourite. There are subtle cameras in each corner, and even subtler lamps tucked into little alcoves all along the wall—lamps with dim blue bulbs—positioned so they don't cause any glare. By their glow I can see the curved and fluted ceiling that arches high above, and the lancet windows, three to a side, all now shuttered tight against the day, thank the gods.

There's a set of large double doors to my left, painted black, with the word "Crimson" engraved in the centre of each, in blood red. Naturally. Down the hall on the right, where the taller lad took the other, is another, smaller door signposted 'PRIVATE', and straight ahead is a stairway, leading down.

It hits me then. I almost killed that boy. Wanted to kill him. Wanted to take it all. I thought I had more control, had fooled myself into thinking I'd mastered the thing inside. But I've obviously been lying to myself. Again. First Grace, now this boy.

Grace. I have to call her. Make sure she's okay. Shame moves over for worry. The demons said they were going to my place first. But they won't find anything there. Nothing that could lead them to her, anyway. At least I don't think so.

With a groan, I struggle to my feet, clenching an arm around my broken ribs. Even after nearly killing the boy, I'm still horribly wounded, and horribly hungry. The fresh blood is good, but won't start to heal me until the sun sets. And I'll need more. The sinews in my legs strain and creak as I stand, serving up a volley of pain that ricochets around the rest of my body, and I bite back a moan as the young man comes back. Again, he does that nodding, bowing thing, giving me a polite smile as he stops a few feet away.

"This way, Miss."

He gestures for me to follow him, down the long hall to the stairs.

I nod, pushing myself forward, using the wall for support and wincing at every step.

"I need a phone."

He walks just ahead of me, inclining his head at my request.

"There's one in your room. Everything's being made ready for you now."

We reach the stairs, and he turns to give me another polite smile before leading the way down to what looks like a cellar. I study him as the darkness calms me and I can think more clearly. He's very pretty. Sandy hair, with sun-kissed skin and a boyishly sensual face. His English is impeccable, but accented east. I'd say he's Russian. He's in incredible shape, for a mortal. I'd guess him to be a dancer, or a martial artist. Given his apparent position in this place, I'm betting it's the latter. He's also being fed a constant supply of our blood. I can smell it on him, can tell by his eyes, not to mention his strength. I try to reach out, mentally—to sense his emotions, but all I get is dizzy, and have to stop for a moment, leaning my head against the cool stone of the cellar wall. He turns and waits for me, looking concerned.

"Do you need help? I can carry you to your room, if you wish?"

That's sweet, even if it's just his training, and perhaps his addiction talking. Hoping for a favour or not, it's not many mortals who, knowing what we are, would offer to carry us to bed. Shaking my head, I give him a wry smile.

"I'll be okay. Thanks."

He nods, and, once I stand up, leads the way again, down the stone steps to a very sturdy looking and very locked door, which he unlocks with an equally sturdy-looking key. He steps through, then turns with another polite smile.

"Please—come in."

Inviting me in, even though a vampire owns this place, and I could come in without an invitation. Still. It's nice.

I smile in return, and follow him down another short set of steps into the softly lit lobby of what looks for all the world like a posh boutique hotel. Plush carpets, soft chairs and sofas; low tables with magazines and newspapers neatly stacked for browsing, a bookcase all along one wall filled with old and interesting titles, and a few well-placed expensive works of art. There's even a baby grand as the centrepiece of the room. Everything is black and red down here as well, but this is a somehow muted version. Understated and modern. I still don't like it, but it's not that bad.

My guide leads me down a softly carpeted corridor with seven doors; three on either side, and one at the end.

Stopping before the next to last on the left, he opens it, and steps inside first.

"Please come in, this room is yours."

I step inside and take a good look around. It's a suite, more red and black, although this one is accented in shades of purple and gold. The room we're in is a sitting room; two couches, a flat-screen telly, a small bookcase. To my right is a kitchenette with a sink, hob, microwave and a small fridge. Beyond is a short hall, leading to a full bath, and the bedroom. Big bed, four-poster, looks comfortable—although at this point, I'd happily sleep on a concrete slab. The phone's beside the bed. I move toward it, then realise he's followed me. Like he's waiting for me to do or say something.

As I turn to look at him, I realise I've no idea how this works. It's been a very long time since I've had to seek shelter with my own kind. I must look as confused as I feel, because he does that little bow thing again.

"Do you need anything else before you rest?"

I shake my head—then stop myself. Blood. I'll need to feed again. What I have in me now will start to heal me as soon as the sun sets, but it'll be used up quickly, and I'll wake up starving. Which has happened way too often lately.

I take a breath to ask, but my guide must see the hunger in me—because before I get an awkward word out, he leads me back out of the bedroom and across to the fridge, tugging it open to reveal three neat stacks of bagged and typed blood.

"For emergencies."

He smiles again as I stare. Why, when they had bagged blood, did he let me nearly kill his companion? I look back to him and know the answer immediately. It's in his eyes, in the way he looks at me, the way he defers. He let me attack his friend because that's what we do. His employers. His masters. Whatever we are to him, he accepts it and goes about his life, such as it is.

Christ.

I walk slowly across to the fridge, pulling out three bags and flopping them on the counter. Then I stop and turn to him as he moves back toward the door.

"Thank you." Just because he expects me to be a killer doesn't mean I have to be rude. I offer him a grateful smile. "What's your name?"

He smiles in return, and maybe it's my imagination, but it seems more genuine this time.

"Artem, Miss—but everyone calls me Temi"

I was right. Russian. "Thank you, Temi. Please, call me Rue."

He smiles further, and I get a glimpse of his fragile humanity. Still there then. That's good. I think.

He gestures toward my ruined clothes as he leaves. "I'll have some new clothing purchased for you. It'll be ready for you when you wake up. There will most likely be others here come evening. If you need anything else, just dial 'one' on your phone. You'll get me."

He gives me one more of those little bows, then he leaves, shutting the door behind him.

I turn back to the IV bags in front of me, grab one up and tear it open with my teeth as I pile the rest by the sink, leaning over the stainless steel to drink. I don't even care about finding a glass and warming the blood. The cold liquid pours down my throat as I lean back and drain bag after bag. Once again, my body takes the blood and turns it, using it, and once again I shiver and close my eyes as it goes careening through me. Stored blood will take even longer to heal me than fresh—but it'll do the job. After three bags I stop to find a glass and warm it up. After five the thing inside stops whimpering. After six I'm not hungry anymore. Instead, I'm full and very, very sleepy.

Tossing the empty bags in the sink, I check the fridge. Three left. Good. Enough for when I wake up. No more risking killing people, no matter how willing they are to feed me.

Exhausted and growing steadily weaker with day-drain, I stumble across to the door and latch it tight. It's got a double deadbolt—and I guess that'll have to do for now. I don't know if I can trust anyone here. But I don't have much of a choice. I head woozily back to the bedroom, stripping off my burnt and bloody clothing as I go.

In a couple of places my jeans are fused to my flesh, and I give a little hiss as I rip them off, skin coming with the cloth. It hurts like hell, but I'll heal. Reaching the bed, I fall across it with a groan. It's all I can do now to stay awake, but I have to call Grace. The old-fashioned phone is on the bedside table, and I lift the receiver and dial Jude. It rings four times before he cautiously picks up.

"Hello?"

He sounds worried. Tense.

"It's me."

"Rue! What's going on? Did you find out anything?"

"Some things. I'll tell you later. Where's Grace—is she okay? Are you both safe?"

"We're safe, and she's here. Hold on."

There's a rustling, and then Grace is on the line, and my heart skips a beat.

"Rue."

She sounds worried and wanting, and hearing her voice makes me sad and happy all at once. Sad that she's worried, and happy that she's okay. Now to keep her that way.

"Hiya."

"Are you okay?"

"I'm grand. Just had to go to ground. Daylight and all."

"Oh. Yeah. Did you find out...what you needed to know?"

Jude must've filled her in. I hope he didn't say too much. Or think too loudly for that matter.

"I found out a few things, but I'll tell you everything when I see you. Are you safe? Did you get some food?"

"Yeah. We're fine. Are you sure you're okay? You sound a bit out of it."

I smile at her worry, leaning back against the pillows, the phone to my ear. A part of me is glad she's worried about me. But I don't want to over-worry her, not when she's there and I'm here. So, I answer truthfully. Just not specifically.

"It's just that it's morning, and I'm tired. But I'm fine. It's safe where I am."

She gives a soft sigh, and I close my eyes. I can feel her worry, and her fear. I wish I could take both away. After a moment, she speaks again.

"Will you come here, later? Tonight?"

I shouldn't. I know I shouldn't. Those demons said they would track me. I'm not sure how they'll do that, but I can't dismiss it. And they're counting on me being with her. On the other hand, there are I-don't-know-how-many other demons, plus this magician person—who may or may not be Grace's boyfriend—already out looking for her. What if they find her, and I'm not there? And I really should tell her what she is. I can't do that over the phone.

She speaks again, and the little somersault my heart does at the sound of her voice tips the scales. "Rue?"

"Yeah. Okay. I have to take care of a couple more things—but I'll head over after."

She breathes a sigh of relief. "Okay. Please be careful. I have a feeling. Like something's not right. Like something bad's about to happen."

I sit up, frowning. "What do you mean? Did you see something? In your mind I mean?"

"No. I haven't slept, so I haven't had any dreams, or whatever. I just have a bad feeling."

I let out a long breath, closing my eyes and willing her to be safe.

"Okay. Try and sleep. I'll call again as soon as I wake up. I promise. But whatever happens, remember, stay in that hotel room, stay with Jude. Don't leave. Don't go anywhere. Please."

There's silence for a moment, then she agrees. "Okay."

"Okay. Put Jude back on?"

"All right."

186

There's a rustle—then Grace again. "Rue?"

"Yeah?"

Another short silence. Like she wants to say something, but can't. Then—

"Be careful."

I smile. "You too."

Another rustle, and Jude comes back on the line.

"Hey."

"Hey. Where are you?"

He gives me the name of a four-star hotel in Ballsbridge.

"Good. Stay there. No one can get to you if you stay in the room. Okay?"

By no one, I mean no demons. Or other things that go bump in the night. I guess a human could. But there's no need to scare either of them at this point.

"Okay, okay. We'll stay put. Are you safe?"

"I'm safe for the day. I'll come by later in the evening. After I wake up. Okay?"

"Okay."

He doesn't sound like he likes it much, but what choice does he have?

"Listen, Jude—don't scare Grace—but those demons, they're hunting both of us. Actively. Hopefully, they'll concentrate on me for now, and don't worry, they won't find me where I am, but please, please, please don't leave that hotel room. And don't let her leave either. And for the love of God, don't invite anyone in. No one, do you understand? They have no way of knowing you're there, as far as I know, but just in case. Please."

"All right. Don't leave. Don't invite anyone in. Got it."

He sounds both exasperated and scared—but I can't help that. Another wave of vertigo washes over me, and I lay back against the pillows, closing my eyes against the feeling. Being awake in the day is not fun.

"Listen, I have to sleep. I'll talk to you when I wake up."

"Okay. Be careful."

I smile. "I always am."

I manage to clunk the receiver back into the cradle before exhaustion takes me over, and I fall gratefully into the warm and welcoming arms of sleep.

Chapter 22

Monster

One hundred and fifty years have passed since the night I leapt from the walls of Babylon, and as each year drifts by like so much dust on the wind, the ache within my soul fades, and fades again. Time has made less of what once was so great a sorrow I thought to die beneath its weight. Or perhaps time has simply made less of me. For I feel with each new night a hollow nothingness begin to take shape within, where once was emotion; and I see, when I dare to glance at polished silver or into still water, behind my demon eyes, a burgeoning monster.

This is the eve of my birth. Tomorrow I am four hundred and twenty-seven years on this earth. My mortal life and four centuries more. I know this, yet cannot fathom it, cannot think too long upon it, for fear I may go mad. And so, I turn away from the knowledge, moving my gaze outward, rather than looking within.

I stand atop the curving wall that marks the boundary of Babylon's necropolis. The city of the dead. A fitting place for us to dwell, we Utukku, in winding tunnels beneath decaying bodies of kings and priests. Only the wealthy dead are buried here, beside the temple. Babylon is bare to the wind and river; unprotected by nature, and is constantly under threat of attack by those who would take the holy seat of power. There is no shelter from the day outside its walls, and no safer place for us than here, amongst its dead.

Over the years we have watched king after king come to rule this great city; each proclaiming on gilded tile their empire to be the greatest ever known. I, however, have seen it all before, and have grown weary of the proclamations of conquerors. It matters little to us. We remain, as Babylon remains.

The people know of us. How could they not? We have walked among them for millennia, watching them, hunting them. They have their myths even as my people did. They call us demons, vengeful spirits; and even number us correctly as seven; telling tales of our deeds around fires, whispering incantations as they pass the necropolis gates, calling on their gods to protect them—which they all too often do not. For we strike swift as the adder, our bite as sharp, our deeds as deadly. Yes, they know of us, and yet they do not know us at all, for even more than ever before, in this great and teeming city, do we walk amongst them, even beside them, seeming by smoking lamplight to be one of them.

Until we let them know we are not.

I have learned many things in this new city; how to manipulate and seduce mortals with deadly intent not the least of my learning. I am, after all, well versed in the art of lovemaking. Even as a mortal I knew it well. A priestess was expected to, and a high priestess beyond all others. But as Utukku I have expanded that knowledge, tempered it with the experience of centuries and sharpened it against the teachings of my brethren, especially those of Lilitu—for she is ever mother and lover to me.

A handful of years after our arrival in this place, Alu decreed that we should seek to better blend with the mortals around us, learning from them, mimicking them, making them believe we are one of them. In this way, he said, we would not so quickly be known for what we are, and would remain safe. For the hunters that drove us from our home in the South had sons, and their sons had sons, and so on, until now there is an entire tribe of hunters, stalking the land.

As yet they have not found us, although the tales claim they have chased us from the southern sea to the far northern mountains where the rivers rise. I do not like to think what creatures they have truly hunted.

More than likely their victims are merely the outcast and mis-born. Whatever the truth behind the tales, though, we seven must take care.

Therefore hidden by remaining seen, at least by night, we walk shadowed streets arm in arm with our prey, smiling as they take us to their homes, acquiescing as they invite us in, watching them while they eat, letting them lead us to their beds; where we then drink them into a dark sleep from which they will never wake.

We may pose for the night as nomads, courtesans, merchants—whatever we need be—and then drift back to these winding tunnels beneath the dead before the dawn. Some of us are better at this pretence than others. I hate the lie. Yet I am the youngest of us, and so the closest to what I once was. It is easy enough for me to assume the role.

Lilitu also has a great gift for this new way of hunting, although I know she is the eldest of us, and the farthest removed from her humanity. Even so, she moves among mortals as if she is one of them, getting closer to them than any of the rest of us, never arousing suspicion until it is far too late. She, at least, does not seem to feel regret or guilt at what she must do to survive. I envy her that freedom from sorrow. Where once I sought to find hurt, to chase after pain, now I more often dream of peace. And do not find it.

Though we seven hunt with greater artistry, I still choose to avoid those mortals I deem innocent. The memory of the child I killed so long ago haunts me. I cannot—I will not—let that happen again. If I must be a monster, if I must kill, then let me kill those I deem unworthy to live. This city teems with huddled, heated masses, and a sinful soul is never far away.

Movement in the silent street below catches my eye, pulling me from my musings once more. It is early spring, and dawn is still several hours away, yet below, in the shadows that gather around the small temple of a god I no longer know, a mortal woman walks the night alone, a small oil lamp held in one trembling hand.

I watch, and wait, listening to her softly anxious breathing. She is worried, frightened—and so she should be. Few dare to walk the night this near to the necropolis. We are not the only beings rumoured to haunt the darkness here. There are stories told of myriad demi-gods and demons, of creatures more animal than human, and of the restless dead. I have myself seen glimpses of beings that are not like us, and yet also are not men. Glimpses only, and not here in this place we call home, but proof enough to make me wonder.

The woman below comes closer, until she is huddled against the very wall upon which I stand.

I crouch down, watching as she follows the wall to the nearest gate, waiting, as—with a last furtive glance back over her shoulder—she ducks inside.

Leaping silently from the wall to the tops of monuments, I follow her progress through the maze of tombs, wondering what could bring someone so obviously terrified to such a place in the dead of night.

Stopping before a freshly built grave, the woman kneels, sets her lamp so she may see, and begins to pull at the mud-brick. Her breath comes in ragged gasps, and I realise that she is sobbing as she digs. I can taste the salt of her tears on the night air, smell the iron tinge of blood and earth as she scrapes skin and breaks fingernails in her frantic digging.

Desire rises in me, but I am more curious than hungry. I move nearer, and nearer still, until I crouch on a monument directly behind the sobbing woman. She is muttering to herself, ragged prayers between sobs, in soft whispers I recognise, and am astonished to hear. Her fevered words are spoken in my own tongue, the melodic language of my people, a language I never thought to hear again from mortal lips. But she cannot be one of my people. They faded away long ago. But if she is not, then what is she? And how has she kept the old words and ways?

Curiosity burns in me as I watch her finish her digging, and, sobs now shuddering through her slight form, take up her lantern and crawl inside. I wait, a moment only, then follow. She has not gone far, nor has she room to, for this passage is new, and holds only a few bodies. I find her kneeling by an alcove that is set into the far wall. As I come near, I see the reason for her sorrow; she kneels beside the swaddled lifeless body of a woman, older than herself, yet similar of feature. Her keening quiets some, as she removes the linen from the face of the woman and kisses her gently, then a great cry escapes her lips, and she leans over the body of what must be her mother, clinging to the body's unmoving breast as she sobs.

I watch and listen for many long moments, struck still as stone by this aching mortal heart, laid bare before me. My own sorrow rises in my breast, triggered by the sight; its distant ache pushing at the nothingness, reminding me what it is to grieve as a human, to feel loss at the end of so short a life.

I step closer, not even knowing what I intend, only that I do not wish to lose this moment. In my need, I become careless and move too close. With a start, she sees me, and gasps aloud, choking on a sob and pressing back against the body, as if to find shelter there. I quickly step away again, into the shadows, trying to show her I mean her no harm.

"Was she your mother?" I ask the question in my own tongue, treasuring the sound and shape of the words, loving the knowledge that they will be understood.

She nods, staring into the darkness as she tries to see who or what it is that I am. Terror fills her, it is palpable, and yet she holds to the body of the woman as if she were still living. After a moment, I move into the circle of lamplight, letting her see me clearly before I speak again.

"I am sorry for your loss."

Her eyes widen, and she makes a holy sign against me. I stop, not because of the gesture, but because I do not wish to frighten her. With her face now tipped to the light, I see that she is young; barely past childhood. Her hair is dark and left wild to fall over darker eyes and dusky skin. She is dressed in the manner of a courtesan—which surprises me again, as this tomb is for the privileged classes, not one such as she, or her relations. Intrigued, I move closer, looking at the body she clings to. An older woman, but not greatly so. Still in the prime of life. Her throat has been slit, and I understand even more the girl's grief. She watches me warily, as I stop a few feet from where she kneels.

"Do not be afraid. I will not harm you."

She does not answer, but only stares and shivers in return, and I realise she must be cold. The earth is damp, and chill. Removing my cloak, I place it around her shoulders. She winces and shrinks back, but calms when I step away again, blinking up at me as she speaks.

"Are you one of the restless dead? Or are you a demon? Have you come to take her from me?" She grips the dead woman tighter, her eyes wide and wild.

I hold up my hands, palms out to face her, trying to calm her grief and fear. "No. I am neither dead, nor demon. And I will not take your mother from you. No one can take her now."

She shakes her head, leaning over the body of the woman once more, and softly stroking a curl of hair that has escaped the muslin wrapping.

"But they did take her. They took her from me." She begins to cry again, lost, aching sobs, bending to the dead woman's chest once again, beating at the unyielding heart within as she calls out for her mother, over and over, like a lost babe.

I am about to step forward again, thinking only to comfort her, when I hear a whisper of movement behind me; a sound so soft the mortal woman does not hear it. I speak without turning, knowing well enough who it is.

"She is mine."

"Is that so, Daughter?" There is a smile in the tone of Lilitu's question, as she softly moves to stand beside me. "And how has she become yours?"

I do not answer. I made the statement without thinking, wanting only to protect the grieving girl. Lilitu laughs softly at my silence, and the sound startles the girl, who looks up to find two of us watching her now. She gives another cry, at first shrinking back in fear, and then abruptly standing up and making holy signs against us, a fierce grief-borne madness in her dark eyes.

"You cannot take her from me! You will not! Be gone, devils, demons—witches! In the name of the god of life, stay away!"

When we do not flee from this tirade, she then drops to her knees, lifting her hands in surrender. "Do not take her, please! Take me in her stead!"

Even I do not see Lilitu move. She stands beside me one moment, and the next she is grasping the girl by the hair, pulling her up from her knees and into her own deathly grasp.

"No!" I cry out, and move almost as swiftly, grasping Lilitu's arm with all my strength. "Do not do this."

She does not move, nor let go of the struggling mortal, only turns to me, her eyes glittering in the flickering lamplight. "Why not, Daughter? What is she to you?"

I look from her to the weeping girl, and back—then drop my hand as I realise I cannot answer with any clarity. Shaking my head, I meet her eyes, and answer honestly. "I do not know. I only know I wish her to live."

She nods, smiling further. "I see. And do you wish her then to be yours?"

I hesitate, knowing full well that she means more than she is saying; that this is some sort of test. "I do not understand your meaning."

She lifts a brow, her tone mocking. "What is there to understand, child? Either you wish her to be yours, or you do not."

My heart sinks within my chest as I realise this is a game I cannot win. And one this mortal girl will certainly lose. I look back again to the girl as she cries and struggles in Lilitu's grasp—all in vain—and make my decision.

"I wish her to be mine."

Lilitu smiles wide, fangs glittering as they lengthen. "Very well, daughter. I will give her to you."

Before I can react, she grasps the girl hard by the hair, pulling back her head and sinking her teeth deep into her throat.

I cry out, as does the girl–once. Then she sinks with a shuddering sigh back into her killer's embrace. I can only watch, blistering anger rising in me as Lilitu drinks deeply, the girl growing still and pale. Then, to my surprise, Lilitu stops, lifting her head and licking her lips as she pushes the now semi-conscious girl into my arms. "Now. Feed her."

I stare at her dumbly, uncomprehending—and she reaches out and grasps my arm, digging her thumbnail like a knife into my wrist. My own blood pools up from the wound as again she nods to the girl. "Feed her. Or kill her. The choice is yours."

Shocked, I look from Lilitu to the blood that drips fast past my fingers to stain the stone floor, and then down to the girl, now barely breathing, and slowly bring my wrist to her lips.

For a moment, nothing happens. My blood spills red across the girl's lips, some small amount seeping past into her mouth, but most of it spilling down her chin and neck. I shake my head, looking again to Lilitu, confusion and anger warring in my breast, but she only smiles her approval. I take a breath to question, even to accuse—but then the girl's mouth closes tight around the wound, and I gasp as she begins to drink from me; softly at first, her lips tentative, testing—and then with a sudden strength she grasps my wrist in both hands, drinking deeply.

It is shocking and strange, the sensation of being fed from, and yet is not unpleasant. It stings slightly, and sends a tingling warmth through my body. I watch her drink from me, fascinated, until a swinging lightness creeps upward from my wrist to the crook of my arm, and further, towards my heart—and then Lilitu is there, pulling the girl gently away.

"That is enough, daughter."

I blink up at her, dazed, to realise I am on my knees on the stone floor. Lilitu nods as she lays the girl softly down beside me.

"You must take care never to give them overmuch. Too much of our blood given may stir the mortal mind to madness, and too much taken will make you weak and unable to heal."

She nods to my wrist and I look down to watch the wound mend, leaving only a smeared trail of scarlet, dark against my pale skin. I am still confused; once again feeling like a child, lost in the dark, as I turn back to the mortal girl beside me, watching the wound in her throat heal, and the colour return to her face. Cold horror uncoils within my breast as I realise the dark power of the blood in my veins.

"What have I done?"

Lilitu's answer is matter-of-fact. "What you wanted. You have made her your own."

Getting to my feet, I glance up to her and then back down to the girl, feeling the hollow within me ebb and flow on the tide of my emotion.

"She is ... she is not ..."

"Like us? No, child, the way of our making is much harder. One night, perhaps, I will teach you. But not this night." She smiles at me, reaching to cradle my face in her cool hands. "This night I have given you a different gift. Someone to care for, to learn from; someone to light the darkness that grows within you. Did you think I did not know?"

I shake my head, blinking back stinging blood tears, as the mortal girl moans and begins to wake. Smiling, Lilitu leans in and kisses me gently, lingering a moment against my lips—and then she is gone.

The mortal girl sits up, looking around in confusion, and then up at me, and I understand then what Lilitu meant when she said I had made this girl my own. For the instant her eyes meet mine, she changes. I can see it in her face. Where moments ago was terror, now is only trust.

Too much trust.

My heart falls. I did not want this. But what can I do? I must be kind to her. Leaning down, I gently take her hand, helping her to stand as she stares around the crypt in wonderment.

"It has grown so light..." Her hand trails up to touch her throat, her dark eyes searching my own, an edge of panic in her voice. "What has happened? Why do I feel so strange? What manner of being are you? Where is the other who was here?"

I take her other hand in mine, holding her gaze to my own as I seek to calm her. "Shhhh. You are safe, and in my care. I will answer your questions. In time."

She looks to me, smiling and nodding with child-like acceptance. I am amazed and appalled at this newfound power, and make a stern vow to myself never to abuse it. To the girl, I smile, taking her arm in mine as I lead her out of the crypt and into the night beyond.

"But first, tell me your name, child, and where you live."

Chapter 23

Black-Eyed and Shark-Toothed

I'm screaming. Only I can't make a sound. But still, I keep on screaming, desperate, terrified. I don't remember how I got here, but I know this place. Fear rises to burn the back of my throat as, just like every time before, the black sand beneath my feet slips away, leaving no purchase.

A warm wind rises, and I feel a sudden searing heat. I look to each impossible horizon as a hundred raging suns boil their way across the charred landscape, leaving smouldering nothingness in their wake.

I turn, trying to run, animal panic rising in the face of annihilating fusion, but my feet won't move, and I cry out, pleading for aid. I feel searing heat upon my back, feel my skin bubble and smoke—and then, a shadow blocks all light, and for a moment I find relief. A cool wind rises, stirring the sand around my feet, soothing my scalded skin, and as it does, I think I hear my name, in a whisper like wind-stirred sand.

"Asharru".

Confused, I look up, but the shadow vanishes, in a sound like the rushing of a thousand wings, and I am blinded by withering light as I am yanked from my feet; caught up once more in the grip of unseen fists.

A burning wind rises and spins around my prone form in a maelstrom of knives; searing, red-bladed knives that flay my flesh to the bone. They cut and burn until there is nothing left. I scream and beg, but faces rise behind the blades, their forms boiling and shifting to become a cavalcade of taunting, leering demons; black-eyed and shark-toothed.

Through the smoke of my burning flesh, I notice writing on the blades. The unfamiliar letters warp, spin and change, and I know, somehow, if I could only read them, if I could only understand what it all means, I will be saved. But then the fists let me go, to fall into the broiling mouth of the sun—and I wake up screaming, torn and blood-stained shreds of bedding in either trembling fist.

Awake. Not burning.

But not in my own bed.

It takes me a few panicked moments to remember where I am, and why. Once I figure it out, and once I stop shaking enough to stand, I stumble to the loo, lean over the sink and turn the tap to cold. Soft blue motion-sensing lights flicker on as I grab a neatly folded hand towel and wash my face. The towels in this place are all dark red. So is the bathrobe on the counter, just as neatly folded and tied with a black silk ribbon. The counter and the basin are black as well—marble—and the sheets and bedding are all red and black.

Practical design here at the Hotel De Vampires.

Leaving the stained cloth in the basin, I walk to the kitchen. I'm hungry. Every muscle burns, and I feel like I've been knocked down by an entire fleet of fully loaded lorries. But I'm in better shape this evening than I was earlier. Physically, at least. Mentally, emotionally, I'm still shook, as images from the nightmare replay through my mind. Running a trembling hand through my soot and blood tangled hair, I head for the fridge. I need to feed. It'll calm me down, keep me healing. I tug open the mini-fridge door—and stand, staring in disbelief.

Not again.

I close my eyes and rub at them, thinking maybe I'm still stuck in the nightmare—but no. When I open them again there's still nothing in front of me but empty shelves. No blood. And I know for a fact I left three full bags there.

Swallowing hard against a clenching fist of anxiety in my chest, I slowly turn to the kitchenette sink. By the dim blue light, I can clearly see the dark stain along the stainless steel, and the wrung-out bags scattered across the counter. That shiver of anxiety grows into a hard, leaden lump of fear and drops to my gut as I walk over to stand and stare down at the dark blood pooled around the drain. All that's left of what I'd saved. I couldn't have done this. I have no memory of doing it. But I know I did. I must have.

Shit.

That's twice now. Which is two times too many.

Hunger hits hard at the heavy scent of blood, and I swipe a finger around the drain and bring it to my lips. Sticky. Cold. But not gone off yet. Good. I wipe up the remaining blood with both hands, sucking it from my fingers then tug out the drain cover, licking it clean before running my fingers around the inside of the drain and getting every last drop I can. Then I rip open all the empty bags, licking the plastic.

It's not much, but it'll stave off the hunger for a little while. They'll have more here. I hope. I'm just licking the last drop from the last bag when there's a polite knock on the door. I'm so jittery it makes me jump. Jesus. Get a grip. Tossing the bag in the sink, I cross to the door as the knock comes again, this time followed by an equally polite voice.

"It's Temi, Miss. I've brought your clothes."

Getting a firm hold on myself, I unlatch the deadbolts and open the door. Temi steps in, carrying six bags from some of the best shops in town. He does that nod-bow thing again, his eyes flickering across my pale and wounded nakedness, lingering for a second on my tattoos, then away and down again, as he puts the bags on the couch.

"Good Evening, Miss. I hope you slept well?"

I nod, walking back over to the kitchen, keeping a safe distance. I'm not starving by any means, but I am hungry, still healing, and I don't exactly trust myself right now.

"I slept fine, thanks."

He nods, pointedly not looking at me now. I always forget how modest most mortals are. He doesn't look uncomfortable, though—just deferential. Even so, I walk back to the loo and grab the bathrobe, tugging it on. When I come back out, he offers a slight smile.

"Would you like me to draw a bath for you, Miss?"

That makes me smile. How very old-fashioned. I shake my head as I walk back over into the kitchen, leaning back against the counter. A twinge of hunger tugs at me again, but I shove it away. Not now.

"That's okay. I'll just have a shower. And it's Rue. Not 'Miss'. Just Rue."

He nods, and gestures to the shopping bags. "I believe these should fit. If anything isn't right, please let me know."

I give him a smile back. "Thanks. I'm sure they'll be fine. How's your friend?"

A shadow passes fast over his features, his smile thinning. "He's fine. Resting."

He turns away and walks back toward the door. Cool and polite again. Maybe I shouldn't have reminded him. I watch him closely as he opens the door, then turns back. "Will there be anything else?"

I notice this time there's no 'miss'. Well, it's a start. And since he asked, "Actually, yes. I'll need more nourishment."

He nods, doing that little half-bow again as he leaves. "I'll get something to you right away." With one last nod—no smile this time—he leaves, shutting the door behind him.

Running a hand through my hair, I sigh and head back to the loo, wincing as the lights flicker on. The headache's back. I rub at my temple as I turn on the tap. A shower will help me calm down and think. Dropping the bathrobe to the floor, I get in. Soon enough the floor of the bath is covered in blood, ash and soot. It takes a bit of scrubbing to get it all off me, and the soapy water stings as it runs over my burns. Everything aches, though less and less, as the remaining blood in my system keeps on healing me.

Hunger clenches in my gut again as I turn off the tap. I'd better get something soon. The more I heal, the hungrier I'll get, and it's not like I have much control over the process. Stepping out of the shower, I wipe the steam from the full-length mirror on the back of the door and take stock. It's bad. I look like I've lost a fight with an angry train. My face is bruised in lovely shades of green and purple, and although my hair was mostly protected from the explosion by my hoodie, it's still badly singed at the ends.

The rest of my body is covered in even more colourful bruises, and some of the deeper cuts and burns are only just beginning to heal. Shaking my head, I look up to meet my own eyes. Something I very rarely do. They're incandescent with hunger, pain and emotion—I expected that—but for a second, as I stare, an alien shadow moves through the silvery blue. I blink, startled—and it's gone.

But it was there.

Fear clenches tight around my heart, and I swallow hard and lean in to my reflection, searching. Remembering. The shadow in the dream. The shadow that spoke my name.

"What are you doing to me?"

But there's no answer. No swimming shadows. Only the hunger-lit blue I've grown so used to. Leaning my forehead against the glass, I let out a long, shaky breath. This is not good. I'm not even sure what 'this' is, or what I can do about it. But I have to keep control. And find some time to think. Time I don't have right now, because right now I have to figure out what the hell the demons want with Grace, and then figure out how to stop them. And I've no real idea how to do either of those things. With a groan, I stand up and walk back into the sitting room.

First thing's first: get dressed.

Shaking my head, then flinching as the headache moves to pound behind my eyes again, I go through the clothes Temi brought. He's good. These all look like they'll fit, and all tend toward my fashion sensibilities; comfort first, style second. There aren't any jeans, which are the staple of my wardrobe—but I like to choose my own anyway—and there are two evening dresses, one red, and one black, with matching heels, lovely and impractical as hell—but other than that, he did pretty well. There are even a couple of pairs of sunglasses and three bottles of some heavy-duty sunblock. Good boy.

After slathering on a good coat of sunblock, I choose a fitted black suit with a white shirt and boots. I'm just tugging on the jacket when there's another knock at the door. Frowning, I shove down another surge of hunger and walk over, opening it abruptly—to a rather anxious-looking girl in a too-short mini and too-high heels. I raise a brow.

"Yes?"

She takes a deep breath, seems about to speak, then she glances at my eyes, stops breathing for a moment, and quickly looks down and away. "I'm...Temi...Artem, I mean, sent me."

Of course he did. I don't know why I was expecting him to show up with a few litres of bagged blood, why would he? Most vampires wouldn't touch the stuff unless they had to. So now what do I do?

As if in answer, a sharp pang of hunger twists through my gut. As I wince and clutch at it, I can hear the girl's frightened heart pounding its staccato rhythm and see the pulse at her throat that follows each beat. Thirst twists dryly up into my mouth and I feel the familiar push of my fangs behind my lips as desire rises to mingle with need.

No.

I turn away from the door, turn my back to the girl, and walk back over to the kitchen. I can't risk it. I hear the door shut quietly behind me, and her footsteps on the carpet.

Her heart is beating so damn loud. It's deafening. She steps closer, then stops. I can feel her emotions without even trying. She's frightened, that's clear enough—but there's something else.

Excitement. Anticipation.

Intrigued, I turn back to her. She works here, after all. It's not like she's an innocent grabbed off the street. She belongs to this place, and to its proprietor, and however scared she seems, I'm sure she's done this before. And I am hungry. But not starving. It's under control. Plus, fresh blood will heal me that much faster. Dull the pain. Besides, I'm meeting Grace later. It'll be much better not to be hungry when I'm around her. I'll just take a little, and let the girl go.

Licking my lips against the ready sharpness behind them, I sit down on the couch, and give her a smile. "Come here."

She obeys, sitting down next to me, her heartbeat drumming in my ears. She's thin, but not too thin. I can probably take a pint or so.

"Closer."

Again, she obeys, scooting over more. Slipping into the old familiar ritual now, having done this a thousand times before—although they haven't always been so willing—I reach over and pull her to me. At the same time, I extend my emotions, taking control of her own, calming her fear and giving her a gentle push into desire.

It couldn't be easier.

She lets out a soft gasp, her pupils dilate, and she leans in as I grasp her wrist, pull her arm up to my lips and sink my fangs into the brachial artery at the crook of her elbow. She cries out once, and then sinks limp against me as her blood pools into my mouth.

It's good. I close my eyes and drink as thought slips away. Sweet heaven. The warm surge quenches my thirst, eases my hunger and sends shivers of healing bliss through my body. So good. And flavoured by that flow of feeling; fear into thrill into want. Her desire feeds my own and we fall together in its grasp. Yes. The rush builds and ebbs and builds again, and I chase it, drinking in ever deeper draughts. Her heart pounds hard against my chest, and I love its struggle. Love it and need it.

As I sink into the dark flood, a matching and familiar darkness uncoils from somewhere deep inside, and I welcome it. This is what I am. I knead at the warmth in my arms, drinking steady and deep. More. Give me more. This high isn't as strong, not as good, doesn't send me reeling like another, like Grace—Grace.

No. I can't do this. Fighting against everything in me that wants to take, and take, I pull away, reluctantly letting the girl go. She moans and flops back against the couch, her arm spilling blood. Shit. Not again. I dash to the loo, coming back with a cloth that I press tight against the wound. She opens her eyes, looking at me woozily.

"That was nice."

I shake my head. "Not really."

She smiles at me as if I hadn't just been in the process of killing her, and leans over to one side, like she means to lie down. Not a good idea.

I slap her gently on the cheek. "Stay awake!" More guilt as I realise I don't even know her name "You need to stay awake, okay?"

Propping her back up to a sitting position, I take her hand and help her press the cloth against her still bleeding arm. "Hold that there. Press tight. I'll be right back."

Christ. What the hell did I think I was doing? Darting into the bedroom, I pick up the phone and dial 1. It rings once before Temi answers.

"This is Artem. How may I help you, Miss?"

We're back to the 'Miss' again. But I don't care right now.

"Temi, listen, will you come and get the girl, please?"

"Certainly, Miss." He hangs up, and I go back to check on the girl.

She seems okay. Pale, dazed, but okay. I stopped in time. This time. But I can't risk it again. It's all too easy for me to slip back into that darkness. And I can't let that happen.

There's a knock on the door, and Temi steps in, nodding deferentially before walking over to the girl and picking her up. I move to help, but he simply lifts her with one am, leaning her over his shoulder and heading back out of the room. I forget how strong constant ingestion of our blood can make humans. I'm left standing, staring after him as he carries her out the door. Before he leaves, he turns back.

"Anthony wants to see you. He's out in the piano room now. Whenever you're ready."

He gives me another nod, this one tempered by a polite smile—and then he's gone.

Anthony. So that's what he's calling himself now. Well, I knew when I came here I'd likely have to see him. Might as well get it over with. I'm still flushed and a little high from the fresh blood—something I'm sure he won't fail to mention—but at least I've healed a bit more now as well.

I head to the door, then turn back. My ruined second-favourite leather jacket is lying on the floor where I dropped it. Grabbing it up, I reach into the inside pocket. Still there. Holding my breath in case it comes unwrapped, I carefully pull out the knife in its scarf, and tuck it into the inside of my boot. Not a great place, but I don't have anywhere better right now, and I'm not about to leave the fucking thing behind.

Tugging my trouser leg down again, I grab up one pair of sunglasses, slip them into my jacket pocket, straighten my suit and head out the door and down the hall to the aptly named piano room, where someone is playing Rachmaninoff's Prelude in C sharp minor. Beautiful.

I know it's him before I walk into the room. No one can play any instrument better than a vampire. And no vampire can play as well as the one sitting at the piano in front of me. I can't help but be moved as I listen, no matter that we've been at odds for over a century now, he and I. He understands music in a way I probably never will. It's a gift he's always had; a gift time has turned to genius. I wait at the edge of the room until he finishes, then walk over as he stands up and turns to me with open arms and a perfect, if somewhat disingenuous smile.

"Hello, Mother."

Chapter 24

Vengeance

Her name is Ku-aya, and she is scarcely fourteen years of age. She was born a child of a courtesan and was raised in modest wealth, and some small privilege. Although, according to class and custom, Ku-aya could never be anything other than a courtesan like her mother and her mother's mother before her; still, she was not unhappy in her life.

She was her mother's only daughter, a child of one of her mother's patrons who, according to the law, had provided her mother with a house of her own, on a hill overlooking the temple complex. Together with their servants, they kept their own ways, old gods, language, and traditions, brought with them generations ago, when their ancestors fled the drought in the southern lands. They lived this way, in peace and harmony with their neighbours, as they had lived for generations.

Every feast day, Ku-aya's family would attend the temple of the goddess, bringing their gifts of food and money to the temple coffers, and spending the hours in prayer and contemplation. Then a new High Priest took over the temple, a man who was stern and cruel. A man her mother instantly disliked. But he liked her mother.

For months he came to their home, at first courting, then bribing, then threatening her mother so that he and he alone could have her. But her mother refused him. The High Priest then forbade the worship of the old gods, over the whole of the city; saying also all had to worship any god only through the temple, and only through him. So, her mother had the family worship in secret, no longer going to the temple.

One night the High Priest came to their home with others. He took what he wanted, and then took her mother's life. And the others took what they wanted from Ku-aya, and the servants. When they were finished, the High Priest had their servants killed, and had her mother's body tossed into the street like that of a dog. Ku-aya alone escaped with her life, her tormentors not caring enough to kill her once they were done with her.

Being a prostitute, and so of a class only slightly higher than a slave, Ku-aya had no recourse against the might of the temple. She paid to have her mother buried well, with what remained of her money, and afterwards had wandered the city for days, lost and bereft of all hope, until finally she had thought to end her own life and join her mother in the land of the wingless dead.

She tells me these things in a voice that is soft and emotionless as we walk the dark city streets, toward her mother's home. My heart breaks for her sorrow and loss, so like my own. I too know what it is to lose a mother, and tell her so. She gazes upon me with absolute trust, no longer showing any fear of me, and I am amazed that I have never before witnessed this power of our blood. I wonder is it only Lilitu who knows of its use, or do the others know as well? Have they too fed their blood to mortals and made them their own? A sharp bitterness rises within, as I am certain they have, and this is but one more truth that has been hidden from me.

Ku-aya keeps talking, her arm entwined in my own, her dark eyes searching mine every few moments, needing assurance—which I give in nods and murmurs of agreement. I am filled with shame as I watch the way she looks to me. It is wrong, what I have done to her, and I know it. Still, she would be dead had I not acted. Lilitu would have killed her simply to teach me a lesson. Of this, I have no doubt. Is it not better that she should live, although enchanted? I cannot help but think this is so, and thus my guilt is lessened. Somewhat.

We reach the foot of the small man-made hill that looks down upon the temple complex, and walk up the tiled road that winds between the ever-larger dwellings of the wealthy; those who are not of the ruling family, yet are still influential enough to have their sprawling residences laid out apart from the rabble below.

Ku-aya stops in front of a white-walled garden, well before we reach the crest of the hill. The ornamental copper gate to the dwelling is shut tight, but I can hear the trickling water of a fountain beyond, and looking in, can see the deep green of fruit trees and hanging plants outlined against a flickering golden lamplight that spills from somewhere further within. I turn to the girl, to find her trembling, her eyes full of tears.

"This is my mother's home. My home. Only it is taken from us. From me. All that is good has been taken from me."
She bends her head, and her grief stirs my own.

I take her hand in mine, and she turns all of her attention to me at my touch. Another wave of wonder washes over me as I realise still more of this newfound power; and although my amazement is still coloured with guilt, the guilt does not linger long, for I know I can use this power for good. At that thought, a warm hope rises in me, that I might help this mortal woman, that I alone can avenge her loss; can give back to her what was taken away. Smiling softly, I reach a pale hand to wipe the tears from her cheek, and incline my head to the gate beyond.

"Save your grief, child. I will return to you what is rightfully yours. Bid me welcome within and let me be the instrument of your vengeance."

She stares at me a moment, bewildered—but then understanding blooms behind her dark eyes and she nods, moving to open the gate of her home and stepping through, then turning back with a deferential bow of her head. "Enter this, my home and my heart, and be most welcome."

It is an old invitation, one used as an invocation to gods of home and hearth; and at those words, a certainty of purpose fills me. I nod my acceptance, and step within.

The garden is a dark, cool and restful place, with ageing fruit trees that arch gently over stone seats and carved statues of gods and winged Anunnaki. The fountain whose gentle fall of water I heard from without is set low into the ground, and is tiled in shimmering blue and gold. The running water flows like silk against the stones in the silver moonlight, and I cannot help but smile.

I like this place. It is good.

Then from within the house beyond comes a soft sound—someone coughs in the night—and Ku-aya grasps my hand tightly, fear colouring her words.

"They are within."

I turn to look at the house, from which golden lamplight glows, and see a shadowed form pass by a window. A thief awake in the night. Troubled by conscience, perhaps?

A smile curves my lips as I move toward the door of the dwelling to stop before the latched door—no barrier to me now—as I am already invited. I hear footsteps within, and turn to Ku-aya, my eyes alight with the anticipation of vengeance, and of blood.

"Do not be afraid. This is your home. Let us take it back."

So saying, I take my hand from hers and push hard against the brass door, which bows inward at the force. The latch within cracks and then breaks, crashing against the opposite wall as the door breaks off its hinges and falls heavily to the floor. I enter the house in a cloud of dust, to the sound of running feet and shouts of alarm.

The first person I encounter is a slave, sent to see what is happening. He screams when he sees me, and I knock him aside with a sweep of my arm. He falls against the far wall and does not rise, and so I move on, deeper into the dwelling.

A woman is next, running from her bed, then screaming and trying to flee. I grasp her by the hair in one hand and feel that sweet familiar pull at my jaw as I draw her head back and bury my fangs in her throat. A heady wash of fear-fed blood floods into me and I welcome it, drinking deeply, letting the darkness rise within; for tonight I am vengeance.

I hear a shout, and then I am struck, once, twice, again. I look up, snarling, my feast interrupted—to find a man standing in front of me, bearing a smoking oil lamp, which he holds high above his head. He is dressed in the garb of a priest, and is making a holy sign against me, as he prays to his gods, over and over again. Fury rises within me like a storm, and, dropping the now unconscious woman to one side, I turn upon him, holding him up against the wall by the throat. The lamp clatters to the tiled floor and sputters out, leaving him blindly blinking in terror as he claws uselessly with both hands against my grip.

I watch, letting him struggle for a few moments, loving the fire that rises within my breast, making me feel alive again; knowing that this night, this hunt is justified. Leaning in then, I bare my fangs, and whisper soft in his ear in my own tongue, knowing that as a priest he will understand.

"I am come from the old gods, whose worship you have forbidden, and whose servants you have murdered. Know you have been judged and have been found wanting."

His eyes open wide in terror, and he tries in vain to scream as I pull him to me and bite deep into his throat, closing my eyes as that dark deluge fills me once more, quenching the burning hollow within my soul. He falls limp as he gives in to my bite, and I drink deeper, and deeper still, until I am dizzy and drunk with blood. Until there is nothing more to take. Only then do I let his body fall to the floor.

I stumble away, swaying and drunk with overfeeding, into a courtyard beyond, seeking more prey, more sinful blood to quench the need within.

But the courtyard is empty. No movement, save for silken tapestries that sway in the desert breeze.

I walk slowly around, still seeking, and then I hear a soft sound from behind, and turn with a snarl to see Ku-aya, her eyes wide and frightened, standing in the doorway—and behind her, one decaying hand resting threateningly upon her shoulder, is a monster. An evil I recognise. Not from my own past, but from Lilitu's harrowed telling.

Chapter 25

Typed and Bagged

"**A**ntonio." I lean in to embrace him with a kiss on either cheek, giving him a wry smile. "I'm not your mother."

He laughs, stepping back to look at me, his blue-green eyes taking in every detail, as always, although his tone remains light, even flippant. "Maker, Mother, whatever. You're the nearest thing I have."

His tone changes, however, as does his expression, to one of actual concern as he reaches to lift my chin in a pale hand, taking in the multitude of still-healing cuts and bruises. "Christ, Rue—you look terrible. What happened?"

I wince as he brushes a bruise. There's no way I'm telling him what's going on. I made him, and I know I can't trust him. Pulling back, I run a hand through my hair and sigh. "Long story. The short of it being I got in the way of a bomb and then got caught out by the sunrise." I shrug, smiling ruefully. "So here I am."

His eyes widen in shock, and for a second I think I see real fear there—but he covers it up quickly, walking across the room to an antique armoire, opening a drawer and rummaging through it. "Ah-ha."

He turns around again, smiling, brandishing a pair of shears as he walks back over. "You're singed." He moves in, lifting the charred ends of my hair. "That will never do. May I?"

I nod, and he quickly and skilfully snips the burnt bits away, letting them fall to the floor, and then scrunching the new ends to softly curl over my shoulders.

He steps back for another look. "Much better."

Smiling again, he meets my eyes, something close to a challenge in his own. "And you've healed more already. Did you like the girl I sent?"

So it was him. I should've known. Dammit.

I hold his gaze, wanting him to know that I know what he's up to. "She was fine."

He smirks. "Good. Let me know if you need any more."

I smile tightly. "I won't."

He laughs, walking over to one of the plush red couches and sitting down gracefully, like a cat, tossing the scissors on the table beside him.

"Whatever. You know, you should be more careful. That boy of mine almost died this morning. If I hadn't been here to feed him..." He shrugs, holding out his hands in front of him and studying his perfectly manicured nails. "I worry about you."

My turn to laugh, as I sit down beside him. "I'm sure you do."

He looks hurt. "I'm serious. You can't keep denying yourself. Look at you. It's making you weak. You're out of control, Rue. Attacking without thinking, like some animal."

Okay, that touches a nerve. I lean toward him, holding his eyes to my own. "I was wounded. Burning. Anyone else would have done the same. Worse. And you know it. Don't make me angry, Antonio. I'm not in the mood to argue with you right now."

Shaking his head, he lifts his hands in a gesture of surrender. "I'm sorry. You're right."

He smiles, changing the subject, done playing games for now. Or at least that particular game. "So, do you like what I've done with the place?"

I take a look around. "It's very...you."

He smiles. "Good. That's the idea."

He settles back into the couch, looking self-satisfied. "You should have seen it before. It was a dungeon. No thought given to comfort, or design. I chose all of this myself." He waves a hand to indicate the decor.

I nod. He always was better at small talk. I never saw the point. Maybe that is the point. Anyway, I need to leave. I have to get back to the car I left last night, then get to Grace. Besides, we don't really have anything to talk about anymore, Antonio and I. There's a gulf between us that just keeps getting wider. It makes me sad, and angry, and I can't deal with it right now.

I stand up. "Look, Antonio..."

But he interrupts me, standing up as well. "Let me give you the tour."

"I need to go."

He lifts a brow. "What's the rush?"

I take a breath to answer, then stop. I can't tell him the truth, and he'll probably sense a lie. I shake my head and smile, willing my body to relax. "No rush. I just want to get home. I'm wrecked."

Suspicion flickers behind his eyes, but he lets it drop, returning my smile. "At least wait until you heal more. Anyway, you can't go yet. I have a present for you."

Okay. It's my turn to raise a brow as he turns and heads upstairs. I follow. Now it's night, and I'm not as wounded, I can pay more attention to my surroundings. The actual sanctuary takes up most of the basement level of the building, occupying what was probably once the safe storage for the import/export company it was originally built to house. As we come up to the first floor, Antonio waves his arm to the black and red decor I noticed last night.

"This is all redone, as the main entrance to the club."

I look around, noting again the black double doors. "The club?"

He grins and walks across to the double doors, throwing them open with gusto. "Welcome to Club Crimson."

I follow him down plush red-carpeted steps into a lavish club setting. Gilded mirrors and marble tables surround a red and black tiled dance floor, above which are suspended banks of disco lights, now dark. Across the room is a stage and a DJ booth, and above that, a spiral staircase leads up to a balcony level, which is cordoned off by a velvet rope. It's all very retro. I turn back to Antonio.

"A nightclub. Really?"

He grins. "Well, I am a vampire, after all. It's de rigueur."

I resist the urge to roll my eyes. "Very trendy. I'm sure you'll do well. But isn't it dangerous?"

His eyes glint with wicked delight. "Dangerous? Rue, it's only dancing."

I shoot him a look. "You know what I mean. Having these many mortals this close to us is—"

"Delicious." He gives me a toothy grin.

Moving across to the dance floor, he spins in a graceful circle. "They drink and drug and dance to their pounding little hearts' content, and we get to take our pick. They're so out of their heads they never remember, and if an accident happens—well, kids these days really ought to be more careful."

I shake my head. "This is wrong, Antonio."

He casts a glance heavenward with an exasperated sigh. "Only to you! Jesus! Stop denying what you are!"

"I'm not denying what I am. I'm changing what I do."

Whirling back to face me, he snarls his frustration, fangs bared, eyes alight. "Then stop denying what I am! What you made me!"

His shouted accusation rings around the empty disco. I say nothing. What can I say? It's the truth. There he stands, perfect and deadly in his anger. A monster of my making. Sorrow fills me again, along with old memories. I loved and hated my own maker, in equal measure, and with good reason. Yet I'm little better. I break the bitter silence with an apology that can never suffice.

"I'm sorry, Antonio."

He glares at me a moment more, then gives me an acerbic smile. "Never mind. We are what we are. Only you used to be such fun."

With a sigh, he leads the way back out of the club. "Come on, I still want to show you your present. Then you can go wherever the hell you're off to."

Shaking my head, I follow him back out into the foyer, down the long hall and through another locked door, which leads to a secured elevator. I watch as he punches in a code and waves me inside. We go up four floors and down another hall which dead-ends at a bookshelf. Only it doesn't.

Antonio shoots me a wink and pulls out a book of fifteenth-century poetry, and the bookshelf glides open into a very sterile and modern hall. I follow him on, through yet another door and into what looks for all the world like a doctor's lounge. There's a door to our right, which leads to a dimly lit hall with more elevators, and another door in front of us. That one has 'Chapel Industries' etched in stark clinical lettering across the front. Antonio just stands there, grinning. Another game. I raise a brow.

He grins further. "Well?"

I look around. "Well, what?"

He reaches into his suit pocket and pulls out a key-card, handing it to me and gesturing to the door in front of us. Frowning at him, and thoroughly tired of his games, I grab the card and press it to the reader at the side of the door. The lock clicks, I push the door open—and am instantly hit by an overwhelming combination of smells: new plastic, sanitised bedding, sterile alcohol, and blood. Lots of blood. Hunger wakes and turns in my gut, and I turn around to Antonio, confused.

"What is this?"

He follows me into the room, smirking. "This is your present. Well, it's mine, but you can use it. Whenever you want. Consider it a perk. A fringe benefit of being my maker."

He winks at me and heads over to a stainless-steel cabinet, which he opens in a spinning cloud of coolant to reveal row upon row of typed and bagged blood.

It's then I realise what this place is. "You've got to be kidding me. You own a blood bank?"

Grabbing up a bag, he tosses it to me, with a grin. "Several, actually. I'm amazed no one else has thought of it. It's surprisingly easy once you get past the government regulations. I just have to make sure everything passes inspection, that I hire the right people who will hire the right people, and that I am several times removed from the whole process."

He grabs another bag, bouncing it in one hand as he shuts the fridge again and walks over, handing it to me.

"This is the building next door. No one even knows I've connected the floors. Most of the blood goes where intended. I simply take a little off the top. For emergencies." He graces me with another grin, loving that he's surprised me. "And for you. Until you come to your senses."

I don't know what to think. Or what to say. I look down at the bags in my hand. Fresh, safe, human blood. I look back up to him, offering a smile. "Thanks."

"You're welcome." He smiles too, a little knowing smile—which is worrying—and heads back toward the door. "That's the tour. I know you have to go. Come on."

I follow him out, still a bit shocked at the revelation and the generosity. It's out of character. Then again, I haven't seen him for the better part of a hundred years. Maybe he's changed. But I doubt it.

We head back downstairs, back into the foyer, where we are greeted by Temi. He nods to both of us deferentially, then turns to Antonio, with a gesture toward the club entrance. "Eve is here."

"Good!" Antonio smiles at me, that glint in his eye again. Another game. Frowning, I follow Temi's gesture as a very pretty blonde walks in from the club. She's dressed to the nines, and she's one of us. She seems startled to see anyone else with Antonio—and does a double-take when she realises what I am. But she recovers well enough, walking over and planting a kiss on his cheek.

"Anthony! It's been so long!"

He laughs and takes her hand, bringing it to his lips with a sly sideways glance at me. She blushes—which means she's recently fed, and she's young. I'd bet she's still in her first century. And by her accent, American. She smiles at him fondly, then turns to me, extending a pale and perfectly manicured hand.

"Hello. I'm Eve."

I take her offered hand as Antonio steps in to introduce us with a flourish. "Evie—this is Rue." He pauses for what I can only assume is dramatic effect. "My maker."

Jesus. How long has he been waiting to do that? The boy has seen far too many vampire films lately. Her reaction is just what I'm certain he wanted: she looks startled and suddenly uncertain; blinks, starts to speak, stops, tries again, then stops again, and then realises I still have her hand. Antonio looks on with growing amusement at her embarrassment.

I forget that I have a reputation among my own kind. It's not entirely undeserved but is highly exaggerated. And I'm certain Antonio has had quite a bit to do with that exaggeration. This girl is too young and inexperienced to know what to do or say, or even if she should do or say anything. Poor thing. Her glance trails to the bags of blood I'm still holding, up over my still bruised face—and then catches me watching. She flushes again, and quickly looks down.

I feel sorry for her then, give her a smile, and let her hand go. "Nice to meet you."

I turn back to Antonio. I don't know what new game he's playing, but I'm not in the mood. "I have to go, Anthony."

I can't help putting slight emphasis on the new version of his name, which he notices, with a sardonic smile. "So soon? But you haven't even seen the club in action!"

I take a breath to reply, but he doesn't pause.

"This is to be the first stop in Europe, for whichever of us needs it. The club will be the hottest thing in Dublin, chock full of delicious, delirious bodies. And Evie here will be my new manager."

"I see." I give her another polite smile, even though I don't really care.

She smiles back at me then turns to Antonio again, apparently deciding that saying nothing about me in my presence is the best tactic. Smart girl. She clears her throat and opens her purse. "Speaking of humans—I have the party favours."

His eyes light up. "Let me see."

She smiles and takes out a neatly packed plastic bag filled with smaller plastic bags, those in turn filled with drugs of various type and quantity. Each bag is stamped with a black symbol. A chaos symbol. A shiver runs down my spine, and I grab her arm as she hands the package over.

"Where'd you get these?"

"Ow!" Her eyes glint with surprise and pain. "You're hurting me!"

Again, I don't care. Gripping her arm tighter, I meet her eyes, making sure she understands the clear threat in mine. "Where did you get the drugs?"

Her eyes flicker to Antonio, but find no help there. He's simply amused by this new twist in his game. Whimpering, and still trying to pull her arm away, she turns back to me. "I have somebody I deal with. A human."

I squeeze her arm. Slightly. "Who and where?"

"Ow! Jesus! His name's Damien, okay? He works out of Ringsend." She tries again to pull her arm away, and then stumbles back as I abruptly let her go.

I turn back to Antonio, who raises a brow, but I don't have the time or the inclination to explain myself right now. "I need a car."

For some reason that makes him smile. "Of course. Temi will drive you wherever you want to go."

I frown. "I can drive myself."

He smirks. "I know. But I've only one car here and I'd really rather have it back tonight. Besides, have you looked in a mirror? You look like shit. People will notice. Seriously, Rue. Take the back seat, let Temi drive."

I glare at him, then relent with a sigh. I don't have the energy to argue with him. "Fine."

He nods to Temi and the latter turns to me. "Will I pack your clothing, Miss?"

"Yeah. Good."

He nods, and heads toward the door. "I'll drive around front." With one more nod to the other two, he leaves, and I turn back to Antonio.

"Thanks. I'm sorry I can't stay."

"No, you're not."

I snarl at him. "You're right. I'm not."

Eve's eyes dart back and forth between us as he glares back. There's that familiar cold charge of anger in the air—and then he laughs it off, all charm and wit again.

"Fine! More for us. Not that you'd want to share in the fun anyway, Mother."

He makes that last word a derisive sneer, and, grabbing up the bag of drugs with one hand and taking Eve's arm in the other, he walks into the club without a backward glance.

Christ. I stare after him for a moment, frowning. I don't know where it went so wrong between us. And I don't have time to try and figure it out right now. I've got to get back to the car I abandoned, then to Grace and Jude, and make sure they're safe. After that—well, after that I can go demon hunting. Just follow the trail of drugs. Like the fucking Yellow Brick Road.

With a sigh, I straighten my suit, check that the dagger is still safe in my boot, run a hand through my hair, and head out into the summer night.

Chapter 26

Fury

Babylon, 1604 BCE

The demon—and that is what he is, of this I have no doubt—sneers, baring rotting teeth behind cracked lips. He is dressed in the garb of a High Priest, or rather, the body he wears is so clothed, and that instant, I realise I was mistaken. The man I just killed was not the one who raped and murdered Ku-aya's mother.

It was this monster.

The stench of decaying flesh fills the room as he steps inside, pushing the terrified girl before him, his hand moving from her shoulder to curl tightly around her neck, broken nails digging into her throat as he speaks.

"Witch spawn. I had wondered when I might meet another of your accursed kind."

I do not answer him. I cannot. Terror holds me fast, and I do not know what to do. The flesh of the body he wears distorts at the presence of the demon beneath, and I do not understand. He steps toward me again, and I step back, desperately trying to think, to remember what Lilitu said of these creatures, trying to recall if she gave me anything to use against him. But I only remember her tears. Her betrayal.

The betrayal of us all.

Then, to my surprise, a wave of burning anger unfurls from deep within my breast, drowning out my fear and filling my mind with a screaming rage that takes my breath away. I think of what this being has done to Lilitu, to myself, my maker and my brethren, and by extension to every mortal whose life was taken to feed our endless hunger. I think of Lilitu's daughter, of the child I killed, of the mother and city I lost, and wave after wave of fury crashes over me, flooding toward this monster that is the very reason I am become what I am.

Then another hatred rises to meet my own; a torrent of feeling that is not mine, and yet in moments becomes so, overtaking my own emotion so that I tremble in the winds of an internal storm. The demon sees this, and misreading, sneers at me, his harsh voice distorting the throat of his stolen body.

"What is the matter, leech? Did you lose your voice in your making? Or do you fear me so that you cannot speak?"

I feel that burning hatred rise into my eyes as I answer, holding tight to the anger within lest I lose all intelligent intent.

"I have my voice, and at least it is mine, and my body my own."

Ku-aya's eyes seek mine, her face filled with terror, but I cannot take my gaze from the demon's. I know the moment I do, he will move to kill her. And so I stand unmoving, staring at him, every fibre of my being on guard.

The demon laughs; a rasping, horrible sound ripped from its rotting throat. "You think to insult me, woman? It is no insult. I drank this one's soul and took his form. It is what I do. At least I am not an accursed half-breed, trapped in flesh, born of a witch-whores magic."

He smirks and clenches his hand tighter around Ku-aya's throat, lifting her off her feet. She chokes and flails in his grip. Anger surges forth in my breast, and I snarl at him, baring my fangs.

"Let her go."

He only lifts her higher, his twisted grip cutting into the flesh of her throat. "This? This whore, a daughter of whores? What do you care whether it lives or dies?"

He steps closer still, holding the struggling girl in mid-air, his eyes solid and shining black as pitch.

"Join me, and I will give you a thousand such mortals to do with what you will. My legions are many, and soon we will again rule this earth.

Serve me, and I will make you whole. No longer will you suffer in darkness, a wretched and broken thing. Bend your will to mine, and I will give you back all that was taken from you."

The fury that rages in my breast spills over, and all thought of caution dissolves in a storm that shudders my voice as I speak.

"I will never serve you! You are nothing! You are Ekkimu; a desolate spirit who wears the body of the dead, who seeks only to deceive and destroy! You say I am cursed, but this is a lie. It is you and your kind that are damned! As long as I shall live you will never reign, not on this earth nor any other! Go back to the waterless desert whence you came, you plague-ridden son of a dog! May your soul descend screaming through sixty-thousand hells!" And I run at him, as fast as I can, my fists raised to fight.

As fast as I can move, he is faster, his free hand sweeping to strike me mid-stride. The blow knocks me from my feet and sends me flying back to crash through the walls of the house and land with a crunch of broken bone on the tiles of the garden without.

Choking on dust and a sudden internal stream of blood, I struggle to my feet. The demon roars and tosses the girl to one side, her limp form tumbling against an inner wall, as he thunders toward me.

Before I can stand, he is upon me again, lifting me by the throat in one hand even as he lifted the mortal girl. His strength is astonishing. I am no match for him. I know it. I choke and struggle like a child in his grip. He grins and draws me close, his fist crushing my throat so that I lose my breath. Desperation moves me then, and I twist against his grasp, kicking upward with both legs and landing a hard knee to his jaw. He reels backwards from the blow, dropping me to land again on the tiles, my head striking hard against a winged statue of a Babylonian god. I see a spinning canopy of stars and feel the stinging flow of blood down my face as my vision reels. No. I must stay awake.

He roars toward me as again I struggle to my knees. Searching madly for anything to use as a weapon, I fumble against the blood-slick marble of the sculpted god. Lifting the heavy statue out of its anchorage, I turn just as he reaches for me, black eyes flashing. With a cry of rage, I swing the idol in an arc against his skull. There is a sickening crunch, and he falls to lie unmoving on the tiles.

Dropping the idol, I stumble across the courtyard to where Ku-aya lies unmoving. She is breathing, but her head is bleeding badly, one arm bent and broken beneath her. Pushing back the pain of my wounds, I kneel and lift her into my arms, bring my wrist to my mouth and bite down, then press the pooling blood against her lips. It takes a moment only for her to drink, and I breathe a sigh of relief, then look back over my shoulder to where the demon lies dead.

Only he is no longer there.

Cursing aloud, I pull away from the still-unconscious girl and stand, searching every shadowed corner. Nothing. A light wind stirs the leaves in the trees that arch above the inner garden, but all the rest is silence. Slowly, cautiously, I move back out into the garden to the spot where he fell. A dark stain glistens in the moonlight, and I crouch down and swipe it with a finger. Blood. But old blood. The blood of the long dead. It smells of decay, and I gag at the foul scent.

Then I hear a rustle of fabric behind me and turn with a snarl to be met with a kick to the face as the demon roars out from the shadows. The blow sends me flying across the flagstones once more, to crash hard into the tiled fountain. Stones crumble and water spills around me as I once again struggle to rise, spitting out a mouthful of blood. But before I can get to my knees, he is upon me again, this time wielding a broken bronze ornamental spear, ripped from another of the statues. I roll out of the way as he strikes down with the dull spearhead, missing me by a hairsbreadth. With a howl of rage, he lifts the spear again, striking down. Again, I roll, and again, he misses.

Fear courses through me now, overtaking anger. He is strong. And fast. His skin stretches out of all proportion as the demon beneath bends stolen flesh to his will.

I struggle to my feet, moving fast as he pulls the spearhead from the shattered tiles, and strides toward me. With a cry, I run for him again, snarling, but he swings the spear shaft around, so fast I cannot avoid the blow—and smashes it like a club against my side, breaking my ribs and knocking the breath from me.

I fall to my knees, gasping for air. He laughs above me and kicks me roughly over. I struggle to move, to breathe, anything, but I am helpless, and can only stare up in witness to my fate. The demon grins at my futile struggles, then lifts the spear high—and plunges the dull spearhead through my breast and on into the earth beneath, the broken shaft quivering at the shock of the blow.

If I thought I knew pain before I was wrong. A hot flow of blood erupts from my broken lips, and all breath deserts me as my lungs wither within my chest. Above me, the demon leers.

He will kill me now, I know it. The body he is wearing is torn and stretched impossibly by the efforts of the evil spirit beneath, and his skull is crushed where I struck him, but it has made little difference. He has won. He crouches beside me, watching as I drown slowly in my own blood.

"You should know, Witch spawn, that I did not wish to kill you. On the contrary, I bear neither you nor your maker ill will. All I wanted was this small place of power among these wretched apes, a place from which to direct the fates of men. The whores of this house defied me, and so met their end. As shall you."

He stands up then, and grasps the broken spear in one hand, wrenching it from my chest.

My vision shudders, then blurs and narrows, until all I see is his leering, evil face as he swings the spearhead high above his head to bring all his weight to bear into the blow.

It is a blow that never lands. For suddenly, a shimmering blade flashes out from the darkness behind him. I watch his eyes grow first wide, then dull, fading from black to ghostly white as his head loosens slowly from his neck, falling to bounce from his shoulder to the ground, and roll to a stop beside my own. There is a rushing sound, like an angry wind battling a cliff face—and then the spear he still holds in directionless hands becomes too much a weight for his aimless body, and he tumbles over backwards, landing with a crash, cold and still and dead upon the broken tiles.

Stunned, I watch as Lilitu steps out of the darkness, a shining bronze sword in one hand, its blade stained black with the demon's blood, her eyes alight as they meet my own.

"You must take their head, Daughter. Anything less and they will never cease."

Chapter 27

Safe and Sound

The stolen demon car is right where I left it: parked neatly at the curb, two streets away from Grace's now half-exploded house. Right where I left it, safe and sound—and clamped.

"Jesus Christ."

"Sorry, Miss?" Temi turns from the front with that same polite, inquisitive look. I shake my head, wondering if he is ever anything other than perfectly urbane.

"Never mind. Pull up over there."

I have him park Antonio's town car up the street while I scope out the area. No one seems to be about. I check laneways, rooftops, and windows. Nothing. Nothing except those cameras. Got to risk it anyway.

"Wait here."

Temi nods, and I get out, taking another long look around before heading across to the boot of the demon car. I give a sharp tug, and it pops loose with a ping of metal. Easy. I grab my bag, slam down the broken hood, which doesn't shut anymore—oh well, not my car—and, moving quickly, dart back across the street and into the backseat of the town car. To any watching human eyes or cameras, I'd be nothing but a blur. I open the bag as Temi pulls the car back onto the road.

"Where to now, Miss?"

"Ballsbridge. The Park Hotel."

A small knot of anxiety curls up in my gut. I need to see Grace, make sure she's okay, and I have to tell her about her house. And her friends. And what she is. None of which will be easy. With a sigh, I double-check the contents of my bag. All there. I tug out the remaining IV bags leftover from yesterday. Christ, it seems longer. Amazingly, they're still cold enough to be okay. I add in the two bags Antonio gave me and zip up the backpack again. Five bags. I'm still healing, and am already hungry because of it. Five will only last me a couple of nights, if even. I'll have to be careful around Grace. Can't get too close. Can't lose control. Leaning back against the seat, I close my eyes, trying to come up with a plan. Think, Rue—think.

Okay.

The demons at Grace's house said they would track me to find her. Starting back at my place. I've no idea how they plan to do that. For all I know they can sniff me out like a pack of dogs. Then again, I was right under their ugly noses last night and they didn't know it at all. So maybe they can't. Anyway, it doesn't matter. It's me tracking them now. Follow the drugs. After I make sure Grace is okay.

I just hope I can find them before they find me.

Opening my eyes, I sit up as Temi turns the car into the curve of the hotel driveway. A valet steps up to open the car door but Temi beats him to it, moving around with the exceptional speed that our blood bestows. He's so fast the valet starts and stumbles back, all apologies. Poor guy.

I put on my new shades before I step out of the car. I don't have my usual hoodie and I know my face is still pretty bruised. Not to mention I'm growing hungrier by the minute and I'm sure my eyes show it. I'll need to feed before I see Grace. I turn to Temi as he gets the bags.

"Can I use your phone?"

He nods once, reaching into his suit jacket and producing his mobile. I smile my thanks and dial Jude, walking away a few feet as I do so. It rings twice before he answers.

"Hello?"

"It's me. I'm downstairs. What room are you in?"

"Rue! Thank God. We're in five-oh-eight. Fifth floor."

"I'll be there in a minute." I hang up, walk back, and hand the phone back to Temi, but he shakes his head and hands it back. "Keep it, Miss. I have others. My number is programmed in if you need anything else."

"Thanks." Taking my bags from him, I shove the phone in my pocket and pull out a stack of cash from the backpack, handing it over. "Do me a favour and get me a room on the fifth floor. Two—no, three nights. Five-oh-seven, five-oh-nine or five-ten. Whichever's free."

Again, that polite nod, and he heads to the desk as I make a slow circuit of the lobby. It's a nice hotel. There are a few patrons in the residents' bar—what looks like the remnants of a wedding party—but at this late hour even they're relatively quiet. No one stands out or smells like demon. Which is good. Hunger rises again at the sight and smell of humans so near, and I turn away from them as Temi walks over, handing me a key card.

"Room five-ten." He hands me back most of the cash. "Enough of a tip for no questions, and a do not disturb request."

Nice. He's very good, this boy. But he belongs to Antonio. I can't forget that. I'm sure he'll report back where he dropped me, and everything I've done. Nothing I can do about that. Time to send him back.

"Listen, thanks for driving me and all. And give Antonio—Anthony—my thanks."

He smiles that same polite smile, and leaves, with a last deferential nod. I watch until he turns the car out of the lot and onto the street beyond, then I grab my bags and head for the lobby restrooms.

Checking to make sure the loo is empty, I dart into a stall and latch it behind. Hungry. My fangs push against my lip as I rip one of the IV bags open and knock it back, drinking deeply. Gods. The blood is cold and empty, but even so, it sends sweet relief cascading through me; quenching the thirst, quieting the remaining aches and pains. I drain the bag then open another. Two should help me face Grace, dull the craving and let me heal a bit more.

I rip the bags apart, licking the plastic clean, then lean back against the stall door as the slow surge of cold blood moves through me. Nice. I needed that. Folding both bags neatly, I shove them into my bag to recycle later somewhere. I hate tossing plastic. I need the earth to be liveable for the long haul.

Stepping out of the stall, I face the mirror, removing my sunglasses and taking a quick inventory. Looking better. The cuts and scratches are gone, and the bruises are fading to a splotchy pale purple and green. I should be fully healed in a couple of nights if I can stay well fed. Not bad for being blown up.

I give my reflection a wry smile and replace the sunglasses just as a woman bursts drunkenly through the door. When she sees me she gasps, then hiccups and bursts into laughter before muttering a slurred apology and stumbling into a stall.

Raising a brow, I stand there a moment, listening as she fumbles and bangs against the walls. Temptation rises, catching me off guard as the thing inside uncoils and whispers need. Fresh human blood would taste that much better, heal me that much faster, make me that much stronger. I wouldn't have to kill her. Simply take what I need and go. She's so drunk she'll never even know. I can feel the heat rise from her flushed skin, hear her pounding heart—even through the closed stall door. Then with a start, I realise I'm standing at that door, one hand reaching to rip it open.

No.

This isn't me. Backing away, I grab my bags and leave the loo. Fast. Christ. What was I thinking? I'm not even hungry right now. Fuck. This is how it starts. The more I have the more I want. The more it wants.

Shit.

Walking back through the lobby, I swipe the key card to activate the lift control pad and press the up arrow. I can hear the carriage whir into motion from above, and I listen as it brakes once, opens, closes and whirs down again. The indicator dings, and the doors open to spill out two more wedding party guests, by the look of them. A man and a woman, both looking pleased and guilty in equal measures. They head to the bar, never even seeing me as I slip past them into the waiting lift.

I punch the gilded button for floor five, then lean back against the mirrored walls as the doors shut and the lift dings and whirs upwards again. Okay. I can do this. I'm in control. Just have to be vigilant. The lift dings again and the doors slide open. Fifth floor. Stepping out, I take a cautious look around before following the numbers and arrows down the empty hall. I find my room, but that can wait. First things first. Taking a deep and calming breath, I set my will against the thing inside, shoving it back and down as I knock on the door next to mine.

Quick footsteps, a pause—then Jude's voice at the door, cautious. "Yes?"

"It's me."

There's a click as he unbolts the door and jerks it open. "Rue! Thank god!"

He steps back, opening the door further, and starting to speak again, but I stop him before he can go there.

"Don't invite me in."

He pauses mid-gesture, confused. "What?"

"Don't. Invite. Me in." I reach up and remove my sunglasses, folding them and putting them in my jacket pocket before looking back up to meet his eyes. After a moment he nods his understanding, just as Grace appears behind him, bleary-eyed with lack of sleep and worry, but otherwise unharmed. I smile at the sight of her. I can't help it.

"Hiya."

She smiles in return, sweet—and cautious. Which means the effects of my blood are wearing off. Which is a good thing. So why am I suddenly sad? Shake it off Rue, she's not for you.

"Sorry. It took me longer to get here than I thought it would."

She frowns as she sees the bruises on my face, concern darkening her eyes. "What happened to you? Why don't you come—"

"Stop." I interrupt her before she can finish the invitation, accidental or no. "You can't let me in."

She frowns. "What? Why?"

Leaning against the outer frame of the door, as close as I dare get, I stand and look at her a moment. Even exhausted and stressed, she's beautiful. My heart catches in my throat as her eyes seek my own, waiting for an answer. I sigh.

"Because once I'm in, other things can come in, and you're no longer safe." I look back to Jude. "Either of you."

He glowers at me. "So, what're you going to do, stand there all night?"

I smile. "Yes."

He rolls his eyes heavenward. "And when morning comes?"

"I'll go to my room." I pull out the key card, waving it at him. "Right next door."

He shakes his head but looks slightly less annoyed with me, at least.

I give him another smile. "Don't worry so much."

"Don't get hurt so much." He glares, lifting a hand to indicate my bruised face. "What happened to you, anyway?"

"Long story. I'll tell you later. Right now, I need to talk to Grace." I hand him my bag and give him the key card along with a meaningful look. "Why don't you take a break. Get some sleep. You can use my room."

He gives me a long stare, and for a moment I think he's going to argue—but then he sighs, grabs the bag and key card from me and heads to my room. I watch him go, then think of something.

"Wait. Here ..."

Bending down, I pull up my trouser leg and gingerly take out the dagger, still wrapped in its scarf, and hold it out to him. "Take this for me. Please."

He stands a moment, staring at the bundle in my hand, then at me. I know he knows what it is by the look on his face. I give him what's meant to be a reassuring smile, and with an exasperated sigh, he walks over, takes the knife, then heads back to my room. I wait until the door clicks shut behind him before turning back to Grace.

Gods, she smells good. Desire blooms through me, and I have to close my eyes for fear she'll see, and be afraid. Not that she shouldn't be. After a second or two, the temptation subsides with a whimper, and I can open my eyes and talk to her again.

"How're you holding up?"

She shrugs. "Okay, I guess. I don't know."

Those hazel eyes search my own, trail over my new clothes, my face and its bruises, my hair. She reaches out gently, touching the curling ends, the back of her hand brushing against my cheek. "You cut your hair."

Her touch sends another shiver of desire down my spine. I shrug, trying to keep my tone casual, although what I feel is anything but.

"It got burnt. It'll grow back."

She nods and gives me a soft, shy smile. "I like it." Then she frowns, her eyes dark with fear and worry. "What happened to you? Where did you go? Did you find anything out?"

I nod, settling into my standing lean against the doorframe. After all, I'm going to be here awhile.

"I did. A few things. That's part of what I need to talk to you about. As to what happened to me, well that was part of the finding things out."

I give her a wry smile, and, taking a deep breath, tell her everything that happened since I left the two of them, leaving out only the bits with Antonio. She listens, without interruption—only a giving short gasp when I tell her how I found her friends, and another when I tell her about the explosion. When I'm done, her eyes are wide, dark and brimming with tears, and her hand has crept up to cover her mouth. She stares at me in silence for a few long minutes—then starts pacing back and forth in the doorway, shaking her head.

"I don't understand. This can't be happening."

I realise with a sinking feeling that A: the calming effects of my blood are wearing off pretty quickly, B: she's still in shock from everything that happened earlier, C: I've just made that worse, and D: I haven't even told her what she is yet. Shit.

"Grace."

She stops pacing and looks up, and the shock and sorrow on her face breaks my heart.

"I'm so sorry."

Closing her eyes, she rubs at them with a shaking sigh. "It's not your fault."

"I know. Still. I'm sorry about your house. About your friends."

Opening her eyes again, she shakes her head, her lips a tight line. "They weren't like—what you said—when I found them."

I nod. "I figured."

She glances up at me, but her gaze is inward. "They were in the kitchen and sitting room, but not... laid out like you saw. They were just lying like they'd fallen. Dead. But there was no blood. Just these holes..."

"Puncture wounds. At the artery." I finish for her. "I saw. I think that was done to make you think it was me."

She stares at me in utter confusion. "But why?"

I shake my head. "I'm not sure about the why, but I think the whole thing was a trap. Back on the rooftop, those demons called me 'bait'. It was a setup. To catch you."

"Me?" She shakes her head, her eyes searching my own as she asks the question I'm finally going to have to answer. "Why do they want me?"

She might hate me, after this. After she realises I've known all along. She has reason enough to already. But I have to tell her. It's time.

"Because you're an angel."

Chapter 28

Lilitu

Babylon, 1604 BCE

Setting the sword to one side, Lilitu kneels and lifts me into her arms, as she has done so many times before. Gasping, and still struggling to breathe, I stare at her, shock and pain tearing through me in turns.

"How...?"

"Shhhhh." Sitting down beside me, she gently lifts my head, tipping my lips to her upturned wrist. "I will explain, in time, all that you need to know. But now drink, Daughter. Drink from me and heal."

And so I drink, closing my eyes and sinking my fangs into her pale flesh. Once again, her blood courses through me, dark and powerful as the sea. I am lost to it in seconds, reaching up to grasp her wrist in both hands, drinking deeply, all thought fading beneath that cardinal tide. She lets me drink for a few long moments, her blood healing me in wave after wave, and then she pulls her wrist away. I reach for more, but she pushes me back.

"Enough."

It is a stern warning, and it brings me to my senses. I sit up, wincing as the gaping wound in my chest closes over and my broken bones begin to re-knit.

Lilitu stands, moving across the courtyard and on through the shattered wall of the house to where Ku-aya lies, still unconscious. I struggle to my feet, holding an arm around my slowly healing ribs as I follow her within. She kneels by Ku-aya's side a moment, her hand on the girl's chest, then she nods to me.

"Come. Cary the girl within. We have much to do before dawn, and it would be best if she were not in the way."

I frown from her to the girl and back, but I am still in shock, and sorely wounded; so numbly obey.

Grimacing with pain that pounds through my sinews as I heal, I lift Ku-aya into my arms and carry her into a bedchamber. Placing her gently on a bed, I draw the coverlet up around her sleeping form. I watch her a moment before turning away and walking back out to where Lilitu now stands over the slave I struck down—was it only moments ago? It seems a lifetime.

I watch as she lifts his unconscious form into her arms, letting his head fall back and sinking her fangs deep into his throat. This one will not be saved. She drinks until there is no more to take, and then lets his body slip to the floor, looking to me as she licks the blood from her lips.

"Now the woman."

She nods across to the woman I had attacked when the human priest interrupted my feeding. I frown and move down the hallway toward her unmoving form. I thought that I had killed her. And now I have no desire to. I turn to Lilitu, who looks at me sternly, her eyes glinting emerald fire in the flickering lamplight.

"You must clean up after yourself, Asharru. No one can be left to speak of what happened here this night. End what you began."

I stare down at the body of the woman, whom I see now is dressed in the style of a courtesan. Bought for the night, not knowing it would be her last. I frown to Lilitu, wanting to argue, but she simply stares at me, and I know she is right. Kneeling, I lift the woman into my arms, and, as Lilitu did with the servant, sink my fangs into her throat, at the place where the blood flows fast and deep. It takes only moments until she is dead. Her life's blood moves in me, healing me further, and I lay her body back down, then look to Lilitu, who has moved to stand beside me.

"Good. Now carry her down into the low streets. Leave her body to the river, and do not let yourself be seen. I will take care of the slave, and the other." She nods toward the body of the demon, and I follow her gaze, then look back to her, a thousand questions burning on my lips.

She shakes her head, seeing the questions in my eyes. "Do as I say, Daughter. When you return, I will be here, and will answer all that you ask."

What can I do but obey? Leaning down, I lift the dead woman into my arms and carry her out through the ruined courtyard and into the street beyond. I keep to the shadows, moving as swiftly as I can; avoiding the circles cast by lamplight. Those lights grow ever fewer as I cross the bridge into the western quarter, and move into the low streets near the river, into the lesser city; the quarter called Kumar.

Here is where I usually hunt, among the beggars and drunkards, mercenaries and thieves. Not all who dwell here are sinners—many more in the richer streets above deal in deceit and murder—but the wages of such sins are often spent here, and here the victims are more commonly found. No one will think twice at the finding of another body, of another harlot.

I walk to the riverbank, where the banners of trader's tents flutter in the breeze. The city is so silent in these hours before dawn, I could believe it abandoned. I find a shadowed inlet, a pace removed from the path above, and walk a few steps out among the reeds. There I kneel and let the woman's body go. I watch as she sinks into the water, then turn and wade back to the shore, walking back through the darkened streets, my heart heavy, my soul in shrouded in shame.

Again, I have killed an innocent, and this time I've no other to blame. I was neither starving, nor blind with emotion. No. I let the darkness within take hold, gave it free rein, and willingly. And what is more, I enjoyed it. Revelled in the killing, relished the freedom to take what prey I wanted, without care of consequence or conscience. Is this then, what I am? A monster, a devil? No better than the demon in the garden above? These dark thoughts follow behind me, haunting my every step as I walk back up through winding streets to Ku-aya's home, where Lilitu awaits my return.

Entering through the bronze gate, I stop at the spot where the demon fell. The body is no longer there. I did not expect it to be. Lilitu said she would take care of the rest and I am certain she has. Frowning, I walk in through the broken wall to find her standing beside the bed where Ku-aya still sleeps. I stop in the doorway of the room, watching. Waiting for her to acknowledge me—which she does not.

Instead, she stands, her back to me, ignoring me until a burning fury fills my breast; until I am clenching my fists with angry impatience. Only then does she turn and move toward me with a soft smile, as if she has just noticed my presence.

"Good. You have returned. Come, we must repair the damage to the wall, and the garden beyond, as best we can. People will have heard the sounds of your battle with the demon; and although they did not dare to venture into the dark to see, they will not have such qualms come morning."

She moves past me, through the house and back into the courtyard where she begins to clear the broken tiles. I stand there a moment, un-moving; dumbfounded and incredulous; then I follow, my anger building with each step.

"How is it you can be so cold after all that has happened? 'Repair the wall', you say?" I step close to her, fists clenched, my voice shaking despite my best efforts to control the storm of my emotions. "I nearly died this night! That...that vile creature nearly ended me! And why? Because I did not know of him! Because you did not see fit to tell me that his kind still walk this earth! Why? Do you not care at all? Does my life mean so little to you? Why do you purposefully keep me in ignorance as if I were a simple-minded child?" My voice breaks, and I must stop speaking, full as I am with fury.

Lilitu stands and turns to look at me, and I watch a great tide of sadness rise into her countenance. She stays silent, and calm until all my anger breaks into despair, and tears rise unbidden. Only then does she speak.

"Your life means all to me, Daughter. Surely you know this by now. I have told you it was I who chose you, I who watched you grow and change. But I have not told you it was I who saved you that night, I who called upon your brethren to come and take you from your death."

She sighs, reaching a pale hand to wipe away the tears that fall to stain my cheek. "I have loved you, as I have loved no other. You would not have died tonight, Asharru, for I would never allow it."

I know then, what I should have known sooner. Lilitu had followed as I left the catacombs with Ku-aya. She followed and watched, as she has so often done all my life.

I swallow hard and hold her gaze. "You knew."

She smiles. "No. I suspected. I was not certain until I followed you within." She steps away from me and sets about clearing the broken tiles again. "I am surprised that you did not sense the demon's presence before you ever came into this place. I could smell his stench before I entered the gate."

I stare at her. "You knew there was a demon within, and yet you let me enter, let me hunt the humans unknowing, let him attack..."

I stop, bitter realisation growing.

"You used me! Used me as a lure!"

Fury builds in me again, so swiftly I cannot control it. Snarling, I strike her, shoving her hard with all my strength. She hits the already damaged wall and falls to the tiles in a cloud of mud-brick and dust. But I am not done. Fangs bared now, I leap upon her, beating and striking her as hard as I can, rage and betrayal burning through my soul.

"This is nothing more than a game to you, and all of us mere playthings! You think you can do whatever it is you wish! You say that you love me, but this is a lie! You could not love me and treat me so! You are a witch! A liar—a monster! Murderer! Child-slayer! You are no better than the demon that made you!"

As soon as the words are out of my mouth, I regret them. Shock and sorrow cascade over me, and I sit back, shaking and ashamed, my hand to my mouth in horror, my anger swiftly spent.

Lilitu sits up, slowly, her face and arms scratched and bleeding from where I have hit her, many times over. I look down, afraid to meet her eyes, certain that her fury will fall upon me, and the punishment will be severe.

But she says not a word. In silence, she gets to her feet, and in silence brushes the dust from her linens. Then she moves back across the garden, continuing to clear the broken tiles and shattered stone. I sit, for a moment more, and then I too stand, moving across to help her, shame rising within my breast in a drowning flood. We clean and clear in utter silence, save for the occasional sound of the shifting of stone—until all signs of the battle are erased; until only the broken wall of the house beyond is left to tell the tale.

Lilitu walks across the garden then, and sits down on an ornately carved stone bench under the softly curving branches of an ancient olive tree. I follow, stopping to stand beside her, fists clenched and waiting. Long moments pass before she looks up and when our eyes meet, my heart breaks at the sorrow in her own.

Instantly, I drop to my knees, bowing my head in shame. "Forgive me. Please. I did not mean to speak so harshly to you."

She remains silent for a moment more, and then speaks, her voice soft and even. "That is not true, Asharru. You meant every word you spoke, in your anger, in your pain. You feel that I have betrayed you. And perhaps you are right."

I lift my head, blinking up at her in confusion.

She meets my questioning gaze with a sad smile. "Perhaps I did use you, Daughter. For that, I am filled with sorrow, and beg your forgiveness." She reaches to touch my face, her eyes dark and serious as she repeats her request.

"Forgive me, child."

I nod, my heart heavy with shame. "I forgive you."

She smiles. "And I also forgive you. Now. Come." Reaching out, she takes my hand and pulls me up to sit beside her. "You have said I have kept things from you, and you are right. I have. But it was only that I did not wish to burden your young mind with knowledge that you did not need. For make no mistake—knowledge is a burdensome thing."

She sighs and entwines her fingers through my own. "Do not think less of me Daughter. I see now that I was wrong to keep these things from you."

I shake my head, my heart filling up again with love for her, all anger fading away. "I will never think less of you. You only did what you thought you must do. But please do not treat me as a child any longer. I have lived long enough now by your side, surely you must see that I am able to bear the burden of your knowledge."

I smile up to her, yearning, fearful, hopeful. She holds my gaze to her own, searching my eyes, my face, and then, as if satisfied at what she sees, she nods. "Very well Daughter. It is time you were told the rest of the tale."

Chapter 29

Hand or Heart

Grace just stands there in the doorway, staring at me for a few long moments. Then she takes a shaky breath, lets it out, takes another breath, and finally manages to speak.

"What do you mean, I'm an 'angel'?"

"Just what I said." This might be hard for her, but she has to understand. "You're an angel. An actual angel. At least in part. You're Nephilim. The rare result of angelic-human relations."

She shakes her head, her eyes dark with confusion. "I don't understand. I can't be. No. That's impossible."

"Why?" I hold her gaze. "Why is it any more impossible than anything else? Why is it more impossible than what's happened to you over the last few days? Than your dreams, your visions, than the demons? Than me?"

She looks up at me, trembling, tears welling up in her eyes. "But angels aren't real."

I smile. "Angels are rare, but they are real. Very real. And you are one."

She's still shaking her head, but I can tell she knows it's true. Her next question comes out in a ragged whisper, past quivering lips. "But...how do you know?"

Dammit. I knew she'd ask that. And I know I have to answer. Even though I wish I could somehow avoid it, even though she'll probably hate me for it. With a sigh, I meet her gaze and give her the truth. "I know because I've fed from you. And I've fed from an angel once before. You smell the same. Taste the same. Your blood's the same."

For a moment I think she might pass out. All the colour drains from her cheeks. "You knew. All along, you knew."

I can't lie to her anymore. "Yes."

Hurt passes over her face like a dark cloud—and I have just enough time to see the tears well up in those lovely eyes before she steps back into the room, and slams the door in my face.

"Grace!"

I reach out to stop her without thinking, and am instantly in searing agony as my hand crosses the threshold. Pulling away with a cry, I stumble back against the opposite wall as a shock wave of residual pain rockets up my arm. "Shit!"

I slide down to sit against the wall, tears stinging my eyes. I don't know what hurts more, my hand or my heart. She hates me, just like I knew she would. Christ. And she has every fucking right to. I could've told her sooner. Should've. Shit. Shit Shit!

I swipe angrily at the tears with my left hand, nursing my right against my chest as my blood begins to cool back down. Way to go Rue. Now what the fuck're you going to do? Leaning back, I close my eyes and knock my head against the wall a few frustrated times. Not that it does any good, but it makes me feel better. Some. Then I hear the door open again, and lift my head to see Grace standing over me.

"What happened?"

I nod to the doorway. "I tried to stop you. From shutting the door, I mean. My hand crossed over and the blood began to boil in my veins." I hold out my hand, which is still red, but has finally stopped throbbing.

She frowns. "Jesus. Are you okay?"

"Yeah." I finally manage a smile. "I'm fine. Go back inside."

She shakes her head, her eyes dark with confusion and concern. "No. I'll stay out here with you."

I give her a sideways glance, noting that she's well able to argue with me. My blood must be wearing off a bit.

"I'd rather you stayed inside."

She shoots a look at my hand. "Would that happen to anyone—anything—else that was uninvited?"

"Probably. That or something similar."

She nods. "Then I'll stay out here with you. If anything happens, I'll go back in." She sighs and walks over to sit down beside me; knees up, back against the wall. "You should've told me."

I nod. "I know."

She tips her head forward to meet my eyes. "Why didn't you?"

I shrug, wincing, as I'm still not fully healed and shrugging hurts. "I was trying to protect you. I thought if I could find out more first, maybe it'd be easier on you." I lean back again, closing my eyes. "I'm sorry."

She's quiet for so long I'm sure she's thinking of ways to tell me she hates me—until I feel her warm hand cover my own, and look to her in surprise as she smiles sad and soft, reading my mind yet again. "I don't hate you, Rue."

My heart does a silly little leap of hope as she continues.

"Maybe I should." She shrugs. "But I can't. I tried—and maybe I did, for a moment, when I thought you killed everyone. I thought I needed to. But I couldn't keep hating you after that, and I don't hate you now."

That hope rises inside me like a balloon, until the thought occurs that this is probably the lingering effects of my blood talking. Then guilt and sorrow curl a cold fist around my heart, that balloon of hope bursts, and I have to close my eyes against another rising tide of tears. Shit. Buck up, Rue. This isn't about you. Stop feeling so damn sorry for yourself and get on with it.

Leaning in like she's read my mind yet again, Grace gives my hand a gentle squeeze, and so I take a shaky breath, open my eyes, and give her a grateful smile. Even if it is only my blood talking, at least she doesn't hate me right now.

"Thanks."

She gives me a soft smile in return, then she goes all serious.

"So. Tell me what you know about angels."

I lean back against the wall. "I don't know that much. Like I said, angels are rare. Rarer than anything else, as far as I know." I turn to face her. "And you're the only one like you I've ever met."

She frowns. "But you said you drank from an angel before."

I nod. "I did. Wings, light, the works. A long time ago. She saved my life."

She nods, leaning in, her eyes locked to mine as I go on.

"It was in Poland, during The Great War. I was running from hunters. They had tracked me for months, never letting up, and I was so tired of it all. Anyway, it was just before the Battle of Bolimov. They'd wounded me—quite badly—and they were running me into the sunrise. I sought what I thought was my last refuge on the steps of a tiny bombed-out church in a ruined village in the middle of nowhere. It was as far as I could go, wounded and weak as I was."

I lean back against the wall, seeing it all so clearly in my mind's eye; the snow falling all around that little abandoned village, the half-burnt church at the edge of a dark wood, the sound of hunters not far behind me; far too many for me to fight off. The dark stain of my own red blood on new snow. The certain feeling that it was finally my time to die.

"I lay there, wondering if the sun would get me first, or the hunters, when I felt something lift me, and carry me inside. Into the church. Away from hunters. Away from the sun."

I smile softly to Grace, still amazed by the memory.

"She turned the hunters away. I don't know how, or why, but they were there and then—they weren't. Then she fed me with what could only have been her own blood. To this night I'm unclear what exactly happened. I only know that what I drank was blood, but somehow also like light. But it didn't burn me. It was unspeakably powerful." I look to her. "Yours is the same. Lighter than hers, or softer maybe. It's hard to describe, and I don't understand how it works. You are after all still human. But your blood is angelic."

Even talking about her blood stirs that dark desire inside, and I have to look away for a moment, staring down at her hand on mine.

"After that, I healed. Quickly. I think she stayed with me for the day; I've a vague recollection of sleeping in her arms, but when I woke up, I was alone, in the crypts beneath the church. She was gone, and I've never met another since." I look up again, to meet her eyes. "Until you."

She shakes her head, her eyes full of questions. "Why did she save you?"

I shrug. "I've no idea."

"Did you try to find out?"

I nod. "I did. I searched for her everywhere, read everything I could get my hands on about angels, talked to anyone I thought might know..."

She leans in. "And?"

"And nothing. I never saw her again, and none of the books I found told me anything specific." I sigh. Better tell her everything. "But vampires have their own ideas about angels and their ilk."

She frowns, but stays quiet, listening, so I go on, hating what I'm about to tell her.

"They say, if you drink the blood of an angel, or their offspring, it'll cure the vampiric condition."

She stares at me for a moment. "I take it that's not true."

I have to smile. "Obviously. However, it does make us able to withstand the light of the sun for a little longer, go longer without feeding, and it heals any wound very quickly. Plus, it's very...desirable." I look over to her. "There are vampires that spend all their time hunting things like you."

She takes a long breath, eyes dark and fearful, swallowing hard before she asks her next question.

"And you? Have you...hunted...things like me?"

I smile sadly. "No. Not in the way you mean. I looked for my angel everywhere, but not for her blood." I lean back again, against the wall, thinking. "I don't know what I would have done if I'd found her. I just needed to see her again." I shrug. "Anyway, I never found her, and most of whatever else I learned you probably know as well, from your own studies."

She shakes her head. "I don't know. I know some. But there's not much written about angels having children. I mean, in the Bible there's that widely misinterpreted bit about the 'Sons of God...'"

"Taking wives from the 'Daughters of Men.'" I finish for her. "In Genesis."

She nods, her eyes lighting up as she shares her knowledge. "Yes. And since every other time that phrase 'the Sons of God' is used, it refers to angels, we have a biblical reference. But their offspring were supposedly evil." She frowns.

I shake my head. "That's only one culture's interpretation of an ancient story. Angels are older than that. Much older. There are children and messengers of the gods in every culture, going back millennia. They're often depicted as winged. Even haloed. And they were said to have had children with human women. The line is strong; the angelic gift is carried in the blood over generations. Widen your search beyond things called angels to things like angels, and there's a lot more information, going back a long, long way."

She agrees, eyes distant, musing. "Okay, yeah. In Egypt and Babylon, lots of gods were depicted with wings—and even before that, in other Mesopotamian cultures, there were hundreds of winged beings, going as far back as Sumer."

I smile softly, nodding, loving that she knows these things, and wanting so much for her to know me. Wishing she could. "The Anunnaki."

A sudden melancholy fills me, as I recall the great murals in the temple complex of Ur, and the tiled and jewelled depictions of our divine teachers; remembering how I used to trace the gilded figures, memorizing every tale told.

How I used to believe.

She nods, caught up in the academic discussion of mythology. I can see that she loves it, and that makes her all the more amazing. "But they were more gods than angels."

I shake my head. "Not really. At least not in the way you think. They are more demigods. The sons and daughters of gods; the teachers of men.

They are divine, but less so than gods, and are more loved and respected than worshipped and feared. Like angels."

I smile to her, but in my mind's eye I see so clearly the face of my mother, hear her voice as she recites the names, realms and ranks of the gods and their children. Closing my eyes, I hold tight to the vision, and for a moment I can almost smell the hot sun baking the mud-brick steps of the temple; can almost feel the cool tiles under its shadow beneath my fingertips.

I hardly dare to breathe, not wanting the memory to fade, but I can't hold on to it. My mother's face burns away, and is replaced with Lilitu's; blood tears staining her pale cheeks as she reaches for me, and the commingled images bring such sadness and loss to my heart that a new flood spills from my eyes before I can stop it. Startled back to the present, I wipe at the tears and realise Grace has gone quiet. I look over to find her staring at me, very still and very pale.

"What's wrong?"

She swallows hard, her eyes searching my own. "How old are you?"

My turn to go quiet. Shit. She must've picked something up from my mind, or something I said. Shit, shit. I wasn't paying attention and forgot to be careful.

Then it hits me. I don't want to be careful. Not with her, not with the truth about me, not about who I am and where I came from. I want to tell her about my past; about love and loss, hope and dreams. I want to tell her everything. Because I want her to know me. Holding on to her gaze like a lifeline, and hoping so hard for her acceptance I think my heart will crack under the pressure—I take a deep breath, and tell her the truth.

"I am four thousand years old. And a bit."

If I thought she went pale before, I was wrong. Her heart races as she stares at me in utter astonishment. "My god."

My own heart is pounding. I don't know how she's taking this; her emotions are a swirling unreadable storm, and I'm so afraid she'll break.

I don't tell humans how old I am for a reason. They can't handle it. Can't wrap their minds around it. Even I try not to think about it too much, and I've lived it. I look at her, looking at me with something pretty close to horror, and I don't even try to stop the tears that begin to spill from my eyes.

"My god." She shakes her head, her lips parted and trembling. Then she looks down to my hand, still wrapped in hers, and her expression changes. No. Not horrified. Amazed.

She picks up my hand, and I let her, watching as she touches me in wonderment, turning my hand over and over in her own and then looking up at me with such awe I have to laugh through my tears.

She smiles, and moves around to face me, reaching out to touch my face; her fingers tracing the curve of my jaw, up to my brow, back down my cheek to my lips, lingering there.

Hunger and desire move in me at her touch, and I feel its fire rise behind my eyes. Only this time I don't hide it from her. I want her to see me, for all that I am.

Her eyes widen, and she takes a sharp breath in, but she doesn't turn away. As our eyes meet, I feel her storming emotions; wonder, fear, doubt, and a growing need that echoes my own.

I don't dare move. I can't. I don't know what will happen if I do. So, I sit perfectly still, watching her watch me, letting her touch me—which she does, over and over again; my face, my ears, my neck, my hands, my arms—like I'm something precious. She sits back, staring at me for a few more long moments, then she leans in slowly across my lap, and softly presses her lips against my own. Her heart is beating so hard that her lips shake with each pulse. Amazed, and finally able to move, I pull her into my arms, returning the kiss gratefully. Passion rises into the storm of our emotion, and I welcome it, kissing her deeply, wanting nothing more and nothing less than to remain in this moment.

Then I taste her blood on my lips, and that darkness wells up inside, wanting more, wanting her. Needing her. I grip her tightly to me, pulling her deeper into the kiss as I feel that familiar tug in my jaw. My fangs pierce her lip, just a little—and I drink, moaning as sweet spiralling pleasure spills slowly into me.

She sighs, giving in to the kiss; and so I drink more, sinking into the high, my hands searching under her clothes to find her skin, soft and hot with need. She gasps at my touch, her desire firing mine and mine hers and I forget where we are, forget everything else but this moment and her in my arms. She presses hard against me, kissing me back hungrily and I drink deeper, causing her to sink into the pleasure of the bite. So good. So very, very good. I don't want to ever stop. The thing inside whispers to take more, more; to take it all—but then something else pushes at me, at the whispering thing within, a soft warning, gentle but insistent, bringing me back from the edge, reminding me who I am, and I recognise, for the first time, her mind in part of that push. Pulling gently away from the kiss, I lick her blood from my lips—my turn to stare at her in wonder.

She opens her eyes with a shudder, breathing hard and flushed with pleasure, and licks gingerly at her lips where I've punctured them several times over. I wince at the damage and lift a hand to touch the wounds. "I'm sorry."

She gives me a slow, sweet smile, "It's okay. I'll heal."

Her eyes are beautiful, and I smile back, leaning against the wall and sinking into the soft, swinging high of her blood, loving it as it moves through me. She straightens her clothes and then tips her head to one side, watching me.

"Your bruises are fading."

I nod, resting my hand on her leg. "Your blood is incredible."

She studies me again; her eyes following the contour of my face, moving down across my body, then back up to meet my own.

"You're Sumerian."

It isn't a question, but I answer anyway.

"I am." It feels strange to say it out loud.

"Jesus." She shakes her head, eyes full of wonder. "What's it like, to live so long?"

I smile as she echoes the question I once asked of another. "I don't know. Honestly, I don't think about it too much. My life passes by in moments, like any other. Time is not the enemy."

She raises a brow "What is?

"Apathy."

She nods, moving off my lap to settle beside me again, closer this time, taking my hand again and entwining her fingers in my own.

After a moment she bends her head to rest against my shoulder, and I close my eyes as my heart lifts in pure aching joy. Her hair is warm and soft and smells of vanilla and sunlight. So good. Her blood spins through me like the sweetest song, healing the last of my wounds and making me feel sleepy, peaceful. Good.

We sit like that for a little while, then she makes a little surprised sound, and I open my eyes, turning to her as she softly touches her lips with her other hand.

"They've healed already." She looks at me, amazed, and I swallow hard as I remember she still has a lot of my blood in her veins. It's healing her. Making her accept me. Making her want me.

Shit.

I can't believe I let myself forget. Tears threaten again, but I shove the sorrow away, deep inside, angry with myself, and meet her eyes. Time to be honest. She deserves the truth.

"It's my blood. You still have quite a bit in you. It'll take a couple of weeks to wear off."

She nods, frowning, and I know she doesn't fully understand, so I explain further. "It'll heal you. Make you stronger, faster—and it can make you want me. Make you...have feelings...for me."

I stop, closing my eyes as shame and guilt rise to my chest. None of it was real. I did this to her. Clenching my fist at my side, driving my nails so hard into my palm they draw blood, I open my eyes again, forcing myself to meet her gaze. So sweet. So innocent. She'll hate me. But I have to make her understand.

"Remember, back at my place? My blood can make you addicted to me. Make you need me, need to be around me. What just happened, what happened before...it's my blood. In you. I'm sorry."

I turn away then, leaning back once more against the hallway wall, as crashing disappointment drowns me. Jesus Christ Rue, did you really think she could love you? Sorrow rises to drown me, tears streaming down my face, and I let them, past caring. Then I realise she's still holding my hand. I look over to find that she was waiting for me to look, her eyes still soft, no anger or hate in them, only a little sadness. And then she surprises me again.

"What does my blood do to you?"

I swallow hard. "It makes me stronger, heal faster, less susceptible to the sun. And it makes me want more. More of you. All of the time."

She smiles further. "In my book, that makes us even. Don't you think?"

I stare at her for a long time, wondering if her ready acceptance is real, or if it's still my blood talking. I don't know.

I hope it's the former, but that coldness inside is sure it's the latter.

She gives me another soft smile then, and squeezes my hand before letting it go, nodding to the far end of the hall, where a picture window looks out over the park.

"It's getting light already."

I turn to look. "Yeah. Must be about five." I get to my feet, slowly, still woozy from her blood. "The sun won't be up for a few minutes yet, but we should both try to get some sleep."

Quenching the guilt and doubt inside me, I reach down to help her up. And then, out of the corner of my eye, I see a flicker of movement in the shadows at the opposite end of the hall, and feel a cold finger of warning move up my spine.

"Get back in the room."

She looks up at me, confused. "What?"

The flicker of movement grows in size, becoming a dense patch of swirling darkness that twists, first in on itself, then outward. The pressure in the hallway changes, and I feel my ears pop in response. The darkness grows larger and darker as I watch, until it is a spinning, gaping maelstrom, swallowing all light and sound around it; until there is an impossible black hole in the middle of the fucking hotel hallway.

"Get back in the room, now!"

No time. I grab Grace by one arm, swinging her up and throwing her across the hall into her hotel room, just as the first of them steps out of that swirling vortex.

They're here. The demons. They've found us.

Chapter 30

Ritual

Babylon, 1604 BCE

Lilitu looks to me as she settles back on the carved bench, leaning against the olive tree that curves overhead. "I have told you I went mad for a time, after the curse of my making. After the death of my child."

I nod, leaning in as she continues.

"Without the bonds of awareness to rein it in, the thirst and hunger that so plagues us all took over my mind, and I was lost to it for many years. I have no true memory of that time; only vague images of night upon harrowing night of hunger, blood and darkness."

She sighs, looking down at her hand, still entwined in mine.

"When I finally came back to myself, when thought and humanity returned and I began to fathom what it was I had become, I was at first overcome with sorrow. But that sorrow soon became determination. I thought to find a way to break the curse. After all, it was I who had created it, I who had set the spell in motion. I was certain it would be within my ability to release myself from the horror that had become my life."

She pauses a moment only, then goes on.

"Gathering what herbs and sacred objects I could find, I set about my work, desperate to set right what I had done. I tried every ritual, every spell, every prayer and cure I knew. To no avail. Magic had abandoned me. I no longer had access to the power of the elements, could not even feel the energies of the earth. And thus the curse held fast."

"Yet still I tried, travelling the land by night, searching out new knowledge, seeking out the sacred places, thinking to find an answer in the realms of the gods. But no answer came. The gods themselves were deaf to my pleas. Still, I could not give up, for the search itself gave me purpose, a reason for being. I travelled far from the land where I was born, moving east, over the mountains, and beyond; hunting only when hunger threatened to overtake me, keeping always to the edges of society. I moved from village to village by night, and slept in mountain caves or dug into the earth itself by day."

She stops, looking to me in acknowledgement of common experience before she carries on.

"Years passed me by like nights, and nights like moments only, and I began to note the changes wrought in me by the curse. I did not age; not since the moment of my making, and I was strong, far stronger than any mortal could be. I could see by moonlit night as well as if it were mid-day, could move short distances faster than the wind, and travel longer distances at great speeds without tiring, as long as I fed. Always I had to feed. To hunt. To kill."

She holds my gaze, that ancient grief in her eyes so familiar now.

"I tried to go without, and when I starved and grew weak, tried then gain sustenance from the blood of animals. But I only made myself ill. I needed the blood of men to sustain me. The curse I had set upon myself. My own words used against me. "

"The fact filled me with an endless, aching sorrow, but as each night passed, and I continued to search for a way to break the spell, I began to feel that each human life was a sacrifice to my quest. I treated my prey accordingly, taking great care to choose well each and every offering, blessing them as they died. And so I continued, always seeking, year upon year—until I began to understand that the dark curse I had created could never be broken."

Again, she stops, her eyes flashing with a rising light of anger, no longer seeing to the courtyard around us, but rather the distant past.

"I was filled then, with a righteous fury. I vowed to find the demons that had done this to me; every one, and to take my vengeance upon them."

"I began my search anew, hunting not only for blood, but for any evidence of the demons' passage. I felt that they still walked this earth, for their leader had told me they were trapped here, and I knew he had not lied. I knew also that they sought power, and worked to manipulate men of position among the humans they so hated, using, and at times possessing them completely."

"I travelled back the way I had come, retracing my steps to that first village, seeking to find the demons that had so cruelly created me. Along the way, I also changed the way I hunted, moving ever closer to humans; watching them, listening to them, even walking among them when the moon was dark: learning that I could be near and yet unknown for what I was, as I sat by their fires, and listened to their tales."

She lifts her eyes to mine once more as she carries on. "And as I listened, I heard stories bitterly familiar to me. Tales of monsters, of demons, of creatures neither animal nor man but both; of good and evil spirits that walked the night beyond and took the form of men by day. I also heard tales of a woman, cold and pale as death itself; who walked the night beyond the fires and hunted the unwary traveller."

She smiles knowingly. "You see, Asharru, we are never wholly unknown, no matter how we try to hide. It was with that thought in mind that I came into the place where I had been remade."

"I was shocked to find the once-small village replaced by a thriving town, the mud-brick wall extending around its border higher than three of the tallest men together, its wooden gates shut tight and guarded against the night by men with spears at the ready. Never had I seen so large a gathering of men. This was no longer a village, but a city. Truly, the first of its kind."

She nods, but not to me—rather to the past, as she goes on.

"I moved past the guards easily enough; as a shadow in the night, and soon found myself wandering through a tangle of streets bounded by market stalls where even at the late hour, some vendors still showed their wares. Torches blazed on posts high above the streets, their flickering light and billowing smoke casting the crowded mud-brick dwellings in shadow and fire. For a moment I believed I had stumbled from my waking life into the nightmare world of the walking dead. Then a muttering crowd of mortal men hurried past me, brushing by me with an intensity of purpose and direction that pulled me from my shock and bade me follow. So follow I did."

"The men rushed through ever-widening streets, deeper into the city, and as they walked they were joined by more men, then women, and children—until all the citadel were gathered in a great murmuring mass at the foot of a mud-brick temple, built up high in the very centre of the city."

She pauses and looks to me. "It was not a temple as you would understand, daughter, not so grand nor so high as those your own people built, and never so mountainous as the great temples here, in Babylon—and yet to me, it was vast; wider and taller than any building I had ever seen."

"The great gathering of people stopped then, and I stopped with them, watching, holding my growing hunger and thirst at bay as I waited with the rest, following their collective gaze to the top of the temple, where four torches blazed around a high stone platform."

"And then, from all around us, drums began to pound an insistent rhythm into the fire-lit night, and a great hush came over the crowd. I stepped forward, moving closer to the temple steps, not knowing what was to come, but wanting to clearly see whatever it might be."

"No sooner had I reached the bottom step than a great shout went up from the surrounding crowd, and I looked to the platform above to see a man, wearing a golden mask carved in the shape of a lizard's head. He was dressed in long white robes that were dyed and woven in dazzling patterns of red and gold, and as he stepped out into the light of the torches, another shout went up from the crowd. I stared at the people around me, at their faces turned as one in adoration—and then I looked back up as the drums stopped, and the man above raised his hands into the air."

"Another great shout from the crowd rang out, and then a different drumbeat began, steady and slow, as through the crowd a slow parade of men walked forward and up the temple steps; men bearing great baskets, overflowing with grain, with fruit and all manner of food. I watched in amazement as the many foods of the city were taken up the steps and laid before the man in the mask, and then watched further as more men came, these leading frightened and struggling animals, two by two up the temple steps."

"I watched as the animals were led and held one by one before the man in the mask, watched as the crowd began to sway and whisper in excitement, watched as the man took out a curving copper dagger, and slit the animals' throats one by one. The crowd shouted and chanted, in a language like my own and yet not; the thundering drums growing faster, and louder, as the sacrificial blood flowed down the temple steps."

"I was stunned. I understood the man above to be a priest—but never, in all the days before my making, never had I seen such waste, such a ritual of death. And yet even as the last animal fell under the knife, the man was not finished. Another roar from the crowd went up around me as the drums once again fell silent, and a chill of horror rose within me at what I then beheld."

"A boy, no more than twelve years old—younger than my own youngest son when last I saw him—covered in bruises and bound tight, was led stumbling up the steps. As he reached the top, he was forced by his captors to lay on the dais in front of the priest. I knew what was to come then, and my hunger rose within me even as my conscience grew ill. This was not for the benefit of the gods. No gods I had ever known would have demanded such a sacrifice."

"The crowd cheered with joy as the priest lifted the shining copper dagger above his head so that it blazed in the light of the torches, holding it high until the masses surrounding me screamed for the finish. And then he stabbed the knife down swift and strong, plunging the blade deep into the boy's heart. The crowd shouted and writhed in ecstatic devotion as the drums began again, the ritual done and the celebration beginning. Yet all my attention was on the platform above, and the priest in the mask."

"With thirst raging in me at the sight and scent of blood, I climbed the steps above the writhing crowd, watching as slaves gathered up the sacrifices and took them away. And yet the priest did not leave. Instead, he remained, hidden by the movement of the slaves around him, kneeling over the body of the boy. I moved closer, driven by hunger as much as curiosity."

"As I did so I saw the priest reach up, remove his mask and lean in to the boy, until his face was almost touching the boy's own. I could not clearly see, and so I moved closer. I could see then, that the boy was not yet dead. He was still struggling to breathe, even as his life's blood poured from his wounds. As I watched in growing horror, the priest leaned in, and lifted the boy into his arms."

She pauses, her eyes flashing bright with the memory. After a moment she continues.

"I could not fathom what he was doing. Was he going to save the boy? Or kill him? In my curiosity, I crept ever nearer, and nearer still, until I was only a few steps from them both. I watched as the priest grasped the boy's face in both his hands, leaning as if to kiss the dying youth; but then, to my horror, he opened his own mouth, impossibly wide, showing rotting teeth, and then—I cannot describe this any clearer—he drank the boy's soul."

"I saw it, so clearly, even through the fire, smoke and blood. A spirit, shimmering like silver mist in the night air, curled as smoke from the boy's mouth, and the priest drew it into his own with an intake of breath. I knew then the priest was not a man at all. Fear and disbelief washed over me, rooting me to the spot as the boy shuddered once, twice—and then died. Then the demon rose to his feet, turned his head, and—with eyes sickeningly familiar and impossibly black—looked straight at me."

Chapter 31

Broken and Bloody

The first of them out of that black hole lifts a sawed-off shotgun, and I throw myself to one side as a volley of shot explodes down the hall. The first misses, as does the second—but the third blasts through my left shoulder, knocking the breath from me and slamming me against the wall.

Grace screams, and I look over. She's still struggling to get up from where I threw her, her face full of fear. Holding up my right hand as my left arm heals, I shout at her, hoping she'll obey.

"Stay there!"

Turning back to face the demons, I find four of them walking toward me, and one more stepping out from the vortex. All of them are wearing big male bodies, and all are using demonic strength, their stolen flesh twisted by the demons within. Big ugly bastards. And five of them. Guess they thought I'd put up a fight.

Better not disappoint, so.

Shoving myself up from the wall, I snarl and run right for them. Shotgun Boy brings the barrel up again, but I'm ready. As he fires, I dodge, and the shot misses by half a metre.

Keeping the momentum, I leap to the right and launch myself off the wall, kicking up and out. The forward kick catches the nearest demon off guard, and his windpipe collapses under the heel of my boot. That's what heels are for.

He goes down, hard, but I've no time to check if he's staying down, now I'm in their midst. I hear doors open and slam shut again amid screams from hotel guests as I spin around, moving as fast as I can, landing another hard kick to the knee of one, then dodging a meaty fist from another.

I duck under a blow meant for my head as another grazes my cheek, splitting it open. Snarling, I whip around, smashing my elbow into the nearest jaw. There is a resounding crack as bone shatters beneath the blow, and the demon falls backwards, knocking into Shotgun Boy, both stumbling off-balance.

The fifth demon swings for me, and I duck under again, connecting with a blow of my own to his gut, but he strikes back, hitting me with a fist like solid stone, and I go flying against the wall, ribs cracking as I bounce off the plaster and fall to the floor.

Then I hear Jude shout my name, and look to see him running from his room. I scream, leaping to my feet and turning to stop him.

"No!"

Too late. There is a crack of gunfire beside me and I watch in horror as Jude falls to the floor and doesn't move, a dark bloom of blood spilling from his head.

Fury rockets through me, and the thing inside wakes and begins to howl. I give it free rein as I run for the one with the gun, slamming him back against the opposite wall with all my strength. Plaster and dust rain down around us as he hits hard, sending the artwork on either side of us crashing to the floor in a cascade of glass and wood.

He hangs on to the gun, and fires into my abdomen, but I don't even feel it. I knock his hand hard against the wall, and the gun goes clunking to the floor as I shove my right forearm against his throat and push. He hisses at me, his mouth opening impossibly wide to show rotting, broken teeth. I bare fangs, snarl back and press harder. The bones in his neck snap and a dark satisfaction fills me at the sound—but then I'm grabbed from behind by another two of them, pulling me back.

Fuck them. Fuck them all.

Snarling, I swing my legs forward and take three steps up the wall, bending my knees and kicking off as hard as I can. The move throws all three of us back to the floor and dislocates my already wounded shoulder. Ignoring the pain, I roll to my knees and turn on the demon to my right as he struggles up, punching the heel of my right palm as hard as I can into his solar plexus. He gasps and goes wide-eyed, momentarily paralysed, and I swing back around, throwing myself sideways as another shot thunders past my head, missing by inches. I hit the ground and keep rolling, until I smack into the wall, hard. Something crunches and slices into my right arm.

The glass.

Searching quickly for the largest shard, I grab it up and spin around to the other demon as he's getting to his feet. Leaping on him with a roar of rage, I knock him onto his back and pin him there, shoving the sharpest edge of the broken glass straight into his throat and pushing it down through his neck with all my strength. Shooting pain erupts from my shoulder and blood pours from my gut, but I ignore it all, shredding both hands as I push. He struggles against me, gurgling and shoving at me as the glass slices down, but I only growl and push harder, until a fountain of rancid blood erupts from his throat, covering my face, chest and arms. It seems to take forever before his head finally lops to one side, a ragged bit of flesh and sinew still holding it to his neck—but the spine is severed. It's enough. There's an angry rushing sound and the lights in the hall spark and pop as the demon quits the body.

That's one.

I get to my knees—and feel day-drain seep into my limbs. Sunrise. Shit. I start to shake, blood gushing freely from a half-dozen wounds as I stop healing abruptly. Both my hands are cut to the bone, my left arm is throbbing and useless, and waves of weakness and vertigo wash over me. No. Can't stop. Have to keep going.

I struggle to get up, trying to push myself off the headless body with my right hand, but then I hear the unmistakable sound of guns being cocked and readied—and look up to see four remaining demons pointing four guns at me point-blank.

Shit.

Grace screams, and once again I throw myself out of the way. Too late. A volley of shots ring out in quick succession. The first catches my side as I turn, ripping a fresh hole through my gut. The second tears through my back, exploding out through my chest, as do the third, fourth and fifth. I'm already falling as the sixth blasts through my right shoulder, and I land face down beside the headless demon corpse, my blood mingling with his to soak the posh hotel carpet.

A ringing silence settles, and I struggle to stay conscious as the world spins sideways. Got to get up. I try and make my limbs obey, but they won't. The thing inside begins to whine, a high-pitched squealing in my head, as hunger carves a burning hollow in my core. I try to draw breath, but blood fills my lungs, and I choke on the bubbling flood. Everything around me warps and fades as darkness taunts the edges of my awareness, circling inwards, calling me into nothingness. But as sight fades sound grows louder, and I become aware that someone is crying. Sobbing. Grace. Grace needs me. Clarity returns.

Get up, Rue. Get up, get up!

Moaning, I push against the blackness that threatens to take me over, and struggle to my knees; shoving myself up with the broken remains of my right arm, hissing with the effort. I turn back toward the dark shapes that loom around me, swaying there, trying to focus. To fight.

Then I hear someone laugh, as if from very far away. "Seven hells, she just doesn't quit!"

I recognise that voice. It's Mr In Charge, the one from Grace's house. The one that set the bomb. He moves closer, and I feel the metal of the shotgun barrel push hot against my forehead. I can barely see, but I manage a glare in his general direction.

"Fuck you." My voice sounds thick and slurred to my ears, but at least the meaning is clear.

He laughs again and curls his finger around the trigger.

"Wait." Another voice I recognise. Cold and mean. Knife Boy. From the stairs of my house. Same voice, different body. "I want her."

A pause, then— "Fine." Mr In Charge again. "But you fucking finish the job this time."

He grunts, pulls the shotgun back, flips it over and before I can react, smashes the butt of the gun into my face. I go flying backwards to the floor, nose broken and streaming blood.

My vision spins into a single point of quickly fading light as he speaks again. "Pick her up. Come on. Let's go."

Rough hands grab me up on either side and drag me down the hall, toward Grace's room. I try to fight against their grip, but I'm weak and hanging by a thread. Pain rockets through me from everywhere at once, and I long to give in to the darkness. But I can't. Have to stay. For Grace.

They stop across from her room, holding me up against the wall where she and I sat, only moments before. I hear her soft sobs, and manage to lift my head. She's there, on her knees just inside the doorway, her face stained with tears, her eyes so sad and terrified it breaks my heart.

I've failed her. And Jude. These demons are here because of me. I knew they were hunting me, and selfishly I came to see her anyway. I've caused this. The knowledge tears through me more painfully than any bullet, and tears fall to merge with the rest of the blood dripping from my face. My vision blurs to red, as my gaze finds hers, and I try to tell her I'm sorry, so sorry—but I can't find the air to speak, and choke again on the burning flow that erupts at the effort.

Grace shakes her head, getting to her feet, her voice little more than a whisper as she looks to me, somehow understanding. "It's okay. It's not your fault, Rue. None of this is."

I can't believe she's comforting me, and shake my head, trying again to speak, but then Mr In Charge is there, smiling cruelly as she stumbles back, away from the door.

"Actually, it is her fault."

He turns back to me, a grin splitting his blackened lips. "Went to your flat, leech. Tracked you from there. The things you can do these days with human magic and a little bit of blood." He grins further. "Too bad about

your place though. I'm afraid we started a little fire. Books burn so easily."
He laughs, and the others join in.

Anger burns in me, and I snarl at him, fighting against the grip of the
two holding me; but only choke and gasp more as I struggle—which in
turn makes the demons laugh harder. Mr In Charge sneers as he walks
back toward Grace.

"Come on, girlie. Say goodbye to the half-breed. It's time to go." He
steps across the threshold as she backs away—and then he screams,
stumbling back into the hall, his face, nose, ears and eyes pouring smoke.
I'd laugh if I could. He howls, and wipes at his eyes, then rounds on me
with equal amounts of anger and incredulity.

"You didn't go in!"

I meet his anger head-on, taking some small delight in his pain. I draw
a burning breath and manage a bloody grin as I spit out the words, "Fuck
you. You fuck."

He roars rage, punching me hard in the gut. A new shock of pain explodes, doubling me over in the grip of the two that hold me. The world
shudders as I fight to breathe. I hear him speak, musing, seemingly to
himself.

"She didn't go in. Why the fuck didn't she go in?" He turns to Grace,
black eyes searching her face. "What the hell was she doing with you?"

I focus past him, fighting to lift my head again. Grace. Hold on. It's a
struggle, but I finally manage to look up.

She's there. On the far side of her room now, back against the window.
Tears stream down her face but she's staying put. She nods to me, then
turns to face Mr In Charge, glaring at him with an anger that belies her
terror.

"Fuck you."

I grin again. Good girl.

Mr In Charge laughs, his burnt lips splitting open and oozing pus.
"Maybe later pretty baby. If there's anything left of you once the boss is
done."

He frowns at me, then looks back to Grace as slow understanding ripples across his face.

"Christ's nails." Dark delight lights his face as he laughs and turns to the others. "Lezzer leech love. How cute!" He turns back to me, with a mocking leer. "What happened, Half-Breed? Hmmm? Did you fall for our little angel? Not that I blame you, she is a tasty little treat!"

He leans back against Grace's doorway, his face twisted, voice mocking as he winks at her. "And you? Do you love this stinking blood-junkie? She's demon you know. Just like us. A weak and tainted version, but demon nonetheless. Angel loves Demon. How very Romeo and Juliet. Or should that be Juliet and Julie?"

Grace glares at him, pressing back as far as she can, but her eyes flit to mine for a split second, and I know he reads in them the same thing I do.

Shit.

He laughs and spins back, wrapping a charred hand around my throat and shoving my head back against the wall, black eyes filled with twisted delight. "What did you do to her? Did you make her love you? What's the matter, leech? Were you lonely? Did you think the little angel could make it all better?"

Letting go, he steps back and hits me again, knocking me sideways so hard that the two holding me struggle to jerk me back upright as he spits his hate in my face.

"Fucking disgusting."

He nods to Knife Boy, who has been standing silently to one side, watching. Waiting. "Kill her."

Knife Boy smiles, steps forward—and Grace screams, running toward us. "No!"

Mr In Charge grins at me, and my heart sinks.

No.

I snarl at him, anger spinning through me as I try to fight again against the two that hold me. No good. Too weak. Knife Boy pulls a long serrated black and silver blade from a sheath at his belt. I focus on Grace, struggling to see her past the surrounding demons.

Knife Boy nods to the two holding me, and they grip me tighter. He steps close, grabbing a handful of my hair and yanking my head back. "Where were we, leech? Oh yeah, I remember! Right here."

He lifts the knife, setting the edge against my exposed throat and slowly pressing in. I feel my blood well against the blade and Grace screams again, her voice closer. Too close. "No! Stop!"

Knife Boy stops, but keeps the blade pressed to my throat. I ignore him, and the knife; looking past him to Grace as she stops just inside her room, inches away from Mr In Charge, who is smiling, watching it all unfold.

"Grace." My vision swims but I push through pain, feeling her panic, her fear, trying to get her to listen, to obey, choking the words out past the blade. "Grace. It's okay. Stay there. Please."

Mr In Charge laughs again. "Yes, do stay there. This'll be a sight to see. Do you know the best way to kill a leech, girlie? It's simple: You take off their head. Now, I know what you're thinking: that'll kill almost anything! Well, that's true, but it's a sure-fire way to kill one of them." He gestures to me. "And from what I hear, when they die it can be fucking amazing. Some melt, some explode, some just disappear! Poof! It depends on the leech, and several variables. I think it has something to do with how old they are. Am I right, Half-breed?" He walks back over. "How old are you, anyway? A hundred? Two? Five? Will you melt? Or explode? Or just—" he snaps his fingers— "disappear?" He turns back to Grace again. "What do you think?"

She ignores him, looking instead to me, and when those sweet eyes meet mine, my heart shatters.

Mr In Charge nods to Knife Boy again, and as he pushes the knife deeper in, I ignore him, holding Grace's gaze to mine, with all the will I have left, trying to stop her, gagging as the knife slices slowly into my throat, gasping past pain.

"Grace. No."

But she looks away, turning instead to Mr In Charge, her eyes dark and filled with certainty; her voice hardly more than a whisper. "Stop. Please. I'll go with you."

He laughs and nods to knife boy, who reluctantly steps back. Mr In Charge grins his triumph to me, then turns, holding out his hand to Grace. "I knew you'd see reason. Come on then."

She hesitates, glancing from him to me to Knife Boy and back. "You won't hurt her anymore. You'll let her go. Let her live."

He rolls his eyes heavenward, nodding. "Yes, we'll let the leech go. Don't worry. Now come on."

"No!" I cry out in horror as she steps across the threshold, placing her hand in his. "Grace!"

He laughs and grabs her hard, wrapping a rotting hand around her arm and pulling her roughly away as he nods back to the others. "Come on lads. The boss is waiting. Let's get back so he can get on with it."

The two that were holding me let me fall to the floor, where I immediately try to get to my feet, tears clouding my vision. The two join Mr In Charge, following after as he drags Grace toward the spinning black morass. No. Gritting my teeth, I struggle to my knees. Have to stop them. Beside me, Knife Boy is laughing as I cry out again. "Grace!"

She turns and looks over her shoulder, eyes filled with tears, giving me that soft sad smile as she shakes her head. Mr In Charge looks back as well, just before stepping into the vortex, and nods to Knife Boy.

"The Half-Breed's all yours. Just make sure you kill her this time, once you're done playing."

Grace's eyes grow wide, horror filling her face, as she screams. "No! You said you wouldn't hurt her! Rue...Rue!"

Crying and clawing, she tries to fight her way back, but they're ready for this. The other two move in, and all three of them grab her, carrying her kicking and screaming through that fucking black hole, which closes abruptly after them, her screams echoing in the empty hall.

No.

Grace.

Screaming in anger and pain, I manage somehow to get to my feet, and, using the wall for support, stumble down the hall after them. I don't get far. Something hits me hard in my lower back, and my legs go out from under me, agony blooming through every nerve as I fall to the floor again, gasping and unable to move.

Knife Boy laughs as he reaches down and grabs me by the hair, dragging me back up the hall toward the window at the end, where a square of sunlight is steadily growing brighter against the hotel carpet. I claw at his grip, at the floor, at anything—grief and rage screaming through me, but I'm too weak. I can't fight him. Tossing me down into the light, he straddles me, pinning my arms to the floor with his knees. Sitting on my hips, he takes out that long knife again, turning it over and over so it glints in the light as my skin singes and smokes.

"Now you can burn just like before, leech. Of course, it's not the same, I know. The other knife was better." He tips his head to one side, a swirling madness in his demon eyes. "What did you do with it, bitch?"

I spit a mouthful of blood at him, rage boiling. "I threw it in the Liffey. Go fetch."

His eyes grow impossibly blacker, and he snarls as he lifts the blade, plunging it deep and slicing up, down, then up again. I scream as the knife rips through me, my skin splitting, then burning in the sunlight. My flesh sears first red, then black; suffocating white smoke curling from my face as the demon arcs the knife down again, and again, stabbing and slicing my burning flesh, over and over, laughing maniacally all the while.

I scream until my voice burns away, and consciousness retreats from this final onslaught. I'm done. Crippled, bleeding, burning; no strength left. My lashes and lids burn, leaving my naked eyes to smoulder. Blinded, I struggle to breathe, choking on the thick smoke that pours from my skin. The thing inside turns inwards in panic, its screams filling my mind, driving me toward madness as it begins to feed upon my soul.

Then the nightmare erupts around me, and I'm falling into a thousand clawed hands; hands that become chains; binding, breaking, burning—

holding me prone before a punishing sun. All sound fades to a high-pitched ringing, and as the fire rages in, I think of Grace.

How I love her. How I failed her. Blood tears slip from my eyes and are set to a bouncing boil against my face. I'm dying. I whisper Grace's name once more, sending my love on the wings of the gods, and with it a prayer, as I have not prayed in four thousand years. And then I give in, waiting for the sun to burn me away into darkness.

Chapter 32

Rage

Lilitu shudders at the memory, gripping my hand tight as she continues. "The demon's black eyes met and held my own, and in that moment, I knew that he knew me, and had known I was there all along."

"Terror and anger gripped my heart at once, the emotions rising in me so fast and strong that all movement and speech was taken from me for a moment; a moment in which the demon dropped the dead boy to the ground, and walked slowly over to stand before me, grinning, his black teeth gleaming."

"'I had wondered when we would meet again, witch.' He tipped his head to one side, studying me with those black eyes. 'I see your curse still holds. Your magic was strong—much stronger than even I could have guessed.'"

"At his words, spoken in that hated voice that had echoed in my memory for so long, the terror that had held me fast in place gave way to fury, and I felt my fangs push against my lips as I snarled my rage."

"'You! You have done this to me. It was your dark magic that changed me that night. Your vile trickery!'"

"He laughed at my words, his voice causing bile to rise to my throat. 'You are wrong, witch. I may have pushed you into my brother's prison, that much is true, but the magic was yours alone; the curse woven from your words. It was you who killed your child. I had no part in that.'"

She looks up, eyes shimmering with remembered anger.

"I did not think, only leapt upon him in animal fury, striking and clawing at him. But I was as a child in the face of his strength. He struck me with one hand, and I went flying backwards, crashing down the steps of the temple to the ground below. I felt bones break, felt my head strike hard against stone, tasted blood on my lips. The pain of my fall surprised me. I struggled to rise, and was confused when I could not. My own blood poured into my eyes from where my head had struck the stone, making me half blind. It was the first time I had been hurt since my making, the first time I knew I could be hurt so, and the shock of it took my breath from me."

She pauses in her telling, her eyes dark with the memories behind them.

"The crowd around screamed and backed away as I fell among them, startled from their celebrations by my sudden appearance."

"As my body began to heal itself, I crawled to my knees, reaching to the crowd around me for aid. I begged them for help, cried out for them to see their priest for what he truly was—monster, demon—but they only backed away, many making holy signs against me, much as they did against you, during those first nights."

I nod, shame and sorrow moving in my breast at the memory. I say nothing, however, and after a moment, she continues.

"The demon came down the steps toward me then, having replaced his lizard-god mask. Wounded as I was, unable to stand, all I could do was watch as the people bowed and made way for him. I could not see his face, behind the mask, but I could feel his delight at my pain as he pulled me up by my hair, and dragged me back up the steps to the platform at the top of the temple."

She closes her eyes, the dark memory etched upon her face. "I struggled to fight him, crying out to the people that he was the evil, not I—but they gave neither answer nor aid, only gathered to watch, as the demon flung me to the platform atop the temple, throwing me down amongst the blood of man and beast. Again, I struggled to rise, and again he struck me, then again, and yet again; until I lay bloodied and helpless on the stone, unable even to draw breath."

She pauses again in her telling, eyes dark.

"You must understand, Daughter, I knew not then how to fight, for unlike you I had no one to teach me, and until that moment I had no need to learn. Understand also that I had not even a fraction of the strength I have now; nor even as much as you have. For as we age, we grow stronger, but I was young, and foolish, and no match for the demon that stood over me, his voice mocking from beneath the mask."

"'Now, witch—now shall you know pain. For I will not kill you so quickly as the rest. You who are my brother's curse made flesh.'"

"So saying, he took up the copper dagger in one hand, and me by the hair again in the other. There was a great shout from the gathered crowd below, as he lifted the dagger high, and, even as he had done with the boy only moments before, plunged it deep into my chest."

Again she shudders, and takes her hand from my own, pressing it tight to her breast.

"The blade pierced my heart, and all thought ran from my mind at the agony. I could not breathe, could barely see. Time seemed to slow and then stop altogether as the demon pushed me back against the stone, removing his mask as he leaned down against me."

"'No, Witch. You will not die. I will not allow it.'"

"He then wrenched the blade from my breast, my blood spilling from the wound in a furious flood. Tossing the blade to one side, he struck me again, then pressed himself down against me, until his black eyes were mere inches from my own."

"'What if I should take your soul, witch? Would the taste of mortal flesh still linger upon your spirit? Or would you taste of my brother, of the curse you wrought and wear?'"

"Leering at me, he leaned in closer, and closer still, parting his lips and breathing in, as if to take from me the very essence of my being, as I had seen him do to the boy only moments before."

"I was helpless, weak and wounded, unable to fight, unable to free myself from his vile grasp. My body was healing, I could feel as much, but without blood I knew I would surely die, my vengeance unrealised, all my striving for nothing. But then, instead of my essence moving into him with that intake of breath as the boy's had done, a feeling moved in me. An emotion; cold, dark, and familiar. I felt its seething hatred, twisting up from deep within, and then turning outward; carrying with it a growing, burning rage that exploded from my breast, lending me strength."

"Snarling with renewed fury, I bared my fangs and bit down into the demon's throat. The dead blood of his stolen flesh spilled into me and I spat it out as he roared and rolled away; grasping the spurting wound in one hand, while with the other he reached for the discarded blade."

She opens her eyes again, a dark light moving behind them as she holds my gaze, my heart pounding to her tale.

"His hand never found it. For I moved then as I knew how to move, so swiftly he did not see until his hand was already severed at the wrist, more black blood flowing forth. Again and again I brought down that blade, until the copper was bent and dulled, until the demon's blood covered the platform where we stood. Yet still he did not die. Then that burning rage so moved in me that with a cry I brought the blade down hard and fast, bringing all my strength into the blow—and severed his head from his body."

She pauses, a dark smile curving her lips.

"And then—he was no more. The body he had worn fell to the stones, the flesh turning black, rotting away even as his head rolled from the platform to tumble down the steps and land amid the shocked and silent crowd. A dark wind rose around me, blowing past me and then away as I stood, blade in hand, wounded, bleeding; triumphant."

The smile that curves her lips turns then, into one colder, darker.

"Of course, the crowd did not remain silent. In me, they saw a demon. One that had taken their priest from them. A sound began among them, a muttering that soon turned to a roar. And so, I ran. As fast as I could. From the temple into the city streets, blade in hand, not hiding what I was, but instead snarling and tearing through the crowd like a beast. Most screamed and ran from me, but some men took up arms and gave chase. To no avail. None could catch me. The rage within carried me away, beyond the city gates and on, into the wild darkness of the night."

"I found shelter in a mountain cave, and there I slept the next day, and the next. When I could move again, I hunted, taking my prey from the men who would have hunted me. And yet I did not kill them all, so their tales, like their numbers, grew. I moved on, far from that city, to another, and another still. Time passed. I remained."

She stops then, her smile becoming softer, lighter as she lets the memory go.

I sit in silence for a moment, waiting for her to go on, and when she does not, I grow impatient, and give voice to the questions that burn in me, all unanswered.

"But what of the demons? Surely there were others? Did you seek them out?"

She smiles, nodding.

"Yes, there were other demons. And yes, I sought them out. I have killed many, but there are many more. They are legion, and not so easy to dispatch. Remember, the flesh they wear is stolen, as they themselves have no flesh. Taking their heads only forces them from the bodies they wear. In time they find another to possess, and so you must kill them again. And again."

I am astonished by this, and dismayed. "But how then do you destroy them? Did you not destroy the one that is...within you?"

I frown, realising for the first time that I have not thought long about this. If Lilitu is demon imprisoned in flesh, then so are we. But how? Questions build within my breast, each leading to another.

Lilitu shakes her head, her eyes growing dark again. "I did not destroy him. Only changed him. Into what I am. Into what we all are. I do not know how that change was wrought, only that I wrought it, and that I can neither undo it, nor do it again. I can only share it."

I frown, so many questions raging within that I barely take a breath as they spill from my lips. "But what of the one here, this night? He knew you, I know he did, for he named me 'Witch spawn'. Was he the one who betrayed you? The one who made you? What of the rage in you? Whence did it come? And what of the hunters? Did they not seek you out even as they now seek us? Why did you not kill them all when they were fewer?"

Lilitu laughs aloud. "So many questions, child! I do not have all the answers you seek. But I will give what answers I can. First, yes. The demon here this night was that very one. The vile, evil one who trapped and tricked me; who shackled me—shackled all of us—with this curse we forever bear. Him I will never forget, no matter what skin he wears, no matter how many centuries pass. I will always know him. And I will always kill him."

She smiles, a bitter twist of her lips that does not reach her eyes.

"As I have said, the demons do not die, only return, again and again; wearing human flesh as we wear clothing. That is why I needed to entrap him, to take his head, and send his spirit seeking shelter. Which I pray he is long in finding."

She takes a breath, looking around us at the silent garden. "As to the rage in me that night, I do not know where it came from. Perhaps it was my own fury, brought up by the demon's abuses." She shrugs. "And the hunters...yes, they sought me out, as they are always seeking us. As to why I did not kill them all? Surely, Asharru, you know the answer yourself. Do they deserve to die simply because they are? Or do you think I so easily kill without thought, without mercy? Is that how you think of me?"

At her words I am instantly ashamed, and I bow my head. "No. I do not. I misspoke. Forgive me."

She smiles, gives my hand a gentle squeeze, then stands up. "You are forgiven, Daughter. Now. That is enough for one night. Heed the sky. The dawn approaches. Come to shelter and rest the day with me. Tomorrow night we will return to your mortal girl, to make her safe, and keep her well—as truly she is yours to keep."

She pulls me up from the bench then, keeping my hand entwined in her own as together we walk back to the city of the dead.

Chapter 33

Burn and Die

Darkness. Heavy and thick, like a blanket of snow in the blackest of winters. It covers me completely, as I drift toward the land of the Winged Dead. All thought is gone, as my mind loses itself, and fades away to silence. Peace.

Then the peace is broken by a sharp jolt, and crashing thunder. Lost and blind, I am jerked roughly back from the edge of death. Someone is calling. Over and over. My mother, calling my name. No. Lilitu? No. It can't be. Alu, come back to carry me beneath the earth to a maze of catacombs filled with tapestries of shimmering light.

My name. Someone is saying my name. Over and over. A voice I know. The darkness stops its inward march, and begins a slow retreat.

Feeling returns. Pain returns. Someone is lifting me, into strong warm arms. Away from the fire. Away from the sun. A door slams behind me, then another, and I feel something cool and smooth against my skin as I am laid gently down. Someone says my name, again and again, someone who is crying and praying, crying and praying.

I drift away on the sound, wondering idly if the gods listen to the prayers of the Wingless Dead.

Then someone lifts my head, speaking softly, and past the soot and smoke, I smell the sweet tang of blood. Everything spins away as the blessed liquid pours past my lips, and down my throat. I drink, not caring who is speaking or why, not caring that the blood is cold, only caring that it is blood. Sweet, fire-quenching blood. The thing inside wakes in a rush, turning outward in animal need, and I whimper, reaching out. More. I need more. And more comes, cold again. I moan, drinking deeply. So good. I drink more, reaching out again for the source of the flow, wanting to bring it to me, to take it all—and finding nothing there. Confusion then, as it stops. A voice. Clearer this time. Familiar.

"It's okay. You're safe. There isn't any more, but I'll get you some. Shhhh. It's okay. Rest now. You're okay."

I can hear tears behind the words. I fight to see who is speaking, but I can't. Still blinded. The blood moves through me, waking me, bringing me back. I draw a ragged breath. "Who?"

"Shhhh. Rest. You're hurt." The voice breaks away in a sob, and I try to lift my hand, trying to find who is speaking. Awake. I'm awake. Alive. But Grace.

Sorrow crashes over me, and I try to rise, choking out her name. "Grace. They took her. My fault, it's my fault ..."

A hand takes mine, and another pushes against my chest, gently forcing me back down. "I know. I know. We'll get her back. It's okay. Just rest. You need to heal. It's day, but you're safe. Please, just sleep. You need to sleep."

I shake my head, trying to sit up, but again I'm pushed back, and I can't fight. Too weak. Once again, consciousness slips away and once again I give in, laying back against the cool surface beneath me. Yes. Rest. Sleep. I hear a sigh, and feel a hand smooth my hair, over and over as I sink back into darkness one more time, my last thought that of Grace crying out my name.

Grace.

I'm falling. Falling through a night blacker than any I have known. I try to scream, but no sound comes out. I try again, and again; as I fall, and fall. I've no sense of time, of space. I can't see, and flail in animal panic.

And then I hit the ground. Sight returns, painfully bright. High hills of sand stretch out before me in endless waves against a sky so blue it burns to white in my vision. Along the far horizon is a ribbon of shimmering blue, surrounded by green. The river, its fertile banks sparkling in the sun.

The sun.

With a cry, I spin around, desperately seeking shelter from the burning sky. But there is no shelter. Neither tree nor stone to break the endless sea of sand. My skin begins to smoke, white swirls wafting from my hands up into the blue, and as I look down, I realise I am naked, exposed to my fate. I fall to my knees, digging frantically at the sand. But although I dig, and dig, scraping at the ground until my hands are raw, more sand falls back into the hole than I can claw out, and I finally have to stop, exhausted and defeated. Falling back against the ground, I sob into a foetal curl as my skin burns from red to black. No shelter. Nothing to do but burn and die.

"Asharru."

I jolt at the sound of my name, clenching smoking fists as I crawl to my knees and turn to face this new torment. Then I stop, astonished at what I see.

The Anunnaki stands above me, shadowy wings curling high above his shoulders, black against the bright sky behind. His skin is a luminous white, and it shimmers in the light like mother-of-pearl. His hair falls long over his shoulders, in silken waves as black as his wings. But his eyes—his eyes are a silvery mercurial blue, and as they meet my own, I know that I know him. I've seen those eyes stare back at me from a thousand mirrors.

He repeats my name, his voice resonant as thunder. "Asharru."

Swallowing hard against the lump of fear that rises in my throat, I struggle to my feet. As I do, he steps closer, stretching his wings wide, so I am sheltered in their shade. I shudder a sigh of relief at the respite, despite its origin, looking up at the dark god from Lilitu's tale, the one with whom I am so familiar. My hunger and thirst, the demon within, made flesh.

"Who...who are you?" I ask even though I know and fear the answer.

He smiles, a slight curl of his lip that doesn't reach his eyes. "You know. Do not pretend. I am you, as you are me."

A low wind stirs the surrounding sand, lifting the feathers on his wings and whipping my hair around my face. Behind him, the sky grows brighter, and I lift my hand to shield my eyes.

"What is this place? Where have you taken me?"

"It is you who have taken me." He lifts a radiant arm, gesturing wide. "This is the landscape of your mind. In its creation I had no part, save for that part of me that is you."

His words echo and drift around me, ringing like discordant bells. I feel suddenly weak. Panic builds in my chest, and I shake my head, swaying on my feet.

"No. This isn't right." My head pounds and I feel I have forgotten something. Something important. "No..."

The Anunnaki steps toward me, and I stumble back—trying to get away—but he simply reaches out a hand, lifting me to face him. I am helpless as a babe in his grasp, lost in his gaze as he leans in, as if to kiss me, his lips brushing against my own as he speaks.

"Heed my words, Asharru. Be the willing weak no more. Drink the blood that flows. We are awake, after too long a sleep. It is time. Take the blade. Wield it. We will give you names."

With that he lets me go, and I fall onto the drifting sand. The sky grows bright again, and I cry out as I feel the bite of the sun on my back. Again, I struggle to my feet, wiping at my eyes as they sting and tear in the smoke rising from my skin. I wheel around, searching desperately for the Anunnaki, but he is gone. A whimper escapes my lips as I cast about for shelter, but find none. Only the whispering hills of sand, stretching endlessly in all directions. I cry out, screaming for him to return, to help me—and then, a sudden shadow moves across the land.

The wind stirs the sand at my feet and carries with it the unmistakable scent of water. Lifting my head to the sky, I see dark, impossible clouds speeding towards me, turning burning blue to boiling black. Thunder crashes hard above, and the ground beneath me shudders in sympathy. Rain begins to pour, soothing my smouldering flesh; rivulets spinning around my feet as the water feeds the thirsty sand. Thunder roars once more, its fury deafening. On its heels lightning strikes, stabbing into the sand inches from where I stand. The darkness erupts in blue-white light, and I am thrown several feet into the air, landing hard, face down against a smooth surface.

Gasping for breath, I roll to my knees, shivering in air that has become suddenly, impossibly cold. I wipe the rain from my eyes as another spear of lightning arcs across the trembling sky—and gasp aloud. All around where I kneel, the sand has turned to glass, black and perfect. A solid obsidian sea. Another peal of thunder, another lightning strike, and I think I see movement beneath me. Pale forms, reaching. Another crash, another blinding flash, and I see a face, hear a scream. Grace. No.

"Grace!"

I cry out, pounding against the glass with all my strength, but nothing happens. It's too solid, too strong. Another flash, and I see her; honey hair floating up around her head like a halo, reaching for me as she sinks away into the darkness.

"Grace!"

Frantic, I search around for something, anything to use to break the glass. Another flash, and something glints nearby. With a cry I dive for whatever it is, my hand closing around metal that is first freezing, then searing. I scream and drop it to clatter coldly against the surface of the glass, my hand smoking. Another flash rips through the night, and I look to see what I have dropped, knowing already. The knife. Its black-edged crimson steel shimmers in the storm's light, the letters etched along the blade flashing silver-bright. They shift and twist through every language known until they come to rest on my own; the symbols burning against my vision.

'Should you wield with will this blade...'

The symbols shift and bend again, shape and meaning moving through time. Steeling myself against the pain I know will come, I reach down and curl my fist around the hilt. Tendrils of fire shoot up my arm, leaving wisps of white smoke in their wake, but I grit my teeth, lift the knife high—and stab it down into the solid sea with all my strength.

The black glass screams as the blade sinks hilt deep, and my hand erupts in flames. I cry out, letting go of the knife as I fall back, clutching my burning hand to my chest. There is another crash overhead, then an answering boom from beneath the glass.

The ebony sea cracks, jagged fissures splintering in every direction outward from the knife. There is a moment of perfect silence—and then the sea explodes around me; shards of black glass flying in a thousand directions, cutting and shredding through my skin. I scream as I am ripped apart, each savage gash spitting fire. I am burning, bleeding, limbless, as I sink beneath the impossible sea. No. This can't be happening. Grace. I have to save her. I try to fight, screaming her name over and over, gasping for air, struggling against my fate with limbs that are no longer there— and then I jolt awake.

Pain explodes through every nerve, and my vision swims and blurs. Light. Too bright. The sun? No. What?

A vague form leans over me. "Shhhh. It's okay. It's just me."

I choke on air that burns through my lungs as I gasp up, still half-caught in the nightmare. A warm hand presses me back down against a smooth cool surface.

"Stay still. You're hurt. Here—"

A rustle of fabric, and a sudden sharp sweet tang of iron.

Blood.

Something cold is pressed against my lips and I drink without another thought—and the blood's gone in seconds. I reach out, toward whoever, whatever. My hand finds the cold thing again, and this time I grasp it in both hands, moaning with relief as I bring it to my lips and drink it in one go. Again, I reach out, whimpering, needing—and again the cold thing is there. But the blood is warm. Yes. I gulp it down, gasping, needing as it spills into me, again, and again. It moves through me sluggishly. Not enough. Senses return, and through still clouded eyes I see movement. Feel warmth. Hear a heartbeat. Smell blood. More.

Animal need lends me strength, and I lunge for whatever is there. My hands grasp something soft and struggling. Alive. Yes. Snarling, I fight to bring whatever it is to my mouth, fangs bared and ready. I need this. Something crashes, and someone cries out in fear and beats at me, punching and kicking in desperation. Weak as I am, they almost get away, but I growl and grab, clawing them closer. I smell their fear, hear their heart-beat pulsing their blood to me. All for me.

Then I am struck on the side of the head by something cold and heavy; something that knocks me back against another hard surface, leaving me reeling, stunned.

Awake.

Moaning, head throbbing, I blink in light that is far too bright as every-thing slowly comes into focus.

The first thing I see is light, humming and headache bright, encased in a crystal lampshade, set onto the wall above a gilt-framed mirror. The mir-ror is hanging above a gold-tapped marble sink, and in that sink is a pile of empty IV bags. Past the sink is an ornate toilet, with its tank lid miss-ing, and past that, crouching against the back of the door, head bandaged, face and arms scratched and bleeding, eyes wide and filled with tears and the lid of the commode held in front of him like a shield—is Jude.

Chapter 34

Brethren

Babylon, 1595 BCE

I do not know if I love Ku-aya. But I have grown very fond of her. I have watched as she has changed, even as I have not. She has grown older and calmer, and although at times madness still shimmers behind those dark eyes, it seems she has found some small peace in her existence.

I cannot help but feel I have contributed somewhat to that peace. Her home is her own, I have made certain of that, and have given her wealth enough so that she need not sell her body, if she does not wish to. I keep her safe by night, and she, in her turn, and in her way, keeps watch over me by day.

Over the years I have taken on the role of teacher, of caretaker, and of lover to her. Her warmth and life do much to quiet the bitter hollow within, even as Lilitu said. And if I regret the constant gifting of my blood to the girl, and the near worship it engenders; then her loving eyes are quick to help me forget.

I have come to enjoy life again, and in Ku-aya's presence, time has slowed its pace for me. Together we spend hours conversing in our native tongue. I have taught her all I learned as Priestess, and she has taught me to laugh, and to remember what it is to be human.

She does not yet know the entirety of what I am, but she seems satisfied with what understanding she has, and I am loathe to spoil her innocence with too much truth. Such is the ease I feel with her, that I have even taken, of late, to spending a day's sleep in the heavily curtained inner room she made ready as a gift for me, safe and sheltered from the sun.

Lilitu has taught me how I might drink from the girl without killing her, now and again. It is not easy. I must always take care that I am well fed before, or the risk is too great. But this knowledge is a revelation for me, and I hold it near my heart.

The years pass swiftly so, each night blending into the next, and the next again. Some of my brethren also have taken mortals as their own, and more and more we seven no longer spend our days in sleep beside Babylon's high-born dead, but rather in the beds and houses of the living.

And so we go on, and so we stay the same.

This night I wake early, as has always been my want, the last arm of the dying sun still reaching for the moon as I rise from my bed. I watch the night bloom across the city from the curtained balcony of my chamber, listening to the soft sounds of the surrounding house; the wind that whispers the leaves of the trees in the courtyard, the gentle spilling of water against the stone of the fountain.

Below me, I hear Ku-aya walking softly from room to room and through the inner courtyard, lighting lamps, candles and incense. The heavy scent rises to fill the night and reminds me of home. It is good.

I close my eyes and let a smile curve my lips, feeling close to a peace I have not felt since the night of my making. And then another sound rises above the others; the faintest whisper of cloth, the slightest scuff of sandal on tile—and that phantom peace is gone, disappearing like a drop of water in a desert of sand. No other could hear her. Even I would not unless she wished me to.

"Lilitu."

I greet her, but do not turn from my gaze out the window as she steps behind me, wrapping pale arms around my waist and leaning in to brush a kiss against the nape of my neck.

"Daughter." Her lips caress my skin as she speaks, causing a small shiver to race up my spine. "Come and hunt with me tonight."

I woke in thirst and hunger, as I always do, but my need was not great. Indeed, I had thought not to hunt tonight, but to remain with Ku-aya, passing time in gentle conversation.

And yet, at Lilitu's words, dark need uncoils within me, waking with an impatient whine, as if at her bidding. Closing my eyes, I clench my fist and shove back at the hunger, wanting to deny it, hoping so for that fleeting peace to return—but all my wishes are in vain. Such peace is not mine to keep. My thirst will never be truly quenched, my hunger never fully satisfied.

Turning in Lilitu's embrace, I meet her shimmering eyes and knowing smile with a sigh of resignation.

"Where do you wish to hunt?"

Her smile grows wider, showing a hint of fangs already extended. "I will show you."

So saying, she moves away, stepping across to the edge of the balcony, and leaping down into the garden below.

I follow, hesitating a moment only, then jumping down to land lightly on the tiles near the fountain. Lilitu is already at the gate, and she turns and smiles at me again before slipping out into the shadowed street. I follow, moving fast to keep pace. She slips through the night like a shadow. No mortal eye could see her, and even I find it difficult to follow as she speeds through ever-narrowing streets toward the Northern gate.

The gate stands open, as it is yet early evening; the way beyond lit by a hundred blazing torches and guarded by soldiers bearing tall spears. Lilitu slows her pace as she walks past, enough to blend with the tide of mortal traders, farmers, merchants and travellers that flow into and out of the city every night. I follow suit, pulling the flowing cloth of my garment to cover my head as I pass beneath the blazing torches—but there is no need. The soldiers pay no heed as we walk beneath their bored gaze, through the milling crowds and out of the city, into the velvet darkness of the desert night.

Once we are out beyond walls and fields, beyond the squat houses of farmers and workers, beyond even the sprawling burial grounds of Babylon's more common dead, I expect Lilitu to stop; to explain what we are doing, whom we are hunting—yet she does not. Rather, as we move beyond the scope of mortal eyes she once again picks up speed, moving across the low ground and over rolling hills like the wind.

Before long she is speeding miles upriver, and once more I am hard pushed to follow. The night is black, the sky above so dark with cloud that even I cannot see clearly, and soon I am frustrated, hungry, and fighting a growing anger. I stop, searching the darkness around for any sign of her, but I find nothing. See nothing. Hear nothing but the distant movement of water, lapping soft against a muddy shore. The river, not too far away. I can smell the water in the air; water, and an acrid, bitter smell. Smoke.

No sooner do I smell it than I hear it; a low and distant murmur, like the incessant humming of a thousand bees. And more, the soft singing scrape of metal on stone, the whisper of leather against skin, the muffled clump of a hoof on sand, the creak and groan of a chariot wheel.

Somewhere, very near, there is an army in waiting.

"They number in the thousands."

I jump, startled by Lilitu's sudden appearance out of the darkness beside me. She smiles, her eyes shimmering with emerald incandescence.

"The largest army I have ever seen. And I have seen many, in my time. As of two or three nations united. They have marched downriver from lands in the North, come to plunder and spoil. On the morrow, they march for Babylon."

I frown, shaking my head. "Babylon will not fall. No army could breach the walls. No matter how great their number."

She smiles darkly in response, and walks further into the night, up the banks of the river. I know she expects me to follow, and after a moment, I do. As we crest the gently sloping hill, the clouds above give way to silver starlight, and I cannot help but gasp at what I see. The great river shimmers below, in its slow mercurial spill across the land, and there, encamped along either bank, is an army such as I have never seen.

A thousand tents and more stretch out below us, pitched so close together they seem an endless field of fluttering white. All around the tents are small fires, dotted through the night like so many flickering stars; and around those fires are men. Thousands upon thousands of men. Men sitting in circles, men talking, eating, praying; men sharpening swords and spears, men readying chariots and horses while still more men load ox-wagons with the thick wooden beams of siege towers; and yet more ready bows, ropes, ladders and slings. All of them, ready for war.

Ready for conquest.

I turn to Lilitu in disbelief, my heart sinking low in my chest. "They are too many. What shall we do? The city will not stand."

She turns to me, her eyes glittering in the light of a thousand fires. "Indeed, it will not. As to what we shall do? We shall leave. This very night. Alu has commanded it."

I frown. "Leave? But why? Should we rather not stay, hidden and safe within the catacombs? Armies have come before, and none have disturbed the dead, they would not dare."

She shakes her head. "Armies have come before, yes, but none like this. This one will not leave even the dead to rest. Nor us. Come. There is more I must show you."

So saying, she leads the way down the desert slope, angling toward the river, and the eastern flank of the army. Again, I follow, swift and silent, until we move behind the tents, shadow to shadow, seeming no more than shadows ourselves.

She does not stop until we crest another low rise, and find below another encampment, set some small distance from the rest. These tents are not as many, a hundred or so, but the camp is far quieter, the men below sitting silent by their fires. Watchful. Ready. Waiting.

Puzzled, I turn to Lilitu. "Why are these set apart from the rest?"

In answer, she only shakes her head, puts a pale finger to her lips and nods across to the banner that is hung above the entrance to this separate camp, its embroidered cloth swinging in the cool night breeze. I follow her gaze, frowning at the fluttering cloth below—at first unable to make it out. But then the clouds above us part once more, and I can see the symbol embroidered on the fabric, blood red on a field of white. A curving snake, the sacred symbol of the Goddess, the very same that is marked upon both my arms—impaled by a spear, the two together making the shape of a cross upon the silken white field.

I shake my head, a cold tide of uncertainty rising in my chest. "What does it mean? Who are these men?"

She turns to meet my questioning gaze, her eyes flashing reflected moonlight. "They call themselves 'The Brethren', and they number here more than two hundred men."

Those eyes grow cold, her gaze drifting over the men and tents below. "They are hunters, Asharru. Sons and sons and sons again, of the same few that have harried us for centuries. Only those few have now become many." Her cool gaze travels back to me. "Too many."

I swallow back a sudden tide of fear. "They have come for us, then."

She nods, although it was not a question. "They have. Alu believes it is they who have brought this army to our gates. I am not so certain. But whatever the reason, they are here, and we cannot stand against so many."

"Alu believes..." I repeat her words, angry denial building in my breast. "Do you mean to say he knew of these 'Brethren'? As did you? How long has this been? How long have you both known? And why did you not see fit to tell us?" With each accusing question, my fury builds. "Or do the others already know? Am I, yet again, the last to be told?"

Lilitu shakes her head, lifting a hand to silence my tirade. "Always you are so quick to anger, Daughter. So quick to judge." She sighs, shaking her head. "I will answer your questions, as I always do, but not here."

So saying, she looks cautiously back over the encampment below, and then takes my arm, leading me down the hill and back toward the river. A twinge of fear shivers up my spine at the sight of the murmuring midnight water, the memory of suffocating beneath its shimmering surface all too fresh in my mind.

She does not release my arm until we stand in the thickness of reeds and tall grasses at the water's edge. Only then does she let me go, moving to sit down on a fallen log, carried here on a long-ago flood from the far away mountains to the north. I stand watching her a moment, anger and impatience stirring in my breast. Only when she turns to me with a raised brow, do I acquiesce, and move to sit beside her. She waits until I am settled before she speaks, her voice low.

"You must learn patience, child. I admire your will, and your fire—but I fear it will be your undoing." She sighs and gazes across the black expanse of the river. "You are not the last to be told, but rather, are the first, after Alu, and myself. We have both known for over a century now, that the numbers of these hunters were growing, that they had come together, and were calling more men to their banner and cause. And not only men. They have in their company magi. I know not how many."

My anger abandons me at her words. "Magi? What do you mean?"

She turns to me, her eyes dark. "Men who wield magic as their weapon, and use it to track us; men who intend to destroy us with powers we can neither command nor comprehend."

That cold fear rises once more, moving from my stomach to my throat, and I seek for solace, searching those eyes I know so well. "But surely you could fight them? You were once a wielder of such powers; you have told me as much!"

"I was, once." She nods her lips a tight line. "No longer. As I have also told you, that power left me the moment I became what I am. What we all are. We cannot use magic, daughter. Its powers are lost to us. But it can still be used against us." She nods, back over her shoulder, toward the waiting army. "And it will be. Alu tells me there are certain of these men that have been preparing for generations; teaching their sons and their sons of sons how to find and fight us, learning our every way and weakness."

I shake my head, still struggling to understand. "What do you mean Alu tells you? How does my maker know these things?" I search her face; certain she is not telling me all the truth there is to tell.

She sighs, staring down at the cool earth beneath our feet for a moment before lifting her head again. "You are always questioning all things, child. The answers may not always please you."

At that moment I do not care, and lean forward, taking her pale hand in my own. "Whether it pleases me or not, I wish to know."

"Very well. Alu knows this because he was once one of them. Before I made him one of us."

Chapter 35

Shaking and Exhausted

"Jude?" The word comes out in a scratchy croak. I swallow hard against the taste of sulphur at the back of my throat and try again. "How?"

I squint my eyes closed and back open again as everything comes more clearly into focus, not quite believing what I'm seeing; certain I'm still caught in the dream. Then I try to move—and the blinding shock of pain that rockets through every limb lets me know beyond any doubt that I'm awake, that this is real, and that somehow, Jude's alive.

He lets out a long breath, blinking back tears and slowly setting the loo lid down on the floor beside him before moving cautiously nearer to where I'm lying. In what I now know to be a bathtub.

"Rue?"

He looks scared, and now that I can see, I realise he's banged up pretty bad. There's a bandage on his head, and scratches and teeth marks all over his hands and arms. Shit.

"I'm sorry."

"It's okay."

"It's not okay." I try to move again, and manage to pull myself up to a sitting position, against the back of the bath. I have to stop then, closing my eyes as an overpowering wave of dizziness and nausea washes over me. It's a moment before I can open them again, and when I do, Jude's there, leaning over me.

"You should try to stay still. You're hurt—"

"I'll heal." I give him a tight-lipped smile. "What happened? How are you okay? I saw you fall. I thought..." The words catch in my throat as the memory of that moment, and all that happened after, replays in my mind.

Jude sighs again, and sits back against the wall. "Honestly, I've no idea. I heard the gunshots and ran to help you. I don't know what I was thinking. I wasn't, I guess." He stops, frowning and shaking his head before continuing. "I heard you shout, saw you turn, saw the demon with the gun, and then everything just...slowed down. I never heard the shot. But what I felt was like someone shoved me, hard to one side. Out of the way. I felt a burning at the side of my head. And then nothing."

He closes eyes red and rimmed with tears. "It must've only grazed me. When I woke up, Grace was gone, and that...that thing...was killing you. Stabbing you. You were burning. I didn't know what to do..."

He stops, bending his head to his hand and rubbing his forehead, as if he could rub the memory away.

"Then I remembered the gun. I ran and got it, and came back out and saw you there. Not moving. And he was still stabbing you, over and over. I just walked over and shot him. In the head. I killed him."

He winces as he says it, his eyes welling with tears, his voice shaking as he continues.

"There was a sound, like wind. And then nothing. But you were still burning. I had to get you out of the sun. I could hear shouts, sirens. So, I picked you up, brought you in here, fed you the rest of the blood from your bag..."

He stops again, lifting his head and meeting my eyes. "You were so hurt. Not healing. Not even breathing. I thought...I thought I'd lost you." He closes his eyes and bends his head to both hands as tears stream down his face. He wipes at them roughly and clears his throat.

"There was a fire then, in the hall. I think it was maybe your blood?" He looks to me, then continues. "Anyway, they evacuated the hotel. I had to leave you here. You'd started breathing again, but were out cold, so I shut you in here and left. Then the fire department came, and then the cops."

He sighs, leaning back against the wall. "They saw my head. Bleeding. So I lied. I said there was a gunfight, gangs maybe, and that I'd tried to stop them and was shot at. I said I hid in my room after that. Said I was scared." He gives me a wry smile. "That part was true at least."

I manage a shaky smile back. He looks at me a long moment, then continues.

"Anyway, they believed me, and had paramedics stitch me up. They wanted to send me to the hospital, but I wouldn't let them. Said I wanted to help up here. To pray." He shrugs. "Priest privilege. They let me back in, and I came back to check on you. I knew I had to get you more blood, but I couldn't leave you. I watched you all day, and then last night you started to heal. But today you still didn't wake up. So...I used the knife, and one of the teacups..."

He trails off again, holding up his wrist, which is wrapped in gauze. Christ.

"How much did you give me?"

He shrugs. "I dunno. A few cups full. I'm okay though. Now that you are." He gives me a shaky smile.

"Jesus, Jude."

I shake my head, and immediately regret the movement as another flood of nausea cascades over me. Daytime vertigo. I moan and lean back against the tub. Jude moves back over, worry colouring his eyes.

"You should stay still. Rest more."

"No. I have to go after them." I look to him, heartache clenching cold around my chest. "Grace...it's my fault. Everything..." Sorrow chokes me, and my voice breaks.

Jude shakes his head, taking my hand in his own. "We will go after them. And we'll get her back. But Rue, it's still daylight. And you're in no condition—"

"I'm fine." I interrupt him with what we both know is a lie, shove down the grief, and attempt to push myself to my feet. Every nerve, joint and muscle is screaming, and my freshly healed wounds open again as I move, but I don't care. I get to my knees before I have to stop, another wave of dizziness crashing over me. I sway and Jude reaches out to steady me.

"You're not fine."

I hold his gaze. "I have to find her."

He stares at me in silence for a minute, then gives a reluctant nod. "Okay. But let's get you cleaned up first. I got some extra bandages from the paramedics. They'll help a bit at least. Hold you together. Until you can heal more."

I give him as much of a smile as I can. "Thanks."

He smiles. "Anytime."

He takes my arm and helps me to my feet. It takes forever, and hurts so bad I'm gasping by the time I'm up, but at least I'm standing. I stay there, leaning against the shower wall, as Jude turns on the water, leaving it to run as he starts to gently remove my burnt and bloody clothes. I help as much as I can, but it takes a long time to get me undressed, and longer still to clean my wounds.

By the time we're done, I'm shaking and exhausted, and Jude doesn't look much better than I feel. The bandage on his head is wet and new blood is seeping through—and the sight and scent of it sends a sudden pang of hunger ripping through me. Without warning, the thing inside wakes up and begins to scream. I gasp and shove Jude away, turning my face to the wall as I feel need rise into my eyes.

He stumbles back, confused. "What's wrong?"

I keep my face to the wall, closing my eyes and clenching my fists as I fight against the thing inside, pushing against the raging hunger and thirst with all my might.

Jude steps closer, not understanding. "Rue?"

I hold up my hand to stop him. "Don't...please. Your head's bleeding."

"Oh." He steps back, putting a hand to his bandage. "Shit."

He moves away quickly, out of the loo, leaving me to get a grip on myself. It takes a bit, but eventually the need subsides, and the screaming in my head fades to a persistent but bearable whine.

Breathing a sigh of relief, I slowly step from the bath, keeping one arm on the wall. It takes me a few minutes, but I manage to get myself over to the mirror to take stock. Jude wasn't exaggerating. This is bad. My skin is raw, thin, and red where it was burnt, and the cuts and bullet wounds are oozing blood with every breath I take.

My broken bones have re-knit, but are still fragile, my entire body is one big bruise, and my eyes are blazing. Even if I had a steady supply of fresh blood, this badly wounded it'd take me a quite a while to heal completely. Even Grace's blood might take a little time.

Grace.

A new surge of loss wells up from my chest at the thought of her—just as Jude cautiously comes back in, and I turn away from my reflection, blinking back blood tears.

"Sorry about that." He walks over with a new bandage on his head, and no blood in sight. He's carrying a few more packs of bandages, some antiseptic cream, and my backpack with my clothes, all of which he hands over. "I didn't realise…"

I toss the bag and cream down, take the bandages from him and start to unwrap the sterile packaging. "It's not your fault. Anyway, it's me who should apologise."

He frowns. "It's okay. You can't help it."

I sigh and stop unwrapping. He doesn't get it. The reality of what I am. And that's my fault. I've never been fully honest with him, not about my past, not about the things I've done, the thousands I've killed. The times I've enjoyed it. Because of this I think he sees me as some sort of tragic hero. Like a character from one of those ridiculous modern vampire films rather than the monster I've been. The monster I still am. And if I'm honest with myself, I don't mind his skewed view of me. I've even taken advantage of it. I meet his gaze, shaking my head.

"You saved my life, and I attacked you, hurt you. I'm sorry Jude. Forgive me. For everything."

I can't go into all of what 'everything' is right now. No time. But maybe later, sometime, I'll have the chance to tell him the truth about it all, and he can make up his own mind whether to stay my friend. Or not.

He sighs and shrugs. "Okay. I forgive you. Now turn around."

Kneeling, he opens the antiseptic cream and starts to slather it on the worst of my cuts. It stinks to high heaven.

"Jude."

He hmms, at me, intent on what he's doing.

"Jude." I wince as he presses on a deep cut a tad too hard.

"Yeah?" He reaches to take another handful of the cream, spreading it across a laceration along my hip.

"Jude!"

"What?" He stands up, looking at me. Finally.

"That won't help."

He frowns. "It will. I mean, I know it won't stop the bleeding or anything, but it'll help prevent infection—"

"I don't get infections." I interrupt him. "And it won't help me heal. Even the bandages are only a stop-gap. I won't really heal until the sun sets. And not without blood."

He swallows hard, and his eyes well up. "Oh."

I close my eyes as another wave of vertigo sweeps over me, reaching out to brace myself against the wall until it passes. When it does, and I look at him again. He's staring at me, his eyes full of concern. I sigh.

"Okay. Maybe it'll help a little bit."

It won't. But it makes him happy. He finishes putting the cream on all my cuts and gashes, then helps me unwrap the long strips of sterile cotton, wrapping them tightly around each wound. When we're done, I look a lot like a mummy. But at least the bandages will soak up the blood. For a bit.

I give Jude a tight smile and pick up my backpack, rummaging for sunblock. "What time is it?"

He reaches to help me balance as I gingerly pull on a pair of jeans. "Almost eight."

"Shit."

Late summer evening. Which means the sun won't set for a couple of hours. As if to hammer that fact home, another wave of weakness washes over me. I have to lean on the counter for a moment, and Jude reaches out a hand to steady me again.

"You okay?"

"Yeah. Fine." I open my eyes as the nausea passes. "What's the weather like?"

"Cloudy. I think. Hang on." He leaves the loo for a moment, and I hear a curtain being pulled back, then shut again. He comes back in, nodding. "Yeah, pretty overcast. Looks like rain."

I nod and wince as I slather sunblock on any still-exposed skin, then pull a t-shirt and hoodie out of the bag. I tug them on and lean back again against the sink, resting while Jude picks up the remains of my ruined clothes, and cleans up the tub and floor. He tosses everything into the bin, then takes up the bin itself.

"What's the plan?"

I stand, biting back a groan. "To get out of here, find the demons, and get Grace back."

He nods, and lets out a long breath. "Okay. Let's start with getting out of here. The hotel is full of cops, they've sealed off this floor, and right outside the door are a bunch of forensic lads. They know I'm here, but how're we going to get you past them?"

I frown, and run a hand through my hair, thinking a minute. Then it comes to me. "The window."

Jude stares. "Rue—we're five storeys up!"

"I know that." I shoot him a look. "You walk down, let the cops know you're leaving, get the car, and back it up below. As close as you can."

He just stares. "It's daytime."

"It's cloudy. I'll have more time. Enough to get into the boot, which you will have open for me."

He folds his arms over his chest, eyes dark. "You're in no shape to climb down five storeys. No. There has to be a better way."

"There isn't. And who said anything about climbing?"

It takes him a moment, then he gets it and freaks. "No! No way are you jumping! You're hurt already!"

I shake my head. "I'll be fine. I've done it before. From higher. Don't worry. Just have the car ready. Okay?"

He glares at me for a furious minute, then sighs, angrily giving in. "Fine."

He turns and storms out of the loo. I grab the backpack and follow, steadying myself against the wall every few steps. The room is blessedly dark, although some light seeps in from around the curtained window. Thankfully it doesn't reach the bed. I sit down with a groan, and rummage in the bag for my last pair of decent boots, my third favourite jacket, and some sunglasses. While I'm at it, I look to make sure the bag of demon drugs is still there. Which it is. Good.

Pulling on the boots reminds me, and I look over to where Jude stands watching me worriedly.

"Where's the knife?"

He walks across to the head of the bed and pulls it out from under the mattress, still wrapped in the scarf. He stares at it a moment before handing it over to me gingerly. I take it from him, reminded of the dream, the blade, the ever-shifting lettering. I don't know what it means. If it means anything at all. But I can't leave the bloody thing behind. Making sure it's securely wrapped up, I tuck it in my inside jacket pocket, then look back at Jude.

"And the gun?"

He looks at me blankly. "What gun?"

"The gun I gave you? The one you shot the demon with?"

"Oh." Sorrow moves across his face as he reaches under the pillow and pulls out the handgun.

I hold out my hand, and after a moment, he walks over and places the handgun in my palm. I eject the magazine to see several rounds are still in it, pop it back in, and hand the gun back to him.

He hesitates—looking at it, but not taking it.

"You didn't shoot a human being, Jude."

He shrugs. "I know."

"The human soul in that body was long gone.'

He nods.

"That demon would have killed me if you hadn't shot him."

He looks up to meet my eyes then, and I give him a tight smile. "Take it. I feel better knowing you have it."

He takes it then, with a sigh—shoving it into his belt, then looking back to me.

"What now?"

"Tell me what's down there?" I nod to the window and Jude walks over, pulls the curtain an inch or so aside and peers below.

"It's quiet enough. No cops, not on this side. There's the park below, then a hedge and a wall by the lot. If you can get over the wall, I think I can get pretty close."

"Good." Taking a deep breath, I clench my jaw and stand up. It hurts, but I hold it together. Jude's lips are set in a tight line—but he doesn't argue anymore, only picks up my bags and the car keys from the bedside locker.

"Where to then?"

"Ringsend. Looking for a dealer named Damien. But I'll do the asking around. Okay?"

He lifts a brow, takes a breath to argue, then just sighs and nods. "Okay. Give me five minutes."

Heading to the door, he turns back. "Rue?"

"Yeah?"

He gives me a sad smile. "Be careful."

I can't manage much of a smile back, but I say it anyway. I know he needs me to.

"I always am."

He nods, smiles at me a moment longer—then turns and opens the door, just wide enough for him to exit. It clicks shut behind him, and in the silence that follows I can hear the murmur of voices in the hall beyond, the shutter-clicks of cameras and the rustling of plastic and cloth.

Forensics. Collecting evidence from bodies and blood. Demon blood. My blood. In that hallway not all of it will burn away. Which means the cops will be able to swab and collect it, along with whatever security footage the hotel might have. Of me. Shit. Shit shit shit!

But there's nothing I can do about it now. Have to keep going. Have to find the demons and save Grace.

Grace.

Gods. The memory of those last few moments, of her screaming my name as they carried her away, washes over me in a sickening rush. Anger and loss rise into my throat again, and tears sting my eyes.

Fuck.

Angrily, I swipe at the tears. No. I'm going to get her back. Biting back a groan, I put the sunglasses on and walk across to the window, waiting another couple of minutes there. The line of light around the curtain hurts my eyes even with the sunglasses—but at least it's muted grey, instead of burning gold. Still. This is going to hurt. There's no getting around it. And whatever happens, I won't heal, not until nightfall. Shit. Another wave of vertigo washes over me, and I close my eyes, reaching to steady myself against the wall. A minute more. Come on, come on.

Then I hear a car below, and engine rev; once, twice—three times. Okay. That's him. Time to go. Taking a deep breath, I pull up my hood, then reach up and jerk open the curtains in one quick motion. Grey daylight crashes over me, stinging my eyes and tingling painfully across my already burnt skin. Tears well up again, but I blink them away as I open the window to its hotel set limit—which is about six inches.

Great.

I shove at the glass as hard as I can. Nothing. Too weak. Fuck. Standing up again, I brace for pain and give the window a quick kick. The whole thing pops out with a loud crack, then shatters to the ground below in a tangle of glass and metal. Shit! I glance back over my shoulder at the door, then shake my head and crawl up onto the window ledge. If they heard me, then they heard me. No time.

I crouch on the ledge for a second, looking down. It's just like Jude said. Herbert Park stretches out below me; a soft grassy slope winding into paths and trees. The park is separated from the hotel lot by a low iron-topped stone wall and a small hedge—and Jude has parked the Merc as close as he can to that. About twenty feet from where I'll land.

I hope.

If I was in the best shape, and if it was dark, this would be simple. But I'm not, and it isn't. I study the probably-not-as-soft-as-it-looks slope of grass below, and wish, not for the first time, that vampires really could fly. It would make things a hell of a lot easier.

Behind me there is a pounding on the door. Shit. Time to go. I take another deep breath, let it out—and leap. I hear a crash and a shout behind me, and then I hit the ground. Hard.

I roll as I hit, knees bent, head tucked, but it doesn't do much good. Several somethings inside snap at the impact, and my right knee dislocates with a bone-jarring crunch. I grab my knee with both hands and shove it back into place, pain exploding through every joint. Move. Move! A cry from above, and then I'm running, fast as I can. Across the muddy grass, up over the wall, through the hedge to the car. Jude's already pulling away, but the boot's open.

I take a running leap, grab the edge of the boot in both hands and pull. I get a blurred glimpse of running bodies in the distance, shouting, waving—but then I'm in, and Jude's speeding up. Reaching up, I slam the boot shut above me as we spin out of the lot, leaving the yelling and running behind.

Carpeted blackness settles in around me, and I sink back into it, shoving the bag into a corner, then curling up and wrapping my arms tight around my wounds.

I'm bleeding again. I can feel the blood soaking the bandages into my clothes, but I don't care. I can't fight the day-drain any longer. Blessed darkness holds me, and I give in to it gladly, the rumbling engine and humming wheels beneath me becoming an odd lullaby that rocks me away into a dense, exhausted sleep.

Chapter 36

Goddess

Lilitu's statement stuns me into a shocked silence. All I can do is sit and stare as her words sink in. Alu, a hunter. Lilitu his maker. Long have I wondered whether Alu was Lilitu's creation. What other could claim him if we seven are truly the only of our kind, and he the maker of us all, save her? She who sits before me so calm, so knowing. So ancient.

In that moment, I consider her as I never have before; her slight, even delicate form belying the power that lies beneath; the demon curse borne in her blood. A curse she then bestowed upon another. Alu. And he upon my brethren. Upon me. But how?

Curiosity stirs in me and I stir from my thoughts to find her watching me. She smiles knowingly, as if yet again she has read my mind.

"Yes, Daughter. I am Alu's maker, and thus mother to you all. You will say I should have told you sooner, and perhaps you are right; but understand, Asharru, this knowledge is not given lightly. What I am about to tell you none of your brethren know, nor shall they. Do you understand?"

I nod. "I will not breathe a word of what you say. Neither to my brethren, nor any living creature."

She squeezes my hand in her own, giving me a slight smile as she begins.

"I have told you how I became what I am, of the cruel and terrible magic that bound the dark god to my flesh. And I have told you of what came after, of the years of madness I suffered, of searching for a cure, and of battling the demon that made me what I am."

I nod, recalling all too well the things she has told me. After a moment, she goes on.

"I have told you also that I was cursed and hunted by people thereafter, and you asked me why I did not destroy those first hunters, do you remember?"

"I do. You told me that they did not deserve to die, simply for what they were."

She smiles. "Yes. No more than do we. Neither death, nor life is about deserving, no matter how we may judge, nor what we may tell ourselves. Surely, daughter, you must know this by now."

She holds my gaze until I must swallow hard against the tide of guilt that rises at the certain knowledge that I have killed so often upon that very judgement. Telling myself that those I prey upon deserve their fate while deep in my heart of hearts I doubt, and am afraid. Afraid that despite all my justifications, I am a demon. A monster. No better than those I deem fit to die.

Tears fill my eyes as I am reminded once more what I am, and I have to look away, unable to answer, and grateful when she takes up her tale again, seeming to take no notice of my grief.

"As I have told you, I fled far and fast away from that first city, and those first hunters, finding shelter in the mountains, then moving on, from village to village, and city to city, seeking always to hide from the eyes of men."

She stares out across the night-black water. "And yet I could not remain hidden for long. Hunger always drove me to hunt again, and wherever I hunted, those who hunted me were not far behind. Always they were tracking me, hounding me. And so I wandered as does the wolf in the night, never lingering; taking for my prey the shepherd in his watch, the trader in his camp, the guard at the gate."

"Whomever I would chance to come upon would not live to see the morn. It was with little wonder then, that once again I heard whispers in the night, stories told by firelight of a demon-woman, haunting the forests and mountain passes, hunting the wicked or foolish."

She glances to me. "As I travelled further south, the stories grew in both glory and horror, until, depending on the teller, they had me either a Demon or beast; a hideous monster, or a temptress; a drinker of souls, or a devourer of babes."

I wince as she says the last, and look down, unable to meet her gaze as I recall shouting in anger that same accusation, not so long ago. A moment passes, and then she sighs, placing a cool hand on the back of my neck, gently.

"Those dark stories stung my heart, all the more because of the small seed of truth behind the words."

I search her eyes to see if yet again, she has read my thoughts—and she smiles, soft, resigned.

After another moment's silence, she takes her hand away as she continues her tale.

"Months went by, then years, decades, centuries. The villages I passed were cities when I returned to them again. And still, I kept on, until I had crossed the length and breadth of this land, from the desert to the west to the eastern mountains, from the northern plains to the southern sea. Yet always the hunters followed. Over years their numbers had grown, although nowhere near the numbers now gathered below. Still, they were enough to worry and harry me. And so I kept moving."

She pauses a moment, her gaze following the river's endless flow toward the distant sea.

"So it was that I came again into the southern plains, once more into the land of my birth; only to find a new people there, come from the east to settle the land and build their cities upon the bones of those that had gone before. Of my own people and language there was no sign, only a word or phrase here and there, familiar and foreign."

She sighs, and I am reminded again of my own loss, my own people gone, my own language nearly dead, and my heart warms at the thought of Ku-aya and our conversations. I realise how much I care for the girl. How much I need to protect her.

After a moments silence, Lilitu carries on. "I was saddened by this loss, reminding me as it did that I was no longer one of mankind; that they moved and changed with time while I stayed the same. Unchanged, perfect. And terrible."

She looks to me and I nod, understanding all too well. After another moment, she smiles sadly.

"Yet I could not dwell long in grief. As always, hunger drove me to hunt, and the hunt drove me on, city to city, never lingering more than a night or two, for fear the hunters would find me."

She gazes out again across the river. "I went on that way, sheltering in the wild places by day, hunting in the cites by night, losing myself to this new existence, night upon night, and, as it does, time passed. Seasons came and went, but I paid little heed, for all seasons to me were blood and darkness."

She gives me a dark smile. "And then it began to rain. And rain. Slowly at first; then to such extent that even I took note. Rivers overflowed their banks, their once pure waters thick with mud. Lowlands became sodden, then impassable. The people whispered of demons and gods, of anger and sacrifice. Many of my daytime resting places became flooded, and I was forced to seek shelter within the cities themselves, sleeping as we do now, with the dead."

"Travel became difficult, even for me, so I stayed within reach of a few cites, taking prey only when hunger drove me to near-desperation, for fear of drawing hunters down upon me."

"My fear was not unfounded. For it was then that a new band of hunters rose up in the land; strong, young, determined and led by a glorious warrior from the distant north. A warrior with hair the colour of night and eyes like ice. It was whispered he was after the demon-woman of legend; for he swore it was she who caused the waters to rise. It was said he would not rest until he found her."

She glances up, eyes glinting. "And find me he did. But he was too late, for the world as we knew it was about to come to an end. Although it did not happen quite as the tales tell. It started slowly."

"First, the earth grew restless, with violent storms and trembling deep beneath the hills. And then the waters rose. Rivers broke their banks, killing herds and crops; lakes grew, lapping at the villages built along their shores. Whispers of fear and anger grew louder, as people grew suspicious and wary. No longer could I hunt in the smaller villages and towns, and risk the notice of watchful eyes. So I made my way to the largest of the cities, where I could lose myself and my dark need among the shadows."

A dark smile curves her lips. "There it was that Alu and his hunters found me."

I sit, open-mouthed in rapt attention, as she continues.

"I had been hunting night upon night, to no avail. Few ventured from their homes in those times. And yet hunger drove me on, until, one night, just before dawn, I finally found my prey in a young man on his own, hurrying through the narrow streets. Intent on his destination, he took no notice of his surroundings, nor of me, watching, waiting. As he made his way down a narrow passage by the temple, I took him."

"You may not know this, daughter, for until now you have had little to fear, but we are vulnerable when we feed. The blood entrances us, distracting us from our surroundings. From danger. So it was with me that night, for as I quenched my thirst I became deaf and blind to all else. It was then that the hunters attacked."

She pauses briefly, her eyes filled with the shadows of the past.

"They fell upon me first from above, ensnaring me in a weighted net of the kind used to trap the lions in the plains. Of course, it did not hold me, for as soon as I came to my senses, I let go my prey, ripping through the net as if it were so much thread. But I was too late, and they were too many. They set upon me from all sides, stabbing and slicing me with sword and spear."

She nods to me. "Although I had by this time begun to test my strength, even so, I had not yet learned to fight, as I still had no one to teach me. The men that attacked me were seasoned hunters, trained to kill. I had greater speed, and strength, but it mattered not. Within minutes I was sorely wounded—and day was fast approaching. I now know that is what the hunters had planned. They were counting on the rising sun to give them their victory over the 'demoness'."

She smiles darkly. "It was a victory nearly achieved. But as I fought them into the breaking dawn, an unnatural darkness swept over the sky, and with it a roar unlike anything I had ever heard. The air became choked with ash that fell like snow, and then a great and terrible shaking began. The ground began to tremble and slip from beneath our feet like water. The buildings could not stand upon earth that was not still, and so they fell, raining brick and mortar all around us."

"The men broke off their attack with shouts and screams of fear as they fell, or were felled by crumbling stone. I did not pause to wonder at the respite, but took the opportunity as a gift from the gods, and ran, as fast and as far as I could, away from the hunters, away from the crumbling city and the screams of people waking to terror."

A shadow passes over her face, lingering in her eyes.

"I ran on and on, beyond the city walls as they fell to dust, leaving behind the cries of dying men. I ran until the shaking stopped, beyond the fields that surrounded the city, and further still, toward the sea, until my wounds overcame me, and I could run no more."

She closes her eyes as if against the memory, and takes my hand.

"I fell to my knees there, upon the sand, weeping in pain and fear. The shaking had stopped, although the darkness remained, and the air was thick with acrid smoke, as from a thousand fires. Ash fell from the sky like hot snow, muting even the pounding of my own heart, and in the silence, I could hear a low rumbling, at the edge of my hearing."

"It was a sound I had never heard before, and it distracted me enough for me to notice that the sand upon which I knelt was wet. And strewn with clumps of salt, seaweed, and gasping, dying fish. It took a moment for me to realise what it meant, and when I did, fear wrapped a cold fist around my heart. I had run, all unknowing, far beyond the place where the shore should have been, and the sea—the sea was gone. It was then that I knew what the sound was. Struggling to my feet, I looked in horror toward the grey horizon."

She turns to me, and I hardly dare breathe as she continues.

"That thundering roar was a wall of water, speeding toward the valley—toward me—with terrible intent. I had no time to think. The impossible wave roared like a thousand beasts as it barrelled toward me. I turned and ran, as fast as I could, back the way I had come, back to the village, forgetting the hunters, forgetting my wounds, forgetting even the dawn; my only thought to save the people from this horrible fate."

She holds tight to my hand, and I to hers, as she carries on.

"I reached the village, the water crashing through the valley only moments behind. People were already out in the streets, stunned and stumbling through rubble, and I screamed at them to run, run—but they just stared at me, blind to their fate. Still, I screamed, snarling at them, cursing and pushing at them to flee—but then the water was upon us, and even I was powerless to escape its fury."

She shudders, her eyes dark.

"The waters slammed into me with the force of a hundred chariots, spinning me around like a leaf caught in a storm, and then pulling me down into watery darkness. I thrashed and fought, gasped and choked on mud and debris; tried to swim, to raise my head above the thrashing waves, to grasp onto any hold—to no avail. Everything was swept before the deluge, and I was as helpless as any in its path."

Lifting her head, she looks out once more across the dark expanse of water beside us.

"The rushing water carried me away, far from the city, tossing and turning me as it roared through village and valley. At some point I was struck hard, by some detritus borne in the water, and I lost consciousness."

Again, she pauses, and I watch her watch the river for a few long moments before she continues.

"When I woke, it was to darkness, and an eerie, empty silence. It took me several moments to realise I was buried beneath a tangle of mud and rubble. I tried to move and cried out as blinding pain seared through my body. Then memory returned, of shaking earth and shattering wave. Hunger and panic twisted together in my core, and I clawed and shoved at the rubble, frantically pushing and pulling my way out, until at last I was able to drag myself up to lie gasping in the mud."

She squeezes my hand tight, as if to take courage from the present before recalling the horror of the past.

"It was a long moment before I could lift my head and take stock of my wounds, which were many. My chest was crushed, burning with every breath, and my left leg was torn open, white bone showing through the wound. I was bleeding from a hundred smaller wounds as well. Worse, I did not have enough blood left in me to heal, and hunger was raging through me with every weakening beat of my heart. I had to feed, and soon."

She lets out a long breath, turning those emerald eyes to mine once more.

"I struggled to my feet, steadying myself against the battered trunk of an age-old tree, uprooted and bent in two, as if by the careless hand of some giant child. It was still day, or it should have been, I could feel it. And yet all was dark. Smoke and ash still filled the air, and far to the west the sky burned red, as if all the mountains were wreathed in flame. I stood at the head of the valley where the wave had carried me, and had then reversed its ravaging course, leaving behind nothing but mud and death."

"Gone were the whispering green grasses; gone were lush forests and fruitful orchards. Gone also animals, both wild and tame. Neither bird nor beast survived. I gazed down over the valley, struggling to see through the smoke to where village after village once stood, their bustling streets and markets usually full to overflowing. All gone. Nothing remained. No one. All that had been, was washed away. All save me."

Crimson tears well into her eyes, and I swallow hard against an echo of my own loss, as she continues.

"Sorrow overcame me then, and I fell to my knees once more, sobbing my grief into the drowned earth. It was then, between my own cries, that I heard it. A sound so faint that as I gasped up to better hear I thought I had imagined it—but no. Again, it came, and again. A voice. Crying for aid."

"Once more I struggled to my feet, and on, through the rubble toward the sound, moving as swift as the mud and my wounds would allow, all thought of sorrow gone. In moments I reached the source of the sound, and stopped, horror returning tenfold. The sound came from a boy— young, perhaps twelve years, not more—whose body was caught impossibly against the trunk of a tree. The branches of the tree were stripped clean—all but three, and those three pieced the boy's shoulder, chest and thigh. Blood seeped from around the protruding branches and at the sight and smell of it my hunger raged anew."

She pauses, this time to wipe away a crimson tear as it spills down her cheek.

"He would not have lived. I know that now. Yet I cannot say I knew it then. It took a moment only. He never saw me, never knew what was happening, of that I am certain. And as his blood flowed into me, I began to hear more sounds; sobs and cries of wounded men, women and children, all around the valley."

She smiles, a curve of her lip that implies no mirth.

"I took a great many wounded to their rest in that unnatural night, each death filling me, until I was sated. Then, as true night fell, and I began to heal, I made my way down the valley to where the waters had birthed a new sea, and there I found more survivors, some wounded, some not at all, making their way along the new shoreline, some huddled and shaking, some calling for loved ones lost."

"These, I helped, as I could, gathering firewood or building shelters from fallen trees. A few times, these ones knew me for what I was, or at least what they thought me to be, for they named me so, in whispers of gratitude. Not destroyer, but saviour. Not demon, but goddess."

Chapter 37

Fear and Sorrow

S omeone is shaking me, saying my name, over and over. But I'm
sleeping. So tired. My limbs are heavy, weighted, my eyelids leaden.
I need to sleep. Just sleep. But they're still shaking me. Still speaking. Insistent. Annoying.

Slowly, I come to, back to consciousness. I lick lips that have gone all dry, and croak out an answer.

"Yeah. Okay! I'm awake. I'm awake!"

I force my eyes to open and uncurl into a sitting position. Jude is frowning above me.

"Are you sure you're able for this?"

"I'm fine." Grimacing in pain, I crawl out of the boot. It takes for-fucking-ever, but I finally stand up, wincing at the square of cloudy daylight above.

We're in a laneway, parked in the relative shadow of a skip, but it's nowhere near being dark yet. Shit. Another wave of vertigo floods over me and I sway and grab the side of the skip to steady myself. Jude sighs, but says nothing. Which is wise, as I'm not in the greatest of moods. After a minute, the vertigo passes.

"What time is it?"

He looks at his watch. "Half nine."

I nod. "Okay. Where are we?"

He gestures over his shoulder. "Cambridge Road. Across from the park. I figured it was a good place to start."

"Yeah. Good." I run a hand through my hair, trying to shake the daytime fog from my mind. The movement only wakes the hammering headache that's been dogging me for nights now. The pain promptly joins the rest, moving to pound right behind my already stinging eyes. "Fuck."

"What's wrong?"

"Nothing. Headache."

He frowns. "Do vampires even get headaches?"

That's a good question. But I can't stop to think about it now, and his insistent concern is getting on my nerves. "I don't know. I do know that I'm a vampire and I have a headache. Okay?"

He grimaces and shrugs, not looking convinced, but doesn't argue. "Okay."

I reach in and rummage through the bag for the smaller baggie of drugs, tugging it open and taking out a random handful, before zipping both bags closed and tossing them into the back seat. I slam the doors and the boot shut, and nod to Jude, who shoves the keys in his pocket and stares at me. "Now what?"

I give him a tight smile, showing him the handful of drugs. "Now I go get someone's attention."

He frowns. "I'm coming with you."

"No, you're not." I shake my head. "You're going to stay here, safe. And wait for me. I won't be long."

He glares at me. "Rue, I'm coming with you. You're hurt. What if something happens?"

I sigh. "Nothing's going to happen. I'm just going to find this Damien and ask him a couple of questions."

"Right." He lets out a humourless laugh, "Because drug dealers just love to answer questions. Oh, and I don't work with addicts or anything. Yeah, I won't be useful at all."

I glare at him for an angry few seconds, then give in. "Fine. Follow me then. Bring the gun. But stay a bit behind. Okay? Happy?"

He frowns at me a moment, then just shakes his head, leans in and grabs the gun from the glove box, tucking it into his belt. I shove the drugs in my pocket, straighten my sunglasses and pull up my hood; then head out of the lane, across the street and into the park.

Ringsend has changed a good bit lately. It used to be a fishing village, some of the old cottages still standing in neat rows along Pigeon House Road. Then, in the 70's it turned rough, with criminal gangs dealing in the drug trade fighting over these streets so close to the docks. In the boom years it changed again, got cleaned up and built up; shiny new high rises towering over tiny old cottages. And now it's begun a slow decline again, new gangs moving in, dealing drugs new and old from street corners and pubs.

It's toward one of those pubs I head, cutting across the park, my shoulders hunched against the bright grey sky above, each step stabbing through every joint. In the state I'm in; weak, hungry, tired, and hurting; limping, hugging broken ribs, my skin pale and bruised, I look a lot like a junkie—and I'm about to take advantage of that fact.

With Jude trailing me, I leap over a low wall and cut across a narrow street into a dark pub. A rush of relief washes over me as I get out from under the light of day. Hurrying in, I duck into a snug at the back, where I sit, bouncing one knee, shifting my weight, and looking around like I want something.

It takes less than a minute for the barman to come over. "You can't be here."

I duck my head and shuffle a bit, back and forth, feigning nervousness. "I'm looking for Damien."

He snorts, and picks me up by the collar of my jacket, shoving me out the door. "I don't care if you're looking for the devil himself, you're not looking here!"

I bristle and tense, but then let myself be manhandled, keeping up the act. I mutter and whine protests, making sure I holler Damien's name a few times as he shoves me out the door.

The door slams in my face, just as another nauseating wave of vertigo crashes over me. I reach out and grab the side of the building, waiting for it to pass, which it does, as Jude comes walking up. He meets my eyes, dark worry in his own, but I shake my head, and walk away, down the street, heading for the next pub. Jude stares after me a moment, then walks into the pub I just left. Well, 'left' is putting it gracefully.

Hunching up once more against the day, I shuffle down the street and turn the corner, making sure I'm seen. A few youths yell out obscenities and whistles, and some go running by me, jumping out at me as they pass, but I ignore them. I'm hunting bigger prey.

The next pub is far too trendy, so I pass it by, but the one after is promisingly dingy, and has the infinitely creative name of 'Ringsend Bar' under a 'For sale, with licence' sign. I shove through the double doors. It's lovely and dark. No snugs here, only an old oak bar and a half-dozen well-worn tables. The few patrons within look up at me as I enter, and then back to their pints, completely disinterested. Good.

I walk to the bar and nod to the barman, who comes over slowly, not seeming too bothered.

"All right?"

I sniff and look around before answering, pretending paranoia. "I'm looking for Damien."

The barman shrugs, wiping the already as-clean-as-its-going-to-get counter and looking sideways, then back at me. "Damien? Don't know him."

Lying. Good. This is the place. I pout at him with an impatient sigh, adopting as non-threatening a posture as I can. Only a junkie, and a girl at that. Not dangerous at all.

"Come on. They said I could find him here. I've got something for him. Okay?"

He stares at me a moment, then nods across to a table in the back. "Wait over there."

He takes out his mobile and I shuffle to the table, sitting down with a sigh that I don't have to exaggerate. Everything aches, and the blood I had earlier isn't doing anything at all under the light of day. Hunger stirs in my gut, cold and hollow. I stifle a groan and clench one fist into my abdomen, shoving the thing inside back down; pushing back at its insistent whine in my head. Not now.

The barman hangs up the phone and gives me a nod. "Out back."

That was fast. I nod back, standing up again, all my limbs protesting at the movement. Biting back pain, I head to the back just as Jude walks in the front. Good timing. Hesitating just long enough to make sure he sees where I'm going, I put my sunglasses on again and push through the back door.

Instantly I'm accosted by a tall, skinny, blonde boy in a blue and white tracksuit, who grabs me by the shoulders, turns me around and shoves me hard against the wall of the pub doing a very poor imitation of frisk search, missing the drugs in my pocket, but taking the opportunity to cop a quick feel. Anger flares in me, but I shove it down with all my will, feigning fear as he jerks me back around to face him.

"Who the fuck're you?"

"I need to talk to Damien. I've got something for him."

"Oh yeah?" He looks me up and down. "What've you got?"

I sniff, straightening my jacket and sunglasses. Can't let him see my eyes. I can feel them blazing with need and rising fury. "I want to talk to Damien."

Tracksuit sniffs and shrugs, shoving his hands in his pockets. "Damien's not here. You can talk to me."

Nice try. "No. Only Damien."

He smirks. "Yeah? You sure about this now?"

I nod, shifting my weight to one hip and shoving my hands in my pockets in mimicry of his own stance. He doesn't notice, but the act tips the scales in my direction.

With another shrug he turns away, gesturing me to follow. "Come on then!"

I follow him across an eighteenth-century courtyard that has changed little since. The crumbling outbuildings of a long-abandoned manor house enclose a courtyard filled with bins and tyres, boxes and crates, rusted parts of cars and less identifiable things. Stray cats peek out suspiciously from the shadows; freeze, stare, and disappear. At the rear of the courtyard is an ancient weeping willow, and beside it, a tiny church, done in neo-gothic style; its stained-glass windows broken, its iron cross bent and swinging from the steeple.

Tracksuit gestures me into an old building opposite the back entrance of the pub. It looks like it was once the kitchen, with a big wooden door opening onto the courtyard and a faint smell of grain, wine, mould and damp. It's blessedly dark; only one dim lamp hanging overhead, and I can't help breathing a sigh of relief.

Inside, seated around an old oak table—on which there are a scales, a handgun, and hundreds of plastic baggies of the same drugs I have in my pocket—are two more men. Young men. Early twenties at best. Tracksuit nods to the darker of the two and slides the doors shut us as the shorter man slowly stands up. All of this is supposed to scare me, I realise.

But I'm sick of playing scared.

I reach up and remove my sunglasses, tucking them into my inside pocket, no longer caring what these assholes might see. "Which one of you is Damien?"

The darker one starts. "Jesus Christ, look at her eyes!"

The shorter of the two looks over at him with a sneer. "Chill. It's only contacts." He turns to Tracksuit Boy behind me. "What the fuck is this?"

Tracksuit shrugs and backs up a couple of steps, and the shorter one leers back at me and repeats his friend's earlier query. "Who the fuck're you?"

I smile, taking a couple of steps toward him. "It doesn't matter who I am. What matters is what I want."

Both men look at me incredulously for a moment, then the shorter one laughs, and they all follow suit. As the laughter dies down, the shorter one—must be Damien—takes a few steps closer, his hands curling into fists.

"Oh yeah?" He licks his lips and trails his gaze up and down my body, then he laughs again, leering. "So what do you want then, you crazy junkie bitch?"

His eyes are too bright, his forehead glistening with a sheen of sweat, and I can smell a sweet, heady aroma oozing from his pores. Cocaine.

This boy is high as a kite.

I smile. "I want to know where you get your gear."

His leering smile fades, replaced by a look of suspicion. "What?"

I take another step toward him, until we're only inches apart, and nod toward the table. "Those drugs. I want to know where you get them, and who you get them from."

His heartbeat thunders hard in my ears, driven by the drug in his veins. Hunger flares up again, strong and fast—and the thing inside begins to whine. Insistent. Needful.

I listen to it.

The darker boy at the table looks nervously back and forth between me, Damien, and Tracksuit Boy, licking his lips. Damien for his part looks menacing. He puts his right hand in his jacket pocket, his fingers curling around something. I follow the movement with a glance. See the outline of a knife. Stupid boy. He still doesn't see me as a threat. He grins over to his mates, then back, laughing, trying to distract—then he moves. I see it coming, but I let him play, the thing inside me rising in delicious darkness; waiting, stalking. Relishing the game.

He jerks out the knife and presses it against my face with one hand, while with the other he shoves me back against the wall, hard. I feel my wounds open and start to bleed again as he sneers at me.

"Oh Yeah? Why don't we talk about what I want, bitch!"

Just then, through every fibre of my body, I feel the sun sink beneath the horizon. I shudder as day-drain fades and power returns to my limbs. Yes. The thing inside whispers sweet want and I let it—loving that familiar pull in my jaw.

Leaning my head in toward his, I give him a slow grin. "I don't think so."

His eyes widen at what he sees, and I move, gripping his palm and bending his hand back until his wrist snaps. He screams and the knife clatters to the floor. I throw him to the ground as the taller one lunges across the table for the gun. He never reaches it. In the next second I'm there, grabbing it up and striking it hard against the side of his head. He crumples backwards to the floor and doesn't get up. I spin around to Tracksuit Boy, who is sprinting for the door, and cut him off mid-stride, pressing the muzzle of the gun against his forehead.

"Don't."

Damien is whimpering on the floor, nursing his broken wrist. I smile to Tracksuit Boy as he slowly backs away to the far wall, then move back around to face my wounded prey.

He stares up at me, his face gone very pale. "What...what do you want?"

"I told you. I want to know where you get your drugs."

He stares, shaking his head and licking his lips. "What?"

I take a step closer. "Your supplier."

He shakes his head, swallowing and cradling his hand against his chest. "I don't know what you mean."

I smile. I can smell his fear, feel his drug-addled confusion, hear his heart beating hard, and Tracksuit Boy's as well, as he backs into a corner, blubbering. Their pounding rhythms stumble over each other. Hunger builds in me with each delicious beat, and the thing inside begins to purr in expectation. I walk across to the table, shoving a bag of miscellaneous pharmaceuticals around with the barrel of the gun. "These drugs. That you sell."

Putting my left hand in my pocket, I pull out the handful of the drugs I stole from the demon on the roof. "Just like these. I want to know who you get them from."

I move in a slow circle around the table, then back to stand above him again, tossing the baggies down around him. He winces and tries to back away, but he's already against the wall. I squat down in front of him, meeting his eyes.

"I'm waiting."

He closes his eyes, setting his jaw against what must be a very painful injury, and then looks up again. "Fuck you."

Wrong answer.

The thing inside howls in triumph as I give it full control. Yes. I drop the gun and attack, picking him up and slamming him hard against the wall. Jerking his head back by his hair, I sink my fangs deep into his throat, where the flow is strongest. He cries out once, then falls limp in my grasp as I drink deeply. Gods. Yes.

His blood spins into me in a scarlet current, hot and sweet and good. So good. I shudder and swallow, releasing my hunger, relieving my thirst, as I sink down with him to the floor. More. The fresh blood surges through me, healing me, sending me floating. Yes. A storm of emotion pounds into me with every pulse, his fear and drug-fed bliss spicing every mouthful. His heart beats hard against mine, pulsing, struggling; every beat for me. Only for me.

Moaning, I knead his arms, his chest, as his heart pounds frantically, then falters. More. The coke hits then, cool fire blooming through my veins, mingling with the warmth of the blood-high. Sweet gods. I pull him into my arms, wringing and pressing his flesh until the beat is no longer steady, the pulsing stream no longer flowing. More. His heartbeat slows, stumbles. More. Reeling with want, I drink until I am swinging, warm and flushed. Until there is no more to take. I shudder and sigh as the thing inside grows quiet, settling into contented silence.

Thought returns, slowly at first, then in a rush of awareness, and I gasp up, letting my prey fall to the floor. Someone makes a small sound, and I look around, momentarily confused—and then I see.

Jude is there, eyes dark. He has the gun I gave him in one shaking hand, and he is pointing it at Tracksuit Boy, who is still cowering in the corner. Across the room the other, darker boy lies in a crumpled heap by the table, pale and still and bleeding from his nose and ears—and beside me, on the floor, not breathing, blood dripping sluggishly from two deep puncture wounds at his throat, is the dealer. Damien.

Comprehension comes crashing, and I push myself away, only to stumble and fall, still dizzy with blood and coke. No. No. I shake my head, looking from Jude to the dealer and back again in vain denial of the truth.

"No...I didn't mean..."

Shit. Shit shit shit!

With a cry, I lift Damien by the shoulders, holding his head, biting down hard into my own wrist, and placing the warm flow over his lips.

"Comeon comeon comeon..."

Even as I try I know it won't work. His face is slack and grey, his pulse non-existent. He's too far gone. I've killed him.

After a minute of trying, I let him go, and stand up again, letting my blood spill to the floor as my wrist heals. Bitter shame rises to drown me, shame that spins outward into blinding fury. With a roar I turn on Tracksuit Boy; lifting him up by the throat and shoving him hard against the far wall. I hear his ribs crack, hear him scream, feel the warm trickle as his bladder releases—and then Jude is there, shouting and pulling at me, but I don't care. I snarl at the boy as he blubbers and begs.

"Where do you get the drugs? Tell me! Where do they come from?"

He gags and chokes out the words as he pulls in vain against my grip. "The old glass factory, the bottle house, down Pigeon House Road! Some guys there, big guys, a gang, I don't know, we always just meet them at the gates—please, please don't kill me!"

I tremble with rage, holding him there, furious—at the demons, at myself, and at him as he sobs and begs for his life, which I want so much to take. Then Jude whispers my name, and I look to see the love in his eyes clouded by fear and sorrow.

Shit.

I let go, and the blubbering boy falls to the floor, gasping and crying. I stand above him, leaning my forehead against the wall. Shit shit shit. I didn't want this. Ever again.

But here it is.

Leaning down, I pick up the still weeping boy with one hand, push his head back with the other, bare fangs, and bite carefully into his jugular, keeping a firm grip on myself. He shudders and goes limp against me, and Jude calls out my name harshly, but I ignore him. This has to be done. I close my eyes and take one deep shuddering drink. Enough to make room. Then I pull away.

Still holding him up with one hand, I bite into my wrist once more and place the wound hard against his mouth, giving him a little shake.

"Drink."

He comes to, his eyes growing wide as he obeys, his lips closing around the wound. At first, he licks at the blood cautiously, then he drinks with more force. I let him take a few gulps, then pull away, holding him back as my wrist heals, watching. waiting.

It doesn't take long, weak-willed as he is. He shudders, licking his lips and staring at my wrist—then he looks up to me, his pupils wide, eyes filling with worship.

I let him go. "Stay there. Stay quiet."

He nods vigorously and stands up against the wall, watching every move I make as I walk across to the gun I dropped, then stand over Damien's lifeless form. Taking aim, I fire twice; once into his chest and once into his neck, the shots reverberating loudly in the confined space, the bullet to his neck obliterating any trace of a bite wound. Then I walk over to the darker boy, stand back a metre or so and fire two shots into his chest. He was dying anyway, but I still feel like shit.

Rubbing the gun clean with my t-shit, I walk back over to Tracksuit boy and place it in his hand, pressing his fingers firmly around it, and holding his gaze, force a smile I don't feel.

"I need you to do something for me."

He nods, smiling back. "Anything."

"After we leave, you're going to call an ambulance. You're going to wait here until they come and you're going to tell them that Damien—" I gesture across to the gang leader's body, "—went crazy, accusing you and him—" I gesture to the darker boy, "—of stealing."

Tracksuit nods, hanging on my every word as I continue.

"Tell them that Damien first hit, then shot your friend there." Again I nod across to the darker boy. "And that he was going to shoot you, but you got the gun from him and you shot him in self-defence. Okay?"

"In self-defence." He nods again, only wanting to please.

"Good." I give him another smile. "You're going to tell them, and the cops, and anyone else this. And you won't ever mention myself or my friend being here." I motion to Jude.

He shakes his head. "You were never here."

I smile and pat his shoulder. "That's right. Thank you."

He nods, and keeps nodding, whispering my instructions to himself as I step away, tug my hood up, put my sunglasses back on and look to Jude.

"Let's go."

He blinks, his face pale with shock, but I don't wait. Leaving the muttering boy and the bodies behind, I walk out of the building, back through the pub, where the patrons are pretending they didn't hear a thing; back out into the street and on across the park to the car.

The sky is fading from muted grey to indigo, and the fresh blood speeds through my veins, healing me further as I wait by the car. After a few minutes, Jude comes up and hands me the keys without a word. I unlock the car, duck into the driver's side, slam the door, and sit there, shaking.

Jude gets in the passenger side, frowning and concerned. "You okay?"

I can't believe he's asking me that, and sorrow rises in my chest at his question, smothering anger and causing tears to burn behind my eyes. The cocaine high fades as my body absorbs it and the chemical depression that follows only adds to my guilt.

I shake my head, trying to get that anger back. Trying, and failing. "No."

Swallowing hard against suffocating self-loathing, I stare straight ahead, reaching up and splaying my fingers out across the steering wheel, staring at the paleness of my skin. I have to be honest. This isn't a bloody fairy tale. I'm a monster. A killer. No matter how hard I try not to be. And it's high time Jude knows it.

"I'm sorry. Sorry you had to see that, so sorry that I did it. But it's done. It's done and I can't take it back." My voice breaks against the last word, and I stop, unable to continue.

Jude looks over, shaking his head, his eyes rimmed with tears. Then he reaches to wrap my hand in his own, his skin so dark against mine. We sit in silence for a moment, as the night gathers around us. Then a police car wails by, followed by another, the lights and sirens splitting the night and the moment in two; and I shove my sorrow and shame down into the darkness of my heart and start the car, wheeling out of the lane and down the road to Pigeon House Road, and the abandoned glass factory.

Chapter 38

Judgement

L ilitu's smile turns triumphant, her eyes glinting brightly as she
continues her tale.

"I helped the survivors of the deluge on into the night, and further
still, until a red sun rose in the east, and the unnatural night paled toward
day.

"Then exhaustion fell over me like a coverlet, and I left to find shelter.
There were caves among the hills surrounding the valley, hidden deep in
the shadows of the rock, and I made my way toward one I knew well. The
night grew pallid as I walked, although no true day broke through the acrid sky; still, I was glad when I found the cave untouched by the flood and
made my way into cool darkness. Sheltered, safe ... yet not alone."

She pauses, and I lean in, enthralled as she carries on.

"As I travelled deeper into the cave, I heard the unmistakable sound of
someone breathing. Sharp gasps of fear and pain that echoed in ragged
whispers around the rocky tunnels. Intrigued, I made my way further in,
to find a huddled shape, half-hidden against a curving rock. As I drew
near, I saw that it was one of those who had hunted me the night before.
And he was dying."

The clouds once again lift their veil from the face of the moon, casting
her in soft blue light as she continues.

"I could smell his blood and fear as I circled him, watching him struggle against his fate. Anger stirred in my breast, as I recalled the way he

and his companions had hunted and harried me across all the land, how they had wounded me and driven me into the dawn."

"Indeed, if it were not for the intervention of the gods, this one and his ilk would have ended me, and for no more reason than their fathers had sought to do the same, and their fathers before them. The injustice burned in my mind, and I moved closer, baring fangs and thinking to take his life as payment for my suffering—when a thought arose in my mind; a thought that had never occurred to me until that moment."

Once again, she turns those glittering eyes upon me.

"I cannot say, even to this night, how I came to the thought— it was as if some other birthed the idea within my mind—but there, in that hillside cave, standing over the dying form of one who had so tormented me, it came to me, pure and perfect in its simplicity."

She holds my gaze to her own, her eyes growing dark as above us the moon hides her face once more, casting us both in shadow.

"I would take his blood even as mine was taken, and give him the dark curse in recompense. It was so easy, so obvious, why had I not thought of it before? The dark god whom I had unmade was bound by my words to a prison of flesh. To me. That was true. But the spell said nothing of there being a single prison. A prisoner can be moved and yet remain a prisoner. It is simply the cage that changes. At that moment, I laughed aloud. After centuries of searching, of working, of yearning for release, I had found it. And in the unlikeliest of circumstance."

She smiles darkly and after a moment, carries on.

"At first, I did not know how I would do this, or if I even could. But dark purpose moved in me, and, even as I doubted, showed me the way. A vision passed before my eyes, and I recalled the moment of my making as if it had only just come to pass; the laughter of the demon as he tore open my throat, the horror as my blood poured from me into the mouth of the blood-black storm, the torment and terror as that same storm poured into me like a living thing, changing me, remaking me. And as I remembered, I knew. As it had been done to me, so must I do."

I watch her closely as she stares into the past.

"I wasted no time in the doing. Before the hunter took his next gasping breath, I was upon him. He cried out and tried to fight me, to no avail, as I wrapped him in my arms and buried my fangs in his throat, drinking quickly, deeply; taking his life even as mine was taken. I sank to the ground with him in my arms, and drank until his heart fell silent; until the flow of his blood slowed to less than a trickle. Only then did I lift my head, letting his cooling body fall heavy against my breast."

"I waited a moment as his blood sped through me, watched as he began to die...and then I bit into my own wrist. I let my blood pool to the surface a moment before pressing the wound to his lips."

She looks to me once more, a shadow in her eyes.

"I did not know what to expect in that moment. A storm, thunder and lightning together, the hand of the gods turned toward me as the curse lifted. I was prepared for any of these. But not for what followed."

She pauses, and though I recall the moment of my making as if it were yesterday, and so know some of what she will say, still, I hold my breath to hear it said.

"At first, nothing happened. The hunter lay in my arms, still and dead as my blood spilt over his lips and down his chin. Then, all at once, his lips parted, and he let out a breath—then he grasped my arm and began to drink. Slowly, at first, then deeply, desperately."

A dark smile plays across her lips.

"Having never been fed from before, I was not prepared for the feeling. It overcame me, that sweet-swinging heaviness, and before I knew what had happened, I had fallen to the floor of the cave, weak and trembling. It was all I could do to pull myself from his grasp."

Her gaze grows distant and dark as she carries on.

"He fell silent then, and as I pulled myself up to lean against the stone, I watched. Waiting. Wondering what I had wrought."

She glances at me once more, then quickly away, a tremor in her voice.

"I could not have known what was to follow. The hunter drew a rasping gasp of air—and then he began to scream and shudder, his limbs thrashing against the hard stone, again and again, his spine arching backwards, as if to break. I was terrified, and pulled myself back against the far wall, watching as the curse worked through him, filled with growing sorrow at what I had done."

Looking down, she takes my hand, twining her fingers through mine as she has so often done.

"So distracted was I by the horror of his pain, I noticed nothing else. Until his screams abruptly fell silent, and I felt my own hunger pulling in my gut, and my fangs press sharp against my lip. I was unchanged."

She grasps my hand tightly.

"I lost myself then in a way I had not in centuries. Fury and denial mingled with need, and I attacked him again, taking my blood from his body and then feeding him once more, willing myself to stay awake, whispering words of power, all I could recall from the night of my own making."

"Again, I was made weak from the loss of blood, and again as I watched, he thrashed and screamed, begging, pleading against the curse. And yet I remained the same. And so again I took from him, more this time, until I was thick and bloated with his blood."

"Once more I fed him from my wrist, this time screaming those words of power, willing the curse upon him with all my might. I fed him until I fell to the ground beside him, drained and trembling. He screamed and flailed, begging, pleading for release, and I closed my eyes, praying for the same."

She pauses, her face pale and stained with blood tears, swallowing hard before she continues.

"I think I lost consciousness then, and for how long I do not know; only that when I awoke it was to a burning hunger, and an empty cave. The hunter was gone, but the curse was not. I remained as I was, demon, monster, unchanging and eternal. The curse had not been lifted; only multiplied."

"I cried out then, screaming my grief into the night, until I had no more voice to scream. And then, I dragged myself up and out of the cave. Into my endless night, to hunt, to feed...and to find the one I had made."

She turns then, and as I meet her gaze, I see the past slip from her eyes. It takes me a moment to realise her story is told. I am left hanging on her last words, trembling with questions that pour from my lips.

"What then? Did you find him? What happened when you did? Was he angry? Please, Lilitu, tell me!"

She sighs and stands, brushing sand from her linens as if she had not just shown me a hundred hunters at the gates; had not just told me that my maker once was one of them.

"Yes, Daughter, I found him. All I had to do was follow the trail of destruction wrought once more by my hand, even if that hand was extended through another's actions. And yes, when I found him, he was angry. But more than that, he was confused, hurting; lost in what he had become. As you once were."

She smiles softly.

"And, just as I taught you, I taught him, telling him all I knew of what he had become, all that I had learned over the centuries."

She walks the few feet to the water's edge and stares out across its dark expanse once more.

"For a long while Alu despised what he had become, and hated me for what I had done to him. But, eventually, he came to see that it was as much gift as curse."

"He was stronger, faster, more powerful than any warrior in all the lands. This pleased him greatly, and thus seemed to outweigh any grief he might have felt at the taking of life to feed the hunger within. He was, after all, a hunter, and a hunter he remained."

She gives me a wry smile.

"I learned as much from him as he did from me. He taught me the skills of battle; from spear and dagger to bow and barehanded combat. All of those things your brethren have taught you, Alu taught us first."

She walks back over her smile growing softer.

"We travelled together across all the lands, moving from village to village as the people rebuilt. We hunted together, sheltered together, and gradually, learned to love one another, in our own way. For the first time since my making, I was not alone. And it was good."

"Surviving the hunters and the deluge taught me the importance of having a haven, an enduring shelter; near enough to men that we could hunt freely, yet also difficult for any mortal to find. We searched for centuries for such a place, until we came at last to those same caverns near the city of your birth. The place of your making."

I stare up sharply at that—and she nods, answering my question before I ask it.

"Yes, Daughter, it was Alu and I who first discovered those winding caves, we who walked those tombs of kings long dead, and it was I who found and repaired that tapestry you so love."

She smiles back out across the rippling water as she carries on.

"In those early nights, your city was little more than a mud-walled village. The great empire of your people was not even a dream. And yet, as they always do, people began to build and build again, stronger walls and higher temples. Until village begat city, city begat kingdom and kingdom begat empire. And all this we watched, as time went on without us. Or perhaps, despite us."

She moves away then, from the river's edge, extending her hand.

"Come, Asharru. The night is short, my tale is done. We must make haste if we would make our escape before the dawn."

I stand and take her hand without thought, distracted by the thousand questions that spin through my mind, trying to discern which I should voice. We walk in silence for some time, until three questions push in front of the rest to escape my lips.

"But what of the others, what of my brethren? When were they made? Was it the same with each?"

She shakes her head.

"Those questions are not mine to answer, daughter, nor shall I. If you must know, then you can ask your brethren yourself, and perhaps they will answer. Once we are safe away from this city, and those who would destroy us."

Heaviness builds in my chest and settles around my heart. I can ask, but I do not think I will get the answers I seek. None of the others have been as forthcoming as Lilitu. Especially not Alu, whom I am certain hates me more with each passing night. I nod and walk on across the sand, with a sigh.

"I will tell Ku-aya to make ready what possessions she can carry."

"No." She stops me, mid-stride, her pale hand grasping my arm. "The girl cannot come."

"What?" I turn back to face her, anger rising. "Why not?"

"Think, child. She is a mortal woman. We must flee, tonight. We must move like the wind to be far enough away by dawn that these hunters will not find us."

I shake my head.

"I will not leave her. Not to an army of soldiers, ready to conquer, to take what they will." The grief of the loss of my city, of my mother, of my own life rises to my mind; the memory strong and sudden as I glare at her. "I will not leave her behind."

She stares back at me, for a lingering moment, a certain softness in her face. I think perhaps she will hear me, permit me to bring the mortal girl I have grown so fond of, but then her face grows stern, even cold.

"No. I am sorry, Daughter, but leave her you must. You have not the strength yet to carry her, and I cannot carry you and her both, should the need arise."

There is a tone to her voice, a mocking shadow behind her eyes, and I know she refers to the journey from my city to this one, so long ago now, reminding me of my weakness and shame. Cold anger rises in my breast, and I step close to her, spitting sudden fury.

"The need will not arise. Far be it from me to ask for help from you! Leave, if you will! I will find my own way from this place, I will keep Ku-aya by my side, and none of you shall stop me!"

She smiles, unaffected by my outburst. "Go then. Do what you will. As you always do."

I barely hear her words as I turn away in a rage, speeding back over the shifting sands.

The image of the waiting army of hunters spins in my mind, along with Ku-aya's sweet trusting smile. I cannot leave her here to die, I will not. Tears rise to my eyes as old memories mingle with new fear. Marauding men that raze and rape, shadows in fire and smoke, my mother and sisters ravaged. No. I will never let them take her.

I do not even know what it is that I will do until I reach the city gates.

Lilitu's words echo in my mind. Do as I will. As I always do. Even as she has done. She chose to make Alu, and chose me for him to make. A choice made and a new life given. And then, I know what I will do. What I must do. I stop, just inside the gates, my anger fading in the face of the choice I am about to make. Yes. I will make Ku-aya like us. Like me. I will change her, save her as I was once saved.

It is the only way.

Chapter 39

Human and Not

The sun is well and truly set by the time I wheel the car into Pigeon House Road, heading east toward the docks and the dark expanse of sea.

Jude has been silent the whole way down, his eyes dark, his lips set in a thin line. I can tell he's worried, and I know he's probably in shock from all that's happened, and afraid. Afraid of me. A familiar ache settles in around my heart, but I don't have time to deal with it right now. Right now, I have to find Grace and get her back.

I take a quick left a street before my destination, avoiding the new roundabout that would drop me right onto the main road that borders the old glass factory; opting instead to go around the long way, deep into the industrial docklands that straddle either side of the river.

Parking the Merc in the relative shelter between two sleeping juggernauts, their trailers stacked with containers ready to move in the morning, I shut off the engine, then turn to Jude.

"Give me the gun."

He pops open the glove compartment and hands it over, frowning as I check how many bullets are left in the magazine.

"What're you going to do?"

Satisfied that there are eight bullets left, I slide one into the chamber before handing it back to him.

"First, I'm going to head over there and take a look around. Then I'll decide what to do."

He frowns down at the gun, then back at me. "I'm coming with you."

"No, you're not."

"Rue—" He starts to argue, but I cut him off.

"No. I need you here."

"But I can't do anything from here!"

I shake my head. "You wouldn't be able to do much out there, anyway. You won't be able to see, not well, and I'll be moving fast. You won't be able to keep up."

He glares across at me, eyes angry and afraid all at once. "I can't just sit here."

"Yes, you can." I give him a tight smile. "I need you to. I need to know you're safe. Okay? Use the gun if you need to. Aim for the head. And if I'm not back in half an hour, get the hell out of here."

With that, I stand up before he can argue anymore, or change his mind and follow. Running as fast as I can, I break the chain of a nearby gate, ducking into the maze of the shipyard beyond, zigzagging toward the old factory road.

Row upon row of shipping containers rise above me, in double and triple stacks, blotting out the dim glow of the city. There's a chill in the air as a cool wind rises off the sea, and as I round the last corner it gusts against me, stirring my hair. As it does, I catch a scent, brief and familiar. Demons. So the boy wasn't lying. Good. But I'd better have a look before I leap. I climb up the dark side of the nearest stack of containers, keeping low as I reach the top and look out across the street to the lot.

The old glass factory was once the largest and most successful in Western Europe. An icon of industry, it employed thousands in the manufacture and supply of glass bottles of all shapes, colours and sizes. Now it's nothing more than a massive empty lot hidden behind a reinforced plywood fence and bolted metal gates, waiting for someone to come along and turn it into something else. It's been vacant long enough now that gorse, wild lilac and curling briars have colonised the edges, but I can see over them well enough to get a decent look inside.

Most of the larger buildings have been razed, with only a few outbuildings still standing. Some of those are on this end, but there are a couple of larger ones on the far side as well. All the buildings are dwarfed by massive piles of rubble and broken glass, scooped up by machinery and left until someone decides what to do with them. Which apparently someone has.

Demons, dozens of them, armed with containers of all sizes, are scooping up the broken glass and bucket-brigading it to the middle of the lot, where a huge pit has been dug—deep enough so I can't see the bottom from here. Bucket after bucket of broken glass is being poured into the pit, in streams of green, white, brown and blue, glinting dully in the streetlight. Under the scraping of buckets and the clinking of glass, I can hear a low male voice, muttering something I can't quite make out, over and over again, like a prayer.

I can't see who or where, and I've no idea what they're doing. But I'm betting whatever it is, it's not good.

And I'm going to have to get closer. Fast.

Leaning over the edge, I do a quick scan of the ground below before taking a deep breath against what I know is going to hurt, and jumping, soaking the landing into my knees. It's only forty or so feet this time, but the jolt still forces a whimper from my lips. I wince, hoping no one heard, and make a dash for the darkest section of the fence, tugging myself up, over and into the gap between it and the outbuildings beyond. I stop there, crouched low, one arm around my aching ribs.

The smell of demon is stronger here. Sickeningly strong. I can hear them, on the other side of the building, footsteps and voices close by and further away, hear the clink of broken glass filling bucket after bucket. I wait a moment, holding still as the wind rises again, stirring rubbish around my feet, listening as it howls low around the edges of the buildings beside me. And then, I catch it. Another scent, achingly sweet, then gone. Vanilla. Grace. Grace is here. Somewhere.

My heart catches in my throat as a deep ache that has nothing to do with broken bones or bruises wraps tight around my chest. I have to find her.

Standing up, I do a quick assessment of my surroundings. I'm in a long, narrow gap about a half a meter wide, where the old buildings don't quite meet the new fence. The space extends for several meters to my right, ending near a high metal gate. Beyond that is the wide-open lot, stretching out to the fence opposite. The wind dies down again, and as it does, I can hear a low steady humming, somewhere close—and something else. Someone crying. Very near. And very familiar. I heard that same sobbing in my house, three nights ago. Grace. She's here. But where?

The wind rises again, and this time carries voices in its wake. Male voices, more than a few, and the sound of footsteps and arguments echo across the lot, drowning out the sound of crying. Shit. Got to get closer. Frowning, I move along the gap, skirting piles of broken glass and battered wooden pallets left to rot. Near the last building, there's so much rubbish piled up I have to press myself against the brick wall to get by, and then I hear it again. That soft sobbing. Grace. She's there. Inside. Right next to me.

Closing my eyes, I lean my forehead against the rough brick and listen, focusing; blocking out all other sound. There. Crying, choking on a sob, crying again. My heart aches, and I open my eyes, looking up and around for a way inside. There are no windows on this side of the building, but in the dim light I can make out a space about twenty feet up, where the old aluminium roof has warped up and away from the brick. It's a tiny space, but it'll let me see in. As long as I can get to it.

Moving quickly, and being as quiet as I can, I scan the wall for finger holds, then, ignoring the protesting of my bruised limbs, begin to climb. It's easier than Babylon. The old bricks shift and some crumble under my weight, and I wince and climb faster.

At the top, I grasp the edge of the opening and pull myself up and over to the roof above. My still-wounded shoulder stabs as the tendons tear again, and I bite through my own lip to keep from crying out. I lie there for a moment, holding still. But no one comes. No shout of alarm, nothing.

Letting out a long breath, and keeping as low a profile as possible, I scoot back over to the edge, peering over it into the space between roof and wall.

It's dark inside. Very dark. It takes a moment for my eyes to adjust, and even then, I can't see inside that well. But I can hear. And smell. The scent of vanilla wafts up through the opening, tugging at my heart. Grace. But she's not sobbing anymore. Just breathing, fast and shallow. Terrified. She must have heard me climb up. I can hear her heart, pounding. And then she moves, and I see her.

She's sitting near the wall, only a little to the right of where I am. I hear the clinking of metal on metal. Chains. They've got her chained to something, but she seems otherwise unharmed. I don't smell her blood, only the sweet scent of her hair, underneath the stench of demon. What I can see, clear enough that it burns in my vision, is the salt circle that has been drawn on the stone floor around her, with various symbols at cardinal points. Magic. Keeping her in. Keeping anything else out.

She's staring wide-eyed into the surrounding darkness, and I suddenly realise that if I can barely see in there, then she can't see at all. They have her chained in the dark like an animal. My heart burns with anger, but there's no time to indulge it. I have to get her out of here and worry about killing the bastards who did this to her later. Leaning further forward, I take a breath to whisper her name, calm her down—but before I can, I hear voices and footsteps coming closer. Several pairs of them. Shit.

I pull back away from the opening as the door opens and slams shut, hard enough to shake the whole building, and I hear a male voice, soft and absurdly pleasant, greet her by name.

"Hello, Grace."

I hear her gasp, then hear footsteps move across the floor, and the clink of chains again. I have to see what's happening. I creep back toward the edge of the roof.

There's a dim light on in the room now, and I can see Grace, just below me. Her wrists are handcuffed to a trailing chain that's fastened to a hook in the stone floor, right in the centre of the chalk circle, and she's staring in shock at someone toward the front of the building; someone just out of my line of sight. Then that someone moves forward, and a snaking feeling of recognition trails up my spine and into my throat. It's the man from the photo in Grace's house. Thomas.

Grace echoes my thought aloud, confusion colouring her voice.

"Thomas?"

He moves further into the light, stepping right into the circle without hesitation.

"Sorry about the accommodation, dear. We've had to improvise." He smiles and moves closer, holding out his arms as if to embrace her. He looks the same as he did in the photo. Dark eyes, dark hair, greying at the temples, neatly trimmed facial hair, dark clothes. All in all, he is handsome and well put together. But there's something off about him.

Something not quite right.

He reeks of demon, for one, and the way he's walking and talking—I can't put my finger on it, but it's as if he's not entirely there. Apparently, Grace notices too. She backs away, as far as the chain will allow.

Frowning, I shift my weight and dare to scoot forward a bit more, trying to see who, or what else is in the room with them. I know more than one of them came in, but I don't know how many more, and no matter how much I crane to see further into the building, I can't, not without giving myself away. Fuck. I can't risk doing anything. Not yet.

I watch Grace as she gulps back her fear, her eyes darting back and forth between Thomas and whomever else is there as he tips his head to one side, talking to her like a parent to a bold child.

"You've given us quite a difficult time, Gracie. I am sorry that it had to happen this way. I never wanted to hurt you."

She swallows hard, and steps back until the chain that holds her is taut. "I don't understand. Why are you doing this? Why are you with these...these..."

"These Demons?" He finishes for her, throwing a glance back over his shoulder. "They are crass, I'll admit, but they are useful. Very useful." He smiles again, "Oh, Gracie, I have missed you."

Moving even closer, he reaches out and touches her cheek. She winces and tries to back away from him, but she has nowhere left to go, and can't fight against him as he leans in, grabs her by the hair, and kisses her roughly. Anger blazes through me so strong that I feel my fangs push against my lip. At the same time, the dagger in my jacket pocket presses uncomfortably against my chest. Damn the thing. I shift my weight and breathe. Have to stay calm. Just wait, and listen.

He pulls back, letting her go—and for a moment his eyes seem to absorb the light, as he bends his head to one side, considering. I blink and look again, but his eyes are normal. Human. What the fuck?

"What's the matter? You used to like it when I kissed you. At least you acted like you did."

He sighs and turns away, walking in a little half-circle around her, glancing back over his shoulder again at his companions as they snigger. I listen. There are at least two. Maybe more. I still can't tell, and I swear to god the dagger in my pocket is growing warmer by the second. But he's talking again, still pacing around her.

"They told me about you and the half-breed. Disgusting." He shakes his head at her. "Don't get me wrong, I'm fine with the lesbian thing. If you had wanted to bring a girl home, you should've told me. College is a time to explore after all...but a fucking leech?"

He whirls back around, slapping her hard across the face. My anger explodes to rage, and I clench my fists against the urge to burst through the roof and rip his fucking heart out. No. Stay calm. Breathe, Rue. Breathe, dammit. I shove my anger down and shift my weight again away from the dagger.

Below me, Thomas steps away again as Grace sinks to the floor, blinking back tears, one hand to her face. He straightens his jacket, frowning down at her.

"I am disappointed in you, Grace. Really, I am." He sighs. "But I guess it's not your fault. You always were so trusting. So naïve." He smiles again. "It's all over now, anyway. The leech is dead. And you're back where you belong."

351

Grace looks up at him, her eyes blazing through her tears. "Why are you doing this? What do you want?"

He grins. "That's simple, darling. I want your blood. To heal the world."

"What?" I think it as Grace says it, her voice shaking. "What do you mean?"

He sighs again. "I suppose it's only right you know. Now it's all come together. Where to begin?"

He starts pacing again, hands behind his back like he's giving a lecture. "As you may have figured out, I am something of a magician. Not the prestidigitation kind, mind—no, I mean, as I am certain you know, real magic. Sorcery. And I'm good at it. Like this circle, around you. I made it, to protect you. Nothing can get in or out, except me."

He glances at Grace as if she's supposed to say something. But she doesn't, and after a moment he goes on.

"Anyway, as I've told you, all my life, I could see far more of the world than anyone around me. Like you, I knew the world the way it really was; could see all the creatures within it, dead and alive, human and not. I also saw, from a very young age, the way mankind and their ilk have ruined this world."

He smiles, his voice coloured with the madness of extreme belief. "And I wanted to fix it."

There is a muttering of agreement from the demons behind him, and I listen, still trying to gauge how many there are. But I can't tell. Shit. The knife is now hot against my chest, and growing hotter by the second. Fuck. I clench a fist and try to arch my ribcage away from it as Thomas carries on.

"I tried so many things over the years. I studied history, mythology, all religions and superstitions. First, I tried to make things better on my own. After university, I became an activist, going around the world and protesting, volunteering for one cause after another. I've been arrested in six different countries. Did you know that? And all for standing up against injustice, standing against those who ravage and rape this planet and its poor. I tried to stop them. Tried to change things. But no matter how hard

I tried, things always got worse. When I got a bit older, I decided to teach, to try and influence the minds of the young, to guide them, to help them make the world better. But nothing worked. Most of my students just graduate and quickly become part of the problem. Creating more of a mess. More greed, more callousness, more damage." He sighs, shaking his head as he continues.

"Then I discovered magic. Real magic. Learning it let me bend the world, let me change reality with a word. Finally, I had control. And I was certain with magic I could find a cure. I studied all the texts, visited all the mystics, learned all the rituals and spells."

He smiles again, his eyes glinting in the semi-darkness. "Magic is a powerful force. Limited only by the physicality of the wielder. And I became a powerful magician."

He leans down in front of Grace, speaking to her like a father to a child. "Even so, I could not affect enough change. Oh, I could bend people to my will, and have done, on many occasions, but it wasn't enough. I still couldn't change enough. I needed more power. So, I decided to recruit." He starts pacing again, gesturing as if speaking to hundreds of adoring students instead of one tearful prisoner.

"I'd learned of groups of people who called themselves hunters; descendants of a family of humans with certain abilities—and decided to assemble my own team. Through my work as a professor, I got to meet a plethora of young, impressionable minds, and with my vision, I could choose those I deemed most helpful. And they were good. Really."

"It was great to have them around, to do the menial tasks, while I concentrated on the real work. I taught them how to see, really see; taught them how to track and hunt, all the while skimming their power from them, using it to fuel my own. But none were as strong as I'd hoped." He stops, looking at Grace. "And then I found you."

He walks to her again, leaning down and reaching a hand to cup her chin. She tries to pull away, but he holds her roughly there, his eyes flashing. "So beautiful. And so talented. With your vision, and your sight..." He sighs. "I'm going to miss you when all is said and done."

Rage blooms in me again as he pulls her close and kisses her once more, slowly. A slow pounding begins in my head. He lets go with a smile, not seeming to notice as Grace wipes her mouth, her eyes full of tears. I clench my fists and force myself to be calm as he continues.

"It's hard to believe it's only been a year since we met. So much has happened." He smiles. "It wasn't long after you came into my life that he came to me."

"I'd been communing with spirits for quite some time. But I'd never spoken to one so great. So powerful. The Master. A prince of demons. He told me what he was. What you were. What I could be. Then he told me what he needed me to do." He stops, letting out a low breath. "The power he showed me, Grace. The good I could do with it! I couldn't let it pass me by. So, I followed his instruction. And, once I'd invited him in, he taught me so much; gave me so much. And I gave back. Gave him my body to use when he wanted."

He frowns. "That took some doing. Giving it over without giving it up. But I raised the power. Drew him into my body, fed him with other souls instead of mine. It's a perfect arrangement. I have his power, and he has my magic. And of course, we had to make sure we had you."

Grace chokes back a sob, and speaks, her voice shaking with fear and grief. "What...what are you talking about, Thomas?"

He answers, speaking slowly, patronisingly.

"You, Grace, are special. So special. And I don't know how much that damn leech told you, but your blood is even more special. You see, Gracie, you have celestial blood. Angelic, for lack of a better word. Some believe Christ was an angel, do you know that? Of course, you do, how silly of me. You were my student after all."

He nods to her, in a sickeningly fatherly fashion.

"His blood saved all of mankind, so they say, and there is some truth in the myth. The bloodline you carry is more than flesh, more than cells and proteins. I don't pretend to know the why or how of it, but somehow celestial blood also carries an echo of the first moment. The first breath. The seed of creation."

He pauses a moment, squatting down until he's at eye level with her. "It's powerful stuff, Gracie. Very powerful stuff."

He stands up, pacing again. "I don't have time to tell you everything, and it's long and boring anyway, but suffice to say, this world is broken, and has been for a very long time. It's filthy, filled with things that are half-human, and with humans that have rejected every gift and opportunity they've been given. With your blood and my power, we can change this. We can make the world again. Make it better."

Gods. He's mad. A power-mad magician with his own personal gang of demons. Jesus Christ. Grace gapes at him, the expression on her face echoing my thoughts. But he doesn't seem to notice as he rants on.

"You won't be here to see it. Sorry about that. And while I'm at it, I'm terribly sorry about the way we had to go about getting you here. You see, we had to get rid of your guardian first."

He pauses expectantly, but she just stares up at him, completely confused. For that matter, so am I. He waits another few seconds, then rolls his eyes and continues talking, condescendingly.

"You should already know this, Grace. Every person has a guardian. Well, almost every person. Spirit, Angel, whatever. They come and they go, sometimes near us and sometimes not. But someone like you, someone so special—one of their own, so to speak—you are watched over twenty-four-seven. But there's a way around that."

He stops, smiling at her like he's waiting for a reaction, but she just keeps staring, and after a moment, he continues.

"We had to make you hate. They can't bear hate in a human. And you are still mostly human. It actually drives them away for a time. It's an anathema to them—like silver to werewolves or sunlight to vampires. Isn't that amazing? I figured that out months ago, but I never knew it would work so well!"

He grins at her.

"I had to feed the master more souls, and needed blood to call the others here, and I knew it would be the opportunity to give you something to hate. You'd been so obsessed with that vampire I thought she'd be the perfect focus. So I killed the rest of our little crew—they were useless any-way—and made sure to frame your vampire." He grins. "I still can't believe how well it worked! For a moment, you hated that leech. And that hatred drove your guardian away."

My heart sinks. It's all my fault. If I hadn't been so out of it all summer, hadn't been so sloppy in the first place, she never would've found me, and he wouldn't have had the opportunity to get to her. Fuck. Fuck! Guilt and shame rise in a choking storm and angry tears spring to my eyes. I shift my weight to wipe them away, and the knife singes into my ribcage. Shit. I pull away from it as much as I can without making noise, as he goes on.

"I wanted to grab you then. That was the plan. But someone royally fucked that up!" He throws a glare back over his shoulder again. "Anyway, it doesn't matter. It worked out fine. Better even. I used their bodies and their blood in a summoning ritual, to call the others to me, and they're all on the way. Soon, we can begin."

Grace blinks hard against her tears, her voice a trembling whisper. "Begin what?"

Thomas grins, and this time alongside the madness in his eyes swirls a sickening, light-absorbing darkness. His skin ripples, his lips stretching way too wide as his voice cracks and bends to a deep, vertigo-inducing, inhuman pitch. "Begin the ritual that will end in your sacrifice, my dear. We are very grateful to you, little angel. Your blood will make us whole again."

The demon that is somehow also Thomas grins, Grace cries out in fear and denial—and rage explodes through me like a hurricane, rising from my veins, deafening and drowning me in a swirling morass of fury that is not my own. The thing inside screams and screams until my head feels like it's splitting in two. I clench my jaw to keep from crying out and clasp my hands to my head, desperately trying to hold it together.

The knife in my jacket grows hotter until I can no longer stand it. Shit shit! I sit up, digging one hand into my pocket and wrenching out the scarf-wrapped bundle, letting it drop beside me on the roof as I lie back down, gasping, blinded by blood tears. It's all I can do not to cry out as I struggle to regain control over the wailing fury screaming through my head. It takes a good five minutes, during which I can't see or hear a thing, but gradually the screaming fades to a steady whine, the whine to a whimper, and the whimper to a whisper. Then, as swiftly as it came, it's gone—leaving me with a splitting headache, but in control again at least.

There's movement below, and the sound of chains being moved. Then the door opens and shuts and a new voice says something about someone coming, and then the Thomas-demon speaks again.

"Good. Let them in. Watch her. It's time to begin. What was lost will be returned to us."

More movement, and I hear the chains clinking, then the door opens again, and I scoot over to the other side of the roof, laying out flat so I can see without being seen, as the Thomas-demon leaves, accompanied by one other.

I watch as they walk across toward the centre of the lot. Several other demons are gathered around the edge of the glass-filled pit, watching, laughing, talking. I count a dozen. Too many. Have to think. Have to get Grace out of here.

Scooting back over to the hole in the roof, I peer in again as best I can. Grace is sitting back in the corner, her head in her hands, softly sobbing. I can't see past this side of the room, and they aren't making any noise but by my count there are two demons in there, watching her. Not to mention that fucking sorcerous boundary. I can smell the magic from here, and I've no doubt of its strength. No way I'm getting over that line, even if I could get rid of the demons guarding her without raising an alarm.

I pull away from the edge of the roof, trying to think past the pounding in my head.

I need a plan, and a good one. Something. Anything. I'm just running over possible options, and discarding every one, when I hear the distant rumble of a big engine out on the streets beyond. Not that unusual in this part of town, or even at this time of night, but as the sounds speed nearer, I can tell it's more than one truck. A lot more. And they're barrelling closer by the minute. A shout goes up from the demons inside, and I hear footsteps running toward the gate. The gate right beside me. Shit. If they see me, I'm dead.

Pressing myself down as flat as I can against the roof, I scoot back to the outer edge and watch as two of the demons unlock the gate and tug it open. The metal doors crash back against the fence with a deep metallic boom, and I hold my breath, as first one semi-truck, then two, enter the lot and drive in a slow circle around the edge. Half a dozen smaller lorries, vans and cars follow the semis in.

They drive around the inside fence before screeching to a halt, throwing up dust and rubble as the doors of each vehicle burst open to disgorge a flood of demons. Out of the cars and off the backs of trucks they climb, ugly and stinking, their stolen human bodies in various states of decay. There are a hundred at least, and all of them heading toward the centre of the lot, where Thomas stands triumphant, half-demon, half madman, holding court at the edge of the pit.

His last words echo around my head, as I watch the demons stream in. He said her sacrifice would make them whole again. Memory rushes back, to the tale at the edge of the Euphrates. Lilitu's tale. The beginning of it all.

The demon told her they'd been torn from their true forms. Made weak, powerless. Rooted to time and place. If they are made whole again, somehow—Jesus.

Lilitu saw one, whole. In this world. The one she cursed and remade. Into what she became. Into what I am. I remember the look in her eyes when she spoke of him.

This can't be happening.

Futile fury burns through me, my heartbeat racing in time with my pounding head. There're too many. I have to save Grace, have to stop them, but I can't see any way to do it that isn't suicide. I need to find some help.

No. Fuck that.

I need to find an army.

Chapter 40

Gift

A s I walk through the winding streets of Babylon, I ponder my decision, a curious excitement blooming within my breast. I can do this. I must. Ku-aya has been my constant companion for a decade and has served me well all the while.

Yes. I will give her this gift, and take her with me.

And yet, as I make my way up the hill to the house she and I share, a shadow of uncertainty haunts the edge of my conscience, whispering it is no gift I mean to bestow. When have I ever felt it so? Perhaps I should not do this. Perhaps there is another way.

No. As I open the gate and walk into the courtyard of our home, I shove all doubt angrily away. There is no other way. An army stands ready outside the city, men in their hundreds ready to rape and kill. I will not leave Ku-aya to that fate. I cannot.

Anticipation thrills through my veins, causing a quiver in my voice as I push through the wide brass doors and call out her name.

She answers from within and I find her in an inner room, making ready the bed she and I have slept in these past years. I say her name again, softly, and she turns with a giving smile. I take a moment to gaze upon her, this woman-child, so young. So innocent. Again, that shiver of doubt pulls at me, and again I push it away, down into the darkness of my heart.

Ku-aya still smiles, confused by my silence, and so I return the smile, taking her hand in my own and guiding her to sit beside me upon the bed.

"There you are. I wanted to find you, child. I must speak with you."

She nods and meets my gaze, her own so trusting.

"What is it?"

I squeeze her hand, noting how warm it is, feeling her blood pulse under her skin as I tell her what I have seen, of the vast army gathered near the city, of the band of hunters within that force, and of our need to swiftly flee.

She reacts much as I thought she would; as she always has since that first night she drank my blood. With pure obedience, not a thought for herself.

"Then we shall go. Wherever you wish. Tell me what you would take, and I will make ready."

She moves to stand, but I keep her hand, pulling her back.

"Wait."

Again, she obeys, sitting back down and looking to me expectantly.

This is the moment. I know it, know what I must do, but know not how to begin. What will I say? How will I tell her? I take a breath to speak—but she interrupts, her eyes soft and giving.

"Do you hunger, beloved?"

Relief pours through me, and I nod. She smiles, and lies down beside me, pulling her hair away from her shoulders, closing her eyes, and tipping her chin so that the pulsing river of blood is bare to my need.

It will be thus, then. No words at all. The familiar twinge of desire pulls in my gut and mingles with heady anticipation as I lean in, and softly, as so many times before, sink my fangs into the curve of her throat.

But this time is not like the others. The crimson tide floods into me, and I take it, drinking deeply each dark surge. Ku-aya shudders and sighs in my arms, sinking heavily down to the bed beneath me, and so I gather her into my arms, still drinking, more, and yet more—until her heart pounds in a desperate struggle, then falters and fades. Until I can feel her breath against my cheek no more.

Only then do I lift my head, licking my lips. Her blood thunders in my veins, and as I gaze upon her, so pale and still, I feel a stabbing of sorrow that pierces my very soul. I have killed her. She who has so loved me. Doubt crashes in once more, following sorrow, but I shove it away with a cry, biting down hard into my own wrist and placing the wound against her lips.

Moments pass like hours. What if this does not work? What if I cannot bring about the change? What if I am too young, my blood too weak?

No. It must work. I close my eyes and will it so, whispering a prayer to all gods, new and old, whether they hear me or no.

And then, her lips part and she begins to drink. Softly at first, and then more deeply, with a shuddering sigh.

I gasp with relief, and then with tingling pleasure as she reaches to grasp my wrist in both hands, drinking more, and still more. The room spins around us, and I sink into the silken softness of the bed linen, as my vision blurs and fades, my mind adrift.

Then that peace is shattered by a piercing scream, and as I come to my senses, I realise that I have fallen to the floor, and that Ku-aya is shrieking, her body writhing on violent spasms on the bed.

I get to my feet and stumble to her side, reaching to grasp her arms, her legs, anything, to hold her down. I am weak with the loss of blood; blood that now burns through her body. The memory of my own making flood back in a torrent; the searing pain beneath my skin, the seemingly endless suffering.

As I struggle to hold her, apprehension grows. I do not know how long this may take. Nor if it may take. Another memory, on the heels of the last; Lilitu saying 'Not many can endure the making.' What if Ku-aya is one who cannot?

Oh, gods. What have I begun?

Dread clutches cold fingers around my heart, and in growing desperation, I hold the girl hard against the bed and lean across her writhing form, baring fangs once more and drinking deeply from the crook of her arm.

As soon as I bite down her struggling ceases, as her blood once more pours into me. I drink recklessly, reeling between quickening flow and quivering fear. Again, I take all that I can from her, and more; until she is lying pale and still. Again, I sink my fangs into my own flesh, puncturing my wrist and pressing it to her lips. Again, she drinks, and I will myself to stay aware through the soft pleasure of her feeding. Long moments pass in sweet stillness—and then her body erupts in a frenzy of pain.

There are words this time, amongst the screams, and as I reach to wind the bedclothes around her limbs, binding her clawing hands and thrashing legs, she opens eyes filled with agony, and begs for release.

Once more, I recall the horror of my making; the torment, the voices in the dark. Words whispered at my making. But what words? I do not recall. And then I do. The curse from Lilitu's telling. Kneeling beside her shuddering form, I smooth her hair and whisper the words in my own tongue, the tongue we share. And then, as her suffering goes on, I whisper words of comfort, encouragement. Words of love. But she does not heed them, only screams and pleads, her voice ragged and breaking, her body writhing so I fear her bones will break.

I cannot bear this. Blood tears blind me as once more I lean over her, and once more bite down, this time at the bend of her wrist.

Again, she falls silent, as I drink, in great, shuddering draughts, until there is no more to take. For the third time then, I bite into my own wrist, drawing out the flow, and pressing it against her rapidly cooling lips.

This time there is no silence. At once, she drinks, so deeply that I am cast adrift in an instant. I fall on the bed beside her as sound and vision waver and fade and are drawn away into darkness.

Some part of me is aware of a roar like wind, or the sea pounding against a rocky shore, far away and fading, but I cannot bring myself out of the darkness that enfolds me to hear, and eventually, all sound and meaning slip away, until I too slip away. Into nothing.

Then comes pain, sharp and stinging, through the nothing—once, twice—and I am aware that Lilitu stands above me, her open hand raised to strike me again, her eyes dark and unreadable.

Seeing I am awake, she drops her hand and lets me go. I fall back onto the bed, too weak to move, my body heavy as lead, my heart pounding erratically in my breast. As I come back to consciousness, I see the bedclothes, torn and bloodied around me, the gilded curtains shredded into pieces. I blink and stare, trembling, not comprehending. Where is Ku-aya?

I struggle to sit up, my arms shaking. So weak. I reach to Lilitu for help, but she steps away from me. Grasping a bedpost, I pull myself to my feet and stand, gasping with the effort.

There is an eerie silence in the house, and as I stare around the room, I see that the tapestry I so love is torn from its place by the door, and the door itself hangs outward, half-broken from its hinges.

I hear sounds without; screams and cries in the streets beyond. I look once more to Lilitu, for aid, and answer, as I have always done. But she only shakes her head, her eyes dark; a stabbing disappointment in their depths.

"Oh, daughter. What have you done?"

Chapter 41

Heaven and Hell

As more and more demons gather in the centre of the lot, I scoot backwards again to the edge of the roof. Their voices and the revving engines blend into a dull roar, inducing a nauseating hammering in my head.

Fuck. I don't want to leave Grace, but I have to get back to Jude, and then—and then I don't know what. But I've got to come up with something. And I don't have much time. Gingerly, I reach for the knife to find it's cooled down some, but it's still warm, even through the scarf.

Shaking my head, I tuck it into my inside jacket pocket again and slip down off the edge of the roof, letting myself drop into the gap below. My battered joints twinge as I land on my feet, but I'm ready for it this time and manage not to cry out. My head is pounding so hard I have to close my eyes and lean against the side of the building. I can hear Grace inside, softly sobbing. I so don't want to leave her. But I have to. I have to find help, have to get her out of here to somewhere safe. And fast.

I move back down the narrow gap toward the shadowed bit of fence where I came in, wincing with every step. As I do, a loud cheer goes up from the demons inside.

Taking advantage of their apparent distraction, I leap to grip the top of the fence and throw myself back over to land on the street beyond. Can't stop. I run back to the shipyard, up and over that fence into the maze of containers and back to the gates, the car, and Jude.

He starts when I appear beside him, nearly jumping out of his skin as I tug open the passenger door and duck inside.

"Dammit, Rue, you scared the—" He stops himself as I lean forward, gripping my splitting head in both hands.

"Are you okay? What happened? Did you find Grace? What's going on?"

I hold a hand up to stop the flood of questions, each one sending a volley of pain ricocheting through my head. Shit. To top it off, I'm hungry again. My wounded body is using up the blood I had too fast. My fangs press hard against my lip, and all I can hear for a moment is Jude's thundering heart, and the blood cascading through his veins. The thing inside snakes awake and begins a needful, insistent whine as my mouth goes dry and my gut twists into knots.

No, no, no!

Biting back a groan I focus all my will on shoving it down and away. It takes a couple of minutes—that much more difficult to fight it after giving into it not so long ago—but I succeed. Just. The pain slowly fades to a bearable ache, the hunger dulls, and the thing inside falls silent. I sit up, leaning back against the seat with a sigh.

"I'm fine. And she's in there. Along with a hundred or so demons."

He listens with an expression of growing horror as I tell him everything I've just seen and heard. When I'm done, he swallows hard, his eyes dark.

"What can we do? Call the guards?"

"No. They'd be massacred. No cops. No humans."

He shakes his head. "Then what?"

I frown, trying to think. "I don't know. There's so fucking many of them."

Another jolt stabs behind my eyes and I rub at them, trying to think. I need to find help. A lot of help. My mind races, considering every possibility and rejecting it. I could go back to the sanctuary, could ask Antonio, but I don't trust him not to turn on me, or Grace, and besides, there aren't enough vampires in Dublin to make a dent in those demons, even if they would do me the favour of joining in my fight. Which they probably wouldn't. No. No good. And I don't know the other Others in this town well enough to go searching, never mind asking. Unless—

A glimmer of an idea arises, and I latch onto it, sitting up.

Jude looks at me. "What?"

I open the door and get out. He frowns.

"What is it?"

"No time." Pulling the front seat forward, I lean into the back and rummage through my bag until I come up with the phone Temi gave me. I check it. Still charged. Good. I push the seat back up and turn to Jude.

"Is your phone okay?"

He checks. "Yeah."

I move around to the driver's side, opening the door and waving him out.

"Good. Listen. I need you to do one thing while I'm gone." I nod to the broken gate in front of us and the freight yard beyond. "At the other end of that yard are some shipping containers. Stacked up. From the top, you can see into the lot.

"I need you to take the gun and climb up, carefully, and keep watch, okay? There's a bit of light in there, enough for you to see. Don't do anything. Just watch, be quiet, and stay low. They're all gathered in the middle now, doing whatever it is they're doing, and they won't notice you if you stay quiet."

I wave my phone at him. "You have this number. It's the one I called you from back at the hotel. Ring if you see Grace, or if there's any trouble. I'll be back as soon as I can. Hopefully with help."

I shove the phone into my pocket as Jude sits back, looks down at the gun in his hand, and back up at me. Then he nods, getting out of the car and shoving the gun in his belt.

"Okay."

"Thanks."

"What're you going to do?"

"I'm going to go ask someone I just met for a favour."

He sighs. "Hurry back."

"I will." I get in the car and start to tug the door shut, but he stops me.

"Rue?"

"Yeah?"

But he doesn't say anything, only stares at me a long moment. I wait, impatient. "What is it?"

He takes a breath, starts to say something, stops, starts again, then shakes his head, with a defeated smile. "Be careful."

I give him a quick smile back. "I always am."

With that I slam the door, start the car and wheel around, tires spitting gravel as I speed down Pigeon house road, through Ringsend and the Docklands and on, through the narrow streets of Irishtown and onto Bridge Street, down through Beggar's Bush and up, speeding the wrong way down one-way streets, but I don't care. Whatever's shorter.

It doesn't take me long. I screech the car to a halt outside Merrion Square Park, getting out and clearing the wrought-iron fence in a running leap, stopping only when I'm right in the centre of the tree-shaded green. Right where I was before. Only this time I'm not leaving so easily. I turn in circles, making my presence known. It might be dangerous, but I don't care. I don't have time for pleasantries. Raising my voice, I call out into the green darkness.

"Hello! Hey! Fairy boy! I'm back! Where are you?"

The park seems to grow darker at the sound of my voice. Above me, the trees whisper and rustle. But there's no sign of the green-eyed boy. Yet. I try again, louder. Ruder.

"Hey! I know you're here! Show yourself asshole!"

Silence. Dark green silence. Fuck. Maybe he's not here. Maybe this was all a stupid useless waste of time. Dammit!

Spinning around, I strike the nearest tree, hard. The old oak shakes, and bark and dead leaves rain down around me as I turn to leave—and then he's there, green eyes glittering in the dark wood. Again, all the surrounding life seems to push forward; to lean toward him as he speaks, his voice low, melodic, and edged with icy anger.

"There was no need to hurt the tree."

I look to him, over to the tree and back. "I'm sorry. Look, I need to—"

I don't get to finish my explanation, however, because just then he lifts his hand, and I can't move. The air around me grows cold and thick. Like cement. I struggle against it, but it grows tighter and tighter until I can't even breathe. I fight to stay conscious as he steps close, with a feral grin.

"Do you need air, vampire? What happens to your kind if you cannot breathe? I wonder."

He clenches his fist, and all the air is forced from my lungs. Everything spins and shrinks to the pinprick of light in his green eyes, and my limbs begin to tingle, then grow numb, until I can't feel, can't think, and everything swings and fades. And then I do think. Of life, and love and regret. Of Grace.

Suddenly he lets me go, and I fall to my knees, gulping air that burns its way back into my lungs. I'm bleeding again. I can feel my blood soak the bandages, sticky and cold against my skin, and the thing inside begins that low whine once more. Constant, needful. Insisting. I struggle to my feet, fangs bared. It's all I can do not to attack him and damn the consequences.

Green eyes is not at all threatened, however. Instead, he looks mildly curious. "You're hurt. Differently to last time. Worse."

I calm myself down, as much as I can. Which isn't much. "Yes. That didn't help."

He shrugs. "Neither did you hitting the tree. We're even. What do you want?"

I decide I don't like him at all. But I need his help. So I have to be nice. "I'm sorry about the tree. I don't have much time. I need a favour."

Something changes behind his eyes at that, and I can't say exactly what. It's like the light of life in him shifts, and an energy rises around us. As if the whole of the park is paying close attention as he tips his head, considering me.

"What kind of favour?"

I sigh. This is a risk. A huge risk. And until now I hadn't thought it through. I have to tell him everything, and he mightn't help me at all. He could decide to quite easily kill me. Or worse, he could side with the demons. I have no idea. But it's a risk I have to take.

"I need help. To fight some demons. A lot of demons."

He raises a brow, and I outline, in brief, what's happening. I tell him about the demons, and the magician, and the overheard plans to re-make the world, and themselves, with a blood sacrifice. Then I take a deep breath and tell him about Grace.

"She's Nephilim. An angel-baby. And they're going to kill her."

He stares at me for a long moment, his expression giving nothing away—then he shrugs, and moves cat-like around the tree, brushing his hand along the bark where I struck it. The tree shivers, once, and the wound in the trunk is healed. Christ. I watch him, waiting, as impatient as I have ever been as he leans back, lounging against the trunk, and finally speaks.

"Why should I care what these demons are doing? Let them war as they have always warred. What is it to us? We dwell between. The squabbles of Heaven and Hell are nothing to us."

His tone is casual, but I sense something underneath. A surge of emotion that I feel, but can't quite name. I don't know what it means, but it makes me angry.

"This isn't Heaven's problem. Or Hell's. These demons are here, now! And they won't stop. I've seen them. I know them. I know what they want, what they need. There is no creation, no beauty in them. They live to destroy!" I gesture to the woods that surround us. "Destroy life. Destroy love. It's what they do. What they are!"

Sorrow clenches around my heart, and I think of Grace, and the demon that is a part of me. The part that wants to destroy her even as I love her. And I know what I just said to try and convince him is absolutely, horribly, true.

Tears well up and I turn away. I feel him watching me, feel his scrutinising silence, but I'm out of words. Wiping roughly at my eyes, I head toward the path back out of the park.

"Going so soon?"

370

I stop but don't turn around. "Yes. There's no time. They've already started."

"And you will take on this army of demons, all on your own?"

His tone is slightly mocking, but I nod, still not turning around. "Yes."

"Why? Why when you are demon-kind yourself?"

I do turn then, fangs bared, snarling through tears as I rage at the darkness within and without. "Because I must! Because I can't give in. I won't! Because in the middle of that demon army is a girl; a sweet, gentle, terrified girl. A girl that breaks my heart, and I will not leave her to die alone in darkness!"

He smiles, oh-so-slowly, green eyes glinting with golden light as the air grows warmer around us.

"Why didn't you tell me you're doing this for love, vampire?" He grins and gracefully stands. "I will take your case to the Midnight Court."

I stop, mid-tirade, thrown by the sudden change of tone. "The what?"

He looks at me like I'm incredibly stupid. "The Midnight Court. I'm not the one in charge here. That would be my lady mother. All decisions have to go through her." He winks at me. "I'm her favourite though, so it's a good bet she'll say yes."

I'm really confused. "Yes to what?"

He rolls his eyes. "Yes to granting you your favour? Help with your demon problem? Are all vampires this dense or is it just you?"

I shake my head, ignoring the insult. "How long will that take?"

He shrugs. "I don't know. A long time, a short time. No time at all. What difference does it make?"

"It makes all the difference!" I shout at him, furious. "This is happening now! Jesus! I have to go."

I turn to leave, but he stops me, suddenly just there, with a very strong hand on my arm. "One more thing."

I glare at him, kicking myself for wasting all this time. "What?"

"A favour granted will require a favour in return."

His words have a ritual ring to them, and the energy around us shifts again. I feel like the trees are holding their breath to listen.

I nod. "Okay, yeah. I'll owe you one. Whatever. Just hurry. Please."

He bows, in a half-mocking, old-fashioned way—then the wind whips up around us, and he's gone, leaving me alone under the canopy of leaves.

Frustration claws at me, as I exit the park, and my head starts to throb again. I have no fucking clue if he will help me or not. And this was my only idea. Fuck. Fuck!

I've got to get back. Jude hasn't called, but that doesn't mean something hasn't happened. I clear the park, leaping the iron fence again, and take stock of the surrounding night. It's around three AM by the feel of it. Which means I've got about two hours before dawn. No time. I run back to the car, gun the engine and wheel back around the way I came. Back to the lot, back to the demons, back to Jude.

Back to Grace.

I don't have any plans. I don't have any help. I just know I have to stop them. I have to save her.

Any damn way I can.

Chapter 42

Burning

Babylon, 1595 BCE

Never have I seen Lilitu look at me so, not even when I caused our exodus from Ur, not even when I named her murderess, child slayer, a decade ago. My heart sinks low in my breast, and I tremble from more than mere physical weakness.

"I...I..." I struggle to find words of explanation, of defence but find none. All my earlier anger is gone, and with it, any certainty. Creeping doubt becomes a torrent of shame, and I can no longer hold her gaze, but instead stare down at the blood-stained bedclothes, tears stinging my eyes.

She moves closer, her voice cold and even. "Look at me, Daughter."

I do not wish to. But I cannot resist the command, and so I raise my head once more to meet her gaze. There is anger there now, and when she speaks, her tone cuts deeper than any sword.

"You have done as you will, as you always have done, without thought of consequence. I told you we could not take the girl. I did not think you would be so foolish as to do this. To make another such as us? Without consulting Alu, or your brethren? Without consulting even me?"

I shake my head, trying once more to defend my actions, but instead of words, a horrible weakness overtakes me. I grasp in desperation at the bedpost as the room tilts sideways, and reach desperately for aid. But my fingers find no purchase, and I cry out as I fall to the floor, my head slamming against the tiles. Pain spears through every limb, and a low whine pounds in my head. My body shudders and I gasp for air that has become abruptly unavailable. The whine in my head becomes a scream of need, and then, to my helpless horror, I feel that need turn in search for sustenance, seeking inward. Beginning to feed upon my mind, my soul, my very self.

Then Lilitu is there above me. I try once more to speak, to plead for forgiveness and aid, but she only shakes her head, and sinks to her knees beside me, the anger in her eyes replaced with sorrow.

"You are too young, too weak, to try and make another. It would have killed you, had I not come. Foolish girl."

She sighs then, and once again offers me her wrist, lifting me to her bosom and placing her flesh against my lips. "Drink, Daughter. Drink and heal. We have much to do."

I do not take even a moment to question, only do as she commands, baring fangs and drinking deeply; gratefully. Once again, her blood surges into me, and once again my need turns outward in relief. The heady spirit courses through me, spilling into bone and sinew, healing my wounds and easing my weakness and sorrow. I close my eyes and cling to her like a needful babe, yet all too soon she pulls away, leaving me sore and wanting.

"Enough. You must heal the rest on your own, and suffer the consequence of your actions, else you will never learn." Pushing me from her lap, she stands and walks toward the door.

"Come. We must find the girl before the others do."

I struggle to my feet, still weak. "What do you mean? Why are the others seeking Ku-aya?"

She shakes her head, eyes dark. "They are not. But they are hunting, and as you did not think to have someone waiting to feed your creation when she awoke, she is even now in the streets beyond, rampaging in blood-starved madness. Do you think your brethren will not find her? And what do you think will happen when they do?"

I frown, still not comprehending. "Surely they will not harm her?"

"And why should they not? They owe her no mercy, nor loyalty. She was not made within their presence, with their knowledge and consent, as were you, as were all your brethren. She is nothing to them."

Cold fear clasps its hand around my already sinking heart. "I did not mean this. I did not know. I only wanted—"

"You only wanted your own way." She interrupts me, her voice low, her face a portrait of disappointment. "As you have always done. And behold what your thoughtlessness has wrought."

I bow my head, tears welling unbidden. "I am sorry."

She steps across, lifting my face in her cool and pale hand, gentle but firm.

"I know you are. But your sorrow will wait. We must hurry if we are to find your progeny before the others do. Come, daughter. Before it is too late."

With that, she moves out the door and down, leaping over the balcony into the inner courtyard, and beyond, out into the garden toward the street. I follow, although she is moving so swiftly I can barely keep pace. Soon enough, however, she stops, kneeling in the shadows that gather at the side of a dark dwelling. I stop by her side, glancing down, and am appalled.

She kneels by the body of a young man, richly attired, his throat torn out completely, as if by some animal. I gape at Lilitu, not understanding— and then she pulls me closer, so I may see. All around the largest wound are smaller wounds, dozens of them; perfectly paired punctures. Like one of us would make. If one of us would be mad enough to attack our prey, over and over, biting like an animal. There is no subtlety here. No swiftness. And certainly, no mercy.

Horrified, I again stare at Lilitu as she lays the body back down in the shadows and stands, her lips a tight line.

"It is as I feared. If you had come to me, I would have told you."

I shake my head, my mind a tangle of weakness and emotion. "Told me?"

She grabs me by my shoulders and gives me a sharp shake, enough to bring my focus fully into the present moment.

"Think, Daughter. The girl was always mad. And feeding her your blood as you have been doing these past years has only fed her lunacy. You know this to be true. I have told you that not everyone can endure the making. I spoke the truth. If there is any weakness, whether of body or mind, in those chosen, our blood will amplify that weakness. This is why you were healed before you were made. Had you not been made whole, the making would have killed you, or worse; left you dying, healing, and dying again, over and over, for eternity."

She pauses, her hands gently squeezing my arms before she continues. "It is why I watched you, all your life; why we watched all of your brethren, Alu and I, long before choosing any of you. We do not choose lightly. If there had been even the slightest seed of madness, in any of your minds, the blood would have forged that lunacy into savage animal frenzy. Until no thought or reason remained. No understanding. Only hunger and thirst. And such creatures will only kill and kill. Without conscience. Without thought. Until they themselves are killed."

With dawning dread, I understand—even so, I must ask. "How do you know this?"

She gazes back at me, her eyes dark with memory and grief. "How do you think, Asharru?"

And then I know. How many of us then, have there been? How many wounded, how many mad? How much suffering has been endured, how many lives ended in terror all for the making of us. Of me. I stare at Lilitu and see, more clearly than ever before, the dark purpose in her eyes. She is truly our mother. She giveth life, and she taketh away.

I am once more unable to meet her endless gaze and bow my head. "I see."

"Good." She slips her arms from my shoulders and takes my hand. "Then you know what must be done."

Just then, a scream pierces the night, further away, near the river. Lilitu glances toward the sound.

"Come. We need only follow the sound of fear."

And with that, she is off, swift as the wind. Again, I am hard pushed to follow, but follow I must, and so I will shaking limbs to move, street to street, shadow to shadow.

Soon enough the torchlight dims, and then we are slipping through the tangle of twisting paths and single-storey mud-brick dwellings that make up the lower quarters by the western gate. The night is not so silent here, in these dark streets. Within their houses men sigh and stir in pre-dawn dreams; no walled gardens here to shelter their sleeping forms from those that haunt the night beyond their wooden doors — above which rest the figures of their gods, carved in fierce forms of protection. Little do they know that protection is not needed. Not from us, not while they remain within.

When they venture without it is another story. A story I am presented with as I round the next corner into a narrow, darkened lane—to find Lilitu standing, one arm stretched behind in warning and the other held before her, palm out, as she faces a growling, wild-eyed Ku-aya.

The girl is covered in blood, and in one hand she holds the dangling body of a young man. He is bleeding from several gaping wounds in his throat, arms and torso—even his face. I do not know how he still lives, and if I am sickened at the sight, I am more so at the state of my once sweet lover, so kind, so giving; now snarling and snapping at Lilitu as she takes a slow step nearer. There is no light of humanity in those eyes, glinting lion-gold against the dim light.

A sob catches in my throat, at what I alone have wrought, and at the sound, Ku-aya turns, snarling and baring fangs, as she backs further into the lane, guarding her prey like a wolf.

"Be still." Lilitu speaks low without taking her eyes from the girl. "The time for sorrow is passed. Her mind is gone, as I had feared. Lost in the making. What is left is only animal, a beast that must be destroyed."

I shake my head in vain denial, staring at the girl who once loved me, trusted me. "No. We cannot."

"We?" Lilitu half turns, keeping one hand outstretched toward the girl. "Not we, daughter. You." So saying, she draws from its scabbard at her side the bronze sword with which she sliced off the demon's head not ten years past, and hands it to me, hilt first.

I look from the blade, to the snarling girl, and back to Lilitu. "No. I cannot do this."

"You must do this." This time she turns to meet my eyes, her own glittering green and cold. No comfort in them now, nor mercy. "Take the blade and take her head. It is the only way."

I take a step forward. The polished bronze glistens in the shivering light, and as if entranced, I reach to take the hilt in one shaking hand. Lilitu nods and moves away, leaving me facing the girl on my own. Ku-aya snarls and snaps at me, fangs bare and bloodied. I take a slow, shaking step forward, heart breaking, fist clenched around the hilt of the blade as I raise it up and behind, ready for the killing blow.

"Strike, daughter. Do it now!" Lilitu's urgent whisper whips through the air behind me, a hissing that seems to linger and grow, until it is all I can hear. I see a bright flash reflected in the blade as I bring it down in a singing arc, a flash met and matched in Ku-aya's animal eyes—and then the world explodes.

Lilitu cries out behind me, and I turn to find the lane and the street behind ablaze, timber frames and market banners billowing ash and fire as they fall. Screams and crashes erupt all around me, followed by the shouts of men and the distant sound of battle drums.

The Army. They've reached the city.

Babylon is burning.

Chapter 43

Flesh and Bone

I'm halfway back to Pigeon House Road when the phone rings, buzzing across the dash. I pick it up and glance at the screen. Jude. A seed of panic takes root in my chest as I hit accept.

"What's wrong?"

But there's no answer. Instead, I hear a muffled scraping sound, then a metallic thunk.

"Jude?"

There are grunts, more thumps, then a yell—and sudden gunshots. Three of them.

"Jude!"

I scream down the phone, panic growing as I hit the gas, screeching around the corner of Bridge Street. Shit, shit! I wheel the car down Bayview Avenue and onto Sean Moore Road, ignoring traffic lights. There are more thumping sounds from the phone, then voices. I shut up, holding my breath as fear twists deep inside. Demons. No no no! I listen as the voices fade, and then all I hear is the empty crackle of a phone left on somewhere in the dark.

Jude.

I throw the phone against the dash, and it shatters into a half dozen pieces. The tyres scream as I wheel the car the wrong way around a round-a-bout and down Pigeon House Road, breaking to a stop behind the freight yard opposite the glass factory again. I'm out of the car and across the yard in seconds, alarm thundering through me. Jude. Hang on.

I'm not even a third of the way when I smell it. Above the stench of demons. Blood.

Jude's blood.

I run through the maze of shipping containers, slowing down when I near the side of the yard nearest the glass factory. The scent of blood is stronger here, along with another smell, lingering heavy in the night air.

Gunpowder.

Moving fast, I climb the nearest stack of containers and look over at the ones along the wall. No Jude. I search all around, in vain denial—and then I see it.

On top of a stack not twenty feet away is a dark stain, and just beyond that, a lumpy silhouette. Not moving. My heart sinks low in my chest. No. Leaping the gap between the two stacks, I kneel beside the body—and am flooded with relief. It's a demon corpse, its head blown half off by a shot at close range. He got one. But they got him.

I'm too late.

All around the top of the container is more blood, Jude's blood, mingling with the seeping black blood of the demon. Too much of it.

No.

Grief and anger storm through me, and I clench my fists hard enough that my nails dig into my palms, blood dripping down my fingers to join the rest on the roof.

Fuck. Fuck! I wheel around, still seeking, hoping against hope.

Jude. Please don't be dead.

Something glints in the light, near the edge of the container. His phone. Cursing, I scramble over and pick it up. It's covered in blood and still blinking with a lost connection. Me. He called me for help. And I wasn't there. I should've made him stay away, made him go home. Kept him safe. Instead, I sent him here.

I did this.

Shaking with guilt and rage, I look out across the road to the glass factory lot. I can't see the whole of it from here, but what I do see is enough.

Demons mill around in small groups, glancing now and again to that big pit dug in the centre.

Like they're waiting for something.

As I watch, a cheer goes up from their midst, and the ones I can see jostle and shove each other, pointing and gesturing at something just out of my line of sight. Then an eerie orange light blooms from the pit, growing brighter and brighter, its reflection lapping around the buildings and walls.

Like it's alive.

I'm running out of time. I can't wait for fairy boy and his help that might never come. It's too late. I've got to stop them myself.

Or die trying.

I feel my fangs press against my lip as I search around the container yard for a weapon. Any weapon. Preferably something sharp.

The fence.

Shoving the phone into my pocket, I leap down from the stack of containers, ignoring the jolt to my bones. Keeping an eye and ear out for any roaming demons, I run across to the fence that borders the container yard. It's a typical modern palisade fence, made up of individual grooved metal stakes slatted together, two inches wide, six feet tall and a few millimetres thick. The galvanised stakes are serrated at the top, to discourage climbing over, and although the edges aren't sharp, they could be.

With a little help.

Grasping the nearest one where it's bolted in, I give a tug, and the bolt pings away across the pavement. Another quick wrench and the stake comes away completely, bringing a second with it. Perfect. Ripping away the strips of metal that hold the two together, I move across to a clear spot of pavement in the middle of the stacks of containers. This'll be noisy, but it can't be helped. If the demons hear me, well then, they hear me.

Laying the stakes down, I stamp each one flat, then pick them up—one in each hand—and spin in a slow circle, first one way, then the other, pushing edges against pavement until metal screams and sparks fly, bouncing away across the ground. It doesn't take long until I have two makeshift blades, with four crudely sharpened edges. They won't last, but they'll have to do.

Slinging the fence-blades over my shoulder, I run back through the maze of containers, leaping the gate and heading out along the road. Above me, the sky is black with cloud. As I move on past rows of parked trucks, a wind rises, heavy with the threat of rain and salty with sea air, stirring the surrounding rubbish in miniature tornadoes and tossing my hair about my face.

There's a storm coming.

I stop in the shadows across the road from the black metal gate that leads into the glass factory. On the other side of that gate is an army of demons. I can hear them clearly now, their muttering mingled voices causing my gut to twist in nausea.

Peering through the gloom, I look down one side of the fence, then the other. They don't seem to be guarding their little gathering at all. Probably because there are so many of them in there, they don't feel like they need to. And they're probably right. Even with surprise on my side, I don't know how many of them I can take out before they overwhelm me.

Probably not enough.

Another cheer goes up from the demons within.

Jude. Grace.

No.

Snarling, I run at the gate, using all my strength as I crash into it, shoulder first, and push. The corrugated metal groans and buckles, then the chain inside snaps, and the gate swings wide, shuddering back against the fence with an echoing clang.

There is a ringing second of silence as a couple of hundred demon eyes turn to stare. I take that second and make it mine, charging full tilt at the nearest group, fangs bared and fence-blades swinging. I take a running leap as I reach the first, bringing all my weight down as I aim between shoulder and head. The metal connects with a meaty thud, and I slice through, cutting his head from his body in one fluid motion. A warm rush of wind flows past as the demon quits the flesh.

One.

Spinning around, I sweep the second blade wide, catching another in the throat. A thick spray of black blood spurts out around the metal as his head falls away.

Two.

I carry through the spin, coming around with the first blade and slicing deep into the exposed Adam's apple of a third demon. I pull down, cleaving through rotting flesh. His eyes widen, then go grey and dull as his head, not quite severed, flops to one side, arteries spurting putrid fluid as he falls.

Three.

I hear curses then, and a shouted warning, and know my advantage is gone.

With a roar, I plunge into their midst, slashing and stabbing. I hack at one to my left, he gasps and stumbles back into another, and they both fall. I hammer the blade down against the first, metal to throat, fetid fluid spewing as his head lops to one side. The second struggles up, cursing as he gropes for his gun.

No.

Stomping my boot against his chest, I stab down, burying the jagged end of the second blade into his open mouth. He gurgles as blood bubbles up around the steel, and I twist the blade hard, left, right—then rip it out along with a clump of festering vertebrae.

Four. Five.

Keep going. I hear a distant roll of thunder, and taste the first kiss of rain on my lips as I turn again, thrusting the second stake into the gut of another as he runs at me. His momentum carries him halfway up the blade. I snarl and shove him back, yanking the stake out as I spin again, one blade out, the other up. If I can hold some space, I might have a chance.

Lightning sears the eastern sky, thunder on its heels. I hear an echoing roar behind as more demons storm in. I duck and step past the first, slicing the blade across the back of his neck. The edge sticks halfway through, no longer sharp, but I tear it away as he falls, kicking the next back into two others as hard as I can, then wheeling on another who barrels in, driving a lead pipe toward my head. I jerk the blade up just in time, steel meeting lead with a shivering clang that shocks its way up my arm, leaving it numb for a second. Shit.

Stumbling back, I somehow manage to bring the second blade up as he pounds the pipe down again, gauging a half-moon chunk out of the steel. With a roar, I run right at him, sliding the blade up the length of the pipe into his hand. The broken edge digs into his fingers, and I press harder, tearing through flesh and bone. He grunts and drops the pipe, and I drive the jagged steel into his gut and push until I am fist deep in blood and bile. I rip the blade back out with all my strength, swinging down again in a shower of reeking, rotting flesh, edge into forehead. Metal bites bone with a satisfying crunch, and he falls backwards into the mud, unmoving.

Six. Seven.

I feel a change in the air behind me and turn to meet a face full of hate. Solid black eyes glare above sneering black lips as a meaty fist pounds toward my face. I take a step back, turning on one heel, bringing the first blade round, slicing hard toward his throat.

But I'm too slow, and the blade's too dull. It bounces off the demon's collar, and I meet his eyes as he reaches up to grab the metal, yanking it hard out of my hand. I let go, bringing the other blade down toward his head, but he parries and sneers, shoving me backwards with incredible strength, just as a volley of gunfire meant for me spews forth from somewhere nearby, hitting him full in the face.

Eight.

I land hard on my back in the gravel and mud as he falls and doesn't get up. Rolling to my feet, I feel the warm seep of blood under my shirt. I'm hit. Doesn't matter. I look around quickly, trying to see Grace or Jude—but then another demon runs at me, and more shots ring out. I duck and feel a burning tug in my left arm.

Another bullet. But I don't care. Switching the second fence-blade into my right hand, I slam it down and the demon recoils, arm dangling, as I stab the blade into his throat. The dulling metal resists, but I wrench it back and forth, carving through with all my might. It works. He gives a gurgling gasp as his head falls slowly away from his shoulders. Another hot rush of air blows past.

Nine.

Shots ring out, and bullets tear at my flesh, ripping into my arms, my legs, my chest—but I can't stop. Won't stop.

Lightning rips through the sky again, and it starts to seriously rain. Moving as fast as I can, I duck and spin, slicing and stabbing at anything that comes near. They're too many. I know it, but I keep swinging, fighting; seeing only raging fists, leering faces and solid black eyes, hearing only screams and shouts and the rapid peal of gunfire, feeling only the blows that connect, fists and feet and bullets amid the stench of fetid flesh and blood, mud and gore. I am covered in it, as again and again I bring the blade around, in, up, across and down; images of past battles fought and won and fought and lost parading through my mind.

Another leering face looms before me, another throat exposed, and I bring the blade up again—but then I look where it's headed, and pull up short, stumbling back.

"Jude?"

The demon with my best friend's face grins and reaches out. I watch, dumb with disbelief as he grasps the blade with both hands and twists. Slippery with water and blood, numb with shock, my fingers lose their grip. And then he has the blade and I don't.

With a triumphant howl, he barrels in, swinging the galvanised steel toward my throat. Shock gives way to self-preservation. I bring both hands up, grab the now-dull and pitted edge and push back, stepping forward until we are only inches apart. I seek his face, his eyes, searching for any sign that the man I know and love might still be in there.

"Jude..."

The demon grins again, his voice that of one of the demons from the roof, three nights ago. The twisted sound coming from a face so familiar breaks my heart.

"Jude's not here anymore."

Then he shoves me, hard. I reach out to grab him, but find only his rosary beads, which break off and tangle around my hand as my feet slip—and then I'm on my back, blinking up. I feel my own warm blood spill into the mud, hear the demon-that-was-Jude laugh, see the look of triumph in his black eyes as he drives the blade down through my chest and on into the mud below, impaling me there. Blood wells up into my throat, and I choke, coughing up a frothing flood.

Consciousness flickers like a broken telly, and I reach up with shaking hands, grabbing at the blade, trying to free myself. The Jude-demon leers, laughing as he squats down and presses the hot black muzzle of a handgun against my forehead.

"Say hello to your friend when you get to hell, half-breed! Oh, wait. You can't. He's not there. He's not anywhere!"

He grins and squeezes his finger slowly against the trigger—and then a voice rings out, with a penetrating and sickeningly familiar resonance.

"Enough!"

Everything stops. The Jude-demon lifts the gun and steps back, and the rest of them move away as well, lowering various weapons as they turn toward the voice. I struggle to breathe as the sea of demons part to make way for the one that speaks, in a voice that pounds like thunder.

"So, witch spawn. We meet again."

Chapter 44

Fall

Babylon, 1595 BCE

Struggling through ash and fire, Ku-aya momentarily forgotten, I scrabble over smoking debris toward the entrance to the lane, searching for Lilitu. Other forms move through the street, coughing as they stumble out of damaged dwellings, crying out for loved ones in the night.

I too call out, straining for an answer. For a few long moments I hear nothing, see no trace—and then, I hear her voice, calling out from across the smouldering street. I turn, relieved—then once more I hear a high-pitched hissing, followed by a booming crash, and more fire falls from the sky; heavy stones flung from slings, and arrows the size of spears, each one trailing flame. Screams erupt all around me, and I dive back into the narrow passage as a smoking arrow strikes hard against the nearby wall, scattering sparks and splattering oil.

A drop of burning oil catches the hem of my linens, and as I gasp and kick at the fire, I am struck and thrown to the ground beneath the snarling, raging beast that was once Ku-aya. The sword clatters from my hand as she attacks with animal savagery, clawing and tearing at my flesh. I struggle to push her away, to free myself and reach the blade, but I am still weak, and in her fury, she traps me beneath her and sinks her fangs deep into my shoulder.

Pain arcs from the wound, followed by curling, rippling pleasure. In an instant, I am slave to its current, sight and sound drifting away. I know a swinging heaviness, and a whispering whine swells in my skull, growing to a pounding wail of need. I struggle to heed it, fighting against the waves of pleasure with all my might—and gasp up, as if from drowning. Met with pain again, I embrace it as it wakes me from paralysed bliss, letting me fight once more to release myself from Ku-aya's savage grasp—and then, shadowy forms dart through the surrounding flames. Weapons flash, voices shout, I feel a sharp jolt, see a flash of fire, and I am free.

In agony, I strive to stand, my bones fragile as threaded dew. I will my shaking hands to flex against the earth, force trembling arms to push, knees to bend, until I am up at the edge of the lane as figures move around me. Men. Shouting in an unfamiliar tongue.

Hunters.

Someone howls, in a voice I know, despite its bestial timbre. Ku-aya.

I struggle to my feet and stumble through the smoke in time to see the men surround her, skewering her cowering form with long spears, over and over as she howls in animal agony. My heart shatters at her cries, and I take a shaking step forward. Then I hear another sound behind me; a clear cry of warning. Lilitu. I turn and peer through smoke to see shadowy forms moving up the street— men, moving in formation, bearing before them that same standard we saw hung over the encampment. Blood red embroidered on white, a serpent pierced by a flaming sword. More of them.

No.

I scramble away over rubble, calling out to Lilitu as I stumble into the street. Around me buildings smoulder, banners burn, and people run screaming, crying, or fall, dying. Once out into the open I wheel around, searching desperately for the woman who has been mother to me more than any other. I call out again, and again—and then I hear it. Faint but certain. My name.

I seek the sound, and find Lilitu, waving from a darkened doorway. My heart lifts and I turn toward her, even as the hunters turn toward me. A cry goes out from within their midst, a shouted word, in a tongue familiar enough for me to discern its meaning. Demon.

Monster.

Fear arcs down my spine as they attack, running with a dozen pointed spearheads. Weak as I am, I am driven back toward the mouth of the lane by the press of so many. As they push on, one man steps from their midst, bearing before him a strip of white cloth which he unfurls in my direction, along with a gesture and a phrase I do not understand. A cheer goes up from the rest at the action, and I see that the strip of cloth bears that same crimson symbol. I do not know what it means, nor why his waving it should fill me with such fear. And yet I am afraid. There are so many. Behind me, the rest of the men turn from their prey—Ku-aya, whose screams are no more—and turn their spear points upon me, still wet with her blood.

Rage blooms through me, and I clench my fists as they surround me. Then the man with the banner utters a single word, pushing his hand toward me, palm out; and to my shock and horror I am at once in an unseen grip that lifts me off my feet, and into the air.

I snarl and struggle as the man steps forward, holding my gaze, his own filled with cruel delight as he lifts his outstretched hand higher, and slowly closes his fist.

I gasp as the invisible hand presses around my limbs, holding me fast—then I cry out as that same hand clenches hard, crushing my arms into my sides. I kick and thrash, to no avail. The hand only grips tighter and tighter, and I fight for breath to scream as my bones crack, pain spearing through me.

And then, without warning, I am free. I fall to the ground, my head striking hard against stone. The sky spins above me, and stars are born and die at the edges of my vision. I taste blood at the back of my throat, and struggle to remain awake. Then I feel strong arms around me, lifting me up. Away.

Lilitu.

Relief floods through me, and I open my eyes to deep concern in her own.

"Daughter? Are you awake?"

I nod, and she sets me down. The world reels around me as my feet find the ground, and I am overwhelmed by a wave of nausea. I close my eyes and must cling to her outstretched arm to keep from falling, but eventually, the sickness passes, and I can stand on my own.

Looking around, I see we are in near-complete darkness. The ground is cold and wet beneath my feet, and I smell water nearby. There is a faint glimmer ahead, as of reflected firelight, and behind, all is dark and cold.

"Where are we?" My voice bounces off the surrounding walls, which are narrow and smooth. Rounded. Lilitu shushes me, and I hear footsteps. Shadows break the flickering light, and someone shouts. The battle still rages, then. I hear weapons clashing, men yelling; the muffled screams of women and children.

Lilitu peers toward the light, her eyes glinting. "We are in the irrigation tunnels, beneath the city."

"Oh." I follow her gaze, to what must be the tunnel entrance. "Thank you, for saving me. I do not know what happened."

She looks back, her jaw tense. "It was not I who saved you. It was Alu. And your brethren. We wait now. For them."

She is still angry with me. I feel an ache in my chest that has little to do with my broken ribs. Then I recall the man with the banner, his hand in the air, the invisible fist.

"What was it that lifted me? I saw nothing, and yet I felt a hand, grasping. Crushing me ..."

She nods. "That was a Magi. As I told you. Allied with the hunters against us, using their magic to trap and kill us. Or worse."

"Worse?" I do not know what would be worse. But my question goes unanswered, for just then, there is a shuffling at the entrance of the tunnel, and Makhir storms in. He is covered in ash and blood, and he snarls as he leaps upon me, fangs bared in fury.

"You!" He strikes me, hard, and I slam into the opposite wall and fall into the muddy water. In an instant he is upon me, dragging me up by my hair with one hand while with the other he draws a bloodied dagger and presses it to my throat. "My brother is dead, and it is your doing! Temple-whore, daughter of whores! I will end you for what you have done!"

I do not understand what is happening. Why is my brother attacking me? But there is no time for comprehension. In one moment I feel his blade slice deep into my flesh, severing my wind-pipe, stealing my breath—and in the next, both blade and brother are gone, and I am left once more on my knees, gasping for air. I feel hot blood spill down my chest and clasp a hand hard against the wound as I struggle to my feet, staring about in the darkness.

The distant torchlight bounces off the water, sending ripples of light and shadow along the walls, and in the shimmering reflection I see Lilitu standing a few feet away, the dagger that was just against my throat in her hand, and the headless body of Makhir at her feet. I gape, my senses reeling, as the body of my brother shudders once, twice—then shrivels and melts, skin from sinew from bone. Then even his bones crumble and fall away with a sigh of dust, into the muddy water.

And Makhir is no more.

I stumble back against the wall, shuddering in shock. Lilitu mutters a curse, wiping the blade on her linens, then gesturing to me.

"Come. We must go."

I try to speak, but no words come, yet I must obey as she grasps my arm and hauls me roughly away from the city and the soldiers; away from the light and the pool of mud and blood that was my brother.

I stumble behind her, made blind by the darkness of the tunnel, dumb by the wound in my throat, numb by the shock of my brother's death. Again, and again I see his snarling face before mine; again and again, I watch that same face fall away to nothing. Dead. We can die. Will die. Horror and fear surge through my breast in smothering waves. And still I run on.

Behind us, the sounds of battle fade away, as before us the passage grows darker still—then, in the narrow distance light blooms, and the tunnel ends. We burst out into the wetlands along the banks of the river, north of the city; the stars above casting the whispering rushes in silver-blue light.

Lilitu lets me go there, and I fall to my knees in the mud, choking against the wound in my throat as it heals enough for me to speak, in a ragged whisper.

"Makhir ..."

She turns, eyes flashing. "Makhir would have killed you. Would you have preferred that I let him?"

I shake my head, blinking back tears, the horror of that moment, of his headless form melting to nothing, etched upon my mind.

Lilitu nods and turns her gaze from me toward the horizon. "Rise, daughter. There is no time to rest. Dawn is near and we must find shelter."

I follow her gaze to see the stars have already faded. Panic shivers up my spine and I stumble to my feet, trembling and weak. Too weak. I have lost so much blood. And the dawning light is sapping what remains of my strength.

Hunger and fatigue pang through me in turns as I struggle to follow Lilitu, who is already moving swiftly along the riverbank. Gripping my linens in one hand, I lurch through the reeds, their long leaves snarling each step as if with intent. As if they would drag me beneath the dark waters to drown. Fear clenches around my heart, and I move faster, limbs shaking with effort, my gaze flitting betwixt murky water and brightening sky.

In my terror I do not see Lilitu has stopped, and run headlong into her stone-like form. I fall again, into the mud, struggling to rise in the tangle of reeds. Then I feel her strong hand around my arm, lifting me up, pulling me close in an unyielding grip.

"Be still."

It is a stern command, and I obey, watching as she stares behind us, back along the river bank toward the city. Listening. Waiting.

She holds me there, both of us silent as death as the water moves sluggishly around us. Small creatures swim, slink and slither past, and a soft breeze rises and falls, whispering its song among the reeds, haunting and discordant. I can hear my heart, each beat laborious and weak; and Lilitu's, strong and sure. Hunger rages at the sound, stabbing through my gut like a knife. I clench a fist against my abdomen, muffling the gasp that rises unbidden to my lips, and Lilitu's grip tightens around my arm.

I am just about to ask her what she heard, why we are waiting here, exposed, when the sun is already swallowing stars, when I hear it. In the distance behind us. Faint at first, then louder. The unmistakable sound of hooves, pounding across sand.

Horses. Coming from the city. Horses, chariots and men. The hunters.

I look to Lilitu, and our eyes meet, her own viridescent as she hisses a single word.

"Run."

She turns and is away while the word still lingers in the air, and I am not far behind, terror filling my chest as I tear through the reeds.

Before us the river narrows, the marsh giving way to scrub brush. Behind us I can smell the smoke of torches, hear the clink and scrape of armour, the pounding hooves of horses and the shouts of men as they gain on us. I turn to look over my shoulder, my foot twists in a tangle of roots, and I fall hard, my ankle cracking as sinews tear. I cry out at the sudden jolt, and try in vain to wrench myself free, but I am too frail, and my trembling hands too slippery with silt and gore.

And then, once more, Lilitu is there, ripping the roots out of the ground and dragging me painfully to my feet. Too late. The men are upon us, horses pounding hooved fury up the riverbank. They reign in, twenty abreast, each one seeking the brightening expanse of water.

One of them gives a triumphant shout, and I know we are seen. Another shout, and the air fills with whistling arrows. I stand, stunned as a gazelle in torchlight, as an arrow finds its mark in my breast. Startled, I stare at the protruding shaft, blinking and too weak to register what has happened. Then, the arrow is ripped out of my chest.

Lilitu.

I grasp blindly for her, darkness circling my mind, as I fall backwards into the reeds; into the water. And then I am taken as on a tide. Away from the men and the fire. Away from shouts and splashes, curses and the screams of animals. All grows ever distant, ever silent, until the water covers me completely. I gulp and choke, as it fills my nose, my mouth, struggling against the force that pulls me, unyielding, ever deeper.

Darkness covers me, and I fight against it, fight to see, to breathe, to live—and then, as suddenly as I was pulled under, I am hauled out, to lay, retching, my face in the cold mud, too spent to move. And yet I am moving. Strong hands lift me, and a soft breeze whispers against my cheek. My head spins and I open my eyes to fading stars above. Their light dances and flickers in rainbow patterns as they and I move, and I feel we are drifting together, the stars and I, both of us borne on a current of sky.

Then all movement stops as I land with a jolt on hard earth in the shadow of a hulking cliff of stone.

Lilitu's face takes shape in front of my reeling vision, a frown creasing her brow. "Can you stand?"

I nod, although I do not know. Still. I must try. Pressing my hands against the cool ground, I labour to my knees, and then, reaching, find sandy stone to cling to, pulling myself to stand, trembling and leaning against the rock.

Lilitu nods approval. "Good. Now climb."

She casts her eyes above us, up and along the jutting outcropping of stone, red in the growing light. Squinting my eyes against the sky, I can see, along the top ridge of the outcropping, a sharp shadow in the stone. No, not a shadow. A cave.

I look back to Lilitu, and she nods. "Swiftly now, daughter. I will follow. The day is upon us, and the hunters will not be far behind."

I need no more encouragement. Gripping fingers and toes in cracks and crags, I pull myself upwards and the face of the escarpment, inch by agonising inch. The sun breaches the horizon as we climb, and although we are on the shadow side of the precipice, the weight of day pulls at me, clouding my mind and making me weaker with each passing moment. My shuddering limbs and burning lungs protest, and once or twice I lose my grip and slip—but Lilitu is always there to catch me, to haul me up and push me onwards, upwards, until I reach the nearest cave, and pull myself, gasping and trembling, into soft, forgiving darkness.

Chapter 45

Love and Loss

Impossible.

My mind reels as I look up to meet the same solid black gaze I last met over three and a half thousand years ago. The face and body are different, but the eyes are unmistakable, and filled with glee as he steps closer, lips curled in a sneer.

"I had thought you dead by now, half-breed."

"Sorry to disappoint you." I choke the words out past a suffocating surge of blood.

The Thomas-demon laughs, a sickening sound that pounds through my head and blurs my vision. "Oh, I am far from disappointed." He leans in, with a delighted grin. "It's perfect. You might even call it fate. Having you here to witness the moment of my triumph." He leans his head to one side. "And exactly as I left you last. Fitting, don't you think?"

Lightning stabs again, and thunder follows, shaking the ground around us. I can feel my whole body begin to shudder, each gasping breath a struggle. I tense trembling limbs, clenching both fists against the blade in my chest, pulling until my palms are shredded to the bone. No good. I'm too weak, my blood is pouring from a dozen wounds, and pain I no longer have action to dull is quaking through me, sending me spinning into shock. Stay conscious. Stay here.

The demon moves closer still, crouching down in front of me, his breath hot in my face. "Whatever happened to the bitch-whore who took my head in that garden? The witch who ate her own child? The first of your wretched kind? What was her name again...?"

My heart stumbles and stutters in my chest. Lilitu. Old feelings flood in, of love and loss, guilt and anger.

"Don't you talk about her. Don't even think about her!"

He laughs again, and it's all I can do not to retch at the sound. I still can't believe it. Here. Now. The demon who began it all. And all I can do is glare my hate as he smiles wicked delight.

"Oh, I think about her all the time. So fascinating, that witch. I have much to thank her for. And you. Oh yes. I have often wondered what I would do if ever we met again."

He stands up, and without warning, rips the fence-blade from my chest. I gasp and curl around the wound, blood pouring freely past my fingers. Consciousness shudders again, darkness licking at the edges of my vision.

No.

I will not give in.

Gasping, I roll onto my side, then crawl to my knees. The whine in my head grows louder, bringing with it an echo of anger not my own. But familiar. I reach for it. Give me strength.

The demon steps back and two of the others stomp over and grab me, yanking me roughly to my feet. The demon lifts the fence-blade in front of him, studying it. "Did you make this?"

I glower at him through vision that blurs and refocuses like a pirated film. He turns the now dull and broken blade this way and that.

"Resourceful. I like it." He nods, then holds the blade out in front of him, leaning back and closing his eyes. I watch in growing horror as his skin ripples, his body shudders; then the demon is gone, and Thomas is there, his all-too-human eyes filled with triumphant hate.

"I too, am resourceful."

He whispers something then, that I don't quite catch, and the fence-blade shivers and quakes once, twice—then melts away to a silvery puddle that falls from his hands to mingle with the mud and blood on the ground.

I stare, blinking blood and water from my eyes, and he grins.

"Just a little trick. Nothing too difficult. But we haven't been properly introduced."

He holds out a hand as if both mine weren't broken, bleeding and held fast.

"I'm Thomas. And you're Rue. Interesting name. You don't hear it much anymore. Is it short for something?"

I won't answer, and I can't move, so I glare my hate in silence.

Thomas shrugs. "Anyway." He takes back his hand and gives me an insincere smile. "I have to thank you for bringing Grace to me. I need her. Well, her blood at least. Powerful stuff, angel blood. But you already knew that, didn't you?" He searches my face. "In fact, you could probably use some blood right about now. I can't give you Grace's. I need that. But..."

He motions to one side, and the demon-crowd parts, letting the one wearing Jude's body step through. Jude. Grief surges through me again, and tears fill my eyes. Thomas smirks.

"Oh yes, your priest! He was a bit of fun for the boys while they waited. They played some sort of game for who'd get to possess him. I guess the souls of the devout are the tastiest. He put up quite a fight, from what I hear."

Then Thomas reaches out, grasping the Jude-demon's forearm. I watch in horror as the flesh of Thomas' human hand ripples, the skin around his thumbnail tearing as the nail curves out in an instant, the demon within forcing it into a long, jagged point, which he digs into the Jude-demon's wrist. A surge of still-red blood spurts out, pooling around the wound and spilling to the ground.

"See?" The demon that was Thomas is back, black eyes pooling as he smiles, stepping back and shoving the Jude-demon forward. "Still fresh."

Hunger thunders in, tearing through my gut and sending a fresh volley of pain rocketing around my head as the thing inside screams need. Every single sense I have is drawn to that scarlet flow, my fangs pushing against parched lips. The Thomas-demon carries on, but I can hardly hear him past the storm inside.

"Of course, the body will begin to rot soon. They just don't last. Not without the soul. And we must drink the soul to take the body." The Jude-demon steps closer, winking at me from Jude's face. No no no no no.

"Usually, anyway. I got around that, with this magician's help. This one's sort of a time-share." The Thomas-demon grins and lifts his arms, presenting his body to me like a new coat. "Not a bad form, really. Weak of course, like all monkeys. But a necessity. For now." He paces again, back and forth behind the Jude-demon. "In a little while, however, none of us will ever have to wear flesh again. The flesh is weak after all."

The demon wearing Jude leers in, lifting his wrist until it's only millimetres from my mouth. No. I turn my face away, but I can still smell it. It smells like Jude.

Jude. Gods. I'm so sorry.

"What's the matter, leech?" The Thomas-demon taunts as those watching snigger. "Aren't you hungry?"

Hungry. I clench my fist around Jude's broken rosary beads until the small cross digs deep into my palm, using the pain, needing it, praying to any god. Take me away. Please. But it's not working. Tears stream down my cheeks as thought slips away like sand in the wind. Desperate, aching need fills me, and I can't fight it anymore.

Leaning forward as much as I can in the grasp of the two that hold me, I bare fangs and reach, shuddering with want as my lips meet the offered wound, shivering at the taste—and then I am struck, hard, across the face, the blow splitting my cheek wide open. The world around me tips sideways and back as I fall and the demons holding me jerk me upright to face Thomas again; human, haughty and sneering.

"Like he said. The flesh is weak."

The gathered demons laugh, and the sound quakes through me as I blink back to awareness. The Jude demon snickers and waves his still bleeding arm tauntingly as he walks away, the demon soul keeping the stolen body upright and moving when it should be dead.

Jude. Dead. My fault. My fault.

No.

Their fault.

I hang on to hate, all I can do as Thomas spins on his heels, gesturing to the two who hold me. They drag me behind him as he walks through the mud toward the pit in the middle of the site. The pit that still flickers with sickening orange light.

Thunder peals again, and the rain pours hard on its heels. Blood seeps from my nose, my lips, my face, my fingertips, and wounds old and new, soaking my clothes and mingling with the rain. The pounding in my head grows worse by the second, and awareness flickers in and out. I close my eyes, saving what strength I have left as I cling to consciousness. Then the demons stop dragging me, shoving me roughly to my knees. I see light past my lids and feel heat against my face.

A lot of heat.

I open my eyes to find I am kneeling at the edge of the pit. It's about twenty metres in diameter, and easily as deep. And it is filled with blistering, boiling, molten glass.

Gods.

I stare in disbelief. All around the edges are jutting, broken pipes, some of them still spitting water that steams away as it hits the bubbling morass below. Fear chills through me, nightmare images fusing with reality as I stare. Then Thomas is there again, grabbing a fistful of my hair and forcing me to look up at him.

"Pay attention, vampire. This is the end of your world."

He lets me go, then walks around to the other side of the pit where he stops, turning slowly around and raising his hands. As he does so, a tremor quakes across his flesh, like a thousand insects crawling beneath his skin, and when he turns, his eyes are solid black and demon again.

The others around fall silent, faces turned toward him as he speaks.

"Brothers! It is time!" His voice sends a shudder of nausea through my gut and the blade in my pocket gets hotter by the second, competing with the heat of the molten glass for attention. I clench my fists in the mud to keep from blacking out as he continues.

"I have called you here, from all corners of this earth. You who have waited so long, abandoned, surviving on the souls of the weak; half-starved as you move from flesh to rotting flesh; fixed in time and place, in this waste of a world!"

A rumble of agreement goes up from the gathered demons as he carries on.

"I know. I too have suffered. And yet I have never stopped searching."

The crowd falls silent again, his sickening voice ringing out around the lot.

"From that first moment, when we were betrayed, torn from our true selves and trapped here, in a world no longer ours; when we were left without form, to scrabble and scratch for what small power we could glean from the minds of these apes that surround us, cursed to wear their stinking flesh to travel even the smallest distance; always, I searched for a way back. And I kept searching. Even after we caught and punished the one who betrayed us."

Here he stops and sneers at me, pausing to allow another angry muttering from the crowd—and I feel a sudden surge of rage, a part of me and yet not; pounding and screaming in my head. I sway on my knees, consciousness darting away from onslaught within and without as he goes on speaking, oblivious.

"And still, I was not satisfied. So, I wandered, as we all wandered, seeking what dominion I could in this wretched world."

There are mutters of agreement from the surrounding demons as he continues.

"As I did, I realised that finding a way back was not what I wanted. I did not want to return to a world to which I was exiled, a world where I—where we—were cursed to toil with a thousand others of our kind, and for what? Some small place in hell? Remember, my brothers. Remember what it was like."

The growl of agreement grows louder.

"Do you want to go back to hell, my brothers?"

Shouts go up, in the negative.

"You do not have to. For I have found a way for us to take back our true forms, take back our power and take back this world; our world—forever!"

He raises his hands, and a cheer goes up from the surrounding demons, my head pounding at the sound. I focus past it. Stay here, Rue. Stay awake. I blink water and blood from my eyes, lowering my head to save strength again as he carries on.

"This pool you see before you, this pit that you have helped to fill—magicked into fire by this magician that I wear," He puts a hand to his face, tugging at Thomas' skin like he's tugging at cloth. "—this is our baptismal font. From fire we were created, by the Word, and by the Word were we also cast out, into fire. But that fire could not harm us, for who, if not we, are the very gods of fire?"

Another shout goes up from the surrounding demons, louder. Then the Thomas-demon speaks again, three worlds that pull all my focus.

"Bring the girl."

I look up as two demons drag Grace forward, her wrists trailing a clinking chain. She's been crying—pale tear trails stand out against the dirt on her face—and she's bleeding from where the chains have worn into her flesh. Fury screams through me and I lunge forward—only to be shoved down again by the two behind me as the Thomas-demon reaches out and grabs the chain, hauling Grace roughly to his side.

The demon crowd cheers as he lifts the chain in one hand, forcing her arms up and out over the pit, while with the other he takes a long knife from a sheath at his belt. He waits then, a long moment, as the crowd falls silent. Behind him, in the east, the sky begins to grow pale as his voice rings around the factory lot.

"Brethren, I give you one of the Word's own! A carrier of creation for our salvation!"

Then, lightning-quick, another shudder quakes across his skin, and he is Thomas again, his voice human, heavy with magic, and coloured with madness.

"For the blood is the life!"

He rips the knife in one quick motion across both Grace's wrists, slicing deep. She cries out and I cry out with her. Her gaze finds mine at the sound, surprise, then realisation rising in her pain-filled eyes.

"Rue." A whisper only, but one so full of hope it breaks my heart. Again, I push against the two that hold me, but it's no good. I'm too weak. Too wounded.

I watch in horror as her blood spills, sizzling into the molten morass below. As soon as the first drop hits, there is a blinding flash, and then a thin line of golden light threads out, branching like lightning, and on, and on; in patterns that loop and line around each other into tangled symbols, too many to count. They burn into my vision, and I have to close my eyes.

When I open them again, it is to Thomas moving his fingers and hands like he's playing an evil mime game of cat's cradle. He speaks then, in liturgical tones; a language it takes me a moment to recognise. And then I do.

Aramaic again.

> *"By the blood of the Word created.*
> *By the same we are renewed.*
> *Within the fire, true form find.*
> *Matter to mind, blood to bind.*
> *In fire and blood reborn!*
> *In fire and blood reborn!*
> *In fire and blood reborn!"*

The rest of the demons take up the chant, and hairs rise on the back of my neck. The temperature around us changes, growing desperately cold, and a cloud of steam rises from the pit, covering all of us in a misty orange mantle.

The knife in my pocket is so hot that it burns me through my jacket. I hiss and use the pain, straining against the grip of the two that hold me.

The golden threads streaming from where Grace's blood hit the molten glass shiver and flare, once, twice—then their heavenly light turns a sickening infected green as the branching lines twist again into symbols of dark, twisted magic.

"Grace!" I shout through the steam. I don't know what good it will do to or if she can even hear me, but I have to try. "Grace! Answer me!"

The steam drifts and for a moment I see her; pale, face drawn, lids fluttering as her blood pours into the pit. No.

"Grace!"

She blinks up at me, and relief pangs through my heart. I smile, tears stinging my eyes, and she gives a faint smile back, then she collapses, falling forward in Thomas' grasp as he leers through the clouds of steam; mad, sweating and triumphant, his voice eerily loud in a sudden silence.

"It is done."

A low ripple of excitement shudders through the crowd, and I am filled with a focused, fatal fury. I snarl at him, fangs bared, fists clenched against the earth.

"I will kill you."

Thomas smirks, and once more his skin quakes, his eyes swirling with demonic blackness, his voice warping down an octave.

"Oh? You, and as they say, what army?"

Just then, the surrounding air grows warmer. Sweeter. At the same time, where my fingers clench in mud and blood, I feel the smallest of movements. As if all the millions of tiny life-forms in those two fistfuls of mud are suddenly moving. Moving toward something. Something Other.

And I know what it is.

I snarl across at him. "This one."

And all hell breaks loose.

There is a flash of silver light—like a sudden burst of moonlight, followed by a low booming groan as the plywood fencing surrounding the lot bows inwards—then explodes in a storm of splinters.

A heavy mist rises from everywhere at once, flooding over and out across the lot, blocking out the rising light; twisting and curling around the gathered demons as they turn and mutter in mass confusion. There is a hail of gunfire, the mist lighting in brief flashes as bullets rip through the night. Close.

Closer still, the sound of metal on metal; the smell of blood, sweet and sour, the grunts and cries of battle. I hear a scream, then another, then more. The demons that hold me let go, and all the hate I've been holding finds release.

Shoving myself to my feet, fangs bared, I run around the side of the pit, towards the Demon that is Thomas. All around me shadows move through the mist, strange shapes; some human, others monstrous and misshapen. All of them there, then gone, as demons howl and scream.

Away to my right there is a sudden explosion of fire, and a serpentine shape whips past. I smell burning flesh. Hear more screams. But I don't care. All I know, all I see, is the Thomas-demon, and Grace, hanging slack in his grasp.

He is glaring wildly through the mist when I reach him, shouting orders left and right.

Howling anger, I launch myself forward, reaching my right hand into my jacket pocket, my fist curling around the knife. The only weapon I have. Yes. My fingers singe, but I don't care. As soon as I touch the hilt my head fills with a rushing, echoing sound, screaming a rage not my own. Stronger. Older. And with it a whisper, faint and yet calling my attention.

A word.

Malephas.

The voice in my head. Urgent. Angry. A flurry of thought. Speak. The knife. The word. No. Not a word. A name. Malephas. The sound moves from my head to my tongue, and I take a burning breath, just as the Thomas-demon whirls to face me, fury curling his lips.

Tearing the knife from my pocket, bits of leather and silk falling away to ash, my fist trailing fire, I raise the dagger high, force my broken lips to move, force the remaining air in my lungs to make sound.

"Malephas!"

And I bring the knife down as hard as I can, the blade sinking hilt-deep into his right shoulder.

He stumbles back, his eyes widening in surprise as he looks to the knife, to me and then to the knife again. I fall to the ground, cradling my blackened and burnt hand; watching as flames arc from the buried blade, ripping out across his flesh, leaving grey trails of ash in their wake. He roars and careens backwards, losing his grip on the chains that hold Grace as he claws at the hilt of the dagger, every touch setting his fingers ablaze.

I turn my focus to Grace, stumbling over as she falls prone, cold and bleeding in the curling mist at the edge of the pit.

"Grace." I lean in, listening for a breath. "Grace!" I press my ear against her chest. There. Slow, and so faint I can barely hear it. But there. A heartbeat. She's alive. Hope blooms, then I hear a bellow behind me and turn in time to meet a kick to the chest. Ribs crack as I fly over Grace's prone form, rolling to a stop several meters away, the mist rippling around me.

Struggling to my feet, I spit blood and bare fangs; fists curled and ready as I turn to face my attacker—but he isn't there. I wheel around, peering through smoke and steam, and I see him at the edge of the pit. His form is a mantle of flame as he lifts Grace in both burning hands, the chains that trail from her wrists dripping with liquid fire as it drizzles from his flesh.

"No!"

I scream, running to stop him, but I'm too far away. Horror shocks through me as he turns and grins revenge, his face an inferno. Then he lifts Grace's prone form over his head—and tosses her into the pit.

I run. All I can see is Grace, falling into the burning morass below, and then I am leaping, reaching. Please. My hands find purchase—her smouldering clothes. I grip tight, then turn mid-air and throw her, as hard as I can, up and away; using every last bit of strength I have.

I watch her rise and disappear, up, through the swirling steam. Rising as I fall, the glow from the pit lighting the mist, surrounding her like a halo as she flies. Like an angel. And that makes me smile. I know a last, lingering moment of love, and a second of pure icy pain.

And then I know nothing at all.

Chapter 46

Flee

I scream awake from a vision of flood and fire, to find a hand covering my mouth, my face. I cannot breathe, cannot see, and fight in panic. "Be still, daughter. It is only a dream, and dreams will pass."

As the vision fades into wakefulness, I open my eyes to find Lilitu above me, and stop my struggles. She looks pale, tired, and weaker than I have ever seen her.

I sit up, gasping for air through burning lungs. She helps me to lean against a wall as I find my breath, and as I do, I taste blood on my lips and know that yet again; she has fed me her own.

Slowly all five senses return, and I realise we are in a narrow cave, some distance back from the mouth. It is dark in the corner where we sit, but I do not need the grey light that seeps through the entrance to tell me it is day without. The feebleness in my limbs and numbness in my mind tells me all. My arms are heavy as sodden wool, and my thoughts are slow to form.

"Where are we?" I stare about the walls and low roof of the place, all of which look like they have been hollowed by human hands.

"In caves, to the North and west of the city. Remember? We ascended as the sun rose." Lilitu stands, slowly, to lean against the wall beside me, closing her eyes and releasing a shuddering sigh.

I nod, recalling the flight from Babylon, the river, the climb. I try to sit up straighter, but the effort only brings agony, and so I give up and rest again. "How long have I slept?"

"Not long. It is only a few hours past dawn, but I had to wake you." Her eyes flash in the half-light as she glances to the opening. "Listen."

I lean my head to one side, listening. I hear my heartbeat, then Lilitu's, faint and slow; hear the shuttle and scrape of tiny creatures in the sand, the faint whisper of water somewhere deeper in the dark, the soft singing of wind around the entrance of the cave, and beyond that—there. A question, a muted answer; the sound of metal scraping leather, the commotion of horses and men. A great many men. And none too far away. The hunters. I look to Lilitu, a cold seed of fear taking root in my spine.

She nods. "It would not have been difficult for them to follow our passage, for you were wounded, and bleeding; and I too harried by the day to hide what traces we left."

I dart a glance around the cave, seeking the dark walls for some escape, but find none. My voice trembles as fear flowers to my throat. "What will we do?"

She closes her eyes, leaning back against the wall, and again I think I have never seen her so frail. The anger that filled her eyes earlier is gone, replaced by a deep weariness. All that has happened the past night floods over me in a surge of confusion, loss, and guilt.

Once more Lilitu has saved me. Thrice over. Once more I am filled with love for her. Truly, she is mother to me. She named me daughter the night I was made, and in truth I am. Flesh of her flesh, made in her image, born of her words, of her blood. And, like a child, I search her face for assurance.

But when she opens her eyes again, there is no comfort there. Only a dark resignation I do not comprehend.

"We will go." She gestures toward the back of the narrow cave, deeper into darkness, toward a darker part, like a stain on the stone. "These caves were formed by wind and weather, but were further shaped by men, not long ago. There is a cleft in the rock, and beyond it, a passage. Where it leads, I do not know, but we cannot remain here."

She leans up from the wall and holds out her hand to help me rise. As she pulls me to my feet, I realise how weakened I am by the day, and how I have not yet even begun to heal, even with the gift of so much of her blood.

Each breath burns in my lungs, my wounds seep dark blood, and as I stumble behind her into the dark, my head spins and I put out a trembling hand to the wall to keep myself from falling. When we reach the fissure, I must stop and lean against the stone to rest, my breath coming in short gasps as I fight against the leaden fragility that overwhelms me.

Lilitu turns, her eyes flashing in the near-complete darkness. "Stay awake, daughter. It is only the feebleness of day. You must fight it." So saying, she peers once more through the cleft in the stone into the darkness beyond, and, with a last look to me, slips into the narrow opening.

Even as she does so, I hear voices from behind, much closer now, and the sound of hands and feet scrabbling against stone. The hunters are climbing the rock face.

Dread rises, and I push myself to my feet, shove myself into the opening and scramble through. The floor on the opposite side is a good bit lower, and I stagger into absolute darkness, balance and bearing lost. I am so used to being able to see in the night, this sightless state fills me with a child's horror, such that I cannot help the whimper that escapes my lips.

"Shhhhhh. Child. Be still." Lilitu's familiar hand grips my arm, steadying me as I find my feet, blinking and blind. The floor here is colder than without, and smooth against my bare feet. I let out a slow breath, and its whisper echoes against walls that are farther apart than the narrower shaft behind. The air is misty and cool, and again I hear water running, singing deep and distant. Then another sound splinters the darkness; a shout and scrape of metal, soon followed by more shouts and a clamouring of limbs, armour and voices.

They have found the cave.

"Flee!" Lilitu's hissing command hangs in the air behind us as she pushes me forward, moving fast.

I lurch and lumber as she shoves me before her, struggling to keep my feet in the pitch-black. I cannot see what is in front of me, nor do I believe can she, yet I must trust and run. The ground beneath our feet grows wetter, and wetter still, until we are splashing through a swiftly running stream. And yet she drives me onwards, faster and further, until I can no longer hear men behind us, and past the terrible fatigue blooms a gem of hope. Surely the hunters are too far behind. Soon enough we will find a way into the open, and when night falls, make our escape, to find Alu and the others.

The others.

The thought wakes the harrowing memory of Makhir, of his attack upon me, and his final death at the hand that now urges me onwards into blackness. I shudder at the memory, trying to bury it, to turn my mind to anything else—and then, Lilitu gives a sharp gasp, and grips my wrist so sudden and tight the bones crack. I cry out in pain and then terror, as the ground beneath my feet ceases to exist, and I am dangling mid-air, with only Lilitu's hand to hold me.

I flail in alarm, scrabbling for any bearing, and manage just to reach my other hand to grasp both her own as she pulls me back up onto the ledge into her arms. We both lay panting there at the edge, water pooling at our feet before spilling away. After a moment, Lilitu moves, and I reach out in panic, gripping her sodden linens. "No. Do not leave me!"

"Hush, daughter. Find your strength." Her cool hand grips my shoulder tight, giving me a firm shake. "I am only trying to feel how wide this cavern may be, and how far the rift extends. I cannot see any more than you, not in this darkness absolute. Be still and calm yourself. I will return."

So saying, she slips away, and I am left to do as she bade; to try to find calm. Cradling my aching wrist against my chest, I close my useless eyes and breathe, a few long, shuddering breaths. I can hear my heartbeat, faint and shallow, and beyond that, the gurgling of water at my feet. I listen as it pools at the brink, and strain my senses to hear it hit the ground below. But I do not hear it hit anything. Only the endless, rippling fall into nothing.

I shudder and pull myself back a few feet, away from the terrible edge, waiting for Lilitu to return, but she does not. I shiver in the cold, my wet linens clinging to my arms and legs. My wrist is not healing. It pounds with pain, and hunger stabs in my belly like a dagger. My thoughts drift, dreamlike and dull as I wait and sink slowly into half-waking. So adrift am I that the sound, when it first echoes at the edges of hearing, becomes a part of a drifting dream where I see, again and again, the face of Makhir, alive, and assailing me, ferocious and fangs bare, attacking me even as his skin melts away with a rasping, scraping sound. I try to defend myself, try to get away, but I cannot move, cannot free myself from his grasp. Again, and again he attacks, shaking me—and then I hear Lilitu's voice, no longer a whisper, but a shout, and realise it is she who is shaking me; and the sound in my dream is not the sound of Makhir's dissolving flesh, but rather the sound of metal on stone. I smell smoke and look behind to see the shivering torch-cast shadows of men approaching, the stabbing flames dancing an evil orange light across the cavern walls.

The hunters. They have found the fissure in the cave wall and are coming through.

Alarm surges through me as I fully awaken, and Lilitu pulls me to my feet. I look to her in horror and vain hope—but she shakes her head, her eyes dark.

"There is no escape. And no time. The rift stretches from wall to wall, and I can find no safe way down."

There is a shout from the cavern behind us, and I start and stare over her shoulder in dread as the torchlight grows brighter, the shadows larger. They are close. I peer around for any escape, any hiding place, but find nothing. Only the glistening rock walls, the swift uncaring stream and the endless black abyss. Panic quickens my breath, and my voice breaks as I seek Lilitu's eyes.

"What will we do?"

But she does not answer, only reaches a cold and pale hand to press against my cheek.

"Listen to me, my daughter. Blood of my blood."

Confusion and fear twist around my heart as she smiles, soft and sad.

"Always, I have told you the truth; yet not the whole of it. This I will tell you now, but first, know that I love you. As I have always loved you. And always will. All I have done has been for love of you. Do not forget."

I nod, wondering dully why she is telling me this now.

She smiles. "Good." She gazes at me a long moment, reaching out to sweep a stray strand of hair from my eyes. "Do not be consumed by darkness in the nights to come, nor linger too long alone. Stay close to the mortal world; move as it moves, change as it changes. Do not be frightened. Find love where you may and learn to cherish it. For love is fleeting, and precious. Remember all that I have taught you, my daughter. My child."

She grips me tight, pulling me near, and over her shoulder the first line of men round the bend. They loose a bellow of triumph as they see us, and begin to run, swords and torches high. But Lilitu does not turn, only draws me into her arms, her lips brushing my cheek as she leans in to whisper a final, crashing truth.

"It was not Alu who made you, Asharru. It was I. You are mine, and mine alone."

I shudder in her arms, shock cascading over me as my mind numbly tries to comprehend her words. Not Alu's, but hers? She holds me a moment more, pressing her mouth to mine in a lingering kiss, quieting the questions that speed to my lips.

Then, still smiling, she pulls away—and shoves me, hard. I scream her name, grasping desperately for her hand, but too late. The last thing I see as I plummet over the edge of the abyss is her face smiling, her eyes shining, and her hair a blood-red halo in the light of a dozen blazing torches.

Chapter 47

Shimmering and Incandescent

Pain.

Every inch of flesh on fire.

Images flash behind entombed eyes; I am Asharru, and I am dying, a dagger in my breast. I am carried into darkness. I am death. I am drowning in a sea of blood; I am buried in burning sand. Hunted. Cursed.

Am I dead?

I am ancient, all-knowing. I love and am loved. I betray and am betrayed. I am forever damned. I am burning, unmade; reborn in flesh and blood.

Always blood.

Hunger moves in me and awakens more agony. I fight to move, to stretch my hand, and my index finger shifts a millimetre. Alive.

I'm alive.

Awake now, panic sets in. I struggle against whatever holds me, try to draw breath, try to scream. Can't breathe. Can't see. My body begins to spasm in the throes of air-starvation, and awareness fades rapidly to a pinpoint of knowing. No. I fight harder, struggling with all my might—and suddenly, there is sound; muffled voices, a shout, then hands, digging, lifting, pulling—and I'm free.

More hands, arms, pulling me up, up into air cool and damp. I fall against a cold wet surface, retching, gasping for breath; my body wracked in impossible agony. Water splashes against my face. Rain. It's raining. I try to open my eyes and rasp out a scream as pain sears through each orb. It's as if they are filled with a thousand shards of glass.

Grace. Where's Grace?

I'm blind, lost; reaching weak and desperate—then a hand grasps my own and I hear a voice. Voices. Arguing. The sound of fire, the smell of smoke and blood. And further away, screams. No. Sirens. The arguing voices grow louder, then one, familiar, cuts across the rest.

"No. Take the mortal to her own kind. I'll take the vampire. But we have to leave. Now."

Sound fades, and darkness swallows me again. When I wake it is to movement. Someone is carrying me. Where? I struggle, try to see, and that familiar voice is there again, melodic, comforting.

"Almost there, vampire."

I spin away again; wake to feel the surrounding air press in, then release and grow warm. There is a heady scent all around. Like a summer night just after rain. But it's not raining anymore. I'm lying face down on the ground. Grass. Damp and sweet. I taste it on my lips, past the taste of blood. Like honey. A breeze blows against my skin, like the softest sigh. Consciousness fades.

Returns.

This time I'm lying on my back, against something soft and giving. There is a warm weight over me, and a heaviness to my limbs. And there is a new voice.

"Drink." Warm flesh is pressed against my lips, and I take it. Bite, drink. Blood spills into me, calming me. Healing me. I shudder, whimpering like a newborn. It moves through me, carrying me away, and I let myself drown in the flood, sinking into it, down and down and down; dark and soft and black.

I'm running. Hunted. Red blood on white snow; falling on stone steps, the distant thunder of guns. The whisper of wings. Her voice. My name. Her blood, like light.

And before; alone in the dark, wounded, lost, betrayed. Her voice. Always there. The Angel. My angel. My mind spins, reeling, moving back through time, before the sands rose, before the seas formed; when this world was new. When we were new. I see her, shining like the sun, reaching for me, whispering.

"Drink."

I feel my wounds begin to heal, in waves of pain and release, over and over again. The sand embedded in my skin falls away. I open my eyes and am met with a barrage of light and colour, too much, too bright. I scream as lightning strikes through every nerve, and darkness takes me again. Darkness that gives way once more to desert. Sweeping sands rise in endless dunes against a starless indigo sky.

I know this place.

Dread fills me, and I whip around, trying to see all ways at once, expecting the monsters to rise, reaching razor-tipped hands to rip me apart until I am no more.

But they do not come.

I am alone.

Turning again, I see a light, glinting at the horizon. I wince, expecting the sun—but no. Night remains. Only the glint, like a shimmering star. I walk toward it, and I am there. Facing a mirror. Freestanding, framed in ebony. I stand, in front of myself. Naked, pale and unchanging. I step closer, staring into my own eyes, their mercurial blue shimmering and incandescent. I lean in. Watching.

Waiting.

Then, I see it. A shadow, moving behind my reflected irises. A shadow of something else. Someone else. I watch as the shadow moves across my right eye, then my left, watch as it ripples across my skin; a dark mother-of-pearl shimmer. I look down at my hand, to find it unchanged, then back to my reflection, watching as its muscles bend and elongate, as its jaw squares and brow firms; watch as its breasts shrink and flatten, becoming muscle; as its shoulders widen and hips narrow.

As female becomes male.

The shimmering shadow moves behind my reflection's form then, and I watch, fascinated, as wings, black as starless night sprout from its shoulder blades, watch as the shadow weaves them wide and strong, until they curve a meter above its head—above his head—feathered ends trailing in the sand at his feet.

Again, I look down at my own body still unchanged—and when I look back, he nods from the mirror. The Anunnaki.

"Asharru."

My name on his lips is greeting, approval and knowledge; and all at once, I know his own.

"Elathan."

He smiles with my eyes, and awed, I reach to touch him. My fingers hit the surface of the mirror, and it ripples, like water. Sound erupts from the glass, ringing and echoing like a tolling bell, growing louder and louder, until it is all I can hear.

I cry out as the ripples circle outward, across the surface of the mirror, across his form and out, over my hand, up my arm and down my body, lapping at the shores of my skin and undulating back and forth until there is no boundary between my reflection and myself; between he and I. Until we are one shivering, shimmering soul; growing brighter and brighter until I can no longer see for brightness—and I gasp awake, struggling in panic against whatever holds me, blinded by light. The sun. I fight to free myself, seeking shadow, shelter, anything.

"Relax, vampire. There's no sun here."

As the voice speaks, the light dims, and I struggle to open eyes that feel like they've been sandpapered and super-glued.

Awake.

I'm awake. Whole. Myself.

Everything comes back in a rush. Grace captured. Jude dead. Possessed. Gone. The demons, the pit of molten glass. The mist, the invisible army, my fury, more than mine, the name in my head, on my lips; the dagger in my hand. In the demon's flesh. The knife burning me, burning him. The demon roaring, Grace falling. Then—

"Grace!"

One thought, spurring me to action. I try to get up again, but am shoved back down by something very strong. I struggle, baring fangs against whoever, whatever holds me, and my eyes finally focus enough to find Fairy Boy. Greeneyes. Holding me back against a bed with very little effort.

I relax, and he steps back. "She's safe."

I lift a hand to rub my eyes and realise I'm shaking. Weak. And everything seems so bright. I wince up at him.

"Where is she?"

"Not here."

What a fount of information. I sit up slowly.

"Where?"

He sighs. "She's safe. In James'."

"The hospital? Is she hurt?" I start to get up again, fear clutching my heart. "Take me to her."

He steps forward again, placing a strong warning hand on my shoulder.

"No."

Anger explodes, cutting through pain. "Let me go!"

I snarl and fight, but he shoves me back against the bed, knocking my head hard against the headboard. Everything spins sideways, a carousel of colour that quickly fades to black.

When I come to, it is to flesh pressed against my lips. Flesh and blood. Yes. Hot blood, pounding through me. Needful and unthinking, I reach and grasp, wrapping my hands around the source, pulling it in. I hear an animal sound above me, and whoever, whatever I am drinking from tries to pull away. No. I grip harder, pull closer, drink deeper, and the animal sound repeats, a grunting growl that turns into a curse.

"Fuck!"

Again, they try to pull away, but need drives me, and I grip harder still, drinking more. Their blood, powerful and strong courses into me, along with an explosion of sensation. Animal instinct mixed with a heady human fear. I hear more curses, shouts—and they are torn from my grasp. Snarling, I reach for more—and then I can't move, can't breathe.

I open my eyes, try to find what it is that has me, but all I can see are two stern, impossibly green eyes, watching me as everything goes black once again.

Music.

Somewhere there's music playing. It wakes me gently, my consciousness rising slowly up from some deep place of sleep.

Awake.

I open my eyes.

It takes a moment to focus, but after a few seconds, I see that I am looking at a window. Inside. Looking out. A gothic window, paned in blown glass that looks centuries old and impossibly clear. Beyond the glass is sky—a purple, twilight sky, filled with shimmering, dancing stars. And by dancing I mean actually dancing. I watch them swing around each other in dizzying patterns. Not possible. I squint my eyes, look again. Still dancing. And somewhere I think I hear faint, musical laughter. The light and sound blend together, warping and swirling around each other, until I feel dizzy, and have to look away.

"Welcome back."

I follow the voice to find Greeneyes leaning gracefully against the wall across the room, watching me.

I try to move, to sit up, only to be met with pain. Like I'm one big bruise. Biting back a groan, I lay back down.

"Where am I?"

"Home. In my world." He bows low, with an old-fashioned and ridiculously graceful flourish that looks somehow appropriate even though he's in jeans and a t-shirt. "Welcome to Arcadia, my lady vampire."

I shoot him what I hope is a withering glance, then gingerly look around.

I'm lying on a bed covered with silks and furs. It is set in the centre of a round room that looks a lot like a castle turret, with curving walls made of stone. But each stone seems to shift shape and change colour and texture constantly. In fact, everything around me is changing. It's as if nothing here is solid. Or inanimate. It makes me dizzy again and I look back to Greeneyes for an explanation, to find him studying me with an enigmatic smile.

"You have interesting dreams, vampire."

I glare at him. "Stop calling me that. My name's Rue. And what do you know about my dreams?"

The memory of the dream drifts past my mind, like sand in the wind. I can't hang onto it. I reach for it and find only the space where it was.

Greeneyes shrugs. "I know dreams. And you weren't dreaming quietly."

I glare at him again, but he only smiles more. So I give up.

"What happened? How did I get here? How long have I been here? How do I get back to Grace?"

"So many questions!" He walks across the room, to a silken colour-shifting chaise lounge, and slants into a graceful cross-legged recline. "Will I answer in order? Or in order of importance?"

"I need to see Grace."

"You can't go yet."

"Why?"

"You're too wounded, too weak. Also, it's the middle of the day there."

"Where?"

He rolls his eyes.

"In your world? Were you listening at all?"

"I was. Right before you knocked me out. Twice."

"I had to. You were delirious. Dangerous. You nearly killed one of my people. And we are notoriously difficult to kill."

The memory returns. Drinking blood, pure and powerful. Animal. I wanted more. I still want more. Shit.

Shame rises and grips my heart. "I'm sorry."

He shrugs. "Don't tell me. Tell her."

"Her?"

"T?" He raises his voice toward the open door, and a young woman steps in. She must've been just outside, and she doesn't come in very far.

She stays there, leaning against the frame, all leather and muscle, with short, shaggy blonde hair, an angular, almost masculine face, and amber eyes. Wolf eyes. Eyes that are currently staring at me with thinly veiled contempt. As I stare back, I notice her right wrist is bandaged, dark blood seeping through the cotton. It steals all my focus for a second. I close my eyes, open them again, and to distract myself I decide to try and sit up. It hurts. A lot. But it works. Moaning, I prop myself up against the bed frame before meeting her gaze.

"I'm sorry." And I mean it. But I don't think she believes me.

She glowers at me for a few more seconds, then across at Greeneyes. "Are we done?"

Her words are coloured by the hint of an accent. Welsh, I think.

He nods. "For now."

She sends one last frown in my direction and disappears back the way she came.

Greeneyes shakes his head. "Don't mind her. The cursed are always out of sorts."

"The cursed?"

He sighs. "Changelings. They're either Cursed or Blessed."

I just look at him, no clue what he's on about, and he shrugs.

"Never mind." He gets up, walks over and sits on the bed. "I was answering your questions. So. After you left the park in such a hurry—and rudely I might add—I went to ask my Lady Mother if she could lend me fifty or so of her knights for your battle. It took some convincing, but of course she said yes. I am her favourite after all. I went to speak to the knights in question—"

I cut him off. "I know you brought your army, and I know you found the factory lot. I meant what happened after that."

He glares at me. "You are impertinent and impatient. I wonder now why I helped you at all."

I breathe out frustration. "I'm sorry. Please continue."

He raises a disapproving eyebrow, considers a moment, then goes on.

"As I was saying, I spoke to the knights in question, and soon enough we were armoured and off to your Glass Factory. Which isn't very far from here, as we travel."

I frown out the window, still unclear where 'here' is, but all I can see is that nerve-wrackingly unfamiliar sky with its ever-changing stars. It makes me nauseous, so I look back at him as he continues.

"When we arrived, I soon saw you had started without me—rude again—and that you had lost."

He gives me another smirk; one I want to rip right off his pretty face. But I bite back the impulse, knowing he's not the enemy.

"Go on."

He shrugs.

"Those demons were not the brightest and had posted no watch. We rode the mist over their walls and defeated them. They never knew what hit them. It was easy."

He grins again, and I wait for him to continue. But he doesn't. I'm quickly losing all patience.

"And then what? Did you get them all? How did I get here? How did Grace get to the hospital? Is she okay? I need to be there."

I try to stand again, this time managing to get to my feet before a wave of weakness knocks me sideways.

I fall, grasping for anything to hold on to, and he's there. Catching me in one arm. He smells of summer and rampant, wild, life—and hunger rises in a sudden storm, so strong I can't stop it. My fangs press against my lips and I grip his arm as he sits me back down, need pounding through me.

"Let go, vampire."

His voice has changed from mild mocking to cold warning, and it pierces through my hunger just enough to find my reason.

I let go.

He sighs and steadies me to sit back down on the bed.

"We routed the demons, killing most. Some few may have gotten away, but not many. My people brought your angel to the hospital, and I brought you here." He studies me, curiously. "You did a very foolish thing, vampire. I almost couldn't change it in time."

"Change...?"

"The molten glass? Back to sand? I had to do it quickly. You gave me no warning, leaping in like that."

I stare at him, remembering. Jumping, reaching Grace, propelling her up, away, and then falling, burning, into the hellish pit.

I should be dead.

Greeneyes stares back at me, watching me remember.

"Yes. I saved your life. You're welcome. And that's two favours you owe me. Three, what with making sure you were fed, and healed. Well, healing."

Again, I notice the surrounding life, the moving stones, the dancing stars, the very air, is suddenly still. Like it's listening in. Taking note. I'm getting the idea that owing one of his kind is not something to take lightly.

I let out a long sigh, and nod. "I owe you one. Three."

He grins and winks. "Good. Now, if you want to see your human, I suggest you get dressed. If we leave soon, we'll get to the nearest waning by your world's dusk."

"The nearest what?"

He looks at me like I'm the stupidest creature he's ever seen.

"Waning? The place where the veil between the worlds is thinnest? Or one place. There are a few. There used to be more, but—never mind. Anyway, something like you can't travel between anywhere else. You're too attached to your skin." He raises an elegant brow. "Although from the way you acted back at the glass factory anyone would think otherwise."

He smirks, and heads for the door, gesturing to the foot of the bed on his way out.

"I left your clothes for you there. From your car. Which we have, by the way. You might want to consider adding some colour to your wardrobe. I'll meet you outside."

With that, he's gone, and I'm alone.

I sit there a minute, gathering my strength before slowly gripping the headboard and pushing myself to my feet. Everything hurts, and everywhere burns, skin to bone, like I've been peeled and stewed. It's another minute before I can let go of the headboard and make my way to the clothes hanging off the end of the bed.

I dress gingerly, wincing as I tug the grey t-shirt and black jeans on over red raw skin. By the time I gently pull on the black hoodie, black leather jacket, socks and motorcycle boots, I'm shaking. But I'm up. Alive.

Greeneyes is waiting in the hall as I exit the room slowly, one hand on the wall to stop myself from falling over.

He frowns. "Maybe you should rest a bit longer, vampire. You don't look at all well."

I shake my head. "I'm fine."

I instantly regret the movement as the floor and ceiling momentarily switch places, and I have to close my eyes and hang on to the wall with both hands. I take a breath, then another—and open my eyes again to find him glaring at me.

"You are not fine."

I straighten up, staring him down as the vertigo passes.

"Take me to Grace."

He glares a moment more, then shrugs and turns away.

"Come on then."

He leads the way along the short hall, down a winding stone staircase and on into a large round throne room. Yep. Castle. And court. Various small groups of murmuring people turn and stare as we walk by. I get the distinct impression I am not quite welcome here, and hurry on in Greeneye's wake, studying the surroundings instead of the inhabitants.

Tapestries adorn every wall, stitched in brilliant colour and sparkling jewels, the figures portrayed in each dazzling scene seeming to turn to watch with disapproval as I follow Green eyes past them. The room opens up as we walk further in, and again I hear music, coming from above. I stare up at an impossible ceiling, curving so high and wide it seems more sky than roof—and dancing in and out among its rafters are more stars;

hundreds, thousands of them, in dozens of colours. And they're all singing.

I watch, entranced, as they spin and sway around each other, in dizzying patterns, faster and faster, their music ringing in my ears and through my head, until it lifts me on a sea of sound, promising every wish come true, every pleasant dream become real; carrying me away on a tide of bliss.

"Stop!"

I open my eyes, jolted back to reality as the music stops abruptly, the stars fading out and darting away, leaving me blinking back tears against a near-overwhelming feeling of loss.

"What...?"

Greeneyes studies me thoughtfully. "I assumed you'd be immune."

"Immune?"

He gestures up, to the now dark and silent ceiling. "Sprites. They're pretty, to be sure, but they can be deadly. To humans, usually. They'll enchant any soul within reach, and drink their dreams dry if they can, leaving nothing but an empty, aimless shell."

I give an involuntary shudder, still feeling the echo of enchantment.

"They drink dreams?"

Greeneyes smiles. "We all do. The little ones simply don't have much self-control, is all. They don't mean any harm."

I'm reminded of his earlier comment on my own dreams and regard him with a whole new wariness.

He shoots me a pointed look, his demeanour shifting like water from casual ease to slightly threatening. "We all have to eat something. Right, vampire?"

I feel the threat and the emphasis and am sure I should agree. "Right."

He nods, all ease again, leading me on past three giant fireplaces and through a grand entrance hall toward two massive carved oak, gold-hinged doors. "Don't worry, they're gone, and you're under my protection. You must still be more human than I thought to attract their attention."

I shrug, looking back over my shoulder as I follow him out the huge doors into the castle grounds—where I stop and stare in abject disbelief.

Stretched out before us is a landscape of startling scale and colour. It's Ireland, no mistake, but no Ireland that I've ever seen. It's bigger, somehow. Deeper. The greens are greener, the blues bluer and the sky—the sky spreads from the lightest silver-kissed lavender at every horizon to a slow deep purple above. An all-encompassing twilight.

Shadows in valleys and under trees drift and change, catching the corner of my gaze and then gone. It is all impossibly, breathtakingly beautiful.

"What is this place?"

"I told you. Arcadia. Twilight. Summerland, Tír na nÓg, The Dreaming. Call it what you will." Greeneyes smiles. "I call it home."

He walks on, leading me down a moss-lined path and out through a walled garden, where he gestures to a shadow that detaches itself from a tree to become the wolf-eyed girl from before.

She fixes me with a glare that could easily kill, then falls into silent step beside us as we walk out beyond what I now know to be a massive castle and grounds, and on over a path that meanders between round tree-topped hills, sheltering small herds of fallow deer.

And suddenly everything seems oddly familiar.

"This is Phoenix Park."

I peer around, noting landmarks that are at once familiar and not.

Wolf-girl smirks, and Greeneyes grins.

"Yes. And also no."

He turns gracefully around, walking backwards and waving his hands to the surroundings.

"This is Phoenix Park, but not as you know it. We are in a world thrice removed. Come and see."

Wolf-girl waits as Greeneyes leads me off the path, and up to the top of a gently sloping hill, from which we can see most of the surrounding parkland.

"Look around. What's missing?"

I look over the familiar landscape of Dublin's largest park—with no footprints of modern man.

"No roads. No cars." I turn west. "No zoo."

Greeneyes smiles slowly. "Exactly. All worlds are reflections of each other. Some—as your world and mine—are close reflections, with only minor differences. Some are more distant. The further apart the worlds the less they resemble one another. Our world is without Cold Iron. Something your world has far too much of."

He moves down the slope again, gesturing me to follow. I do, slowly, and soon enough wolf-girl falls in step beside us again. We walk in silence for a bit, while my impatience grows.

"How much further to this...waning...thing?"

"Not far."

He leads us on, turning off the path after a few yards, through a dew-diamond field bordered by a mist-laden wood.

At the edge of the wood is a solitary oak, standing a few yards in front of its fellow trees; a part of the wood, and yet distinctly apart.

Greeneyes leads us around the wide and gnarled trunk until the three of us are facing the back side of the tree, into which, rather unbelievably, is set a narrow, green, wooden door; rounded top, golden hinges and an elaborate filigreed golden doorknob, right in the centre.

"You're fucking kidding me." I shoot a look at Greeneyes, who grins.

"Hey—this is fairyland. What were you expecting? Come on."

He grasps the doorknob, pushes the door inwards, and steps into the tree. The acrid iron smell of exhaust, rubber, wet pavement and people blasts through the opening, made all the more noticeable by its absence here. Wolf-girl winces and steps back, glaring at me. I guess that she means me to go next—so I take a breath, close my eyes, duck my head, and step through the impossible doorway.

Chapter 48

Sound

Al-Tar Caves, Babylonia

S ound.
A whisper, echoing around me, like wind through river grass. I feel warmth, smell a sweet spicy scent; see, behind closed eyes, a cool blue glow. Like the light of the full moon. And always the sound. Like a distant song, sung by many voices.

No. Listen.

The notes separate. Nearby, ringing, short and hollow, like a drum. Further away, a higher melody, ringing like temple bells, and further still and far above; a sigh, building to a crescendo of release.

Not wind. Not music. Water.

My mind moves. Wakes. Names what I hear. What I feel.

Cold. Wet. Awake.

Where?

As soon as the question rises through the mists of my clouded mind, so too the answer; in broken fragments of memory. Ku-aya and her death. Babylon burning. The hunters. Lilitu. Oh, gods. Lilitu.

With a cry more howl than human, I push myself to my feet, sorrow and fear furthering my mind to lean awareness. I am at the bottom of the pit. And I am standing in a pool of water. Water that is rapidly rising.

I open my eyes to perfect darkness, fear feeding panic as I move slowly forward; reaching out both hands for any hold, any boundary. The water spilling from above has risen to a roar that echoes and pounds around the blackness of the abyss. I look up, seeking the opening I know is above, but I find no hint of light or life. How long have I been here? I do not remember landing—only Lilitu, and the fall. The water continues to swell around me, surging to my knees, and as it rises so does realisation. If I do not find a way out of this place soon, I will drown.

The horror of my last drowning sends me into further panic, and I stumble and splash in every direction, first one way, then another, arms out and shaking, seeking a boundary that must be here. Surely it must. I flounder blindly for what seems forever, and my distraught senses get a shock when I brush up against an object under the water.

Starting back in terror, I slip and fall backwards into the flood, which whorls over my head, as if to possess me. My flailing hands again strike something that rolls from my touch. Many more similar things cover the floor, causing me to stumble and fall as I scramble for purchase. Finally, I find solid ground beneath me, and push myself gasping to my feet, the pooling water now to my thighs.

Biting back terror, I reach beneath the surface, curiosity outweighing fear. My fingers strike one of the objects, and before it can tumble away, I grasp it, lift it up and feel along its surface. It is smooth, and rounded on either end. Like a stick. Or a bone. The thought rises as swift and as cold as the surrounding water, and then I know what I'm holding; what all the objects are that are covering the floor. Bones. Hundreds of bones. I can feel them around my feet, moving, as if still alive.

Moving.

I search frantically along the bottom, reaching down around my ankles—and feel another of the bones tumble by, and another. All moving in the same direction; rolling along the bottom of the abyss. As if they're being pulled. On a current.

A desperate hope fills my heart, and I splash and fumble through the water, following the tumbling bones until I stumble headfirst into what must be, what is—all gods be praised—a wall. Not boundless then, this abyss. Muttering a prayer, I run my hands down along the wall, down under the water which is now level with my waist, seeking, and finding. As far down as I can reach without putting my head under water, I feel it. A breach in the stone near the floor, perhaps two or three hand lengths in width and height, and nearly blocked with bones. Still, I can feel the current as the water is pulled out. Flowing somewhere.

Away from here.

Crying in triumph, I pull at the bones, flinging them through the water, across the pit. As I do, the water spills more freely into the breach, until it is a steady undercurrent; the water around me ceasing to rise as equal amounts flow out as pour in.

The steady flow brings more bones barrelling toward me, until I am in a constant battle to clear the breach, and I know if I do not move now, I will never be free of this watery grave. Whatever the consequence, wherever the rift may lead, it cannot be worse. With a last pull sending skeletal limbs splashing, I stand, draw the deepest breath I can—and thrust myself under the water.

As soon as my head is under, that old fear rises, but I fight it, gripping the sides of the hole with both hands and pulling myself in, sweeping bones out of my way as I push and pull myself through what I now know to be a small passage through the stone; a tunnel that grows steadily smaller, and smaller; the flow of water quickening as its way narrows. I press my shoulders in against each other, narrowing my form as much as I can as I propel myself forward with fingertips and toes, the held breath in my lungs burning, then pounding to escape.

My heart hammers hard in my chest, until my whole body trembles, and then begins to shudder and quake. No. I cannot drown. Not again. Not here. Tears spill from my eyes to join the flow around me as I fight against the releasing of air I know must come. Stars burst across my vision in the blinding blackness, and I feel a weight pressing in like lead, deadening limbs, forcing my chest to sink, my lips to part, expelling air with no more to breathe—and then, the passage opens unforeseen, widening out beyond my reach, and I am borne along with a hundred billowing bones, in the current of a thundering underground river. I flail and grasp for any hold, choking as I gulp in as much water as air.

431

Again, and again, I am spun and wheeled, bashed and battered, until suddenly, and without warning, I am expelled into the night, as from the maw of some mythical giant; spewed forth and tumbling down a rocky crag in a torrent of bones.

My descent ends as abruptly as it began—hard against the wind-hewn back of a broad boulder, my own bones cracking at the impact.

I lie there, drawing the night air into starved lungs, each gasping breath bringing pain, but pain I can bear. For at least I am breathing. Free. Alive.

After a few long moments, I pull myself slowly to my feet, leaning against the boulder for support. I am standing at the stone-strewn head of a deep ravine, hewn by that same stream of water that bore me forth, now racing along its own deep cut in the belly of the gorge. High walls rise to either side; their silhouettes black against a starry sky. Save for the gurgling, bubbling water, the night is silent.

I take it all in, then turn and look behind me; back toward the split in the rock high above, shuddering at the memory of being trapped in watery darkness. Never again. Wincing and wrapping an arm around broken ribs, I move down the rocky slope into the narrow valley.

The bones born with me are scattered all along the ground, the smaller ones snapping underfoot like dry twigs. So many bones. As of the leavings of a great many predators over time; or one large long-lived one. I shudder to think what might have been sharing the black expanse of the cavern with me, grateful that I escaped my prison whole and un-devoured.

The thought brings me to a standstill as upon its heels three others bite; the first being how am I so hale and relatively whole after such a fall? The second, fast behind; how long did I lie there after, at the bottom of the pit? And the third, slicing like a dagger through the others. Where is Lilitu?

Panic gathers at the horizons of my mind as memories descend, hastening over each other in a storm of recollection. The fall of Babylon, the death of Ku-aya, then of Makhir at Lilitu's hand; the hunters tracking us, finding us; the arrow in my breast, Lilitu's blood on my lips, the cave, the hunters upon us, trapping us at the edge of the abyss; Lilitu's eyes, glittering green; her hand against my cheek, her lips on mine, her voice, whispering truth. Revelation.

I am not Alu's child after all. I am Lilitu's. And Lilitu is gone.

A sob escapes my lips as I turn back, looking up at the mountain, past the crevice and its spurting bone-thick water, to the line where the rock face meets the night sky. A glimmer of hope glistens in the shadows of my soul. Perhaps she is not gone. If I can get back, I can find her.

Forcing my battered limbs into action, I scramble back up the rock face, bones and boulders rolling away beneath my feet and hands. Toward the top, the slope grows far steeper, until it is near-vertical, and I am forced to claw my way up, using fingertips and toes from fissure to cleft. Finally, with a last heave to clear the craggy overhang, I reach the top and pull myself to my feet.

The valley below spreads down and out, as far as I can see, starlit shades of barren brown and shadowy grey dotted here and there with darker green, as the water feeds the thirsty vegetation. I peer out to the distant horizon, to a fading line of indigo that tells me I am facing west, and have hours of night before me. I am surprised yet again at how much I have healed already. I am hungry, as always, but not yet starving.

Perhaps then, it has not been so long as I have thought, perhaps this is still Lilitu's blood, moving through me. If so, and it must be so, then perhaps she is still there, in the cave. It cannot be far. Turning east, I hasten over the upland, fear and hope in equal measures surging through me, until I am running, the soles of my feet lacerated by stone, healing, cut and healing again and again, but I do not care. Lilitu. I must find her.

I run and run until I am bought up short by the eastern edge of the plateau. Beneath me the ground fans away into another valley—this one far more familiar. I see the moonlit thread of the Euphrates, and, at a bend as it winds its way south toward my homeland, I can just make out a dim glow that must be Babylon. I am too far away to tell if it is still burning.

Turning back to the cliff face as it descends away from me, I study the rocky escarpment, seeking the cave where first we hid from the hunters and the sun, Lilitu and I. It must be here. She must be here. Pacing along the ridge, I stare at every shadowed overhang, every rupture and rift, but I do not see the opening.

Perhaps I am at the wrong place. Frustrated, fear and panic growing, I walk the bluff from edge to edge, searching again, and again—there. Finally. Halfway down the rock, a shadow darker than the rest, like a scar on the cheek of this earthy giant. And I can see, as I watch for a moment, the orange glint of firelight. My heart goes cold. The hunters.

Fear gives way to fury, and I scramble down the rock face, almost falling in my urgency, heart pounding, fangs bared and battle-ready as I hurl myself through the opening.

Chapter 49

Give and Take

There is a rush of warm wind, and a feeling across my skin like stepping through the thinnest sheet of water; then Dublin erupts around me, a dizzying cacophony of sight and sound and smell, thundering down along with a sudden onslaught of day-drain, sending me reeling.

I stagger, almost fall, and a strong arm grips my own, holding me steady. I open my eyes to meet a wolf-gold glare. This close, the animal heat and life coursing through her is too much, and hunger riots through me, sudden and shocking. My fangs press against my lip as need wars with reason, and I curl my hand around her forearm. She snarls, a wolfish warning—and then Greeneyes grips my shoulder, hard—bringing me back from the edge.

"Play nice, you two,"

His tone is light, yet the intention behind the words is anything but. I let go, and step back, pushing my hunger down with some effort, while fighting to see against the glare of a thankfully cloud-covered sky.

"It's day."

Greeneyes glances up at the sky, then back, his tone flippant. "Yeah. Sorry about that. Must've taken less time getting here than I thought."

Anger courses through me, and I curl my fists, snarling at him. "You could've killed me."

"Oh, come on." He rolls his eyes. "Everyone knows it takes a couple of minutes for one of you to go up in smoke, even on the sunniest of days. I'd have had time to shelter you. Besides—" He fixes me with a look. "If I wanted you dead, you would be. Many times over."

He's right. I'm deep in his debt, and I know it. Plus, I'm in no condition to argue or fight. Every sinew is shaking, and any healing has stopped cold under the onslaught of day. I'm hurting, weak, exhausted, dizzy as fuck, and I need him to take me to Grace. I take a shaky breath and let it go.

"Sorry."

He shrugs and turns to Wolfgirl. "Tamsin. Give her back her knife."

Wolfgirl—Tamsin—glowers at him a moment, but then she walks a few steps back to the tree—which in this world doesn't have a door, only a fire-blackened hollow—reaches up into a nook in the branches, and pulls out the dagger I left burning in the Thomas-Demon's shoulder. I blink, shocked to see it. Shocked they have it. Shocked they left it in a fucking tree.

"How...?"

Greeneyes shrugs. "We found it at the edge of the pit, after the battle. It is yours, isn't it? It has your scent. Or so the wolves say." He turns to Tamsin, and she nods, holding the damn thing out to me.

I take an involuntary step back, and Greeneyes frowns. "Don't you want it?"

I look from him to her to the knife and back. I don't understand why it isn't still in the demon. I shake my head, then close my eyes as a wave of vertigo surges through me. I take a few breaths and wait until it passes to answer.

"I can't touch it."

He raises a brow. "Why?"

"It burns me."

Tamsin smirks. "It doesn't burn me."

I shoot her a glare, and turn to Greeneyes. "Why was it in the tree?"

He rolls his eyes heavenward. "Really? Do vampires read? Like, anything, ever?"

I stare at him, no idea what he's on about, and he shakes his head. "Let me put this in terms you'll understand." He points up into the cloudy sky.

"The sun." He points at me. "Vampire. Bad." He points to the knife. "Cold iron." He points to himself. "Fairy. Equally bad. Capisci?"

Okay, now he's just being an ass.

"I thought that was a myth."

"We're all myths, darling." He gives a graceful shrug. "Anyway, we couldn't bring the knife into Faerie, but we wanted to keep it close. The tree is half in, half out. And a friend. Safest place for something like that."

I try not to think too hard about what he means by the tree being a friend. It makes my head hurt.

Tamsin is still holding out the knife, and, impatience growing, I snatch it out of her hand, thinking if I can grab it quickly enough and shove it in a pocket, it won't have time to burn me. Much. I wince, preparing—but to my utter surprise, it doesn't burn. At all. In fact, it's cold. I stare down at the thing as I turn to over and over in my hand, not understanding.

"I thought you said it would burn you?"

I look up to find Greeneyes watching me.

"It did. I mean...it used to."

"Well. It seems to be behaving now."

"Yeah..." I mutter, completely thrown.

Then Tamsin clears her throat. "Hey, leech. If you're done playing with your knife, we should go." She nods across the field to where a group of mortals are ambling their way toward us, tourist maps in hand.

"Yep! Time to go!" Greeneyes grins and I shake my head, too confused by the knife and too impatient to get to Grace to pay much attention to Wolfgirl's insult. Shoving the cold blade into my jacket pocket, I follow as Greeneyes leads us away across the field and on to the edge of a parking lot, where he stops again.

"Okay, vampire. This is where we part ways. Tams will drive you from here."

I turn to him, surprised, and he grins. "I know, you'll miss me. But I can't slip you sideways, so a car is the next best thing. And I can't drive one. Cold Iron and all."

"Slip me sideways?" I'm still baffled by the knife not burning me; not to mention having just been to a place I didn't think existed, and enchanted by little glowing fairy children for fuck's sake, and Fairy Boy here is not making any sense.

"Never mind." He shrugs. "It's a faster way to travel. Between worlds. Not important." He turns to Tamsin. "Well, go get the car, darling."

Wolfgirl rolls her eyes and stomps off, muttering under her breath, and he winks at me.

"She adores me. And now she's gone—here." He reaches into his pocket and brings out my amulet, still hanging from its silver chain, and Jude's broken rosary beads. "I thought you might want these. It's kind of amazing they weren't burnt up. Then again, it's kind of amazing you weren't burnt up."

He hands me both, and I stare down at them bunched together in my palm, a wave of grief rising.

Jude.

Oh gods, I'm so sorry.

Blinking back tears, I look back up to Greeneyes. "Thanks."

He smiles, shrugs. "No problem. Just keep the amulet hidden from Tamsin. Silver and all."

I nod, putting the two necklaces in my pocket for now, and shoving my grief down and away. No time to cry. I still have to see Grace.

There's a rumble of a large engine behind us, and Tamsin pulls up in an old 4×4. Of course. Greeneyes gestures in her direction. "You're all set so."

I nod and walk the short distance to the car, opening the door, still too lost in grief and worry to pay much attention. "Thanks."

"You're welcome." He smiles and takes a step away as I step up into the car, then he turns back. "Oh—one more thing."

I pause, door ajar. "Yeah?"

"Time does funny things in my world. You've been there three days. But here it's been three weeks."

"What!?"

He shrugs, stepping back into a rising mist and fading from view like the fucking Cheshire cat. "Give or take a day or two..."

He waves a graceful hand and is gone, leaving me staring after him.

"Shut the door." Tamsin's tone is all annoyance.

I slam the door. "What did he mean, it's been three weeks?"

She shrugs, whipping the big car expertly out of the lot. "Just what he said. Time moves differently in different worlds. There it's been three days. Here it's been three weeks."

Anger rises again, burning in my chest and setting my eyes alight. "And neither of you thought this was something I should know? What about Grace? You're telling me she's been in hospital all this time?"

She nods, steering the 4×4 out of the park and onto the road. "She's in a coma."

"What!?"

"Blood loss."

My heart sinks, the memory of Grace's blood spilling into the pit replaying in my mind as she goes on.

"She has some burns as well—second degree, mostly, and some broken bones and of course the cuts on her wrists." She shoots me a sideways look. "They've stitched her up and replaced the volume. She's breathing on her own now, but she's still unresponsive."

"Shit." Fear wraps a cold fist around my heart. I know all too well what blood loss can do to the human brain. "Shit, shit!" I pound a fist into the dash, cracking the hard plastic.

"Christ, calm the fuck down!" Tamsin glares at me as she turns the car onto the quays. "They don't know anything yet. She could be fine. Anyway, we have people in there, looking after her."

We stop at a red, waiting to turn onto the Rory O'More bridge, and she turns to face me, a surprising sympathy in her wolf-gold eyes. "I just want you to be prepared."

The light goes green, and she wheels the car across the bridge and down Waiting Street.

I watch the traffic and buildings go by, drowning under a huge swell of grief and guilt. I did this. All of it. Jude. Grace. I close my eyes against the surge of shame and two tears escape. I swipe them angrily away, wiping the blood on my jeans, thankful for the black.

Tamsin shoots a glance at me but doesn't say anything, just drives on in silence. Soon enough we're rolling down James's street and into the hospital campus. She pulls the 4 x 4 into a parking lot and kills the engine, then sighs and leans over, popping open the dented glove compartment, tugging out two pairs of mirrored sunglasses and handing one to me.

"Put these on. You look like shit. And your eyes are all...weird."

I shove them on, and she stares at me a moment, then nods. "Okay. Come on."

She puts her own sunglasses on, then hops out. After a moment, I follow suit, trailing her slowly up the path and around the corner to the main entrance of the hospital. When we enter through the sliding glass doors, she motions me over to a row of chairs against one wall.

"Be right back."

She heads off to the reception desk, and I wander over and sit down, biting back a groan as my joints scream in protest. Reception is full of people, all full of worry, and paying not a lick of attention to one more sick-looking woman in their midst. Thank the gods.

I sigh and run a hand through my hair, noting for the first time that it's very clean, and smells of summer. Someone must've given me a bath somewhere along the line, while I was out of it. In Fairyland. Gods. I close my eyes and try to remember, but everything's a muddled blur. Even the recent memories—from an hour or so ago—are fading fast. Like a dream. Which is weird. I usually remember everything.

"Hey. Vampire." A boot thumps against the leg of my chair and I look up to meet my reflection in Wolfgirl's mirrored sunglasses. Standing next to her is an older woman—late forties, maybe—dressed as a nurse and smiling down at me.

"Stop that, T. I'm sure she has a name. Don't you, my love?"

Her accent is far thicker than Wolfgirl's, and definitely Welsh—but her shoulder-length hair is the same shade of blonde, and her eyes only a slightly darker gold—dark enough to pass for a normal brown. But I know better. I stand up, holding out my hand.

"Rue."

"Rue." She takes my hand and squeezes it. "A pretty name. Oh, your hands are cold!" She grabs my other hand and rubs both in her own as if to warm them, and for some reason the flood of grief comes rushing back, forming a hard lump in my throat. I swallow hard against it, suddenly very glad of the sunglasses as I feel blood tears sting.

"I'm Arianwen. Lovely to finally meet you." She gives my hands another gentle squeeze, then takes a step closer, studying my face. "You're very pale." She turns to Tamsin. "She's very pale."

Wolfgirl sighs. "Of course, she's pale, mum. She's a fucking vampire."

"Language!" Arianwen tsks and, keeping one of my hands in her own as if I were a child, starts walking down the main hall toward some double doors, taking me with her and talking all the while.

"I knew Órin wouldn't feed you enough. He probably didn't even think about it. Oh, he's lovely, just a bit self-involved. But who can blame him, not his fault, the dear boy, being what he is, he's been horribly spoiled."

She turns to Tamsin, who's been trailing behind like a sullen teen.

"How is our young Prince?"

She shrugs. "He's fine. The usual."

"He did actually. Feed me." I don't know why I feel the need to defend Greeneyes—Órin. Prince Órin, apparently. But I do. "He tried to get me to stay. Heal more. I wanted to leave. I have to see Grace."

Arianwen nods. "And you will. Today, and any other day." She lets go of my hand and smiles again; but this time it's a dangerous, feral smile that doesn't reach her eyes, and I understand.

"Any day."

She nods. "This is my hospital. And although our prince has vouchsafed your being here, I don't know you. But I know what you are. And we can't be too careful these days, can we?"

I shrug, nodding in acquiescence, too exhausted and worried to argue. "I just want to see Grace."

"And so you shall."

She takes my hand once more, and I let myself be led through set after set of automated doors and down several sterile florescent-lit hallways. We pass a nurses' station, staffed with harried-looking nurses who barely look up as we go by. Arianwen leads on, past another station and into a smaller hall, speaking softly all the while.

"We've finally got hold of her family. Well, her father. He was somewhere in the middle-east. He's on his way." She looks at me sideways. I nod, only half listening.

"That's good."

"Yes. We think she'll come out of it. We just don't know when. Or ... how she'll be."

Again, I nod, and she stops talking, leading us on down the hall and stopping in front of a set of red-bordered double doors. "Wait here."

She goes in, leaving me waiting with Wolfgirl, who just stands there, staring at me. "You don't look so good."

I shrug, take a breath, let it out, then reach up and remove the sunglasses, handing them back to her. "Thanks."

She shakes her head. "Keep them."

I fold them up and shove them in my pocket as Arianwen comes back through the doors, giving me a 'come on' gesture.

We follow her through into a darker, quieter hall, bordered on either side by rows of beds, separated from one another and the hall by half-drawn green curtains. Each bed is surrounded by banks of machines that beep and hum softly, wires and tubes leading from each machine to each seriously ill patient. The whole place is permeated with the scent of sterile alcohol, disinfectant, blood, and death.

"This is the ICU."

Arianwen nods, but doesn't say anything as she leads us past another nurses' station, this one staffed by one nurse who looks up as we enter. She smiles at Arianwen, shoots a quick glance at Tamsin, a longer more suspicious one at me, and then purposefully turns her back, focusing on a bank of file cabinets behind the desk.

Arianwen nods to Tamsin, who lingers watchful, while her mother leads me across the hall, to one of the beds.

My heart clenches in my chest, and tears spring into my eyes as I see the bed's occupant, lying pale and still and surrounded by machines that monitor her every breath and heartbeat.

"Grace." I hurry to the side of the bed and stop. An IV tube trails from a vein in the back of her right hand up to a bag that dutifully drips fluids, while on her left index finger a pulse monitor is connected to a softly beeping machine. She's breathing soft and even, but as I reach out instinctively with my mind for her own, I feel nothing. It's like coming up against a wall. No sign of consciousness. Of life. Of her.

No.

Closing my eyes and clenching fists against palms, I try harder; pushing against the nothingness in her mind until I'm dizzy with the effort. For a moment, I think I feel something—a whisper of hope, so deep inside—but then it's gone, and I'm left shaking, exhausted, and defeated by daytime effort.

I open my eyes to find Arianwen watching me as she pushes forward a chair, motioning me to sit.

"I'll give you a moment." She nods, softly closing the curtains around the bed and then leaving us alone.

I scoot the chair up to the bed and sit down, taking Grace's hand and bringing it to my mouth; planting kiss beside the needle that's taped there.

"Grace. I'm so sorry."

I never wanted this. Losing Jude, hurting Grace. Any of it. My last thought, back at the lot, at the pit of fire, was that at least I'd saved her. At least I'd done one good thing. But no. All that, only to have her here like this.

I take a shaky breath and close my eyes, sending the tears that have been welling there a while trailing down my cheeks to drip onto my fingers clasped around her own. I open my eyes and watch the red stain bloom across the white medical tape that holds the IV in place at the back of her hand.

And I know what I have to do.

They've given her blood, but only mortal blood. And a lot of it. So much that I bet her own, angelic blood is drowning in it, unable to heal. It'll take time to rebuild. Time she doesn't have. The longer she's under, the more likely it is she'll be lost.

My blood, on the other hand, doesn't need time. In pure, parasitic form, it instantly re-synthesises any blood I ingest, breaking down and re-writing its DNA, making it mine. And my blood can heal. Will heal.

At this point, it will also make her need me. Desperately, helplessly. I already know she's susceptible to its influence, and every time she takes it, that susceptibility grows. If I give her my blood now, there won't be any honesty between us for weeks. Maybe longer. I'll won't be sure of anything she says or does, because my blood will make her do and say anything to please me. And the longer she's around me, the more she'll want to give, and the longer I'm around her, the more I'll want to take—and give, and take, and take and give, until we're in an endless cycle of addiction to each other.

I don't want that.

Especially not with her. I love her too much.

I look at her, lying there pale and lost, and know.

Standing up, and moving quickly, I open the drawers in the stand under the nearest machine, rummaging around until I find what I'm looking for: a length of iv tubing, tourniquet, needle and catheter.

With a glance over my shoulder to make sure the curtains are well and truly drawn, I shove up my sleeve, tie off the tourniquet, shove the needle with the attached catheter into my vein and the line into the catheter.

Blood flows instantly as I loose the tourniquet, then gently take the IV drip out of Grace's hand, slip the now blood-filled tube from my arm into the catheter there instead, crimp the drip line in one hand, and wait.

I watch as my blood disappears into her vein, watch as the pulse at her throat quickens at the flow, watch as colour blooms back into her cheeks and lips. Watch until I feel dizzy, leaden and weak.

Then I remove the tube from her arm, replace the drip, take the needle and tube out of my arm, wrap them up in the tourniquet and shove the lot into my pocket and sit back down.

Just in time.

Arianwen pulls back the curtain and steps in, giving me a stern but not unkind nod. "The sun's almost set. Time to go."

I stand up, keeping a firm grip on the edge of the chair to keep from falling. Can't let on what I've done. Not to her. Not to anyone. I look back down at Grace, watching my blood move through her body, and my heart clenches hard in my chest.

"Just another minute. Please."

She purses her lips and stares at me a long moment, but then she nods. "One."

She ducks out again, pulling the curtain behind her, and I step close to Grace, taking her hand again.

"Grace. I know you're in there. Listen. You mean more to me than anyone ever has. I didn't think I could feel the way I do about you. I didn't think I could feel so...much...anymore. You've brought me out of myself." I squeeze her hand gently, bringing the backs of her fingers to my lips and closing my eyes, trying to memorise the feeling of them there. "Thank you."

I lay her hand gently back down at her side, and stand up, tears burning as I take the silver amulet of Enki from my pocket and stare at it a moment before wrapping it around her neck and clasping the chain, leaving the charm to lay against the soft rise and fall of her chest. I smile as each breath grows stronger, kiss her gently on the forehead, and look at her a moment longer, before forcing myself to step back.

"I love you. Goodbye."

Turning quickly, I part the curtain and walk away, before my screaming heart can change my mind.

445

Arianwen steps up beside me as I head for the exit, so I shove down the rising tide of grief and force a polite smile.

"Thank you."

She nods.

"You're welcome. When will you be back?"

"I won't."

She stops, looking confused, but I keep heading for the door, willing my feet to move. Tamsin falls into step beside me as I push through the double doors and down the hall. She takes one look at my face and thankfully says nothing, just shadows me back out the way we came in.

I feel the sun set with a shudder of relief through my bones as we exit into the lobby. I'm still weak from the loss of the blood I gave Grace, but with the sun down at least I'll have enough strength to get me through this moment.

The automated doors hiss open and shut again behind me as I step through into the growing night. Once out, I stop, closing my eyes and taking a long, deep breath before moving on, down the path and into the parking lot.

"Hey."

Tamsin has stopped a few feet back. I turn to face her, swallowing back the tears that rise to choke me.

"What?"

She pauses, staring at me a moment. When she speaks again, her tone is gentler.

"Do you need a lift somewhere?"

"I'm okay on my own. Thanks."

She nods, and I start to turn away, then stop.

"Will you keep an eye on her?"

She nods, understanding blooming across her face.

"Thanks." I turn away then, and walk. No idea where—just away; every step breaking my heart a little more, everything in me wanting to turn around. To stay. But I can't. I won't. I love her, and she's better off without me. Everyone's better off without me.

And I'm better off alone.

Chapter 50

Alone

Al-Tar Caves, Babylonia

I am met by a scream of terror, followed by another--that one followed by the fearful bleating of a small herd of goats as the two men watching them leap to their feet, their goats stampeding; some past me over the edge, others deeper into the cave. The two men stand like stone, staring—as do I, as startled as they. No hunters. No Lilitu. What is this?

I recover first, stepping deeper into the cavern toward the older of the two. I see now they are man and boy; a father and son perhaps. Or brothers. The older steps in front of the younger, holding his staff as if to bar my way as he whispers a word that is familiar and yet not.

"What did you say?" My voice sounds course to my ears. Feels strange and rough in my throat. I take another step forward. "Speak!"

I am growing impatient, confusion feeding anger. The older one raises his staff up and out, holding it level, as if such a thing could be a barrier, and speaks again, a tremor in his voice. "Tuwl Shedim!"

I do not know what he is saying, yet his meaning is clear enough. Memory upon memory of the same said against me, different words, different tongues, all the same. Monster. Demon. Get away. As if words could banish me.

I take another step forward, and he shouts the same again, and again, pushing the staff out at me in a white-knuckled grip. I am growing tired of this game. In an instant, I grasp the staff, rip it from his grasp and splinter it in two with one hand, while with the other I clutch his throat, lifting him off the ground, shouting at him in the common tongue.

"Who are you? Where are the men who were here? The soldiers? Where did they go and when? Tell me!"

I shake him, to make him speak, but he only gasps and kicks, eyes gaping as his bladder releases, his heart thundering in his breast, full of fear. Full of blood.

Hunger and thirst scorch through me, and I pull him close, ignoring his struggles as I push aside his hair, press his chin up and away with my thumb, and sink my fangs into that river of red.

Relief settles as I drink and drink; soothing fear, easing pain. I close my eyes at the stream of sensation; taking it all, losing myself in the blessed flood, no thought, no need nor deed but this.

Gradually his heart slows and stops, and I lift my head, lick my lips and lay him down beside his fire. I watch a moment as he dies, then turn to the boy—who is curled into a corner clutching one of his goats; his eyes screwed shut as he sobs and begs in that same oddly familiar tongue. Like a thousand others before him.

All the same.

I walk over and crouch down, watching him in silence. Slowly his sobs subside, and he opens his eyes. I nod to him and he shudders. He is young—ten, perhaps twelve years of age. I smile, speaking softly in the common tongue, my voice my own again, smooth and resonant.

"What is your name?"

He shakes his head, pulling back into his corner, his eyes trailing toward the body by the fire—and so I move ever so slightly, to block the sight.

"No ... look at me. Listen. Tell me your name, boy."

His eyes dart back to mine, and I lean in, willing him to hear me, to answer me, fresh blood singing through my veins, making me mindful of every nuance of his energy. Beyond the hard hammer of his heart and the soft surge of his blood, I sense more. His essence. So near the surface, I feel I can grasp it; as if it is made manifest. Never have I felt such a thing before, not without feeding, or being fed from. It is thrilling and new, and I wonder in that moment, if I can control it. Control him, by guiding his emotions.

Calming myself first with some effort, I then press that calm outwards, toward the boy, holding his gaze and watching him soften, his body relaxing enough so that the goat slips from his grasp and away. It is the simplest task, and I wonder how I have not chanced upon this gift before.

Smiling again, I lay my hand open and flat on my chest, and gently say my name.

"Asharru."

Then I put my hand out, gesturing to him, and repeat my question.

"Your name?"

He chokes back a last sob, his eyes filling with fledgling trust, his voice a broken whisper.

"Dawid."

I nod, smiling further. "Dawid. Good. You speak the common tongue."

He nods, eyes wide and fixed upon my own.

I hold his gaze. "Tell me, Dawid, how long have you been tending your goats in this place?"

He shudders a little. "All my life."

His accent is strange. So thick I can barely understand him. And yet I must know more. I smile, to keep him calm as I question him further.

"Here? On this mountain?"

He nods. "As my father, and his father before him..." His eyes once more flit to the fire, and the cooling body there, so I move nearer to him.

"And in that time, have you ever seen anyone else here, in this place?"

He shakes his head.

"No men? Soldiers? Strangers?"

He shakes his head again.

"What about a woman...smaller than myself, with hair the colour of carmine?"

"No." A whisper this time. "No men. No woman like that. Only..."

He falters, and I feel his fear rise, threatening to shatter the fragile hold I have as he begins once more to tremble. "Only the monster."

"Monster?" I lean in, close enough to feel his breath on my cheek. "What monster?"

His emotions surge, panic building as he gestures deeper into the cave. "They say she lives in darkness, sleeping among the bones of those she has killed. They say she will wake and eat you in the night if you are bad …"

He shudders, and I feel the hold I have on him fracture and fail. His eyes grow wide with dread, and he presses back away from me, as far back against the stone as he can, his sobs renewing, hands out in supplication as he begs and pleads. "Please, please, do not kill me. Please, Shedim. I beg of you. Do not take me to your den of bones! I will be good, I promise!"

Cold, cruel comprehension descends. Shedim. Demon. A monster in the dark, dwelling in her den of bones.

For the first time this night, I look down at my own form, and realise I am covered in mud, mire and blood; my once-white linens black and rotted through, more rags than clothes. My hair hangs in matted dreads to my hips. My hands are foul with filth, my nails like claws. I am a wild thing. A beast.

A monster.

I stand, the knowledge piercing my heart like a knife. How long has it been? I stare down at the boy a moment more, then turn away, leaving him to his goats and his tears.

Climbing down from the cave, I walk back toward the city, lost in dark thoughts. How long? I remember Lilitu's tale, how she lost herself after the horror of her making, living as a beast. No thought, no self, only animal need. To hunt, to feed. To kill.

So many bones. Hundreds. Thousands. How long? Long enough to become legend. A tale told to frighten children into obedience.

Lilitu never knew how long her mind was gone. Months. Years. Centuries, perhaps. Have I too, been lost to the beast for so long? I shudder at the horror of it, trying to push the thought away, but it will not go.

How long?

The night grows darker as I head east, toward the river, and the city beyond. If it still stands. Dread fills my heart as I reach the river, and walk south along its banks, searching the sky for a glimpse of torchlight, seeking the scent of smoke—and then, as I round a long bend, I see it; a dark shadow looming in the night. The wall. Babylon still stands.

Relief surges through me, and I hurry toward my adopted city. Perhaps it has not been so long. Perhaps my brethren are within. Still alive. Perhaps Lilitu is there, waiting for me.

I race toward the gate at the western quarter, slowing to a mortal pace as I advance, to find the way guarded by two spear-wielding men in armour I do not recognise. Crouching in the gloom where the river meets the wall, I gather a few handfuls of reeds and scrub the filth from my skin as best I can, while I watch the guards; listening as they speak to one other in a language I do not know, waiting as the night grows cold around me.

Soon enough, I am rewarded for my patience. One man mutters to the other, hands him his spear, then turns and walks toward the river. Toward me. I pull further into the dark as he strides to the riverbank and lifts his tunic to ease his bladder.

It is a release he never achieves, for in that moment I am upon him, covering his mouth so he cannot scream, dragging him into the shadows, biting into his throat and drinking deep. In moments he is dead, and I strip his lifeless form of helmet, armour and tunic, donning them myself; then I take his dagger and sword, roll his body into the river and run toward the other. He turns in surprise, taking a breath to shout—but I allow him no sound, gripping his throat and shoving him hard against the wall, crushing his larynx as I lean in and drink him dry. It is over quickly, and I enter through the gates in the guise of a soldier, armed with sword and spear and drunk with blood.

No one challenges me as I weave through the streets of the lesser city; past merchants selling wine, courtesans selling themselves, and men and soldiers gathered in small groups, drinking and talking. I listen as I pass, but none are speaking the common tongue, and I cannot understand. I note that no buildings here are scorched or razed. No evidence remaining of the night Babylon burned. So, some time has passed. Yet these mud-brick houses were never so grand as those in the city beyond. They would not take much time to rebuild.

I soothe myself with the thought as I walk on unnoticed across the bridge into the city proper, and the temple complex. More soldiers stand guard at the gates into the temple district, but I duck my head, letting the helmet hide my face, and they nod and wave me within.

It is quieter here, in the sacred quarter. The walls soar above me as I walk between them, not a stone fallen, burned, or damaged. Hope withers as I realise enough time has passed then, to rebuild even here. Still, my brethren may remain within. For who else can withstand the passage of time but us?

Moving swiftly, I abandon spear, helmet and armour, keeping only dagger and sword as I enter the temple courtyard. Once inside, I slip beneath the shadow of the ziggurat, wending my way behind the great temple, out through a lesser gate into the city of the dead.

Dread wars with hope as I enter within, the sweet familiarity of what once was home stirring the disquiet that has haunted me since leaving the cave. This place is thick with memory. I breathe it in as I move between the graves of mortal men, seeking any sign, and finding none. Still, I search, scouring every crypt, catacomb, portal and passage. But all is silent.

And so I search again. And again. Until the sky above grows grey with dawn, and I must rest. It is then I notice one of the tombs nearby is new; the tile upon it inscribed in the sacred language of the temple. Sumerian. I read the name, the title—a priest it seems—and the date of his death.

My heart grows cold. I cannot believe it. The date. It is five hundred years beyond the last night I remember. The night that Babylon burned, the night Ku-aya and Makhir died, the night we ran, Lilitu and I. Out of Babylon and into the past.

Five hundred years. Lost to the beast within.

I fall against the mud-brick of the tomb as my legs collapse beneath me, the weight of time beating down upon me like a hundred-thousand thundering drums. Five hundred years. It is impossible. But there it is. And here I am. And my brethren are gone. But gone where?

Iyar is dead, this I know, and Makhir after him, killed by Lilitu to save me. Yet what of Alu? Eshe? Bion? Perhaps they too are dead, killed by the hunters. Or perhaps they left long ago, thinking I was dead. Perhaps they did not care to seek for me. At any rate, they are gone. But Lilitu—she never would have left me. Again, the last vision I have of her rises in my mind's eye. Lilitu—my maker, casting me over the edge of the abyss. Lilitu, my only mother, smiling wild above me, hair ablaze, as the hunters' torches surround her. Lilitu.

If she did not search for me, nor wait for me, then surely, she is dead.

Grief rises once more, a smothering sorrow I cannot hold. Lilitu, my maker. Not Alu, Lilitu, hiding the truth from me, all this time, and now she is dead, and I cannot even ask her why. Longing and loss rise in a torrent and I sink down, sobbing amongst the detritus of the dead. Tears burn my eyes and sear my throat as I weep and weep as if all the wretchedness in the world is within me.

I do not know how long I remain lost in anguish, but when I finally lift my head, it is to a sky ripe with light. I must find shelter.

Drawing a shuddering breath, I stand, searching through the catacombs until I find a tomb deep within the maze. Pulling back the stone, I slip within, setting the stone back in place and then laying down on the cold hard ground beside a linen-wrapped corpse. A fitting bed for one bereft as I.

Despair dwells bitter in my chest as the weakness of day descends. The last trailing, trembling thought I have as I sink into sleep, is that I am, for the first time in my life, utterly and horribly alone.

Epilogue

Rue

I love winters here. Especially December. The nights are lovely and long; the streets shimmering with Christmas lights. The air is crisp and cold, and the shops and pubs thronged with people shopping, talking, making merry. And none of them paying any attention to me.

I've kept myself busy the past few months, trying not to think about Grace, although I do. Every moment of every night. It was so hard not to go back to her. But I had to keep myself away. It was better—is better—that way.

Wolf girl got in touch two weeks after I left the hospital, bringing my car back. She found me through Greeneyes, who now seems to think he can pop in and out of my life at will. She told me that Grace woke up, and there didn't appear to be any lasting damage. She left the hospital in the care of her father. Wolf girl says she seemed sad but otherwise okay. And that's the last of it. For all I know she's left Ireland.

I hope so, for her sake.

I've spoken with Greeneyes—Órin—a couple of times since. He and his people have seen no trace of the demons that got away. As far as the police and papers are concerned, what they found in the aftermath of the battle at the glass factory lot was just a sick prank; someone having destroyed the fences, dug up some dead bodies, chopped off their heads and left them lying around the site. Greeneyes and his people took away any weapons they found, and the demon bodies were already in various states of decay, so it was a logical--if odd--conclusion. The mystery of it all stayed in the papers for a few weeks—some more sensational rags sporting various 'zombie' headlines—but then something else happened, and the public eye looked elsewhere.

As to what went on in the hotel, I haven't heard a thing. No news, no footage, no viral videos, nothing. Which is either very good, or very bad. Either way, I need to stay aware.

I booked into the Hotel De Vampires for a few nights after everything. I didn't have much choice. I had to move out of my old place after the demons burnt it down. Not that I could've stayed there anyway, with where I lived being common knowledge for gods know how many of them. Although they all seem to have disappeared. I keep scouring the news, the web, papers, radio, for any hint, but there's been nothing.

So, I do nothing.

I've healed, as I always do, and everything is back to normal. No headaches. No nightmares. No blackout blood dumping. I still don't know why I did that, but I try not to think about it too much, now I'm back to the fragile peace within.

I visit the blood bank once a week now after hours, using the key card Antonio gave me and avoiding the club. I've run into Temi often enough, and Antonio's young club manager Eve, but as for Antonio himself, as far as I know, he's away in London.

Just as well.

I bought the pub and old manor house in Ringsend. Yes, I killed someone there—I'll never forget—but maybe the reminder isn't such a bad thing. Plus, it's a good idea for me to keep an eye on the place, considering. My solicitor informed me that there were drug dealers recently arrested there, and he knew there'd been some kind of violence. But nothing else. It seems Tracksuit Boy didn't talk to anyone. But he still might. And someone might believe him. It's better I'm there if anyone comes looking. So I can nip it in the bud.

Anyway, I love the old courtyard, with its half-wild cats and its tiny church. I've closed the pub for the time being, but I've had my solicitor transfer the licence. Maybe I'll open it again. Greeneyes says he'll staff it, but we shall see.

At any rate, it's a good facade to hide behind, as no one can see the full extent of the property from the street. I salvaged a few things from my old flat and moved in as soon as the sale was finalised. I've been rebuilding and remodelling every night since, doing it myself, taking advantage of the growing winter darkness to work and buy supplies.

I still have the knife. I carry it with me everywhere. I don't know why it's not burning me anymore. I have a few theories—the main one being maybe it can only be used once, and then it's dead. I don't know. But I keep it with me because I'd rather know where it is than not. Plus, I might need it again someday. I don't know if I killed Thomas or the demon in him. Malephas. I've asked Greeneyes, and he says he didn't see his body. Or Jude's.

Thinking of Jude makes my heart ache. What happened to him was my fault, there's no question. I got him killed. Worse than killed. And I can't fix it, or make up for it, no matter how much I wish I could. The loss and guilt feel like they might choke me sometimes. I miss him so much. Some nights I wake up thinking I should call him and check in, only to remember I can't. It hurts. A lot.

I've built a little shrine for him on the altar of the tumbledown church. I keep adding things to it. Anything I can find I think he might like. An old hymnal from behind one of the broken pews, some icons and prayer cards like he always used to carry, and a picture of Saint Jude—the Patron Saint of hopeless cases. Our little joke that. No case more hopeless than mine. I'm still wearing his rosary beads. I like them there, around my neck, although it's not lost on me. A symbol of death to replace the one of life I gave to Grace.

An appropriate exchange.

Tonight, I'm in the city centre, meandering down Grafton Street, over the Liffey to O'Connell Street and Henry Street; wandering in and out of bric-a-brac and home and design shops. It's only this time of year I get to go shopping anywhere but online, and it's quite an experience, especially this close to the holidays. The city is thronged with shoppers and tourists from all over the world, the air thick with mingled voices and the heady scent of human.

It's been threatening snow from heavy skies all week, and everyone, including me, is bundled up in scarves and jumpers, hats, coats and boots. It's nice to have the extra layers between myself and them; although I can still hear their mingling heartbeats, feel the life pushing through every vein to the tips of their gloved fingers.

I slip between them in their twos and threes, all busy talking to each other or on their phones, planning dinners and dates and holiday reunions; mindful I don't get too close, or linger near any one of them too long. I never go out hungry these nights, but I have to be careful.

I buy some tiles I like, two bookshelves, and a lamp—scheduling their delivery to the pub, making sure they can deliver after five—then I stroll out of that shop and into an antiques gallery, drawn in by a lovely stained-glass window, displayed in the front. It would be perfect for my little church.

I'm standing inside by the window, studying the glass and waiting my turn to speak to the shopkeeper, when I am struck by the sweet and achingly familiar scent of vanilla, and look up—to find Grace just outside, staring in at me.

I stare back, stunned, a chorus of joy exploding through me, followed quickly by confusion and caution. I watch the same emotions play across her face—but then she smiles, and everything fades but that. I head for the door, as does she, and we meet in the middle, enfolding one another without a word. I hold her tight, breathing her in, again and again, hardly daring to believe it's her. But it is, and she feels like somewhere I was always supposed to be. And I don't want to let her go, ever again.

Then someone else pushes past us through the door, and I want to kill them—but Grace gently extracts herself and mutters an apology, and so I don't kill them, but instead help her pick up her bags and get us both out of the way, out to the street.

I keep on staring at her, taking everything in; her eyes, her lips, her hair, that honey blonde, soft and frizzing like a halo against the lights. It's a little longer now, and her face a little drawn. She's lost weight, and there's a sadness in her eyes, half-hidden behind wire-rimmed glasses. A sadness that wasn't there before.

Guilt pushes its way in again, a sour note in joy, a tightness in my throat. My fault. I swallow against it, surprised by a sudden surge of tears, and I look away, blinking them back. When I look over again, she's staring at me, her eyes searching my own. I don't know what she's looking for, or what she sees, but, after a minute, she puts her hand into her pocket and pulls out the amulet of Enki.

"You left this."

I glance to the amulet and nod. "I wanted you to have it."

She closes her palm around the charm and puts it back in her pocket. When she speaks again, her voice is edged with hurt.

"You left me. When I needed you. I woke up and you weren't there."

There it is. I take a breath, swallow pain. Meet her gaze.

"I couldn't stay."

"Why not?"

"You're better off...I thought..." I stop. Take another breath. Start again. "I think you're better off without me."

"No, I'm not." She glares at me, steps closer, her breath clouding the air in front of us. "And you've no right to make that decision for me. It's selfish. And condescending."

I shake my head. "Grace, I will hurt you. I almost killed you. Twice."

"Yes, and you saved me. Twice."

"You don't know me."

"I want to know you!"

"No, you don't. I'm not a good person. I'm not even a person."

"Yes, you are." She smiles softly, laying her hand on my arm.

Her touch is electric; it sends a shock of desire coursing through me; for her body, her blood. I feel it rise into my eyes and bend close to her, so no one else will see.

"You don't understand. It's not safe. I can't—I want you right now. I want to drink you. I'll want to all the time."

She meets my gaze, and holds it, moving her hand to touch my face. "I don't care. I'm not afraid of you. You're the only thing that doesn't scare me. I need you. And don't you dare tell me it's not real, or only something to do with your blood, or mine, or whatever. It's been six months, and it hasn't gone away. This..." She touches her free hand to her heart, her voice breaking. "This is real."

She pauses to take a breath, cheeks flushed, heart pounding, eyes bright. She's so beautiful. My heart aches.

I close my eyes and press my cheek to her palm; all the reasons for me not to be with her fading in the face of actually being with her. I can't fight it anymore.

I love her.

I open my eyes again to find her own.

"Okay."

She frowns. "Okay, what?"

"Okay, it's real."

"Oh," she takes a breath. "For you too?"

"Yes."

"Oh. Okay."

She breathes out, the breath hanging in the air between us as we stand there, just looking at one another. And then it starts to snow, big fluffy white flakes tumbling down out of the night like the falling feathers of a million unseen angels. She gives a little sigh, steps back, and bends her face to the sky, eyes closed. I watch as a few snowflakes land on her nose and eyelashes, melting into little crystalline pools I want more than anything in the world to kiss from her cheeks. Then she opens her eyes.

"So now what?"

I shrug. "I don't know."

She tilts her head to one side. "Want to get some coffee?"

"No." I smile. "But I'll watch you get some."

She smiles, a slow curve of her lips that lights up her whole face; then she bends down, gathers up her bags in one hand, entwines the other in mine, and we walk into the winter's night.

Together.

GLOSSARY

Ur was an important Sumerian city-state in ancient Mesopotamia, located at the site of modern Tell el-Muqayyar in south Iraq. Although Ur was once a coastal city near the mouth of the Euphrates in the Persian Gulf, the coastline has shifted over time and the city is now well inland, on the south bank of the Euphrates, 16 kilometres (9.9 miles) from Nasiriyah.

Ziggurat (ZIG-u-rat D-stem of Sumerian zaqāru 'to build on a raised area') is a type of massive structure built in ancient Mesopotamia. It has the form of a terraced compound of successively receding stories or levels.

The Ziggurat (or Great Ziggurat) of Ur (Sumerian: e-temen-ní-gùru "Etemenniguru", meaning "temple whose foundation creates aura") is a Neo-Sumerian Ziggurat in what was the city of Ur near Nasiriyah, in present-day Dhi Qar Province, Iraq. The structure was built during the Early Bronze Age (21st century BCE) but had crumbled to ruins by the 6th century BCE of the Neo-Babylonian period.

The udug, later known in Akkadian as the utukku, were an ambiguous class of demons from ancient Mesopotamian mythology who were sometimes thought of as good and sometimes as evil. In exorcism texts, the "good udug" is sometimes invoked against the "evil udug". The word is generally ambiguous and is sometimes used to refer to demons as a whole rather than a specific kind of demon. No visual representations of the udug have yet been identified, but descriptions of it ascribe to it features often given to other ancient Mesopotamian demons: a dark shadow, absence of light surrounding it, poison, and a deafening voice. The surviving ancient Mesopotamian texts giving instructions for exorcizing the evil udug are known as the Udug Hul texts. These texts emphasize the evil udug's role in causing disease and the exorcist's role in curing the disease.

L ilith is a figure in Jewish Mythology, developed earliest in the Babylonian Talmud (3rd to 5th century AD). Lilith is often envisioned as a dangerous demon of the night, who is sexually wanton, and who steals babies in the darkness. Lilith may be linked in part to a historically earlier class of female demons (lilītu) in ancient Mesopotamian religion, found in cuneiform texts of Sumer, the Akkadian Empire, Assyria and Babylonia.

T he sack of Babylon and ancient Near East chronology The date of the sack of Babylon by the Hittites under king Mursili I is considered crucial to the various calculations of the early chronology of the ancient Near East, as it is taken as a fixed point in the discussion. Suggestions for its precise date vary by as much as 230 years, corresponding to the uncertainty regarding the length of the "Dark Age" of the much later Late Bronze Age collapse, resulting in the shift of the entire Bronze Age chronology of Mesopotamia regarding the Egyptian chronology.

N ephilim were the offspring of the 'sons of God' and the 'daughters of men' before the Deluge, according to Genesis 6:1-4. A similar or identical biblical Hebrew term, read as "Nephilim" by some scholars, or as the word "fallen" by others, appears in Ezekiel 32:27.

T he Battle of Bolimów was the first attempt by the Germans at large-scale use of poison gas; the eighteen thousand gas shells they fired proved unsuccessful when the xylyl bromide—a type of tear gas—was blown back at their own lines. The gas caused few, if any, casualties, however, since the cold weather caused it to freeze, rendering it ineffective. The failure of the xylyl bromide caused the German commanders to call off their attack. In response, the Russians sent 11 divisions, led by Vasily Gurko to launch a counter-attack; German artillery repelled the Russian troops, who suffered 40,000 casualties.

ABOUT THE AUTHOR

Aisling Wilder writes Urban and High Fantasy from her home in the West of Ireland, on the edge of windswept Connemara. Blood and Sand is her first novel, and was the winner of the 'Golden Stake' award at the International Vampire Film and Arts Festival 2018

For more information, visit aislingwilder.com